# THIRTEEN STEPS
# DOWN

# By Ruth Rendell

# RUTH RENDELL

# THIRTEEN STEPS DOWN

arrow books

Published by Arrow in 2005

10

Copyright © Kingsmarkham Enterprises Ltd 2004

Kingsmarkham Enterprises Ltd has asserted its right under the Copyright,
Designs and Patents Act, 1988 to be identified as the author of this work

First published in Great Britain in 2004 by Hutchinson

Arrow Books
Random House, 20 Vauxhall Bridge Road,
London SW1V 2SA

www.rbooks.co.uk

Addresses for companies within The Random House Group Limited
can be found at: www.randomhouse.co.uk/offices.htm

The Random House Group Limited Reg. No. 954009

A CIP catalogue record for this book
is available from the British Library

ISBN 9780099474326

The Random House Group Limited supports The Forest
Stewardship Council (FSC), the leading international forest
certification organisation. All our titles that are printed on
Greenpeace approved FSC certified paper carry the FSC logo.
Our paper procurement policy can be found at
www.rbooks.co.uk/environment.

Typeset by Palimpsest Book Production Limited, Polmont, Stirlingshire

Printed and bound in Great Britain by
CPI Bookmarque, Croydon, CR0 4TD

To P. D. James, with affection
and admiration

# Chapter 1

Mix was standing where the street should have been. Or where he thought it should have been. By this time shock and disbelief were past. Bitter disappointment, then rage, filled his body and climbed into his throat, half choking him. How dared they? How could they, whoever they were, destroy what should have been a national monument? The house itself should have been a museum, one of those blue plaques high up on its wall, the garden, lovingly preserved just as it was, part of a tour visiting parties could have made. If they had wanted a curator they need have looked no further than him.

Everything was new, carefully and soullessly designed. 'Soulless' – that was the word and he was proud of himself for thinking it up. The place was *pretty*, he thought in disgust, typical yuppie-land building. The petunias in the flowerbeds particularly enraged him. Of course he knew that some time back before he was born they had changed the name from Rillington Place to Ruston Close but now there wasn't even a Ruston Close any more. He had brought an old map with him but it was useless, harder to find the old streets than searching for the child's features in the fifty-year-old face. Fifty years was right. It would be half a century since Reggie was caught and hanged. If they had to rename the streets, surely they could have put up a sign somewhere which said, *Formerly Rillington Place.* Or something to tell visitors they were in Reggie country. Hundreds must come here, some of them expectant and deeply disappointed, others knowing nothing of the place's history, all of them encountering this smart little enclave of red brick and raised flowerbeds, geraniums and busy lizzies spilling out of window-boxes, and trees chosen for their golden and creamy white foliage.

It was midsummer and a fine day, the sky a cloudless blue. The little grass plots were a bright and lush green, a pink climbing plant draping a rosy cloak over walls cunningly constructed on varying levels. Mix turned away, the choking anger making his heart beat faster and more loudly, thud, thud, thud. If he had known everything had been eradicated, he would never have considered the flat in St Blaise House. He had come to this corner of Notting Hill solely because it had been Reggie's district. Of course he had known the house itself was gone and its neighbours too but still he had been confident the place would be easily recognisable, a street shunned by the faint-hearted, frequented by intelligent enthusiasts like himself. But the feeble, the squeamish, the politically correct had had their way and torn it all down. They would have been laughing at the likes of him, he thought, and triumphant at replacing history with a tasteless housing estate.

The visit itself he had been saving up as a treat for when he was settled in. A treat! How often, when he was a child, had a promised treat turned into a let-down? Too often, he seemed to remember, and it didn't stop when one was grown-up and a responsible person. Still, he wasn't moving again, not after paying Ed and his mate to paint the place and refit the kitchen. He turned his back on the pretty little new houses, the trees and flowerbeds, and walked slowly up Oxford Gardens and across Ladbroke Grove to view the house where Reggie's first victim had had a room. At least that wasn't changed. By the look of it, no one had painted it since the woman's death in 1943. No one seemed to know which room it had been, there were no details in any of the books he'd read. He gazed at the windows, speculating and making guesses, until someone looked out at him and he thought he'd better move on.

St Blaise Avenue was quite up-market where it crossed Oxford Gardens, tree-lined with ornamental cherries, but the further he walked downhill it too went down until it was all sixties local authority housing, dry cleaners and motorcycle spare parts places and corner shops. All except for the terrace on the other side, isolated elegant Victorian, and the big house, the only one like it in the whole neighbourhood that wasn't divided into a dozen flats, St Blaise House. Pity they hadn't pulled that lot down, Mix thought, and left Rillington Place alone.

No cherries here but great dusty plane trees with huge leaves and bark peeling off their trunks. They were partly responsible for making the place so dark. He paused to look at the house, marvelling at its size, as he always did, and wondering why on earth the old woman hadn't sold it to a developer years ago. Three floors high, it was of once-white, now grey, stucco, with steps up to a great front door that was half hidden in the depths of a pillared portico. Above, almost under the eaves, was a circular window quite different from the other oblong windows, being of stained glass, clouded by the accumulation of grime built up over the years since it had last been cleaned.

Mix let himself in. The hallway alone, he had thought when he first saw the place, was big enough for a normal-size flat to fit inside, big, square and dark like everything in there. Big dark chairs with carved backs stood uselessly against the walls, one of them under a huge mirror in a carved wooden frame, its glass all spotted with greenish blots like islands on a map of the sea. Stairs went down to a basement but he had never been in it and as far as he knew no one else had for years and years.

When he came in he always hoped she wouldn't be anywhere about and usually she wasn't, but today he was out of luck. Dressed in her usual garments, long droopy cardigan and skirt with a dipping hemline, she was standing beside a huge carved table which must have weighed a ton, holding up a coloured flyer advertising a Tibetan restaurant. When she saw him she said, 'Good afternoon, Mr Cellini,' in her upper-class drawl, putting, he thought, a lot of scorn into her voice.

When he spoke to Gwendolen Chawcer, when addressing her was unavoidable, he did his best to shock her – so far without marked success.

'You'll never guess where I've been.'

'That is almost a certainty,' she said. 'So it seems pointless to attempt it.'

Sarcastic old bitch. 'Rillington Place,' he said, 'or where it used to be. I wanted to see where Christie

4

buried all those women he killed in his garden but there's not a trace of it left.'

She put the flyer back on the table. No doubt, it would lie there for months. Then she surprised him. 'I went to his house once,' she said, 'when I was young.'

'You did? Why was that?'

He knew she wouldn't be forthcoming and she wasn't. 'I had a reason to go there. The visit lasted no more than half an hour. He was an unpleasant man.'

He couldn't control his excitement. 'What sort of an impression did he make on you? Did you feel you were in the presence of a murderer? Was his wife there?'

She laughed her cold laugh. 'Goodness, Mr Cellini, I've no time to answer all these questions. I have to get on.'

With what? She seldom did anything but read, as far as he knew. She must have read thousands of books, she was always at it. He felt frustrated after her unsatisfactory but provocative response. She might be a mine of information about Reggie but she was too stand-offish to talk about it.

He began to mount the stairs, hating them with a fierce hatred, though they were not narrow or precarious or winding. There were fifty-two and one of the things he disliked about them was that they were composed of three flights, twenty-two in this stretch, seventeen in the next, but thirteen in the top flight. If there was anything which upset Mix more than unpleasant surprises and rude old women, it was the number thirteen. St Blaise House, fortunately, was number 54 St Blaise Avenue.

One day when old Chawcer was out he had

counted the bedrooms, not including his own, and found there were nine. Some were furnished, if you could call it furniture, some were not. The whole place was filthy. In his opinion, no one had done any housework in it for years, though he had seen her flicking about with a feather duster. All that woodwork, carved with shields and swords and helmets, faces and flowers, leaves and garlands and ribbons, lay under an ancient accumulation of dust. Banister was linked to banister and cornice to picture rail by ropes of cobwebs. She had lived here all her long life, first with her parents, then with her dad, then alone. Apart from that he knew nothing about her. He didn't even know how she happened to have three bedrooms on the top floor already converted into a flat.

The stairs grew narrower after the first landing and the last flight, the top one, was tiled, not carpeted. Mix had never seen a staircase of shiny black tiles before but there were many things in Miss Chawcer's house he had never seen before. No matter what kind of shoes he wore, those tiles made a terrible noise, a thump-thumping or a clack-clacking, and his belief was that she had tiled the stairs so that she would be able to tell what time her tenant came in. He had already got into the habit of removing his shoes and continuing in his socks alone. It wasn't that he ever did anything *wrong* but he didn't want her knowing his business.

The stained glass window speckled the top landing with spots of coloured light. It was a picture of a girl looking into a pot with some sort of plant in it. When old Chawcer brought him up here for the first time she had called it the Isabella window and the picture, Isabella and the Pot of

Basil, made very little sense to Mix. As far as he was concerned, basil was something growing in a bag you bought at Tesco. The girl looked ill, her face was the only bit of the glass that was white, and Mix resented having to see her each time he went into or came out of, his flat.

He called his home an apartment but Gwendolen Chawcer called it 'rooms'. She lived in the past, in his opinion, and not thirty or forty years ago like most old people but a hundred years. He had put in the bathroom himself with Ed and his mate's help and fitted the kitchen. He paid for it, so Miss Chawcer couldn't really complain. She ought to have been pleased; it would still be there for the next tenant when he was famous and had moved out. The fact was that she had never been able to see the need for a bathroom. When she was young, she told him, you had a chamber pot in your bedroom and a basin on the washstand and the maid brought you up a jug of hot water.

Mix had a bedroom as well and a large living room, dominated by a huge poster photograph of Nerissa Nash, taken when a newspaper started naming the models as well as the clothes designers. That was in the days when they called her the poor man's Naomi Campbell. They did so no longer. Mix stood in front of the poster, as he often did when he first came in, like a religious contemplating a holy picture, his lips murmuring, 'I love you, I adore you,' instead of prayers.

He was earning good money at Fiterama and he had spent freely on this flat. The chrome-encased television, video and DVD player were on the hire purchase as was most of the kitchen equipment but that, to use one of Ed's favourite expressions, was par for the course, everyone did it. He had paid for the white carpet and grey tweed suite with ready cash, buying the black marble statue of the nude girl on an impulse but not for a moment regretting his purchase. The poster of Nerissa he had had framed in the same chrome finish as the TV. In the black ash shelving he kept his collection of Reggie books: *10 Rillington Place*, *John Reginald Halliday Christie*, *The Christie Legend*, *Murder in Rillington Place* and *Christie's Victims* among many others. Richard Attenborough's film of *10 Rillington Place* he had on video and DVD. It was outrageous, he thought, that one Hollywood movie after another was re-made while you never heard a thing about a re-make of that. The one he possessed he often played and the digital version was even better, clearer and brighter. Richard Attenborough was wonderful, he wasn't arguing about that, but he didn't look much like Reggie. A taller actor was needed with sharper features and burning eyes.

Mix was inclined to day-dream and sometimes he speculated as to whether he would be famous through knowing Nerissa or through his expert knowledge of Reggie. There was probably no one alive today, not even Ludovic Kennedy who had written *the* book, who knew more. It might be his mission in life to reawaken interest in Rillington Place and its most famous occupant, though how this was to come about after what he had seen that afternoon, was as yet a mystery. He would solve it, of course. Perhaps he would write a book about Reggie himself, and not one full of feeble comments on the man's wickedness and depravity. His book would draw attention to the murderer as artist.

It was getting on for six. Mix poured himself his favourite drink. He had invented it himself and called it Boot Camp because it had such a savage kick. It mystified him that no one he had offered it to seemed to share his taste for a double measure of vodka, a glass of Sauvignon and a tablespoonful of Cointreau poured over crushed ice. His fridge was the kind which spewed out the crushed ice all prepared. He was just savouring the first sip when his mobile rang.

It was Colette Gilbert-Bamber to tell him she was desperate to get her treadmill repaired. It might be no more than the electric plug or it might be something bigger. Her husband had gone out but she had had to stay at home because she was expecting an important phone call. Mix knew what all that meant. Being in love with his distant star, his queen and lady, didn't mean he was never to treat himself to a bit of fun. Once he and Nerissa were together, a recognised item, it would be a different thing.

Regretfully but getting his priorities right, Mix put his Boot Camp into the fridge. He cleaned his teeth, gargled with a mouthwash which tasted not unlike his cocktail without the stimulus, and made his way down the stairs. In the midst of the house you wouldn't have guessed how fine the day was and bright and hot the sunshine. Here it was always cold and strangely silent too, it always was. You couldn't hear the Hammersmith and City Line running above ground from Latimer Road to Shepherd's Bush, or the traffic in Ladbroke Grove. The only noise came from the Westway but if you didn't know you wouldn't have imagined you were listening to traffic. It sounded like the sea, like waves breaking on the shore, or what you hear when you hold a big seashell up to your ear, a soft unceasing roar.

These days Gwendolen sometimes needed the help of a magnifying glass to read small print. And, unfortunately, most of the books she wanted to read were printed in what she understood to be called 10-point. Her ordinary glasses couldn't cope with Papa's edition of *The Decline and Fall of the Roman Empire,* for instance, or what she was reading now, a very old copy of *Middlemarch,* published in the nineteenth century.

Like her bedroom above it, the drawing room encompassed the whole depth of the house, a pair of large sash windows overlooking the street, french windows at the back giving onto the garden. When she was reading Gwendolen reclined on a sofa upholstered in dark brown corduroy, its back surmounted with a carved mahogany dragon. The dragon's tail curved round to meet one of the sofa arms, while its head reared up as it snarled at the black marble fireplace. Most of the furniture was rather like that, carved and thickly padded and covered in velvet which was brown or dull green or the dark red of claret, but some was made of dark veined marble with gilt legs. There was a very large mirror on one wall, framed in gilt leaves and fruit and curlicues, which had grown dull with time and lack of care.

Beyond the french windows, open now to the warm evening light, lay the garden. Gwendolen still saw it as it used to be, the lawn closely mown to the smoothness of emerald velvet, the herbaceous border alight with flowers, the trees pruned to make the best of their luxuriant foliage. Or, rather, she saw that it could be like that with a little attention, nothing that couldn't be achieved by a day's work. That the grass was knee high, the flowerbeds a mass of weeds and the trees ruined by dead branches, escaped her notice. The printed word was more real to her than a comfortable interior and pleasing exterior.

Her mind and her memories too were occasionally stronger than the book; then she laid it down to stare at the brownish cobweb-hung ceiling and the dusty prisms on the chandelier, to think and to remember.

The man Cellini she disliked, but that was of small importance. His inelegant conversation had awakened sleeping things, Christie and his murders, Rillington Place, her fear, Dr Reeves and Bertha. It must be at least fifty-two years ago, maybe fifty-three. Rillington Place had been a sordid slum, the terraces of houses with front doors opening on to the street, an iron foundry with a tall chimney at the far end of it. Until she went there she had no idea such places existed. She had led a sheltered life, both before that day and after it. Bertha would have married – those sort of people always did. Probably had a string of children who by now would be middle-aged, the first one of them the cause of her misfortunes.

Why did women behave like that? She had never understood. She had never been tempted. Not even with Dr Reeves. Her feelings for him had always been chaste and honourable, as had his for her. She was sure of that, in spite of his subsequent behaviour. Perhaps, after all, she had chosen the better part.

What on earth made Cellini so interested in Christie? It wasn't a healthy attitude of mind. Gwendolen picked up her book again. Not in this one but in another of George Eliot's, *Adam Bede,* there was a girl who had behaved like Bertha and met a dreadful fate. She read for another half-hour, lost to the world, oblivious to everything but the page in front of her. A footfall above her head alerted her.

Poor as her sight was becoming, Gwendolen's hearing was superb. Not for a woman of her age but for anyone of any age. Her friend Olive Fordyce said she was sure Gwendolen could hear a bat squeak. She listened now. He was coming down the stairs. No doubt he thought she didn't know he took his shoes off in an attempt to come and go secretly. She was not so easily deceived. The lowest flight creaked. Nothing he could do would put a stop to that, she thought triumphantly. She heard him padding across the hall but when he closed the front door it was with a slam that shook the house and caused a whitish flake to drop off the ceiling on to her left foot.

She went to one of the front windows and saw him getting into his car. It was a small blue car and, in her opinion, he kept it absurdly clean. When he had gone she went out to the kitchen, opened the door on an ancient and never-used spin dryer to take out a netting bag which had once held potatoes. The bag was full of keys. No labels were attached to them but she knew very well the shape and colour of the one she wanted. The key in the pocket of her cardigan, she began to mount the stairs.

It was a long way up but she was used to it. She

might be over eighty but she was thin and strong. Never in her life had she had a day's illness. Of course she couldn't climb those stairs as fast as she could fifty years ago but that was only to be expected. Otto was sitting halfway up the top flight, dismembering and eating some small mammal. She took no notice of him nor he of her. The evening sun blazed through the Isabella window and since there was no wind to blow on the glass, a nearly perfect coloured picture of the girl and the pot of basil appeared reflected on the floor, a circular mosaic of reds and blues and purples and greens. Gwendolen stopped to admire it. Rarely indeed was this facsimile so clear and still.

She lingered for only a minute or two before inserting her key in the lock and letting herself into Cellini's flat.

All this white paint was unwise, she thought. It showed every mark. And grey was a bad furnishing colour, cold and stark. She walked into his bedroom, wondering why he bothered to make his bed when he would only have to unmake it at night. Everything was depressingly tidy. Very likely he suffered from that affliction she had read about in a newspaper, Obsessive Compulsive Disorder. The kitchen was just as bad. It looked like one of those on show at the Ideal Home Exhibition, to which Olive had insisted on taking her some time in the eighties. A place for everything and everything in its place, not a packet or tin left on the counter, nothing in the sink. How could anyone live like that?

She opened the door of the fridge. There was very little food to be seen but in the door rack were two bottles of wine and, in the very front of the middle shelf a nearly full glass of something that looked like faintly coloured water. Gwendolen sniffed it. Not water, certainly not. So he drank, did he? She couldn't say she was surprised. Making her way back into the living room, she stopped at the bookshelves. Any books, no matter of what kind, always drew her attention. These were not the sort she would read, perhaps that anyone *should* read. All of them, except for one called *Sex for Men in the 21st Century*, were about Christie. She had scarcely thought about the man for more than forty years and today she seemed not to be able to get away from him.

As for Cellini, this would be another of his obsessions. The more I know people, said Gwendolen, quoting her father, the more I like books. She went downstairs and into the kitchen. There she fetched herself a cheese and pickle sandwich, ready-made from the corner shop, and taking it and a glass of orange juice back to the dragon sofa, she returned to *Middlemarch*.

# Chapter 2

It was a funny part of the world altogether, Mix
hadn't got used to it yet, the Westway to the north
and Wormwood Scrubs and its prison not far
away, a tangle of little winding streets, big houses,
purpose-built blocks, ugly Victorian terraces, Gothic
places more like churches than homes, cottages cunningly designed on different levels to look as if they
had been there for two hundred years, corner shops,
MOT testing centres, garages, meeting halls, real
churches for Holy Catholic Apostolics or Latter Day
Saints and convents for Oblates and Carmelites. The
whole place populated by people whose families
had always been there and people whose families
came from Freetown and Goa and Vilnius and
Beirut and Aleppo.

The Gilbert-Bambers also lived in West Eleven
but the upmarket fashionable part. Their house was
in Lansdowne Walk, not as big as Miss Chawcer's
but more imposing, with Corinthian columns all
along the front and urns with bushes in them on
the balconies. It took Mix no more than five minutes to drive there and another five to park his car
on a meter, costing him nothing after six-thirty.
Colette gave him one of her sexy looks as she
opened the door, a look which wasn't in the least
necessary as both knew why she had sent for him

and what he had come for. For his part, he put up a show of formality, smiling as he marched in with his case of tools and saying it was upstairs if he remembered rightly.

'Of course you remember rightly,' Colette said, giggling.

More stairs but these were wide and shallow and anyway there was only one flight to go up. 'How's Miss Nash these days?'

He'd known she wouldn't like that and she didn't. 'I'm sure she's fine. I haven't seen her for a couple of weeks.'

It was at the Gilbert-Bambers' that he had first met Nerissa Nash. 'Encountered' might be the better word. Until he saw her he had thought Colette beautiful, her slenderness and her long blonde hair and her full lips, even though she'd told him about the collagen implants. The difference between them, he had thought, was that between the Hollywood star and the prettiest girl in the office.

Colette preceded him into the bedroom. What she called her gym was really a dressing room which opened out of it next to the bathroom, and when this house was built had been designed for the master of the house.

'He'd knock on her door when he wanted a bonk,' Colette had explained. 'They were all bonkers in those days. Isn't that funny it's the same word?'

The room was now furnished with a treadmill, a step machine, a stationary bicycle and an elliptical cross-trainer. There was a rack of weights, a rolled-up yoga mat, a turquoise-coloured inflatable ball and a virgin fridge which had never seen the like of Boot Camp but held only sparkling spring water. Mix could see at once why the treadmill wouldn't start. Colette was no fool and was probably well aware of the reason herself.

The machine had a safety device in the form of a key which slotted into a keyhole and a string attached to it with a clip on the other end. You were supposed to fasten it on to your clothes while you used it so that if you fell over the key would be pulled out and the motor stop running. Mix held up the key.

'You didn't put it in.'

'As the actress said to the bishop.'

He thought this rejoinder extremely old hat. He'd heard his stepfather say it a good twenty years ago. 'It won't start unless the key's in,' he said in a toneless voice, intended to show her he didn't think her witty. Still, he should complain. He'd get his fifty-pound call-out fee for just coming here.

He inserted the key, started the machine, ran it up and to delay things a little – why should she have it all her own way? – applied some oil underneath the pedals. Colette switched it off herself and led him back into the bedroom. He sometimes wondered what would happen if the Honourable Hugo Gilbert-Bamber came back unexpectedly but he could always nip back into his clothes and crouch down among the machines with screwdriver and oilcan.

Mix intended to be famous. The only possible life anyone could wish for these days, it seemed to him, was a celebrity's. To be stopped in the street and asked for your autograph, to be forced to travel incognito, to see your picture in the papers, to be in demand by journalists for interviews, to have fans speculate about your sex life, to be quoted in gossip columns. To wear shades when you didn't want to be recognised, to be transported in a limo with tinted windows. To have your own PR person and maybe get Max Clifford to represent you.

It would be best to be famous for something you did which people liked or because they admired you, like he did Nerissa Nash. But fame deriving from some great crime was enviable in a way. What would it feel like to be the man the police smuggle out of a courthouse with a coat over his head because if they saw him the crowd would tear him to pieces? Assassination secured you fame for ever. Only think of the killer of John Lennon, and of President Kennedy, or Princip who shot the Austrian Archduke and started the First World War. But being Nerissa Nash's escort would be better and a lot safer. Soon it would lead to celebrity status, he would be invited on TV chat shows, asked to parties by the Beckhams and Madonna.

Colette had been a model herself, though in a minor league, and marriage to a stockbroker ended her career. But she and Nerissa remained firm friends. Mix had been in the gym/dressing room, fitting a new running belt to the treadmill, on this occasion a legitimate task. There couldn't be any of the other because a hired cook was in the house getting lunch for Nerissa and Colette. The two women came into the bedroom for Colette to show her friend some new creation she had bought for an astronomical sum in a Notting Hill boutique. Whispering and giggling reached Mix's ears. He couldn't be sure but he thought he heard Nerissa warn Colette to be careful about undressing because 'the man' was next door in the gym.

Mix was familiar enough with Colette's ways and tastes to know she wouldn't care if fifty men were in the gym, all gaping at her through the glass door, she'd like it, but he admired Nerissa's modest attitude. You didn't come across much of that these days. Up until then he had never seen her beyond glancing at her photograph in the tabloids. Her voice was so pretty and her laugh so silvery that he was determined to see her. He used a technique he always employed when needing to speak to the lady of the house and, clearing his throat rather loudly, called out, 'Are you there, Mrs Gilbert-Bamber?'

A giggle from Colette answered him, so he wasted no more time and walked into the bedroom. Colette was in scarlet bra and thong but he had seen more of her than that. In his own words, he wasn't bothered. Besides, Colette's friend commanded all his attention. To say she was the most beautiful woman he had ever seen was an understatement. Immediately he felt that all women, to be good to look at, should have long black hair, huge golden eyes and skin the colour of a cappuccino. Apart from all this and her shape, her height and her graceful way of standing, instead of the hauteur he would have expected in her face, he saw a warm sweetness, and when she smiled and said, 'Hi,' he was a lost man.

After that he collected in his scrapbooks every picture of her he saw. He even found her portrait on postcards in a tourist shop in Shepherd's Bush. When there was a film première he waited, sometimes for hours, on the pavement outside the cinema for a glimpse of her alighting from a car. Once he was amply rewarded, having secured a position at the front of the fans. Helped out of the car, she drew her white fur stole round the diaphanous yellow shift she wore and seeing him – recognising him? – bestowed on him a radiant smile.

In one of his fantasies he and she sat in a club, alone at their table, gazing into each other's eyes. A cameraman approached them, then another. Nerissa smiled at the photographers, then at him. She whispered, 'Kiss me,' and he did. It was the most wonderful clinch he had ever had, made even better by the flashes round them and the encouragement of the cameramen. Their kiss was in all the papers next day and the headlines he imagined thrilled him. 'Nerissa and her New Man' and 'Nerissa Seals New Love with a Kiss'. They'd call him 'Michael Cellini, the distinguished criminologist'.

Meanwhile he never saw her in the flesh, that golden flesh so delicately laid on long bones, though he had several times waited outside her house on Campden Hill Square, waiting for a glimpse of her at a window. Colette had told him where she lived, though she had done so reluctantly, and he had asked her if Nerissa had any exercise equipment in her home.

'She goes to the gym.'

'Which gym?' he asked, gently biting her neck the way she liked.

'The nearest, I suppose. What do you want to know for?'

'Just curious,' he said.

He must follow her, he knew that, though it savoured of stalking, which he didn't want to think of in connection with Nerissa. Just once he'd follow her and when he found the gym he'd join. He wasn't as fit as he should be in his job, and why not her gym as well as another?

He had been with Fiterama for nine years, the first eight and a bit at their Birmingham branch. When he came to London and started looking for a place to live, he rented for a while a room in Tufnell Park. Hilldrop Crescent, just round the corner, was another location that fascinated him. They hadn't changed its name, though Dr Crippen who killed his wife and put bits of her under the floor, had lived there. He'd never read anything about Crippen, his crime was so long ago, before the First World War and practically ancient history. Then he saw a television programme about catching criminals by wireless and from that he learnt that Crippen was the first to be caught by this means. He learnt too where he had lived. Something which might be distasteful to another man, or simply of no interest, excited Mix and he went out to take a look. The disappointment he felt when he found the house gone and newer buildings on the site was a precursor of his much deeper bitterness at the destruction of Rillington Place.

It was seeing the film that started him off. He was still living at home then and he watched it on his mother's old black and white television. Never much for reading, he had found the book of the film, as he thought of it, on a stall outside a junk shop. It came as a surprise when he looked at the photographs and saw that John Reginald Halliday Christie looked, not like Attenborough, but far more like himself. Of course he was a lot younger and he didn't wear glasses. He forced himself to look in the mirror long enough to be sure of the resemblance. In a funny way it seemed to bring him and the mass murderer closer together, and it was from that time that he began referring to him in his mind as Reggie rather than Christie. After all, what had he done that was so terrible? Rid the world of a bunch of useless women, hookers and streetwalkers, most of them.

Reggie. The name sounded nice. Sort of warm and friendly. It was no surprise to Mix to discover in his reading that people had liked Reggie, looked up to him and admired him, a lot of them. They had recognised in him a man of power. That was one of the things Mix liked about him, that he was a strong man. He would have made a good father, wouldn't have stood any nonsense from his kids but wouldn't have knocked them about either. That wasn't Reggie's way. Fleetingly, as happened every day, Mix thought of Javy. To his mind, women shouldn't be allowed to give their children stepfathers.

Driving home from Colette's, his thoughts returned to what old Chawcer had told him. He was still amazed by it. She had actually been to Reggie's house. She had met Reggie. To Mix, at his age, Reggie seemed to have lived in a far distant time, in history really, but he realised that was not so for old Chawcer. She must be in her eighties and when Reggie had lived in Rillington Place, had still been young, had been a girl. Now, as all the books said and everyone knew who was interested, Reggie had lured his victims to his house by posing as an abortionist. Therefore, she must have gone to him with that in view. What else?

Because he was himself young in the twenty-first century, Mix thought things had always been the way they were now. Old Chawcer's youth, as far as sexual encounters went, would have been much as his was, love affairs, one-night stands and sex as often as one could get it. Old Chawcer would have been careless, forgotten her pill, as they did, and found herself up the spout. What little Mix knew about the law was concentrated on the liability of exercise equipment manufacturers and retailers for the safety of their products. Of acts making abortion legal he was ignorant, only supposing that when old Chawcer was young you couldn't just go to a hospital and get it done. It stood to reason. If that had been possible Reggie would have been out of business.

The big question was: if she'd been there and in his hands, why was she still alive after fifty years? Maybe he would never know but he longed to find out.

In his flat it was almost entirely quiet. All his windows overlooked sections of flat roof and bits of gables and the wild untended garden at the back. The gardens down here were wildernesses except one and it was neat with mown lawn and rosebeds. Most nights, after it got dark, which happened late, he saw two eyes, bright as green flames, staring up at him out of the dense foliage of the ivy which climbed unrestrainedly over wall and trellis. Old Chawcer went to bed early, he supposed. Because the house stood alone no sound could ever be heard from neighbours. If you slept in the front part, you might sometimes be woken by the shrieks and shouts and bursts of music from cars he'd heard someone call the new cries of London. In the back where he was there was little to disturb you. A child of his time and one who had grown up on a noisy housing estate, he would occasionally have welcomed audible signs of life outside. Here the silent hours passed by as if time and the world had forgotten all about you. Except for the Westway. Like a great grey centipede it marched across west London on its hundred concrete legs, its ceaseless moving burden making sea sounds.

He opened the fridge door. An obsessively tidy person, he thought he had left his Boot Camp precisely in the centre of the middle shelf and two inches in from the front. It was very unlike him to have put it on the left-hand side, pushed up against a Tesco chocolate log. Thoughtfully, he sipped it. He must have been in a hurry to get out, that was the explanation.

His drink half-consumed, he stood in front of Nerissa's picture and said to it, said to *her*, 'I love you. I worship you.' He raised his glass and drank to her. 'You know I adore you.'

# Chapter 3

Gwendolen Chawcer's home in St Blaise Avenue
had been built in 1860 by her grandfather, her
father's father. Notting Hill was countrified then
with lots of open spaces and new building and supposed to be a healthy place to live. The Westway
was not to be thought of for another hundred years,
the first section of the London Underground, the
Metropolitan Railway from Baker Street to
Hammersmith would be built in three years' time,
but the site of the street later called Rillington Place
was open land. Gwendolen's father, the professor,
was born in St Blaise House in the nineties of that
century and she herself in the twenties of the next
one.

The neighbourhood went down and down.
Because it was cheap, immigrants moved in in the
fifties and lived in run-down North Kensington
and Kensal Town, in Powis Square and Golborne
Road, and it was a man from the Caribbean who
found the first body in the Christie case when
taking down a wall in the flat he had moved into.
Hippies and flower people lived up there in the
next two decades. Ladbroke Grove was so familiar
a part of their lives that they called it affectionately,
'the Grove'. In their rented rooms and flats they
grew cannabis in cupboards with ultraviolet light

inside. They dressed in cheesecloth and the concept of the Global Village was born.

Miss Chawcer knew nothing of this. It flowed over her. She was born in St Blaise House, had no brothers or sisters and was educated at home by Professor Chawcer, who had a chair of philology at London University. When she was a little over thirty her mother died. From the first the professor had been against her taking any sort of job, and what the professor was against invariably didn't happen, just as what he was in favour of, did. Someone had to look after him. The maid had left to get married and Gwendolen was a natural to take her place.

It was a strange life she led but a safe one, as any life must be which is without fear or hope or passion or love or change or anxiety about money. The house was very large, on three floors, innumerable rooms opening out of square hallways or long passages, with a great grand staircase consisting of four flights. When it seemed certain Gwendolen would never marry, her father had three rooms on the top floor converted into a self-contained flat for her, with its own hallway, two rooms and a kitchen. The lack of a bathroom had nothing to do with her disinclination to move in. What was the point of being up there when her father was always down in the drawing room and always, it seemed, hungry for his meals or thirsty for a cup of tea? Her unwillingness to go up to the top floor started at that point. She only went up there if she had lost something and had exhausted all other places where it might be.

Nothing had been painted in the rest of the house and no other rooms had been modernised.

Electricity had been installed, but not everywhere, and the place was rewired in the eighties because the existing wiring was dangerous. But where the old cables had been taken out and the new ones inserted, the walls had been plastered up over the holes but no redecoration had been done. Gwendolen said herself she wasn't much of a cleaner. Cleaning bored her. She was happiest when sitting about and reading. She had read thousands of books, seeing no point in doing anything else unless you had to. When she shopped for food, she kept to the old shops as long as she could, and on the departure of the grocer and the butcher and the fishmonger, she went to the new supermarkets without registering that the change had affected her. She liked her food well enough and had made few changes to her diet since she was a young girl, except that with no one to cook for her she barely ate hot meals.

Every afternoon, after lunch, she lay down and rested, reading herself to sleep. She had a radio but no television. The house was full of books, learned works and ancient novels, old bound copies of the *National Geographic* and *Punch*, encyclopaedias long obsolete, dictionaries published in 1906, such collections as *The Bedside Esquire* and *The Mammoth Book of Thrillers, Ghosts and Mysteries*. She had read most of them and some she had re-read. She had acquaintances she had met through the St Blaise and Latimer Residents' Association, and they called themselves her friends. Such relationships are difficult for an only child who has never been to school. She had been away on holidays with the professor, even to foreign countries, and thanks to him she spoke good French and Italian, though with no chance of using either except for reading Montaigne and D'Annunzio, but she had never had a boyfriend. While she had visited the theatre and the cinema, she had never been to a smart restaurant or a club or a dance or a party. She sometimes said to herself that, like Wordsworth's Lucy, 'she dwelt among the untrodden ways' but it was said rather with relief than unhappiness.

The professor lived on into extreme old age, finally dying at the age of ninety-four. For the past few years of his life he had been unable to walk and incontinent, but his brain remained powerful and his demands undiminished. With the occasional assistance of a district nurse, even more occasionally that of a paid carer, Gwendolen looked after him. She never complained. She never showed signs of weariness. She changed his incontinence pads and stripped his bed, thinking only while she did so of getting through it as fast as possible so that she could get back to her book. His meals were brought and the tray later removed in the same spirit. He had brought her up apparently with no other purpose than that she should housekeep for him while he was middle-aged, care for him when he was old and read to keep herself out of mischief.

There had been moments in his life when he had looked at her with a cool unbiased eye and had acknowledged to himself that she was good-looking. He had never seen any other reason for a man to fall in love and marry, or at least wish to marry, than that the woman he chose was beautiful. Intellect, wit, charm, kindliness, a particular talent or warmth of heart, none of these played any part in his choice nor, as far as he knew, in the choice made by other intelligent men. He had married a woman for her looks alone and when he saw those looks in his daughter he became apprehensive. A man might see them too and take her away from him. None did. How could such a man have met her when he invited no one to the house except the doctor, and she went nowhere without her father's being aware of it and watching her with an eagle eye?

But at last he died. He left her comfortably off and he left her the house, now in the eighties a dilapidated mansion half buried among new mewses and closes, small factories, local authority housing, corner shops, debased terraces and street-widening schemes. She was at that time a tall thin woman of sixty-six, whose *belle époque* profile was growing nutcracker-like, her fine Grecian nose pointing markedly towards a jutting chin. Her skin, which had been very fine and white with a delicate flush on the high cheekbones, was a mass of wrinkles. Such skin is sometimes compared to the peel of an apple that has been left lying too long in a warm room. Her blue eyes had faded to pastel grey and her once-fair hair, though still copious, was quite white.

The two elderly women who called themselves her friends, who had red fingernails and tinted hair and dressed in an approximation of current fashion, sometimes said that Miss Chawcer was Victorian in her clothes. This showed only how much they had forgotten of their own youth, for some of Gwendolen's wardrobe could have been placed in 1936 and some in 1953. Many of her coats and dresses were of these vintages and would have fetched a fortune in the shops of Notting Hill Gate where such things were much prized, like the 1953 clothes she had bought for Dr Reeves. But he went away and married someone else. They had been good in their day and were so carefully looked after that they never wore out. Gwendolen Chawcer was a living anachronism.

She had cared for the house less well. To do her justice, she had determined a year or two after the professor died that it should be thoroughly redecorated and even in places refitted. But she was always rather slow in making decisions and by the time she reached the point of looking for a builder, she found she was unable to afford it. Because she had never paid National Insurance and no one had ever made contributions for her, the pension she received was very small. The money her father had left paid annually a diminishing return.

One of her friends, Olive Fordyce, suggested she take a tenant for part of the top floor. At first Gwendolen was appalled but after a time she gradually came round to the idea, but she would never have taken any action herself. It was Mrs Fordyce who found Michael Cellini's advertisement in the *Evening Standard*, who arranged an interview and who sent him round to St Blaise House.

Gwendolen, the Italian speaker, addressed him as Mr Chellini but he, the grandson of an Italian prisoner of war, had always called himself Sellini. She refused to change: she knew what was correct and what was not if he didn't. He would have preferred that they should be Mix and Gwen, he lived in a world in which everyone was on first name terms, and he had suggested it.

'I think not, Mr Cellini,' was all she had said.

It would probably have killed her to be called by her given name, and as for Gwen, only Olive

Fordyce, much to Gwendolen's distaste, used that diminutive. She called him, not her tenant, or even 'the man who rents the flat' but her lodger. When he mentioned her, which was seldom, he called her 'the old bat who owns the place' but on the whole they got on well, largely because the house was so big and they rarely met. Of course, it was early days. He had only been there a fortnight.

At one of their very occasional meetings he had told her he was an engineer. To Miss Chawcer an engineer was a man who built dams and bridges in distant lands but Mr Cellini explained that his job was servicing work-out equipment. She had to ask him what that meant and, not being very articulate, he was obliged to tell her she could view similar machines in the sports department of any large London store. The only London store she ever went to was Harrods and when next there, she made her way to view the exercise equipment. She entered a world she didn't understand, she could see no motive for setting foot on any of these devices and scarcely believed what Cellini had told her. Could he have been, to use a rare example of the professor's inverted commas-surrounded slang, 'pulling her leg'?

Every so often, but not very often, Gwendolen went round the house with a feather duster and a carpet sweeper. She pushed this implement half-heartedly and never emptied its dust container. The vacuum cleaner, bought in 1951, had broken down twenty years before and never been repaired. It sat in the basement among old rolls of carpet, the leaf from a dining table, flattened cardboard boxes, a gramophone from the thirties, a stringless violin of unknown provenance and a basket off the bicycle the professor had once used to ride to Bloomsbury and back. The carpet sweeper deposited dirt as regularly as it picked it up. By the time she reached her own bedroom, dragging the sweeper up the stairs behind her, Gwendolen had grown bored with the whole thing and wanted to get back to whatever she happened to be reading, Balzac all over again or Trollope. She couldn't be bothered to take the carpet sweeper back downstairs so she left it in a corner of her bedroom with the dirty duster draped over its handle; sometimes it would remain there for weeks.

Later that day, at about four, she was expecting Olive Fordyce and her niece for tea. The niece she had never met but Olive said it would be cruel never to let her see where Gwendolen lived, she was 'absolutely mad about' old houses. Just to spend an hour in St Blaise House would make her ecstatic. Gwendolen wasn't doing anything special, apart from re-reading *Le Père Goriot*. She'd go out in a minute and buy a swiss roll from the Indian shop on the corner and maybe a packet of custard creams.

The days when that wouldn't have been good enough were long gone. Years had passed since she had baked or cooked anything more than, say, a scrambled egg, but once every cake eaten in this house, every pie and flapjack and éclair, had been made by her. She particularly remembered a certain swiss roll, the pale creamy-yellow sponge, the raspberry jam, the subtle dusting of powdered sugar. The professor wouldn't tolerate bought cakes. And tea was the favourite meal of all three of them. Tea was what you asked people to partake of if you asked them at all. When Mrs Chawcer was so ill, was slowly and painfully dying, her doctor on his regular visits was always asked to stay to tea. Her mother upstairs in bed and the professor giving a lecture somewhere, Gwendolen found herself alone with Dr Reeves.

Falling in love with him and he with her, she convinced herself, were the most important events of her life. He was younger than she was but not much, not enough, Gwendolen thought, for her mother to put him beyond the pale on grounds of age. Mrs Chawcer disapproved of marriages in which the man was more than two years younger than the woman. In appearance Dr Reeves was boyish with dark curly hair, dark but fiery eyes and an enthusiastic expression. Though thin, he ate enormously of Gwendolen's scones with Cornish cream and home-made strawberry jam, Dundee cake and flapjacks, while she picked delicately at a Marie biscuit. Men didn't like seeing a girl guzzle, Mrs Chawcer said – had almost stopped saying now her daughter was over thirty. Before tea, between mouthfuls and afterwards, Dr Reeves talked. About his profession and his ambitions, about the place in which they lived, the Korean War, the Iron Curtain, and the changing times. Gwendolen talked about these things too, as she had never talked to anyone before, and sometimes about hoping to see more of life, making friends, travelling, seeing the world. And always they talked about her mother dying, how it wouldn't be long, and what would happen afterwards.

Doctors' handwriting is notoriously unreadable. Gwendolen scrutinised the prescriptions he wrote for Mrs Chawcer, trying to decipher his first name. At first she thought it was Jonathan, then Barnabas. The nearest she got was Swithun. Cunningly, she turned the conversation on to names and how important or unimportant they were to their possessors. She liked hers, so long as no one called her Gwen. No one? Who were these people who might inadvertently create for her a diminutive? Her parents were the only ones who didn't call her Miss Chawcer. She said none of this to Dr Reeves but listened avidly for his contribution.

Out it came. 'Stephen's the sort of name that's always all right to have. Fashionable at the moment. For the first time, actually. So, one day, maybe, folks will guess I'm thirty years younger than I am.'

He always called people 'folks'. And he said 'guess' the American way, meaning 'think'. Gwendolen loved these idiosyncrasies. She was delighted to find out his name. Sometimes, in the solitude of her bedroom, she mouthed to herself interesting combinations: Gwendolen Reeves, Mrs Stephen Reeves, G.M. Reeves. If she were American she could call herself Gwendolen Chawcer Reeves, if from parts of Europe, Mrs Doctor Stephen Reeves. To use the servants' word, he was courting her. She was sure of that. What would be the next step? An invitation out somewhere, her mother would probably say. Will you come with me to the theatre, Miss Chawcer? Do you ever go to the pictures, Miss Chawcer? May I call you Gwendolen?

Her mother no longer said anything. She was comatose with morphine. Stephen Reeves came regularly and every time he had tea with Gwendolen. One afternoon, across the cakestand, he called her Gwendolen and asked her to call him Stephen. The professor usually came home to keep an eye on his daughter as they were finishing their portions of Victoria sponge, and Gwendolen noticed that Dr Reeves reverted to Miss Chawcer when her father was present.

She sighed a little. That was half a century ago and now it wasn't Dr Reeves but Olive and her niece who were expected for tea. Gwendolen hadn't invited them for this day, she wouldn't have dreamt of it. They had asked themselves. If she hadn't been tired at the time and even more tired of Olive's company she would have said no. Wishing she had, she went up to the bedroom which had once been her mother's, where in fact her mother had died, but not the one where she had tried out those name combinations, and put on a blue velvet dress with a lace insert at the neckline, once but no longer called a modesty vest. She added pearls and a brooch in the shape of a phoenix rising from the ashes and put her mother's engagement ring on her right hand. She wore it every day and at night put it in the jewel box of silver and chased mirror glass which had also been her mother's.

The niece didn't come. Olive brought her dog instead, a small white poodle with ballet dancer's feet. Gwendolen was annoyed but not much surprised. She had done this before. The dog had a toy with it like a child, only this plaything was a very lifelike white plastic bone. Olive ate two slices of the swiss roll and a great many biscuits and talked about her niece's daughter while Gwendolen thought what a good thing it was the niece hadn't come or there would have been two of them talking about this paragon, her achievements, her wealth, her lovely home and her devotion to her parents. As it was, her day was spoiled. She should have been alone, to think about Stephen, to remember – and perhaps to plan?

Olive was wearing a trouser suit in bright emerald green and a lot of mock-gold jewellery. Kitsch, Gwendolen called it to herself. Olive was too fat and too old to wear trousers or anything in that colour. She was proud of her long fingernails and had lacquered them the same scarlet as her lipstick. Gwendolen stared at lips and nails with the critical and mocking eye of a young girl. She often wondered why she had friends when she rather disliked them and didn't want their company.

'When my great-niece was fourteen she was already five feet ten inches tall,' said Olive. 'My husband was alive then. "If you grow any more," he said to her, "you'll never find a boyfriend. The boys won't go out with a girl taller than them." And what do you think happened? When she was seventeen and over six feet she met this stockbroker. He'd wanted to be an actor but they wouldn't have him because he was six feet six, far too tall for the theatre, so he went into stockbroking and made a packet. The two of them were quite an item. He wanted to marry her but she had her career to think of.'

'How interesting,' said Gwendolen, thinking of Dr Reeves who had once said she was a nice girl and he was awfully fond of her.

'Girls don't have to get married these days like we did.' She seemed to have forgotten Gwendolen's single status and went on blithely, 'They don't feel they're left on the shelf. There's no *status* to marriage any more. I know it's a bold thing to say but if I was young again, I wouldn't get married. Would you?'

'I never did,' said Gwendolen austerely.

'No, that's true,' Olive said as if Gwendolen might have been in some doubt about it. 'Maybe you did the right thing all along.'

But I would have married Stephen Reeves if he'd asked me, Gwendolen thought after Olive had gone and she was clearing up the tea things. We would have been happy, I would have made him happy and I'd have got away from Papa. But he had never asked her. Once he had said he was fond of her, Papa seemed to have made a point of being there, though he could not have overheard. When her mother was dead Stephen signed the death certificate and said that if they wanted Mrs Chawcer cremated they would need a second doctor's signature, so he'd ask his partner to come round.

He didn't say he'd enjoyed all those teas they'd had together or that he'd miss them or her. Therefore she knew he'd come back. Probably there was some rule in medical etiquette that forbade a general practitioner asking the relatives of a patient to go out with him. He was planning on coming back, waiting till after the funeral. Or perhaps he meant to come to the funeral. Gwendolen went through several series of agony because she had omitted to ask him to the funeral. That too might be in the medical etiquette rule book. She couldn't ask her father. They were both supposed to be grieving too much to ask each other anything like that.

Dr Reeves didn't come to the funeral. It was at St Mark's and apart from Gwendolen and her father, only three other people were there: an old cousin of Mrs Chawcer's, their current maid who came because she was religious and the old man next door in St Blaise Avenue. Since he hadn't been at the funeral, Gwendolen was sure Stephen Reeves would just turn up at the house one day. He was leaving it for a little while out of respect for the dead and the mourners. During that week she spent more time, trouble and money on her appearance than she had ever done before or since. She had her hair cut and set, she bought two new dresses, one grey and one dark blue, she experimented with make-up. Everyone else piled it on, especially about the lips and eyelids. For the first time in her life she wore lipstick, bright red, until her father asked her if she'd been kissing a fire engine.

Dr Reeves never came back.

# Chapter 4

For the third time in a week, Mix sat in his car on
Campden Hill Square with the windows shut and
the engine running to keep the air conditioning on.
It was a hot day and getting hotter every minute.
He felt like a stalker and didn't much like it, partly
because it reminded him of Javy. When he was
twelve Javy had caught him looking through a pair
of binoculars that belonged to his elder brother and
beaten him for being a peeping Tom. Useless to say
he hadn't been looking at the woman next door
but at someone's new motorbike parked by the
kerb.

Forget it, he said to himself, put it out of your
mind. He always said that when he started thinking
of his mother and Javy and life at home but he never
really forgot it. Reading *Christie's Victims* would have
passed the time while he waited but he might get
immersed in it and miss her. It must be half an hour
he'd been there, waiting for her to come out, keeping
his eye on her front door or shifting it to the golden
Jaguar parked on her drive. Of course he'd seen her
on previous visits but it had always been with some
man escorting her or she'd been dressed in one of
those semi-transparent shifts she liked so much,
under a fur wrap or sequin-embroidered denim
jacket, or else in skin-tight jeans and stilt heels which

permitted only small mincing steps. On those occasions she got into the chauffeur-driven limo.

It wouldn't be long before a traffic warden appeared and moved him on. Having a client in Campden Hill Square would have been a help but he didn't. Judging by the bronzed, taut-muscled young men who called at several of these houses, the residents mostly had personal trainers. He was wondering if there was any point in staying, he had several calls to make before lunchtime, when a woman out walking a dog banged on the car window. She had a cigarette in her hand and the dog, not much bigger than a Beanie Baby, was wearing a red collar with a diamanté tag hanging from it. They were all rich round here.

'You know,' she said in a voice like Colette Gilbert-Bamber's, 'it's very wrong of you to sit there with your engine on like that. You're polluting the environment.'

'How about you with your fag?' The combination of waiting about and her voice made him angry. 'Why don't you get lost and take that toy on a lead with you?'

She said something about how dared he and marched off, dropping ash. He was on the point of giving up when Nerissa came out of her front door and got into her own car. She wore a rose-pink sleeveless top and white jeans, her hair tied on the top of her head with a pink silk ribbon. Mix thought she looked lovelier than ever, even in the big black shades that half covered her face. Casual suited her. But what kind of fashion didn't?

To follow her was essential, even if it made him late for the appointment he had at twelve in Addison Road. He'd give the woman there a call and say he'd been held up. Nerissa drove into Notting Hill Gate and turned up towards the Portobello Road but avoided it and went on to Westbourne Grove. For once, there was very little traffic, nothing to separate his car from her car or hold them up. Roadworks at the top slowed them both and he saw her put her head out of the window in an attempt to see what was going on. But finally they were through the barriers and past the cones. More suddenly than he expected – she didn't signal – she swung the car into a metered space in a side street, dropped in her coins and ran up to a door with the number 13 Charing Terrace on it and 'Shoshana's Spa and Health Club' in big chrome letters. By then, staring after her, he was holding up a stream of traffic. A chorus of hooting and yells of rage from other drivers at last forced him to move.

He was ten minutes late for the woman in Addison Road. All the way to the back of this big house and down the basement stairs, she lectured him on punctuality as if she were his employer, not his client. Mix nearly told her that, in his opinion, the damage to the climbing machine was caused by disuse, not wear and tear, and he wasn't surprised when he looked at the shape and size of her. But he didn't. She had an elliptical cross-trainer on order from Fiterama Accessories and if he was rude she'd withdraw her custom.

Nothing like that mattered now he'd found the gym Nerissa went to. Pity about the number though. Along with his other occult beliefs and fears, Mix was superstitious, especially about walking under ladders and the number thirteen. He always avoided having anything to do with it when he could. When this phobia or whatever it was had started he didn't know, though it was true that Javy, whom his mother had married on the thirteenth of the month, had his birthday on the thirteenth of April. The day he had beaten Mix so badly it had nearly killed him had very likely been the thirteenth but Mix had been too young then to remember or even to have known.

The Cockatoodle Club in Soho was overheated, smelt of various kinds of smoke and Thai green curry and was none too clean. So, at any rate, said the girl Ed's girlfriend Steph had brought along for Mix. Ed was another rep-engineer at Fiterama and Mix's friend, Steph his live-in partner. The other girl kept running her finger along the chair legs and under the tables and holding it up to show everyone.

'You remind me of my gran,' said Steph.

'A place where people eat ought to be clean.'

'Eat! Chance'd be a fine thing. It's a good three-quarters of an hour since we ordered those prawns.'

The other girl, whose name was Lara, and who had hay fever or something which made her sniff a lot, resumed her finger-dusting of the area below their table. Steph lit a cigarette. Mix, who didn't approve of smoking, calculated that it was her eighth since they had come in here. The music, which was hip-hop, was too loud for normal speech, and to make yourself heard you had to shout. How Steph managed with her damaged lungs, Mix didn't know, imagining the villi all lying prone in there. Just as the waitress appeared with curried prawns for the girls and cottage pie for the men, Lara's questing finger touched his knee and was pulled away as if he'd stung her.

They exchanged resentful looks. What with the noise and this awful girl and the cottage pie smelling as if green curry had got into it, Mix felt like going home. He wasn't very old but he was too old for this. Lara said a waitress dressed like that was an insult to all the women patrons.

'Why? She's lovely. I love her skirt.'

'Yes, you would, Ed. That's my point. More like a belt than a skirt, if you ask me.'

'I didn't ask you,' Ed yelled at the top of his voice. 'As for insults, I'm only looking, I'm not going to screw her.'

'You wish.'

'Oh, shut up,' said Steph, taking Ed's hand affectionately.

No one was much enjoying themselves. But they stayed. Ed bought a bottle of Moravian champagne and he and Steph tried to dance but the tiny floor-space was too crowded, not just to move but to keep upright. Lara started sneezing and had to use her table napkin for a tissue. They didn't leave till two. That was the earliest any of them felt the heavens wouldn't fall if they went home. Mix got into one of his fantasies, a vindictive one this time, in which he gave a lift to Lara but instead of driving her home to Palmers Green – that was a fine distance at this time of night for a bloke who lived in Notting Dale – he imagined taking her up to Victoria Park or London Fields, and pushing her out of the car to find her own way home. If by that time she hadn't been the prey of the homicidal maniacs who allegedly haunted those places. Reggie, he thought, Reggie would have dealt with her.

They proceeded in silence up to Hornsey, Mix

43

imagining Reggie luring her to Rillington Place on the grounds of curing her hay fever with his inhaler which would actually gas her. He'd make her sit in his deckchair and breathe in the chloroform . . .

'Why have you been so horrible?' she asked him after his distant 'Good night' and opening of the passenger door for her. He didn't answer, but turned his face away. She let herself in through the front door of number thirteen – it would be – and banged it loudly after her. There were probably at least ten other occupants of that building and all of them would have woken up. It seemed to Mix that the place was still reverberating when he got back into the driving seat.

The night was cold and out here the windscreens of parked cars had frost on them. He didn't know the area very well, missed his turning and, after driving for what seemed like hours, found himself round the back of King's Cross station. Never mind. He'd take the Marylebone Road and the flyover. Day and night it was busy. Traffic never ceased. But the side streets were deserted, the lamps which should have cheered them making them seem more stark and less safe than darkness.

He had to drive up and down St Blaise Avenue and up again before he found a space in the residents' parking to put his car. If he left it on the yellow line he'd have to be out there before eight-thirty in the morning to move it. At this hour of the night, the street was packed with cars and empty of people. It was so dark between the pillars and inside the portico that it took him a while to find the lock and slide the key into it.

Crossing the hall, he saw himself in the big mirror like a stranger, unrecognisable in the dimness. All the lights on staircase and landings were on time switches and turned themselves off, he'd calculated, after about fifteen seconds. The bulbs in the hanging lamps in hall and stairs being of very low wattage, great pools of darkness lay ahead in the twists and bends. Cursing the length of this staircase, he began to climb. He was very tired and he didn't know why. Perhaps it had something to do with the emotional stress of tracking down Nerissa and discovering where she went, or it was due to that Lara who was such a contrast to her. His legs dragged and the calf muscles began to ache. After two flights, at the first landing, where Miss Chawcer slept behind a big oak door set in a deep recess, the lights grew even dimmer and went out faster. It was impossible to see the top of the next flight. From here the floor above was lost in dense black shadow.

The place was so big and the ceilings so high that it had a creepy feel even on a bright day. By night the flower and fruit carvings on the wood-work turned into gargoyles and in the silence he seemed to hear soft sighs coming from the darkest corners. Mounting slowly because he was as usual panting, he recalled, as one does in such situations, his half-belief in ghosts. He had often said, of some particular old house, that he didn't believe in ghosts but he wouldn't spend a night there for any-thing. The habit he had got into of counting the stairs in this top flight as if he could make the figure twelve or fourteen was hard to break. He seemed to do it automatically once he had pressed the switch at the foot. But he had reached only to three when he seemed to see, in the light's feeble gleam, a figure standing at the top. It was a man, tallish, glasses on its beaky nose catching the coloured light from the Isabella window.

The sound that rose to his mouth came out as a thin whimper, the kind you utter in a bad dream when you think you are screaming loudly. At the same time, he squeezed his eyes shut. With one hand stretched out, he stood there until a darkening inside his eyelids told him the light had gone out again. He took a step backwards, pressed the switch again, opened his eyes and looked. The figure was gone. If it had ever been there, if he hadn't imagined it.

It still took all the nerve he could summon to go up those stairs past the spot where it had stood and across the spots of Isabella light to let himself into his flat.

A bright morning and the terrors of the night dispelled by sunshine. Mix was having a lie-in because it was Saturday. He lay in bed in the stifling warmth of his overheated bedroom, watching a flock of pigeons, a single heron flying low, an aircraft leaving a trail like a string of cloud across the blue sky. Now he could tell himself the figure on the stairs was an hallucination or something caused by that stained glass window. Drink and darkness played strange tricks on the mind. He had drunk quite a bit and that house where she lived being thirteen was the last straw.

Getting up to make tea and take it back with him, he saw Otto far below, a dark chocolate silhouette, sitting on one of the crumbling walls against which ancient trees leant and from which an ancient trellis drooped. In the almost identical wilderness at the end of this garden, two guinea fowl with crinolines of grey feathers pottered among dead weed stalks and brambles. Otto spent hours watching these guinea fowl, plotting how to catch and eat them. Mix had often watched him, disliking the cat but half hoping to witness the hunt and the kill. Keeping the birds was almost certainly illegal but the local authority remained in ignorance of their existence and no neighbour ever told.

He lifted out of a drawer his Nerissa scrapbooks and took them back to bed with him. This bright morning would be a good time to take a photograph of her house and perhaps another of the health club. And there would be a chance of seeing her again. Turning the pages of this collection of Nerissa pictures and cuttings, he slipped into a fantasy of how he could meet her. Really meet her and remind her of their previous encounter. A party would be the sort of occasion he wanted, one that she was attending and to which he could get himself invited. A niggling fear crept into his mind that she might have spotted him outside her house and known it was he following her to the health club. He must be more careful.

Could he persuade Colette Gilbert-Bamber to give a party? More to the point, could he persuade her to invite him to it if she did? The husband, whom he'd never met, was an unknown quantity. Mix had never even seen a picture of him. Maybe he hated parties or only liked the formal kind, full of business people drinking dry wine and fizzy water and talking about gilts and a bear market. Even if the party happened, would he have the nerve to ask Nerissa out? He'd have to take her somewhere fabulous, but he'd started saving up for that, and once he'd been seen out with her –

or, say, three times – he'd be made, the TV offers would start rolling in, the requests for interviews, the invitations to premières.

He must hedge his bets. He'd call the health club this morning and ask about joining. Suppose he found out who her guru was, or her clairvoyant or whatever? That would be easier than a party. He knew she had one. It had been in the papers. He wouldn't have to be invited to a guru's place. He could just go, provided he paid. There were ways of finding out when Nerissa's appointments were and then somehow getting his to precede or follow hers. It wouldn't be all pretending either, it wouldn't just be a ploy. He wouldn't mind seeing someone who knew about the supernatural. If there really were ghosts and spirits and whatever or if sighting them was always in the mind. A guru or a medium could tell him.

Mix finished his tea, closed the scrapbook, and forced himself to walk over to the long mirror that was a cheval-glass framed in stainless steel. He shut his eyes and opened them again. There – nothing and no one behind him, what a mad idea! Naked, he confessed to himself that there was room for improvement. In his job and with his ambition, he ought to have a perfect figure, a six-pack chest, fleshless hips and a small hard bum. Once it had been like that – and would be again, he resolved. All those chips and chocolate bars were to blame. His face was all right. Handsome, according to Colette and others, the features regular, the eyes a steady honest blue. He could tell they admired his fine head of light brown hair with the blond highlights but his skin ought not to be so pale. She would be used to men of perfect physique and magnificent tan. The gym was the answer to that and the tanning place round the corner. He couldn't see his back but he knew the scars were all gone now, anyway. Pity, really. He still nursed a fantasy which had begun when his back was still bleeding, of showing someone – the police, the social services – what Javy had done and seeing him handcuffed and taken away to prison. It was either that or killing him.

For five years Mix had been his mother's darling. He was her only child, his father a boyfriend who had moved out when he was six months old. She was only eighteen and she loved her little son passionately. But not enduringly or exclusively, for when Mix was five she met James Victor Calthorpe, fell for a baby and married him. Javy, as everyone called him, was big and dark and handsome. At first he took very little notice of Mix except to smack him and at first it seemed to the boy that his mother loved him as much as ever. Then the baby was born, a dark-eyed, dark-haired girl they called Shannon. Mix couldn't remember feeling much about the baby or seeing his mother pay her more attention than she paid him but the psychiatrist they made him go to when he was older told him that was his trouble. He resented his mother withdrawing her love from him and transferring it to Shannon. That was why he tried to kill the baby.

Mix remembered nothing about it, nothing about picking up the tomato ketchup bottle and hitting her with it. Or not quite hitting her. Bashing inside the cot but missing. He couldn't remember Javy coming into the room but he remembered the beating Javy gave him. And his mother standing there and watching but doing nothing to stop him.

He had used the leather belt, from his jeans, pulling Mix's T-shirt over his head, lashing at his back till it bled.

That never happened again, though Javy went on smacking him whenever he didn't toe the line. Apart from the psychiatrist talking about it, the only way he knew he had tried to kill Shannon was because Javy was always telling him. He got on quite well with his little sister and with the baby boy Terry who was born a year later, but if ever Javy caught him even disagreeing with Shannon or taking a toy away from her, he'd repeat that story and say how Mix had tried to kill her.

'You'd be dead by now,' he'd say to his daughter, 'but for me stopping that murdering kid.' And to his little son, 'You want to watch him, he'll kill you as soon as look at you.'

That would be a way to get famous, Mix sometimes thought, killing one's stepfather out of revenge. But Javy had left them when he was fourteen. Mix's mother wept and sobbed and had hysterics until Mix got fed up with it and slapped her face.

'I'll give you something to make you cry,' he had shouted in his anger. 'Standing there and watching him beat me up.'

They sent him to the psychiatrist for hitting his mother. A domestic violence perpetrator waiting to happen, was the description he overheard one social worker call him. She was still alive, his mother, not yet fifty, but he'd never see her again.

It was Saturday, so he could park more or less anywhere he could find a space in Westbourne Park Road. As it happened he got on to the same meter as Nerissa had used. Mix was besotted enough to get a thrill out of that, just as he would have from touching something she had touched or reading some sign she had read hours before. He went up to the door and rang the lowest one of a series of bells. The door growled open on to an unprepossessing hallway smelling of incense, a steep and narrow staircase and a smart new lift, all steel and glass like his mirror. It took him up a couple of floors where, to Mix's relief, everything was like itself, streamlined, glittering and sleek. Doors opened off the hallway, labelled Reflexology and Massage and Podiatry. The gym was full of young people labouring away on treadmills and skiers and stationary bikes. Through a big picture window he could see girls in bikinis and men looking the way he wanted to look, either in or sitting round the edge of, a large bubbling Jacuzzi. A thin dark girl in a leotard with an open white coat over it asked him what he wanted. Mix had had an idea. He explained his trade and asked if anyone was needed to service and maintain the machines. His company would consider taking Shoshana's on.

'It's funny you should say that,' said the girl, 'because the guy who was going to do ours let us down yesterday.'

'I think we could fit you in,' said Mix. He asked what rates the defaulters had charged. The answer pleased him. He could undercut that. And he began to think daringly of taking it on privately, strictly against the company's rules, but why should they find out?

'I'll have to ask Madam Shoshana.' She had a faltering voice and the bright nervous eyes of a mouse. 'Would you like to give me a call later?'

'I'll do that small thing. What's your name then?'

'Danila.'

'That's a funny one,' he said.

She looked about sixteen. 'I'm from Bosnia. But I've been here since I was a kid.'

'Bosnia, right.' There had been a war there, he thought vaguely, back some time in the nineties.

'I was afraid for a moment you wanted to join,' said Danila. 'We got a waiting list as long as your arm. Most of them don't come more than four times – that's the usual, four times – but they're on the books, aren't they? They're members.'

Mix was interested in only one member. 'I'll call you later,' he said.

Suppose Nerissa was here now? He wandered along the aisle between the machines. Small television transmitters hung at head height in front of each one and all were showing either a quiz show or a very old Tom and Jerry cartoon. Most were watching the cartoon while pumping or pedalling away. She wasn't there. He wouldn't have had to look closely. She stood out from others like an angel in hell or a rose in a sewer. Those long legs, that gazelle's body, that raven hair, must cause a sensation in here.

Contemplating going to a film, later a drink with Ed in the Kensington Park Hotel, the pub Reggie had used and called KPH, he thought of the figure he had hallucinated on the stairs. Suppose it wasn't an hallucination but a real ghost? Suppose it had been Reggie? His ghost, that is. His spirit, doomed to haunt the environs of where he'd once lived. Mix knew Reggie didn't really look like Richard Attenborough; or like himself, come to that. He'd looked quite different, taller and thinner and older.

There were plenty of photographs in his books. Mix became very frightened when he tried to conjure up an image of the man on the stairs. Besides, he couldn't do it. He just about knew it was a man and not very young and maybe wearing glasses. Yes, he couldn't have made up the glasses, could he? They couldn't have been in his mind.

Reggie might have been in St Blaise House while he was alive. Why not? Miss Chawcer had escaped him but he might have come there after her. Mix, who thoroughly knew the details of Reggie's life after he came to Notting Hill, pictured her going to Rillington Place, as it then was, for an abortion, but getting cold feet and running away. A lucky escape. Had Reggie tried to persuade her to let him do the deed at her own place? No, because he had to get rid of the body. He went there to get her to return . . .

Were there ghosts and if so, was it the murderer whose spirit he had seen? Why had he come back? And why there and not to Rillington Place which had been the graveyard for so many dead women? Why not was pretty obvious. He wouldn't know the place after what they'd done to it, his three-storey Victorian house and all the others like it razed to the ground. All those smart new rows, the trees and the *cheerful* atmosphere would have put him off ever returning. He could have gone to the place in Oxford Gardens where his first victim Ruth Fuerst had had a room. She was the one whose leg bone they had found propping up the fence in Reggie's garden. Or to that of his second, Muriel Eady who had lived in Putney. But St Blaise House was nearer and *unchanged*. He would like that, a house just the same as it had been in the forties and fifties. He'd feel comfortable there and besides, he still had unfinished business to attend to.

She was old now but he wasn't. He was the same age as when they'd hanged him and would always be. What more likely than that he had come back to find old Chawcer and take her back with him to wherever he came from? Don't think like that, stop it, Mix said to himself as he climbed the fifty-two stairs, you'll frighten yourself to death.

# Chapter 5

In her house in Campden Hill Square, Nerissa Nash was getting ready to go to her parents' for supper. If it had been her mum alone she was going to see, say when her dad was at work, she would have put on jeans and boots and an old jumper under her sheepskin. But her dad liked to see her dressed up, he took such pride in her.

Though she had no idea of this, her life was one they didn't begin to understand. If not everyone could lead it, she supposed everyone would want to. It was bounded by the body and the face, hair – lots of it on the head and none anywhere else – clothes, cosmetics, aids to beauty, homoeopathy, work-outs, massage, sparkling water, lettuce, vitamin supplements, alternative medicine, astrology and having her fortune told, the images and activities of other celebrities, her mum and dad and her brothers. Of music she knew very little, of painting, books, opera, ballet, scientific advances and politics she knew nothing and wasn't interested in them. Taking part in fashion shows, she had visited all the major capitals of the world and seen of them only the studios and changing rooms of designers, the inside of clubs and gyms, the premises of masseurs and her own face in the mirrors of cosmeticians. But for one lack in her life, she was extremely happy.

From both parents, somewhere in the genes, she had inherited a sunny disposition, a faculty for enjoying simple pleasures, and a kindly nature. People said of her that Nerissa would do anything to help a friend. Almost everything she did she enjoyed. Especially delightful was sitting at her huge dressing table, a white cotton cape covering her silk shift, her long hair looped back, making up her face. On the CD player Johnny Cash was singing her favourite song, loved by her because it was her dad's preference over all others, the one about the teenage queen, prettiest girl they'd ever seen, she who loved the boy next door, who worked at the candy store. Nerissa identified with this successful beauty in most respects.

Her dad liked her hair hanging loose, so she left it that way. If only it had been cold, she could have worn her new fake fur that was made to look like Arctic fox. No real fur for her, she loved animals too much. The very thought made her shudder. But no, it had better be something thin and silky. She dropped the cape on the floor, inadvertently swept off the dressing table the lid of a pot and three ear-rings. What should she take her parents? She should have bought something but she'd been working out most of the day and hadn't got round to it. Never mind. Two bottles of champagne came out of the drinks cupboard and a jar of cocktail sticks fell out, scattering everywhere. Next that huge box of chocolates Rodney had given her – he was so sweet but was he crazy, thinking she'd so much as look at a chocolate?

Nerissa left a trail of litter behind her through

the house. Even the flowers toppled out of the vases. Magazines tumbled out of the rack, handfuls of tissues spilled onto surfaces and under tables, lamps fell over, glasses broke and odd bits of jewellery glinted from the carpet pile and the windowsills. Lynette, who came to clean, was so well paid she didn't mind. She went about the house, picking everything up, admiring a ring here, a bottle of scent there, and if she was at home, Nerissa would give it to her.

It was raining, the heavy crashing rain of summer. Nerissa put on her white shiny raincoat over her shift and leapt into the car with her champagne and her chocolates, her wet umbrella – white and with a picture of the seafront at Nice on it – slung on to the back seat. She stopped in Holland Park on a double yellow line to buy flowers for her mum, orchids and arum lilies, roses and funny green things the florist couldn't identify. Luck was with her, as it usually was. All the wardens were indoors watching *Casualty* on TV. She was going to be late – when wasn't she? – but Dad wouldn't mind. He liked eating closer to nine than eight.

They lived in Acton, in a street of semi-detached mock-Tudor houses, theirs with an extra bedroom over the garage. Nerissa and her brothers had grown up there, gone to the local schools, visited the local cinema and shopped at the local shops. Both of her brothers were older than Nerissa and both were now married. When she started to make a lot of money, she had wanted to buy her parents a house near her own, perhaps a smart cottage in fashionable Pottery Lane, but they would have none of it. They liked Acton. They liked their neighbours and the neighbourhood and their big garden. All their friends lived nearby and they were staying put. Besides, her father had made three ponds in his garden, one in the front and two in the back, and filled them with goldfish. Where in Pottery Lane would he be able to have three ponds or even one? And the goldfish were very active tonight, enjoying the rain.

It was her father who answered the door. Nerissa threw her arms round him, then round her mother, presented her gifts. These were, as always, received rapturously. She never touched alcohol, she drank bottled water, but now she accepted with pleasure a large cup of Yorkshire tea. You could get very fed up with water thrust at you wherever you went. Her mum always announced dinner in the same way, and uttered it in an atrocious French accent. Nerissa would have wondered what was wrong if she had deviated from this practice.

'Mademoiselle est servie.'

She only ate food like this when she went to her parents' house. The rest of the time she picked at grapefruit and Japanese rice crackers at home or green salad in restaurants. It was a miracle, she sometimes thought, that her insides could weather the shock of digesting thick soup, rolls and butter, roast meat and potatoes, batter pudding and Brussels sprouts, with no ill effects. Her mother thought this was her normal diet.

'My daughter can eat as much as she likes,' she told friends. 'She never puts on a scrap of weight.'

When they had reached the apple charlotte and baked Alaska stage of the meal, Nerissa asked her mother about their neighbours. These people were great friends, as close as cousins.

'Fine, I think,' her mother said. 'I haven't seen much of them for a few days. Sheila's got a new job, I do know that – oh, and Bill's got the all-clear from the hospital.'

'That's good.' Nerissa trod warily. 'And the son? He's still living at home?'

'Darel?' her dad said. 'Such a nice well-mannered boy. He's still at home but Sheila told me he's buying a flat in Docklands. Time to move on, he says.'

Nerissa was unsure whether this was good news for her or bad. While she was having dinner with her parents, she always hoped Darel Jones would come to the door to beg a couple of teabags or return a borrowed book. He never had, though according to her mother, they and the Joneses were always 'in and out of each other's houses'. She thought of him next door, watching television with his parents or maybe out somewhere with another girl. The latter was more likely for a very handsome and charming young man of twenty-eight. She sighed and then smiled to stop her parents noticing.

Guilt seldom troubled Gwendolen. To her mind she led, and had always led, a blameless life of absolute integrity. Entering a tenant's flat in his absence and exploring it seemed to her a landlord's right and if she enjoyed it, so much the better. The only draw-back was her need to rest and take deep breaths between flights.

What a lot he drank! An empty gin bottle and one which had contained vodka and four wine bot-tles had been put into the recycling box since she was last up here. It was evident he didn't eat much at home, the fridge was again nearly empty and smelling of antiseptic. A large leather-bound book lay on the coffee table. Because she could hardly pass a book without opening it, Gwendolen opened this one. Nothing but photographs of a black girl in very short skirts or swimming costumes. Perhaps this was what they meant by pornography; she had never really known.

A copy of the previous day's *Daily Telegraph* was beside the book. Gwendolen rather liked the *Telegraph* and would have bought it herself if it hadn't been so ruinously expensive. It puzzled her that Cellini had bought it. One of those tabloids was surely more his mark and she wouldn't have been surprised to learn that he had been given this copy. Ed had seen an article in it about fitness machines, which especially singled out Fiterama for mention, and passed it on.

Just as she couldn't pass a book without opening it, so Gwendolen found it impossible to see the printed word without reading it. Some of it, that is. Ignoring the fitness machine article, she read the front page, then the next page, managing fairly well but wishing she had her magnifying glass with her. When she reached the births, marriages and deaths, she laid the paper down and went to the door to listen. He hardly ever came back in the middle of the day but it was as well to be careful. How tidy it was! It amused her to think that of the two of them *he* with his cleanliness and fussy ways would be called an old woman while everyone saw her as cultivated and urbane, more like a man really.

She wasn't much interested in marriages and births, she never had been, but she ran her eye – pushed and strained her eye really – down the deaths column. People no longer had any stamina and many younger than herself died every day. Anderson, Arbuthnot, Beresford, Brewster, Brown, Carstairs – she had once known a Mrs Carstairs who lived down the road, but it wasn't her, she was called Diana, not Madeleine. Davis, Edwards, Egan, Fitch, Graham, Kureishi. There were three Nolans, very odd that, it wasn't a common name. Palmer, Pritchard, Rawlings, Reeves – Reeves!

How extraordinary and what a coincidence. This was the first time she had looked at the *Telegraph* for months and what should she find but the announcement of his wife's death. For it certainly was his wife.

*On 15 June, at home, Eileen Margaret, aged 78, beloved wife of Dr Stephen Reeves of Woodstock, Oxon. Funeral 21 June at St Bede's Church, Woodstock. No flowers. Donations to cancer research.*

This small print was terribly hard to read but there was no doubt about it. Would he notice if she cut it out of the paper? Possibly, but what could he do about it if he did? Now to find the scissors. Her own might be in the bathroom cabinet or the oven – seldom used, it made a useful cupboard – or somewhere in the bookshelves, but an old woman like him would keep his in a neatly arranged drawer along with such gadgets as potato peelers and bottle openers. He would be sure to have several of those.

Gwendolen poked about in Mix's kitchen, paying particular attention to the microwave, whose function was a puzzle to her. Did toast come out of it or music? It might even be a very small washing machine. She found the scissors exactly where she thought they would be and cut out the announcement of his wife's death. Downstairs she would be able to study it at leisure with the aid of her magnifying glass.

She was only just in time. As she was descending the bottom flight he let himself in by the front door.

'Good evening, Mr Cellini.'

'Hiya,' said Mix, thinking about her getting pregnant and going for help to Reggie. 'How are you doing? All right?'

When he phoned the spa the girl called Danila told him Madam Shoshana agreed to his servicing the machines. Perhaps he would like to come along some time and bring one of his contracts with him. Mix concocted a contract with *Mix Maintenance* as its headline – he was rather proud of that – and printed out two copies.

Instead of being modified by the passage of time, his fear increased as the days went by. He had never seen the figure on the stairs again, though he fancied sometimes that he heard noises which shouldn't have been there, footsteps in the long passage, a curious rustling sound like someone taking crushed paper out of bags or stuffing it into them, once a strain of music, though that might have come from the street. By night he had to screw up his courage in order to let himself in. And those stairs he had always hated were worse.

Reaching St Blaise House, he forced himself to put his key into the lock and enter the hall, the dim light coming on. Try not to think about it, he told himself as he began to mount, think about Nerissa and about getting fit, the way she'd like you to be

– why not get yourself an exercise bike? Fiterama will let you have it at cost. Go for walks, lift weights. He was always telling clients what marvellous physical benefit they'd get from using the machines. Tell yourself, he thought. And try to be glad about these stairs. Going up them is good exercise too.

Like a kind of therapy, this worked until he came to the landing below the tiled flight. Feeble light, filtered through tree branches and foliage and the grime on the glass, seeped through the Isabella window and touched him with spots of colour as he walked up. It lay on the top floor like a pattern done in smudged chalks and quite still on this windless night. Two long black passages stretched away from the landing, empty and silent, all the doors closed. He switched on the light once more, staring fearfully down the left-hand passage as the cat appeared from out of a door which came open and closed of its own accord. He saw its green eyes glinting as it walked in unconcerned fashion towards him, hissed as it passed him and made for the stairs.

Who or what had opened the door? He plunged into his flat, fumbling for the light switch but at last turning it on. The sudden brightness made him let out his breath in a long, relieved sigh. He'd heard of cats learning to open doors, though these in the flat had knobs, not handles. It might be different out there. Going to look was out of the question. The door in question must have a handle and Otto, who was clever if evil, had learnt to stand on his hind legs and apply to it the pressure of his clawy paw. Who had closed it? Doors close of their own accord, he told himself. It happens all the time.

A cheerful film on television, a not-so-old

Hollywood musical, a mug of hot chocolate with a drop of whisky in it and three Maryland cookies, finished the job of reassurance. Still, once he started on his fitness regime, all that sort of eating and drinking would have to stop. It was warm in the flat but not too hot, 27 degrees. That was the kind of temperature he liked. Warmth, sweet filling food, a thick soft mattress, lazing around, doing nothing – why were all the nice things bad for you?

The cat and its eyes were banished for the duration of the musical. Above his head, outside his front door, he could hear no sound, and when the television was off the silence was disturbed only by the sighing of traffic on the Westway. He felt better. He congratulated himself on his resilience. But in bed, with the bedside lamp off, he thought of the cat and the door again, and although there could be nothing to see, kept his eyes shut against the darkness.

# Chapter 6

Next morning he woke up to awareness that he had
been frightened the night before and for a moment
he had to think why. But fear and the memory of
fear began to fade when he saw the sunshine and
heard children playing in the garden next door to
the guinea fowl man. Otto must have opened the
door himself and it must have shut behind him of
its own volition. He got up, had a shower and,
telling himself it was a good start to a work-out
programme, he set off for a walk. But before starting
he went rather cautiously along the passage
towards the door of the room the cat must have
come out of. Sure enough, the doors down here had
handles. He left, unreasonably relieved, more as if
he'd just had a wonderful piece of news instead of
only finding out what he already knew was true.

Now for a walk. Blow the cobwebs away in more
senses than one, let sunlight and energy into his
life. There was a big Catholic church near the con-
vent and, about to march on past it, he stopped for
a moment to watch the people going in to mass. A
lot of people, more than he'd have thought likely.
A kind of regret came into his mind and a wist-
fulness. Those people wouldn't have his problems,
his doubts and fears. They had their religion, they
had something to turn to, something or someone

to bring them comfort. If they saw a ghost or heard footsteps and doors closing, they'd call out the name of their god or utter the appropriate curse. In stories, that usually worked. He had had religion when he was small and his grandmother was alive to take him to church. But that was long ago and it was all gone now. He'd not thought about it since and didn't believe in any of it. If he went in there and along with them asked someone up in the sky for help, he'd feel such a fool, he'd be embarrassed. Much the same went for asking their vicar – their priest? Mix couldn't imagine how he'd explain to the man or what the man would answer. It was beyond him.

On Monday and Tuesday he was busy at work, and for once was relieved he had work to do. There was a new treadmill coming to a ground-floor flat in Bayswater which he had to set up and demonstrate. Half a dozen steps on that and he was breathless, in spite of his walks. Then all the calls for help with broken-down equipment to answer, e-mails, complaining or demanding. On the second evening he managed a visit to Shoshana's Spa and Health Club, where he told Danila he was making a survey and a servicing plan. This was to put her off the scent. Because he was really looking for Nerissa. He was on the point of asking Danila about her, which were her days for coming to the club, was she a regular visitor, that kind of thing, but he decided it would sound funny. It would sound as if his contracting to look after the club's machines was no more than a ploy to meet the famous model – as indeed it was. He handed over a copy of his contract and left.

On Wednesday evening he went to the Coronet cinema with Ed and Steph and afterwards to the Sun in Splendour for a drink. When the men each had a gin and tonic in front of them and Steph a vodka and blackcurrant, he asked her what he'd been planning, in fact rehearsing, saying to her all day. The elaborate, hedging-of-bets, covert way of asking a simple question got lost and he came out with a few simple words.

'Do you believe in ghosts, Steph?'

She didn't laugh or scoff. 'There's more things in heaven and earth . . .' she began but couldn't remember the rest. 'I think, like, if there's been an awful thing like a murder in a place, the dead person or the killer – well, they may come back and revisit the scene of the crime. It's their energy,' she went on vaguely, 'it kind of hangs around and makes the person – well, *materialise.*'

Just what he thought. He was going to ask her about the mysterious opening and shutting of that door but then he remembered the cat had done it. 'Would it have to be the scene of the crime? I mean, where someone died? Could it be a place where another crime was committed?'

'She's not an expert, Mix,' Ed said. 'She's not a medium.'

Mix took no notice. 'Suppose it was a murderer who'd tried to do another murder but it went wrong? Would he come back to the place where it went wrong?'

'He might,' Steph said rather dubiously, and then, 'Look, is this really happening? That funny old place you live in, is it haunted or what?'

'Funny old place' was right, but Mix didn't much like someone else calling it that. It seemed an insult to his beautiful flat. 'I reckon I may have seen – something,' he said carefully.

'What sort of something?' Ed was agog.

The more sensitive and perhaps intuitive Steph read the expression on Mix's face. 'He doesn't want to talk about it, Ed. I mean, would you? You know what Ed said, Mix. You need help.'

'Do I?'

'Look, I'll tell you what I'll do. I'll let you have a lend of this and you can drive the thing away with it if it comes again.' She unfastened the Gothic cross of purple and black stones which hung round her neck from a silver chain. 'Here, you have it.'

'Oh, no, I might lose it!'

'Not the end of the world if you do. It only cost me fifteen quid. And my mum says I shouldn't wear it, she says it's – what's the word, Ed?'

'Blasphemous,' said Ed.

'That's it, blasphemous. My mum knows a medium and she said it would work. If I needed it. She said *any* cross would work.'

Mix studied the cross. He thought it ugly, the stones so obviously glass, the silver so evidently nickel. But it was a cross and as such might do the trick. If he threw it at Reggie or even if he only held it up in front of him, the ghost might melt away like a spiral of smoke or a genie going back into a bottle.

Gwendolen had found a plastic bone in her bedroom. At first she couldn't think what it was doing there or where it had come from and then she remembered Olive's little dog playing with it. She offered it to Otto, who shrank away with an expression of contempt on his face, as if repelled by the smell of dog. The bone wrapped up in a sheet of newspaper and put inside the washing machine for safe keeping, she waited for Olive to phone and complain about her loss.

With the diminishing of her income, Gwendolen had become very careful with money and disliked spending it on unnecessary phone calls. If Olive wanted her animal's toy, let her phone or come round and fetch it. But the days went by and there was no call and no visit. Gwendolen used the washing machine only when she had accumulated a stack of dirty laundry. When this happened she nearly washed the bone and the newspaper, stuffing the clothes in before she noticed. There were a number of small Asian-run shops as well as the bigger grocers in Ladbroke Grove and Westbourne Grove where she did her shopping, carefully comparing prices – every single penny piece counted – before making up her mind. To reach any of them she had to pass the block of flats where Olive lived. Putting on her good black silk coat with the tiny covered buttons, now some thirty years old, and a small round straw hat because the day looked warm, she set off with the bone in the bottom of her shopping trolley. This was covered in Black Watch tartan and, being only nine years old, quite smart still.

Dropping in on Olive, she rang her bell in the lobby. No answer. Nor did the porter get an answer when she asked him to phone Mrs Fordyce in 11C. He thought he had seen her go out. Gwendolen was extremely annoyed. It was feckless leaving your rubbish in other people's houses and then giving no sign of the social solecism you had committed. She was tempted to drop the bone in its wrapping into the nearest litter bin but a niggling doubt about the validity of doing that stopped her. It might amount to stealing.

After reading, Gwendolen liked shopping best of what she did. Not because of what she bought or the layout of the shops or the friendliness of staff but solely on the grounds of comparing prices and saving money. She was no fool and she knew very well that the amounts she saved on a tin of gravy powder here and a piece of Cheddar cheese there would never amount to more than, say, twenty pence a day. But she acknowledged to herself that it was a game she played and one that made trekking all the way over to the Portobello Road market or up to Sainsbury's a pleasure rather than a chore. Besides, crossing Ladbroke Grove, if she followed a certain route, took her past the house where, all those years ago, Dr Reeves had had his surgery. By now the pain had gone from her memories of him and only a rather delightful nostalgia remained, that and a new hope, brought about by the announcement in the *Telegraph*.

Just after the war the Chawcers had thought of going to Dr Odess. The first symptoms of Mrs Chawcer's illness had showed themselves about that time. But Colville Square was rather a long walk away, while Dr Reeves was in Ladbroke Grove and reached by simply taking Cambridge Gardens. It wasn't till the trial and all the publicity in the newspapers that Gwendolen discovered Dr Odess had been Christie's doctor and had attended him and his wife for years.

She was tempted to go up to the market this morning. The sun was shining and flowers were out everywhere. The council had hung baskets of geraniums on all the lampposts. I wonder what that costs, thought Gwendolen. Sometimes when she went to the market for her vegetables, her cooking apples and her bananas – the only fruit Gwendolen ever ate were bananas and stewed apple – she was able to save a lot and sometimes have forty pence more than she expected in her purse at the end of the day. She stopped outside the four-storey house with basement and with steep stairs climbing to the front door, where Stephen Reeves had practised. It was run-down now, its paint peeling, a pane in a front bay window broken and patched up with a plastic Tesco bag and Sellotape.

Inside there had been the waiting room where she had sat and waited for prescriptions for her mother. In those days doctors had no lights and bells to signify they were ready to receive the next patient, often no receptionist or nurse on the premises. Dr Reeves used to come to the waiting room himself, call out the patient's name and hold the door open for him or her to pass through. Gwendolen never minded how long she had to wait for the prescription to be handed to her for he would do this himself, and might come two or three times into the waiting room to receive the next patient before he did so. She knew he only did this so that he could catch glimpses of her and she have sight of him. He always smiled and the smile for her was different from those directed at others, warmer, wider and somehow more conspiratorial.

It was as if they shared a secret as indeed they did – their love for each other. She hadn't minded having to leave the surgery on her own. He would be at St Blaise House in a day or two and then they would be alone, having tea and talking, talking,

talking. To all intents and purposes they were alone in the house. Bertha the last maid was long gone and by this time domestic workers wanted higher wages than the Chawcers could afford. Mrs Chawcer was asleep, or certainly immobile, upstairs. The professor might be home by five but seldom before, threading his way on the old bicycle through the increasing traffic on the Marylebone Road into the complexities of Bayswater and Notting Hill. It was very quiet in St Blaise House in the fifties while Stephen Reeves and Gwendolen sat side by side and talked and whispered, putting the world right, laughing a little, their hands and knees very close, their eyes meeting. Because of these sessions and the intimacy which had grown up between them, because he had once said he was awfully fond of her, she considered herself irrevocably bound to him. In her mind it was an until-death-us-do-part agreement.

For a long time she had been bitter against him, seeing him as treacherous, a man who had jilted her. If he had never said he loved her in so many words, actions spoke louder. Later on, she had looked at the situation more rationally, understanding that he had no doubt been entangled with this Eileen before he had met her, or before he had got to know her, and had perhaps been threatened with an action for breach of promise. Or her father or brother had threatened him with a horsewhip. Such things happened, she knew from her reading. Duelling, of course, was illegal and long since gone out of fashion. But he must have been inescapably entangled with the woman he had married, so what could he do but marry her? As for her, Gwendolen, she too was tied to him, as good as his wife.

It was interesting, she thought as she pushed her trolley along Westbourne Grove, the number of people she had heard of lately who, widowed or losing their wives in old age, came back to their past and married the sweetheart of their youth. Queenie Winthrop's sister was such a one and so was a certain member of the St Blaise Residents' Association, a Mrs Coburn-French. Of course, Gwendolen was a realist and had to face the fact that women lost their husbands more often than men lost their wives. But sometimes women were the first to die. Look at her father. Not that he had married any long-lost sweetheart, but Mr Iqbal from the Hyderabad Emporium had done just that, meeting outside the mosque in Willesden a lady he had known from the same village in India fifty years before. And now Eileen was dead . . .

Stephen Reeves was a widower now. Would he come back for her? If she had married someone else and that someone had died, she would look for him. The bond between them must be as fixed and enduring for him as it was for her. Perhaps she should take steps to find him . . . ? He might be shy, he might even feel guilty about what he had done and be afraid to face her. Men were such cowards, that was a well-known fact. Look how squeamish the professor had been about taking on any of the tending of her mother when she was so ill.

It was half a century since last she had seen Stephen, or it soon would be. There were ways of finding people these days, much easier and surer ways than when she was young. You did it somehow with a computer. You used this computer and got into something called the 'net' or the 'web' and it would tell you. There were places – there was one in Ladbroke Grove – called Internet cafés. For a long time Gwendolen had thought that meant a place to have coffee in and eat cakes but Olive, laughing stupidly, had set her right. If she went to such a place would she be able to find Stephen Reeves after fifty years?

She thought about all this as she walked home with her shopping. After he had told her she was a nice girl and he was fond of her, she sat up in her bedroom and practised writing her name as it would soon be. *Gwendolen Reeves* or *G.L.Reeves*, she would sign herself, but on invitation cards she would be Mrs Stephen Reeves. *Mrs Stephen Reeves at home* and *Dr and Mrs Stephen Reeves thank you for your kind invitation but regret they cannot accept* . . . As it turned out, these last had been reserved for Eileen. That need not trouble her now, for Eileen was dead. Somehow she knew it hadn't been a happy marriage, in spite of that 'beloved wife'. He had to put it like that, everyone did, it was the convention. Possibly, when he and Eileen quarrelled, as no doubt they often did, he told her he should never have married her.

'I should have married Gwendolen,' he would have said. 'She was my first love.'

Gwendolen had never expressed her feelings to him. It wouldn't have been right for a woman to do that then but things seemed to be different now. He might not know how she felt, he might never have known. Somehow she must manage to tell him and then everything would come right.

# Chapter 7

He had read *Christie's Victims* before but a long time ago, six or seven years ago when he began collecting his Reggie library. Of course he remembered it. But it was still fascinating to retrace his steps through the Notting Hill of those days and through the life of one of the most famous serial killers of all time.

'John Reginald Halliday Christie came to live in London in 1938,' Mix read while eating his breakfast,

and with him came his wife Ethel. He was a curious man. There must be something strange, not to say appalling, about any necrophile. Not only is the idea of necrophilia repugnant to everyone but, in order to indulge his desire, the sufferer from this aberration must, unless he has unlikely access to a morgue, first kill his victims.

Looking at it from the perspective of the twenty-first century, Christie's marriage was not a happy one. Five years after their wedding, Ethel left him and went to live in Sheffield. Their separation lasted for several years until Christie wrote to her, asking her to return to him. After their reunion, she was often away staying with her relatives in the north. Christie had been a cinema operative, a mill-worker and a postman, in connection with which last he was sent to prison for stealing postal orders. Imprisoned again for stealing a car from a Roman Catholic priest who had befriended him, he nevertheless volunteered for the Emergency Reserve of the London Police Force and was accepted in the year he and his wife came to Rillington Place, Notting Hill, West London.

Apparently the police made no inquiries about his past, or if they did their findings were not serious enough to disqualify him, and in 1939 he became a full-time Special Constable. Four years later, while still a policeman, he met the girl who was to be his first murder victim . . .

Reluctantly, Mix raised his eyes and slipped a marker in between the pages. Having told Danila at Shoshana's Spa and Health Club that he would be arriving at ten to service five machines, he had better go. The book, by a certain Charles Q. Dudley, was the fourth or fifth he had read on the Rillington Place murderer and the facts he had just absorbed were already known to him. This he had expected. What he was looking for and expected to find, per-haps halfway through the book, was some hint or suggestion that Christie sometimes visited his prospective victims' homes. Had he noticed any-thing of this sort when he read the book for the first time? He couldn't remember.

Mix was taking the day off in lieu of working on a previous Sunday. It was useless trying to do the

Shoshana job before or after work because these were the least likely times for Nerissa to be there. Models get up very late in the mornings, Mix had read somewhere, while their evenings are occupied with film premières, clubs, public appearances and parties at manor houses in the Home Counties. When the happy time came, he fantasised, he and she would lie in together, maybe until midday or later. A maid would bring breakfast, but not before eleven, and when it came it would be what he had ordered, buck's fizz, caviare on toast and eggs benedict.

He returned to reality and recognised that parking was going to be a problem. He knew that before he got there. Eventually he found a meter and paid for two hours, but it was a long way from the health club. He told himself that all this walking must be improving his figure. Arriving on the dot of ten, he turned his eyes away from the chrome number thirteen and got quickly into the lift. Glancing round the girls and a couple of young men working out, he saw at once that Nerissa wasn't among them. Probably it was a bit early for her. His fussy eye appraised Danila and he decided that though skinny and scared, she wasn't so bad. Knowing her better might help him in his quest.

'Madam Shoshana said to ask you not to fiddle about with the machines the clients are using. I'm only telling you what she said.'

'You can trust me,' he said. 'I know what I'm doing.'

'And she says not to use any oil or stuff like that because if it gets on the clients' gear they're going to go ballistic. It's what she said, not me.'

'I only use invisible fat-free oil,' Mix lied.

He had brought three new belts with him and

spanners for adjusting the parts. Shoshana's hadn't been open very long, so servicing wasn't necessary, but he whiled away the time taking ellipticals apart and checking handlebar positions on stationary bikes. Whatever came out of it, he was really going to squeeze Madam Shoshana for putting him through this tedious business. Pity Danila had been told to keep an eye on him or he'd settle down in a corner and read a bit more of *Christie's Victims*.

Danila was very thin. So was Nerissa but hers was a different kind of thinness. You couldn't see her bones sticking out the way Danila's did. And her face was like a bird's with a beaky nose and not much chin. Still, she had great legs and more tangled-up dark hair than Mix could ever remember seeing on a woman's head. He had almost given up looking for Nerissa that day. It was eleven-fifteen and if he wasn't going to get clamped or towed away or whatever they did round here, he had to be back at the car by ten to twelve.

Danila was sitting behind her counter, drinking a cup of black coffee.

'Would there be another one of those going?'

'There might be but don't say a word, will you?' She disappeared into some inner recesses of the club and came back with coffee, a milk jug and sweetener in little tubular packs. 'Here you are. Shoshana'd kill me if she knew. We're not supposed to give coffee to anyone but staff.'

'You're a star,' said Mix and got a smile. No time like the present, he thought, and keeping his eye on the door in case Nerissa did just happen to come in at eleven-forty, said, 'You feel like having a drink? Say Wednesday or Thursday if you want.'

She was surprised. He would have liked her

78

better if she'd taken such invitations for granted and as her due. 'I don't mind,' she said, and then, spoiling it, 'Are you sure?'

'I'll pick you up then. Where d'you live?'

'Oxford Gardens.' She gave him the number.

'Not far from me,' he said. 'We'll go to KPH,' he said, forgetting she wouldn't know what those initials meant. 'Eight suit you?'

No point, he thought, in spending the whole evening with her. Suppose Nerissa was one of those clients, the ones she'd talked about last time he was here, who only came to the club four times and then lost interest. He mustn't be impatient because she hadn't come today, she wouldn't come every day, no matter how keen she was on fitness. Next week he'd do his servicing on a Wednesday instead of a Tuesday. And maybe he'd psych himself up to walk here. It couldn't be more than a mile.

Olive had forgotten about leaving the bone behind in Gwendolen's house, had hunted for it all round the block's communal gardens and even grubbed about in various bins outside shops. Kylie, the little white dog, had been frantic. So calling on Gwendolen was not to retrieve the bone, but to pour out her heart to a sympathetic ear.

Gwendolen's was never that. It was with some amusement that she listened to her friend's woes. The bone had been sent to Kylie by an American friend who shared Olive's love of poodles. Kylie had adored it from the first. Now it was lost and Olive had no idea what to do, it being impossible to buy such a toy here. Nor would she dare write to her friend in Baltimore, confessing her carelessness and asking for a replacement.

Gwendolen laughed. 'Your troubles are over. It's here.'

'Kylie's bone?'

'You left it here. I did call to give it to you but of course you were out.'

If Olive disliked that 'of course' she gave no sign of it. Gwendolen hunted about for the bone in her dirty cluttered kitchen, finding it at last on top of a heap of newspapers dating from the professor's time and under a twenty-five-year-old pack of vacuum cleaner bags.

'You have made a little dog very happy, Gwen.'

'That's a relief.'

Gwendolen's sarcasm wasn't lost on Olive but she was too happy at the recovery of the bone to take much notice. She went off cheerfully in the direction of Ridgemount Mansions. Gwendolen, who preferred her own company to that of her friends, was glad to see the back of her. In the past few days since she had decided, daringly, to try and find where Stephen Reeves now was, she had considered asking her tenant for help. He possessed a computer. She had seen him carrying it one day when they had met by chance in the hall.

'You'll think I'm asking for trouble carrying this about with me,' he had said, 'but I won't leave it on one of the seats. It'll go in the boot.'

Gwendolen hadn't thought anything like that as she had no idea what he was talking about. 'What is it?'

He looked at her warily, the way the unthinking look at the mentally disturbed. 'It's a PC, isn't it?' Her blank look was maintained. 'A computer, isn't it?' he said desperately.

'Really?' She shrugged her thin old shoulders.

'Then you'd better go and do whatever you have to do with it.'

The information she needed – was it somehow automatically shut up in that thing in the small flat case? Would all of them provide it? Or did you have to have a special kind of machine attached to it? And where was the screen she'd seen on them in shops? She was well aware that Mr Cellini had found her ignorance ridiculous and she was anxious not to make a fool of herself again. Not that there was anything intrinsically foolish in someone who had read the whole of Gibbon and the complete works of Ruskin not knowing how these modern inventions worked. Just the same, she preferred not to ask him. She preferred not asking Olive too. If she went round to Golborne Mansions she would have to witness Kylie's ecstasy, hear the tale of the lost bone all over again and maybe – something she always, unreasonably, dreaded – that paragon of a niece would be there or her mother.

It would do no harm to visit one of those Internet restaurants – no, cafés. She was clever, she knew that. Stephen Reeves had called her an intellectual and even Papa had several times told her she had a good brain for a woman. Surely therefore she could master the handling of one of those computers and get it to disgorge its information. She put on her hat, reflecting on the one Olive had been wearing – bright red grosgrain to match her nails – then the black silk coat and black net gloves because it was hot. Papa had given them to her for her fifty-second birthday and it was wonderful how they had lasted. No need for the trolley today.

It was bright and sunny. All the days this

summer were hot and the temperature was going up. Several young men and girls about the streets were wearing short-sleeved T-shirts and sandals. One girl had a bikini top on and a boy appeared to have left his shirt somewhere, for he was wearing only a vest. Gwendolen shook her head, wondering what her mother would have said if she had tried going outdoors in her brassière.

Nerissa had been to the gym, had an all-over body massage and a facial, and now, once more wearing the dark glasses she had put on to walk here and not be recognised, she was going upstairs to Madam Shoshana.

The stairs were steep and narrow. Covered in brown linoleum of a vintage before Nerissa's mother was born, they had metal rims to the treads which, coming away in places, made tripping likely and the risk of a nasty accident great. She trod carefully. A model friend of hers had fractured her tibia on death-trap stairs and when the break had mended one ankle was noticeably thicker than the other. The stairs smelt nasty, like stale cabbage and cheap burgers, in spite of the little window halfway up being wide open. A very dirty lace curtain blew out and flapped against Nerissa's face. She was used to it. She came here once a week to have her future foretold.

A notice on the sagging brown door said: *Madam Shoshana, Soothsayer. Please knock,* and below this in straggly ballpoint, *(Even if you have appointment).* Nerissa knocked. A low, thrilling voice called out, 'Come.'

The room was the most crowded and cluttered and stuffed with bric-à-brac that Nerissa ever went into. It was also almost too hot even for her and she liked heat. Strange things not only filled the shelves and covered the surfaces but sprouted from the floor and hung from the ceiling. Artificial plants in pots, mostly cypress trees but lilies too and passion flowers, stood about like stalagmites while stalactitic rods and chimes and mobiles and crystal pendants hung from the ceiling. The strangest thing of all was Madam Shoshana herself, a skinny old woman enveloped in layers of robes in many shades, but all of them the colours of a stormy sky, indigo and charcoal, dove grey and slate grey, grubby white and violet, angry blue and silver. Her waist-length yellowish white hair hung in straggly locks over her shoulders and down her back, entangling in places with the silver chains and crystal strings she wore round her neck. Though she had developed a range of cosmetics which she sold on the premises at inflated prices, she never wore make-up herself and looked as if she didn't wash her face much. Nerissa thought her nails looked like birds' talons, not human at all.

The velvet curtains were drawn and, for some reason known only to Madam Shoshana, pinned together in several places with old-fashioned brooches of Celtic design. A number of stuffed birds, dominated by a large white owl, were arranged to stare at the supplicant as she or he entered the room, but perhaps its most disquieting feature was the figure of a man in Merlin-like (or Gandalf-like) grey robes, holding inexplicably a staff of Aesculapias. This waxwork stood behind Madam Shoshana as she sat at her wide marble table as if advising her on ancient lore, witchcraft, necromancy, astrological prognostication or whatever she might require. A single low-wattage table lamp, vaguely art nouveau in design, all pewter and dull stained glass, gave the only light.

On the marble table was arranged a ring of crystals, rose quartz, Iceland spar, amethyst quartz, olivine schist, basalt and lapis lazuli, in the centre of which lay a small round lace mat like a crocheted doily. Shoshana's chair was of ebony inlaid all along the back and arms with white and yellow crystals, but the chair provided for the client was the Windsor type, plain wood, here and there stained with what looked like blood but was probably tomato ketchup.

'Sit.'

Nerissa knew the routine and obeyed. At Madam Shoshana's command she laid her hands, manicured that morning, the nails lacquered a slightly paler gold than the skin of her fingers, on the lace mat in the ring of stones. Shoshana gazed at Nerissa's hands and let her eyes rove in circles from crystal to crystal, rather like a cat following a moving spot of light.

'Tell me which of the sacred stones you can feel drawn closer to your fingers? Which two are gradually drawing towards you?'

It was a source of dismay to Nerissa that she could never feel and certainly not see, any of the crystals moving. She was always reproached for this failure. Madam Shoshana seemed to imply it was due to some insensitivity on her part or to lack of concentration. Certain she would once more be found wanting, she said, 'I think it's the dark blue one and the pink one.'

'Try again.'

'The dark blue one and the green one.'

Shoshana shook her head, more in sorrow than in anger. Some of her clients she had known for years but she never treated them with any more friendship or intimacy than she had done on their first visit. She looked at Nerissa as if she had never seen her before.

'The basalt and the amethyst are in your Ring of Fate today.' Shoshana's voice sounded as if it came from a long way off and long in the past. So might a mummy sound if it could speak. 'Both are pushing hard to break the energy barrier between themselves and your fingers. You must relax and let them come. Relax now and bid them approach you.'

Many times before had Nerissa been through this routine. She tried to let her hands go limp but she was very aware of the white owl and the grey-robed waxwork staring at her, she thought, accusingly. 'Come, come, come,' she intoned. It suddenly occurred to her that this was exactly what an arrogant former boyfriend used to whisper to her while they were making love, and she bit her lip to stop herself giggling.

'Concentrate,' said Shoshana sternly.

Nerissa thought how frightened she would be if she actually saw the basalt and the amethyst move at her bidding. But only Madam Shoshana could see that happening. She began to speak.

'Your fateful balance is badly out of truth. The stones speak of confusion, doubt and fear. They tell me of a dark man, his name beginning with a D. He is your fate, for good or ill. His destiny is to live by water . . . You are pushing the stones away – ah, too late. They have ceased to speak. You see how they shrink as the soul comes out of them.'

The stones looked the same to Nerissa but she knew that was due to her spiritual blindness. Shoshana had told her so on previous occasions. She was too worldly, the soothsayer had said, too preoccupied with her own appearance, with possessions and with artefacts. She wasn't sure what 'artefacts' meant and although she meant to look the word up she always forgot. The stuffed birds and the wizard figure were all looking at her with contempt. Nerissa cast her eyes down, humiliated.

The session was over. Her homework was to pay close attention to the man whose name began with a D and to water with creatures swimming in it, though not fish. She stood up and felt in her bag for her wallet. Madam Shoshana on her feet was rather different from Madam Shoshana sitting down. She became more practical and businesslike, less aware of the soul and more of the pocket.

'Forty-five pounds, please, no euros and no credit cards,' she said, as if the client had never been before.

Nerissa walked thoughtfully along Westbourne Grove. When Madam Shoshana said that the dark man was her fate, her heart had leapt for she was sure she must mean Darel Jones. But suppose she hadn't, suppose she had meant Rodney Devereux?

She could have asked but she'd known it would have been useless. Shoshana would only have said the stones told her no more and implied that this was Nerissa's fault for obstructing them with her energy. As for the water, immediately to mind came the Pacific Rim restaurant Rodney loved and where he was always taking her, though Nerissa didn't like watching the fish swimming about in the huge mirror-backed tanks and ten minutes later eating one of them. She couldn't tell why it was different from just buying fish at Harrods Food Hall and having it later, but somehow it was.

Still, this must be what Shoshana had meant, speaking of it so soon after mentioning the man with the initial D. Of course she had specifically said not fish but there were other things in those tanks, snails with coloured shells and little creeping things and a creature like a water snake. Last time they'd been there she was afraid Rodney would eat the snake and that made her queasy. She'd been on the point of saying to him that she'd never go to Pacific Rim again but for some reason she hadn't. Now she'd have to go there. It was her fate.

Christie's first victim, as far as is known, was a young woman of Austrian origin called Ruth Fuerst. She had been a nurse but when Christie first met her in 1943 was working in a munitions factory and as a part-time prostitute. Whether he first met her while a policeman on the beat or in a café or pub is a matter of doubt, but he claimed that she came to see him in Rillington Place while Ethel Christie was at work in Osram's factory.

No one involved in the case could say if he ever visited her in the single room she rented at 41 Oxford Gardens . . .

Mix looked up from the book, keeping his finger on the page. What an amazing thing! Although he had read every book on Christie he could get hold of, mainly from hunting through secondhand bookshops, none of them had stated precisely where Ruth Fuerst had lived. But here it was, a few houses along the street from the address Danila had given him. If only it had been the same house, he thought with a stab of regret. If only she had had the same room! He imagined going back there with her, maybe screwing her in the very place . . . Still, what he'd discovered made going out with her quite an exciting experience rather than a chore.

He read on. 'Christie killed Ruth Fuerst one day in the middle of August. "She undressed," he said, "and wanted me to have intercourse with her." In his book *10 Rillington Place*, which Mix had among the rest of his library, Ludovic Kennedy, writing that their relationship developed gradually, suggests that it was far more likely she had a straightforward transaction with him, prostitute and client, or granted her favours as his price for not reporting her soliciting in his capacity as a special constable.

'During sexual relations, he strangled her with a piece of rope. Then he wrapped her leopard-skin coat round her' – a fur coat in August! – 'took her into the front room and placed her under the floorboards with the rest of her clothes.

'That same evening, Ethel, who had been away in Sheffield with her relations, arrived home with her brother Henry Waddington who intended to stay the night. Because they had only one bedroom and that was occupied by Christie and Mrs Christie, Henry Waddington slept in the front room, a few feet away from the temporarily interred body of Ruth Fuerst . . .'

Mix had to stop there. He was calling for Danila at eight and he meant to leave early in order to stand outside number 41 and contemplate the house where that first victim had lived. Forty-one Oxford Gardens was on the other side of Ladbroke

Grove, rather shabby, much in need of painting and general refurbishment. No doubt it would now be worth some enormous sum, incredible to its wartime occupants if any of them were still alive. A cat, rather like Otto but older and with a grey muzzle, came over the wall and stopped when it saw Mix staring. Mix shooed it and made a face, but it was streetwise and experienced. It gave him an inscrutable look and strolled slowly into a clump of bushes.

Had Reggie ever stood where he was, then making up his mind, gone up the path and rung the bell? There may have been other occasions when he came here before that final fatal meeting. Hadn't the author of the best-known book on Reggie suggested they had known each other for a long time? Very probably all his relationships with his victims developed gradually. It stood to reason he must sometimes have gone to their places. After all, Ethel Christie was usually at home in Rillington Place and he couldn't always just have met them in cafés and pubs.

Mix was growing more and more convinced that Reggie had visited Gwendolen at St Blaise House. When he first began renting the flat, she had mentioned in passing her mother and father with whom she had lived in those far-off days and she had also mentioned her mother's death soon after the war. The father would have been working as a professor, whatever that meant, certainly that he'd be away from home. Mix could imagine Gwendolen letting Reggie in, taking him into the kitchen for a cup of tea – snob that she was – while they talked about the abortion, her need for it and his ability to perform the operation. Perhaps she couldn't afford the fee Reggie asked, but Mix couldn't remember reading anywhere that he ever charged . . .

Returning to the house where Danila lived, at two minutes after eight, he found her waiting for him just inside the front gate. This didn't please him, it was too much of a sign of desperation. He would have preferred her to keep him waiting, even if it had been half an hour. But now she was with him, dressed up to the nines as his gran used to say, in skin-tight leather trousers, a frilled shirt and a fake leopard-skin jacket. Just like Ruth Fuerst, he thought, and he wondered if Fuerst had looked like this, skinny and dark and sharp-featured. He tried to recall if he'd ever seen photographs of her. They walked up to Ladbroke Grove and the Kensington Park Hotel.

He loved KPH, not because there was anything special about it but because all those years ago Reggie had used it. It was historic. They ought to have a sign up telling the clientele that it had once been the local of west London's most infamous killer. But when you had people ignorant enough to pull down Rillington Place and destroy all signs of that celebrated site, what could you expect?

'You're very quiet,' said Danila, a vodka and blackcurrant in front of her. 'Kayleigh'd want to know if the cat had got your tongue.'

It was an unpleasant reminder of Otto. 'Who's Kayleigh?'

'The girl who does the evening shift at the spa. She's my friend.' When Mix made no reply, she said eagerly – or desperately? – 'I had my fortune told today.'

Mix was going to say he'd no time for that and it was a load of rubbish when he remembered reading how Nerissa patronised faith healers, fortune-tellers and had some guru. Besides, he half believed in ghosts now, didn't he? 'I reckon there may be something in it. There's lots of things we don't know, aren't there? I mean, some of them'll turn out to be scientific all along.'

'That's exactly what I say. Madam Shoshana at the spa does mine. She's the boss but she's a sooth-sayer too, got all sorts of qualifications, letters after her name and all.'

'What did she say?'

'You mustn't laugh. My fate's bound up with a man whose name starts with a C. And I thought, I wonder if it's a chap who does the pedicures at the spa. He's called Charlie, Charlie Owen.'

Mix laughed. 'It might be me.'

'Your name begins with an M.'

'Not my surname.'

'Yeah, but that's an S.'

'No it's not. I ought to know. It's C,E, double-L, I, N, I.'

She stared into his face. 'You're kidding.'

'D'you want another drink?' he said.


On the way back to Oxford Gardens he bought two bottles of California white, cheap offer bin ends, in the wine shop. They drank it on her bed and after-wards Mix didn't think he acquitted himself very well. But what did it matter? They were both drunk and she wasn't the sort of girl for whom you felt you had to put up a good performance. Outside her door, the floor and the ceiling rocked like the waves of the sea, rising and sinking and quivering. Heading for the stairs, clutching the banisters, he stumbled and nearly came to his knees, his jacket falling forward over his head. Adjusting it as best he could and starting down, he passed a man coming up who stood back, unmistakably flinching at a blast from his breath. Another tenant, his fuddled mind conjectured, Middle Eastern chap, sallow face, black moustache, they all looked the same. He didn't look back to see the Middle Eastern chap pick up a small white card, from the landing outside Danila's room.

Mix shambled home through the close humid night. Colder air might have sobered him up a bit but this was like a lukewarm bath. Otto was on the stairs again, washing his face as if he'd just been eating something. To Mix there was something odd and perhaps not pleasant about the cat being up here on the stairs so much. It never happened when he first came. Their dislike was mutual, so he wasn't the attraction. What was?

# Chapter 8

Nerissa was having a party. None of her own friends was invited, not Rodney Devereux or Colette Gilbert-Bamber or the model whose ankle had ended up thicker than the other one, but only her own family and all its extensions. The only outsiders she asked were the Joneses from next door to her parents. She sent one of her beautiful purple cards, lettered in gold, to Mr and Mrs Bill Jones and Mr Darel Jones, and at the foot she wrote in white ink: *Do come, love, Nerissa.*

A nice enough, but rather cold, letter came back from Sheila Jones. It said they couldn't come and that she was sorry, but not why they couldn't. Nerissa had no very high opinion of her own intelligence but even she could read between the lines that Mrs Jones thought the party would be too grand for them with too many smart people attending, too much fashion on show and too much talk about things they wouldn't understand. Nerissa was disappointed and not just because the refusal included Darel. The senior Joneses were the sort of people she liked, straightforward, unassuming and down-to-earth.

If only they understood the sort of party it really was, given for her dad's birthday (which she'd said on the invitation) and that his brothers would be there with their wives, the seven children they had between them, his cousin who was a leading light in the Transport and General Workers' Union, her mum's younger sister, elected last year to Tower Hamlets Council, her mum's elder sister who met and married the sweetheart she hadn't seen for a lifetime, her mum's auntie from Notting Hill, her three baby nieces and her three-year-old nephew, and her grandma, the matriarch born just ninety-two years ago in Africa.

It was the Joneses' loss, Nerissa said defiantly to herself as she and Lynette handed round cups of tea to those who didn't want champagne cocktails. But she admitted silently that it was her loss too, and when Lynette and the TGWU cousin had moved some of the furniture back and dancing began, she imagined the happiness she might have had in Darel's arms, drifting gently round the floor. To make things worse, just as her grandma was telling her an enthralling tale about her own mother and a witch doctor, the phone rang. It was Rodney. Nerissa took the phone into the study and listened impatiently while he asked her why he hadn't been asked to the party and was she mad, entertaining all those relations?

'It's a well-known fact that everyone hates their parents,' said Rodney. 'You know what what's-his-name said. "They fuck you up, your mum and dad."'

'Mine didn't. And whoever it was said it, they were sick.'

'For God's sake, leave them to it, and I'll pick you up in five minutes.'

'I can't, Rod,' said Nerissa. 'My dad's just going to cut the cake.'

She went back to the party and fed the little ones

chocolate biscuits and ice-cream because none of them liked fruit cake.

'You'll have one like that yourself in a couple of years,' said her Tower Hamlets auntie.

'I wish.' Nerissa thought of Darel, out some- where with his girlfriend, no doubt. Maybe even getting engaged to her – now, while she spoke. 'I'll have to get married first.'

'Most of them don't bother any more,' said her auntie from Notting Hill – well, great-auntie really.

'I would,' said Nerissa, wiping a small mouth, open, bird-like, for more.

She put on Johnny Cash singing 'I Walk the Line', turned up the CD player and went to dance with her dad.

Gwendolen would have been horrified and deeply shocked had she known the fantasies her tenant created about her past life. But she had forgotten the brief conversation they had had in the hall on the subject of her visit to 10 Rillington Place. That Mix Cellini had come to believe she had known Christie as well as Ruth Fuerst or Muriel Eady had known him, that she had been a frequent visitor to his house and that he had come here because she needed an abortion, would have humiliated her beyond words. He had gone further, concluding that because she was still alive, she must ultimately have refused Christie's offer of an illegal operation because she couldn't afford to pay for it, and there- fore given birth to a child. A middle-aged man or woman by now – did he or she ever come here, had he, Mix, ever seen this mysterious person? But Gwendolen, mercifully for her, knew nothing of these feverish workings of his mind.

She had been humiliated enough by her visit to the Internet café, where for a time she received no help from anyone. And she was utterly in the dark. Whether other people, all of them very young, expertly using the machines, found her bafflement absurd, she couldn't tell but she felt they did, interpreting the half-smile on a face and the turning away of a head as signs of amused contempt. Although she had paid and she hated wasting money, she would have got up and left, abandoning for ever these means of finding Stephen Reeves. But just as she pushed back her chair in despair a young man who had just come in asked her if she had a problem.

'I am afraid I can't seem to make it . . .'

'What is it you want to know?' he asked.

Would there be any harm in telling this stranger? She would never see him again. And surely he couldn't guess her reason for searching for Stephen Reeves? Deciding to confide in him was one of the biggest decisions of Gwendolen's long life.

'I wish to discover the – er, whereabouts of a Dr Stephen Makepeace Reeves.' She sensed that giving Stephen's age would rouse incredulity in this twenty-year-old but she couldn't help that. 'He would be eighty years old. He's a doctor of medicine and he once practised here in Ladbroke Grove – oh, a long long time ago, fifty years ago.'

If her helper found the request an odd one he gave no sign of it. In spite of her shyness and her very real fear of the computer and what it might do, she was fascinated by the quick sure way he conjured up one picture after another on the screen; columns of text, squares of printing and boxes of information followed one another, unfolding and rolling, and in so many different colours. Then, there he was: *Stephen Makepeace Reeves, 25 Columbia Road, Woodstock, Oxfordshire,* with a phone number and something the young man said was an e-mail address, and then a kind of biography of him, telling her when and where he was born, where he took his medical training, that he had been married to Eileen Summers and they had a son and a daughter. He had left Notting Hill and become a partner in a practice in Oxford, where he had remained until his retirement in 1985. In the years which followed he had written several books on the life of a doctor in a famous university town, one of which had been the forerunner of a television series.

His wife Eileen had sadly died recently, aged seventy-eight. Gwendolen sighed happily and hoped the young man didn't notice. All she wanted now was to be alone but curiosity remained and she had to know.

'Does everyone have something like that in there?' She pointed with one finger close to the screen, half afraid, half hopeful, that her own history might be concealed in its depths.

'Not like that. He's got a website, you see. On account of writing those books, I guess, and getting that stuff on TV.'

Gwendolen hadn't the faintest idea what he was talking about but she thanked him and left. She had shopping to do but not just at present, she couldn't do anything now but *think.* Mr Cellini's car, which had been parked outside when she left, was gone. She was relieved. Although she and he had little contact, the fact that he was in the house, though all the way up there in what her mother had called the attics, slightly interfered with the absolute peace she needed to think in and remember and plan.

For a while she sat in the drawing room where the dusty atmosphere and the smells of fabrics uncleaned for half a century, damp, mildew, flaking plaster and dead insects combined to remind her comfortingly of distant happy times. But something that hadn't been there half a century before, the grind and screech and throb of traffic passing outside the window, sent her upstairs to her bedroom, where things were marginally better.

Otto was lying in front of the fireplace, where ashes from a fire lit in 1975 still lingered in the grate, eating a mouse. He never brought mice to her as a gift, as most cats would to their owners, but took them to his favourite places, bit their heads off and ate as much of the rest of them as he fancied. Gwendolen took no more notice of him than she had ever done, apart from putting his food down, since he had walked into St Blaise House from nowhere a year before. She kicked off her shoes, lay on the bed and pulled the pink silk eiderdown over her feet and legs.

Perhaps she would go to Oxford. Perhaps even, daringly, spend a weekend there. At the Randolph. That was where Papa always stopped if he wasn't invited by the Master of some college to stay in a set designated for distinguished guests. While there she would take a taxi out to Woodstock, though perhaps there was a bus. Taxis were very expensive. Or write a letter. It was usually best, in these circumstances, to write first. On the other hand, she had no previous experience of these circumstances . . .

The music she had been vaguely aware of since she came into the bedroom seemed gradually to increase in volume. It wasn't coming through the wall but through the ceiling. So Mr Cellini must be at home in spite of the absence of his car. Perhaps it had gone to be mended or whatever one did with cars. She went to the door and opened it, annoyed but at the same time rather gratified that her tenant liked *real* music, after all. Whatever he said, that must have been he playing *Lucia* the other day. This time it was a Bach toccata.

Gwendolen would have been incredulous if, before the arrival of Mr Cellini, anyone had told her she would tolerate with patience, and even pleasure, sounds coming from the rented flat. But, really, classical music was another thing, and she didn't have to pay for the electricity used up in playing it. So long as he didn't fancy Prokofiev – she couldn't stand those Russians – she wasn't at all perturbed. Back on the bed, she imagined coming face to face with Stephen Reeves outside the gates of Blenheim Palace. He would know her at once, and taking both her hands in his, tell her she hadn't changed a bit. Then she would show him her mother's engagement ring she wore in place of the one he hadn't given her. Perhaps he would slip it off her finger and transfer it to her left hand. With this ring I thee wed . . .

At Shoshana's Spa, Mix attended to the next batch of machines. It was his fourth visit, he had finished what he was coming to call the 'day job' and got here just before five. On the other occasions he had chosen morning on his day off, early morning before work and the middle of the day in his lunch break, but on none of these visits had he seen Nerissa. Now there was nothing left to do to these machines for at least six months and his only excuse for coming back was to see Danila.

If Mix had his way he would never have set eyes on Danila again. Unfortunately, she very evidently felt the reverse about him. Not an analyst of character, he nevertheless understood she was a loser, a woman with little if any self-esteem, one who was looking for a man to cling to, love and obey as a pet dog might. In him she believed she had found that man. Recognising her, if dimly, as a victim and one who, seeing herself as of no account, merited being treated that way, he was unwilling to spend money on her or take her anywhere she might be seen as with him. He wasn't proud of her flat chest and skinny legs, her weasel face and hungry eyes. Their evening at the Kensington Park Hotel was an isolated visit. Since then he had simply called round at her place in Oxford Gardens with a couple of bottles and spent the evening there.

She regarded him as her boyfriend. He wanted to know if she had told any of her friends about him and she said she hadn't really got any friends. There was Kayleigh, of course, but she hadn't mentioned him to Kayleigh. It might upset her. She hadn't a boyfriend of her own. Danila had only been in London six months. Before that she'd worked at Shoshana's Beauty Zenana in Lincoln.

'Madam Shoshana wanted me to work late but I said I couldn't, I was seeing my boyfriend. I never said it was you on account of you having that contract with her. I thought it would look funny.'

Mix understood that he could drop her whenever he felt like it. There would be no repercussions. Meanwhile he didn't mind shagging her, his body and mind, and hers, desirous and relaxed from the sweetish red wine. In some ways, she was a better option than Colette Gilbert-Bamber who thrashed about, wriggling and biting and shouting instructions. Danila lay passive and yielding, asking nothing, receiving what she could get and smiling as the long shudder passed through her. For such a bony girl, she felt surprisingly soft and when he kissed her, as he occasionally did, her thin lips seemed to swell and grow warm.

But it wasn't enough to hold him, as he told himself when he returned to St Blaise House at midnight, wrapping his dark scarf round his eyes as he climbed the tiled flight blind, in case Reggie's ghost was in the passage. He said nothing about the ghost to Danila but asked her if she knew Ruth Fuerst had lived just down the road.

'Who?'

It was always a surprise to Mix to discover anyone living in Notting Hill not knowing about Christie and his murders. Fifty years ago it may have been, but it was still fresh in the minds of intelligent people. What could you expect from a girl as thick as Danila?

'She was the first woman Christie murdered. She lived at number 41.' He told her about Reggie as they lay on her bed after sex. Ruth Fuerst, Muriel Eady, very probably Beryl Evans and her daughter Geraldine, several others and Ethel Christie herself. All of them strangled and buried in the house or the garden. 'If I was him and you were one of them,' he said. 'I'd have screwed you the moment you were dead.'

'You're kidding me.'

'Oh, no. That's what he did. You can go and see where he lived if you like. It's not far, but it's all changed, not the same.' He didn't offer to show her. 'The old woman my flat belongs to, I mean it's her house, she knew him, they were close, he was going to do an abortion on her but she ran away.'

'You're giving me the creeps, Mix.'

He laughed. 'I'm going to open the other bottle. Don't get up.'

A quarter of an hour before midnight he put his clothes on, a male Cinderella, preparing to be home at the appointed hour. A real dump, he thought, looking round the room, not particularly dirty, but an untidy mess and not a decent piece of furniture to be seen. The curtains looked as if made from a bedsheet, split down the middle. 'You can come to my place next time,' he said, carefully considering the implications and deciding St Blaise House was safe and a lot more comfortable. It amused him to think how impressed she would be. 'About eight on Friday?'

'Can I really?' She looked at him with shining eyes.

What a creep, he thought, hasn't got a clue. He didn't really like her. No, that was wrong. He hated her and he realised why. She reminded him of his mother. Here, in her, was the same weakness and passivity, the same inadequacy – look at the mess in that room of hers. Like his mother, she wasn't good-looking or clever or successful at anything, she hadn't a scrap of pride and she let any man screw her who wanted to. The first time he and she went out she'd let him. To be worth having, women should be hard to get. Not that Colette was but she was a nymphomaniac, all the reps said so.

His anger with his mother was transferring itself to Danila. That was the effect she had on a man, he thought, she made him want to strike her just as his mother did.

He was relieved none of Danila's neighbours were about, no sign of the Middle Eastern man, and he had to tell himself not to be so anxious as he emerged into the cold night air, he wasn't Reggie, he wasn't a murderer fearful of being recognised near the scene of a crime. What did it matter if anyone saw him? They'd forget in five minutes, anyway. Abstractedly, he fingered the cross in his pocket. These days he found he did this more and more, especially when in contact with the number thirteen, passing 13 Oxford Gardens, for instance, or attending to the thirteenth treadmill at Shoshana's.

More deserving of his attention, he thought next day, was getting to know Nerissa. So far he was nowhere. His next move might be to put himself on the Shoshana Spa waiting list for membership. It would be a simple matter to get Danila to move him up the list, move him to the top, even perhaps let him in without his going on it at all. Then he'd be able to go there whenever he liked. And it would be good for him. He had to admit that he wasn't getting very far with his walking or cutting down on junk food. Only half an hour ago, on leaving Colette's, he'd bought a Cadbury's fruit and nut bar and a packet of crisps, all of which had mysteriously been consumed while he sat in the car thinking.

He'd ask Danila on Friday. Correction, he'd *tell* her on Friday, tell her what he wanted and to do it. If he went to the spa every day for a week he'd

be bound to see Nerissa, and once he'd seen her
. . . Mix told himself he was confident in his relations with women and he understood that it was
because of this confidence that he managed to get
the ones he wanted. Mostly. If he were strictly
honest with himself, he'd admit that when it came
to one he really wanted a lot, he wasn't so successful. Why was that? He must remember that and
once he'd met Nerissa, go slowly, carefully. There
was no doubt he wanted her more than he ever
had anyone before. For herself, of course, but also
for the fame she'd bring him.

All this introspection wearied him and as he
drove off to his next call, his mind wandered into a
fantasy of escorting Nerissa to some glittering function, say the Bafta Awards ceremony where they laid
red carpet out on the pavements for the stars to walk
on when they stepped out of their cars. She'd be
wearing a wonderful see-through dress and her own
diamonds and he'd be in a tuxedo, beautifully fitting his new slim figure. Mix had never thought
much about marriage, beyond knowing he didn't
want it, or not yet, not till he was approaching forty
maybe. But now . . . If he played his cards right,
why shouldn't he marry Nerissa? If he was going
to get married one day, who would suit him better
than her and suit him now?

A letter was decided upon. Though it was many
years since she had written a letter and as long
since she had received one, Gwendolen believed
she wrote well. Any piece of prose she produced
would be a joy to read and kindle in the heart of
the recipient a sensation of the good days gone by
when people could spell, wrote good English

without grammatical errors and knew how to construct a sentence. A missive she had been sent by some company purporting to supply her with gas had contained the sentence, 'You will of received our communication.' Of course she had replied in stinging words about the undoubted and rapid failure of any business unwise enough to employ illiterates, but had had no answer.

Now she was writing to Stephen Reeves and finding the task difficult. For the first time in her life she wished she had a television set so that she could have seen his programmes about a country doctor. What a surprise it would have been to see his name come up on the screen! If she had known the series was to be transmitted she could have stood outside the television shop in Westbourne Grove and watched it through the window. As things were, she couldn't write to him as she would have liked to, that she had seen his programmes and enjoyed them. *Watching your stories brought to life on the small screen inspired* – no, prompted, no, encouraged? – *impelled me to write to you after so many years. Although in some doubt as to the author's identity, I acquainted myself with your website which* – it would make him see that she had moved with the times if she mentioned the website. Then Gwendolen remembered that of course she *hadn't* seen the series, she *hadn't* got television, and she must start again.

*Hearing from an acquaintance that you had ventured into the realm of television, I was moved to* – the young man in the Internet café would surely count as an acquaintance. She was anxious not to begin by telling untruths. *I was moved to renew old friendship* – was that too forward? Most people would say

105

fifty years was a long break in any friendship – *I was moved to get in touch with you*. She would have to say why. She would have to say she wanted to see him. Gwendolen screwed up her fifth effort and sat disconsolate. It might be best to concentrate without pen and paper and resolve on her words before starting to write them down.

A serious young man, Darel Jones was handling his move to a Docklands flat with tender care for his parents. Through school and university and his postgraduate studies, he had lived at home and now, at the age of twenty-eight, with a new and much better paid job, it was time to leave. Knowing he must do so before he was thirty, he had been careful once he came of age, to do his own washing and ironing, eat out four times a week, visit his girlfriends' places rather than bring them home for the night, and generally be independent. Thus he trod a fine line, for his mother would willingly and happily have done everything for him, welcomed girls, and forced herself not to apply the double standard, inwardly congratulating him on his choice while condemning them for their unchastity. He had spent at least two evenings a week with his parents, taken them out, gone to the cinema with them, been charming to their friends and scrupulously thanked his mother for performing small services for him. Now he was leaving, to live at the other end of London on his own.

Neither parent had uttered a word of objection but on the eve of his move, the new furniture installed, his clothes in two suitcases in the hall waiting to be put into his car, he saw a tear trickle down his mother's cheek.

'Come on, Mum. Cheer up. Suppose I'd been going to Australia like your chum Mrs What's-hername's son.'

'I didn't say a word,' said Sheila Jones defensively.

'Tears speak louder.'

'What'll you be like when he gets married?' Her husband passed his handkerchief, a move he had made on an average once a week during their thirty-year marriage.

'I hope he will. I know I'm going to love his wife.'

Darel wasn't so sure. 'That's a long way off,' he said. 'Look, I want you both to say you'll come over to dinner on Saturday. I'll be straight by then.'

Sheila began to cheer up. 'Tom and Hazel want us all to go in next door for a drink this evening to say goodbye. I said we would. Nerissa will be there.'

Darel considered, but not for long. 'You go,' he said. 'You can say goodbye for me.'

'Oh, we wouldn't go without you. There'd be no point. Besides, we'd miss our last few precious hours with you.'

If she hadn't said that model would be there he might have agreed. Nerissa Nash – why couldn't she have kept her father's interesting surname? – was very beautiful, any man would admit that, and according to his father, a nice girl. But Darel was wary of the whole celebrity world. He knew of it only from what he read in the newspapers. Since his preferred reading was usually the *Financial Times*, this wasn't much of a guide, but certain emotive words suggestive of that world aroused his distaste: club, fashion, star, public appearance, designer and of course 'celebrity' itself were among them. Someone belonging in that so-called elite must be empty-headed, ignorant, tasteless and shallow. Such people were heading for empty unhappy lives, failed relationships, dysfunctional families, alienated children and a desperate unwillingness to grow old.

What a prig you are, he often told himself, always resolving to be less censorious. The fact remained that he had no wish to extend his acquaintance with Nerissa Nash beyond replying, 'Good evening' to her 'Hi' and raising his hand in a modified wave if he saw her at a distance.

# Chapter 9

It wasn't until the doorbell rang that Mix remembered Danila was coming round. He had forgotten to buy any cheap wine and now he'd have to give her that rather nice Merlot he'd bought for his own private consumption on Sunday night. Spending the evening at home, as he thought alone, he had been enthralled in Chapter 3 of *Christie's Victims*, reading of

> Muriel Eady, a 31-year-old woman, living in Putney and employed at the Ultra Radio Works in Park Royal. On leaving the police for no known reason, Christie had also gone to work there. He and she became friends, insofar as Christie was capable of friendship, and on several occasions she and her fiancé and Christie with Mrs Christie all went out together.
>
> Muriel Eady suffered from chronic rhinitis and Christie claimed to be able to cure her with the aid of an inhalation device of his own invention. When his wife had gone away, once more to have a holiday with her brother in Sheffield, he invited Muriel round, gave her a cup of tea and showed her what he said was the device. However, though it contained

Friar's Balsam, it also, unbeknown to Muriel, admitted a tube attached at the other end to a gas outlet . . .

It had been at this point that he was summoned to answer the door. Old Chawcer had seen no need for an entryphone or even a separate doorbell for the top flat, so on the rare occasions when someone called on him, Mix had to go all the way down the fifty-two stairs and come all the way up again. Old Chawcer never answered the door unless she was expecting a guest, an even less usual event in the evenings, so he was pretty sure she wouldn't let Danila in. For, by the time he had set foot on the top tread of the tiled staircase, he had remembered who this caller must be.

The bell rang twice more before he got there. He needn't have worried about the wine because she had brought two bottles with her, one of Riesling and one of gin. This ought to have pleased him but it didn't. In his view, women shouldn't contribute to the evening's entertainment, no self-respecting woman would, she'd expect the man to pay. Danila's mass of dark hair was bigger and wilder than ever – ridiculous, he thought, it caused her little pinched face to look tiny. Her next move made matters even worse. Having set the bottles down on the hall table, she threw her arms round Mix's neck and kissed him.

'I'm ever so glad to see you. I've been looking forward to this.'

He said nothing but led her up the stairs. Outside Miss Chawcer's bedroom sat Otto, engaged in an all-over wash.

'Oh, what a sweet kitty!' Danila's shriek made

Otto start to his feet and arch his back. 'Is she yours? Isn't she a darling!' She made the mistake of putting out a hand towards Otto's head. He drew back, hissed and lashed at her before running upstairs. 'Oh, I frightened her!'

'Come on,' said Mix.

On the landing outside his front door she asked why it was so dark and said the stained glass window gave her the creeps, but his anger was softened to a mild irritation by her admiration of his flat. She walked round his living room, passing the portrait of Nerissa Nash with just a glance at it and then at him, but adoring everything else. Oh, the window blinds! Oh, the cushions, the furniture, the ornaments, the lampshades! The amazing TV! That lovely grey marble statue of a girl. Who was she?

'Some goddess. Psyche, they called her, when I bought her,' he said. He poured them each a stiff gin with tonic from his fridge and ice from the freezer. He hadn't a lemon.

'You like the apartment, then?'

'It's great. What you must think of my grotty place!'

'I've taken a lot of trouble to get it this way.'

'I'm sure. Why d'you read about awful murders when you've got a lovely place like this?' She had picked up his book, left face-downwards on the arm of the grey tweed sofa. 'Yuck, it's horrible. "She was unconscious and while he strangled her he raped her,"' she read aloud.

'Give that to me.' Mix snatched the book from her. 'Now you've lost my place.'

'I'm sorry. It was just that I . . .'

'All right, never mind. Bring your drink in the bedroom.'

111

They would have to go through all that shrieking and gasping stuff all over again when she saw the furniture and the pictures. Might as well get it over with so that they could get down to what was the reason for her coming at all. He refilled his glass while she wandered round the bedroom in the same sort of ecstasy as she'd shown in the living room. He sipped his drink. It was that good Bombay gin in the blue bottle she'd brought, he had to grant her that. He strolled back, pretending astonishment to see her dressed as she had been two minutes before.

'I reckoned you'd be starkers by now.'

'Mix.' She came up to him. 'Mix, do we always have to start doing it the minute I come? Can't we talk for a bit?'

He was surprised. She was showing initiative for the first time, as if she had some sort of right to an opinion on the order of events. He could see what it was. In her eyes he was her boyfriend now and she was starting to take him for granted. Soon she'd be telling him what to do, not asking him.

'Talk about what?' he said.

'I don't know. Things. You getting the furniture for this place, your job, mine, your lovely cat.'

'It's not my fucking cat!' he almost yelled.

'There's no need to shout.'

She took her clothes off but not the way Mix would have preferred, not like a stripper giving a titillating performance. Danila undressed as she would when she was alone, placing her outer garments over the back of a chair, turning her back on him to take off thong and tights. How he hated tights. And didn't she know wearing a G-string with them was a joke? She left her bra till last, ashamed of her tiny breasts. He thought, I won't see her again, I'll find some other way of getting to know Nerissa.

She went to the bed but he stopped her. 'Wait a minute.' He wasn't going to do it on top of his ivory satin quilt; he lifted it off and folded it. 'All right,' he said.

The look she gave him was subservient but with something in it too of bewilderment. He took off his shoes and trousers but kept his shirt on and his socks. A man didn't have to strip off, that was the woman's role. A simmering anger against her, a cold rage he couldn't quite account for, stopped him taking any trouble and what happened could have been called rape, only she didn't resist. He rolled away from her to finish his drink.

Five minutes later she was walking round the flat again. He heard her say, 'Why d'you have her up there?'

There was no doubt as to what she meant. But 'You mean Nerissa Nash?' he said, to make assurance absolutely sure.

'You fancy her or something?'

Mix got up. Somewhere in him was a prudish streak, legacy perhaps of a childhood among the Seventh Day Adventists. Of course his disapproval rather depended on who it was. Somehow it was all right when it was Colette and it would be more than all right – fantastic – if it had been Nerissa, but in Danila it seemed to smack of defiance, of taking things and him for granted, and of asserting herself. A woman like her knew very well you don't walk about nude the way she was doing in a man's flat unless you have a good reason to call him yours and have a proprietary interest in his place. He

113

took his dressing gown out of the wardrobe and put it round her.

She received it with an ill grace. Like his mother, she sulked when you told her off. Standing in front of the portrait, she pointed to it, actually placing one finger on the glass. '*She's* got practically nothing on. I suppose that's all right.'

Careless of the pain his words might cause, he said, 'She's beautiful.'

Danila said nothing but continued to stare and to keep her finger where she had placed it. Never very tall, she seemed to shrink a little and goose bumps came up on her forearms, uncovered by the dressing-gown sleeves. A great resentment filled him. By her silence and her palpable hurt, she had made him feel awkward.

'D'you want another drink?' he muttered.

'Not just yet.'

He opened the wine bottle. If he kept on at the gin he'd not be able to do it again, and the only point in her being here was to manage it two or three times. With Nerissa, he thought, he'd be inexhaustible. He remembered that there was another point to Danila's visit. He had to ask her about the membership list. Tell her, he corrected himself, a brimming glass of wine in his hand.

'Look, getting to be a member of the spa, I thought . . .'

Slowly, she turned round and he saw tear marks on her face. She took no notice of what he had begun to say. 'I've seen her,' she said.

'Seen who?'

'Her. Nerissa Nash.'

This wasn't at all the way he wanted things to go. If he told her what he expected her to do about

114

the list now, at this moment, she'd understand at once he only aimed to join the spa in order to meet Nerissa. His request would have to be postponed again.

He chose his words carefully. 'Where did you see her, then? In a photo, you mean.'

'No, for real. She goes to Madam Shoshana for a reading of the stones.'

With no idea what she was talking about, he said as if he'd be astonished by the answer yes, 'She's not a member of the spa, is she?'

'Nerissa? Oh, no. With that figure, she must go to a gym somewhere. Somewhere in the West End, I reckon, Mayfair. I'd been to Madam Shoshana for my reading – I get a discount – and I met her coming up the stairs. A Wednesday it was, sometime in July. Ever so nice she was, said hi and it was a lovely day, made you glad to be alive.'

He was stunned. He couldn't speak. He'd wasted weeks going to that place, messed about uselessly with machines that didn't need attention, used up his evenings with this dog of a woman, spent his hard-earned money on her. Her cunningly back-combed and tangled hair had done what it always did during their scuffles, fallen in lank rats' tails. His rage at the shock of discovering Nerissa's true purpose in visiting the spa building had come to boiling point, and it was directed at this girl, this stupid ignorant ugly girl with her rice-white skin and her bony chest. Nerissa didn't even belong to Shoshana's Spa. She'd gone there to see a fortune-teller and no doubt it was a one-off visit.

Quite unaware of his anger, Danila said, 'Mind you, close-to, she's not the supermodel she is in your pic. Her skin's a bit coarse – well, it being so dark, it would be. I reckon whoever took that photo got busy airbrushing . . .'

He didn't hear the end of the sentence. Hatred filled him, joining his anger. That she dared to criticise the most beautiful woman in the world! The insult grated like something scraping at his brain. He reached for some object, anything, to infuse with his rage. His hand closed round the marble Psyche and once more he seemed to hear Javy accusing him of the attack on Shannon, his mother standing by.

Who was it he was about to destroy with this weapon? Javy? His mother? This cringing girl?

'What are you doing?'

She never spoke again, only screamed and made gurgling sounds as he struck her repeatedly about her head with the Psyche. He'd thought blood flowed gently but hers sprayed at him in scarlet fountains. Her eyes remained fixed on his in horror and amazement. He aimed a final blow at her forehead to close those staring eyes.

She fell to the floor, sliding down the portrait to collapse on her back. He dropped the Psyche on to the polished boards. It seemed to make an enormous noise as it fell so that he expected crowds alerted by it to come rushing into the room. But there was no one, of course there was no one. Instead absolute quiet, the silence of a vast desert or an empty house by the sea, waves breaking softly on the shore. The Psyche rolled a little, this way and that way, and was still. The only movement was the slow trickling of her blood down the glass.

# Chapter 10

He went slowly to the window, opened the slats instead of raising the blind, and looked down. Lights in the backs of houses in the street behind, lit the gardens. There was no one about. Nothing stirred, no human being, no cat, no bird. A pale crescent moon had risen in a sky streaked with cloud. Behind his front door he listened. Out there too all was still and silent.

'No one knows anything about it,' he said aloud. 'They don't know what's happened, no one knows but me.' And then, as if someone had accused him and he was defending himself, 'I didn't mean to do it but she asked for it. It just happened.'

His instinct was to shut himself in the bedroom where he couldn't see what he had done, and hide himself. For some time, though with the door still open, he sat on the bed with his head in his hands. The phone ringing frightened him more than anything ever had. He gave a galvanic start so violent that he feared he might have broken a bone. I was wrong and people do know. Police, he thought, someone's phoned them. They heard her scream and me drop the statue. The ringing stopped but started again after a few seconds. This time he had to answer it and he did so in a hoarse, quavering voice.

'You sound as if you've got the dreaded lurgy too,' said Ed.

'I'm OK.'

'Yeah. Well, good. I'm not. I think I've got a virus, so could you do two of my calls tomorrow? They're the important ones.' Ed named the clients and gave their phone numbers. Or Mix supposed that's what he was doing. He couldn't take it in. 'I realise it's Saturday but they won't take long, it's more they want reassuring.'

'OK. Anything you say.'

'That's brilliant. And, Mix, me and Steph are getting engaged Wednesday. I've got to be back to normal for that. Drinks on me in the old Sun at eight-thirty so be there.'

Mix put the phone down. He went slowly back to the living room, feeling his way with his eyes shut. The idea came to him before he opened them that he might have dreamt it all, it was some hideous nightmare. There would be nothing on the floor. She had gone home. Blindly he fumbled his way into an armchair, sat there, facing straight ahead, and the first thing he saw when he opened his eyes was the blood on the glass. It was drying by now. Some of the thin streams had never reached the floor but dried into blackish-crimson lines and globules. What he thought was a sigh became a sob, and a long shudder passed through him.

Had Reggie felt like this? Or was he made of stronger, sterner stuff? That wasn't something Mix wanted to admit to. The girl had asked for it – which seemed to be true of some of Reggie's victims. He knew he must do something. He couldn't just leave her here. If it took him all night, he must clean up and decide what to do about the thing on the floor.

Her eyes, which he had tried to close, remained open under the wound in her forehead, looking up at him. He took a grey linen napkin out of a drawer and laid it over her face. After that it was better.

He was still wearing nothing but his underpants. Some spots of blood had got on to them. He took them off, threw them on the floor and put on jeans and a black sweatshirt. She had fallen beyond the edge of the carpet, so that most of the blood was on the pale polished wood surround, on the walls and on the glass of the portrait. A good thing he had decided to splash out and have it glazed. That he could think like this comforted him. He was recovering. The first thing must be to wrap the body and move it. What was he going to do next? Do with it, he meant. Take it somewhere in the boot of the car, a park or a building site, and dump it? When they found it they wouldn't know he'd done it. No one knew they'd spent any time together.

He found a sheet that would do. When he came to St Blaise House he'd bought all his bedlinen new but he had some left from Tufnell Park days. His tastes had changed from when he was buying red sheets! Still, red was good for this purpose, it wouldn't show blood. Keeping his eyes averted as best he could, he rolled the body up in the sheet. She felt very light and fragile and he wondered if she'd been anorexic. Maybe. He knew very little about her, he hadn't been interested.

When he'd dragged the bundle out into his narrow hall, he fetched a bucket and detergent and cloths from the kitchen and set about cleaning up. He began with the portrait and when it was spotless and gleaming once again, he felt enormously better. His fear had been that some of the blood –

there had been so much – might have got inside the glass and the frame on to Nerissa's photograph, but not a drop had. It occurred to him that the Psyche looked a lot like Nerissa, she might have been the model for it. He washed the figurine in the kitchen sink, under the running tap, first hot water, then cold, the blood sliding off its head and breasts, red water, then pink, then clear.

Just the edge of the carpet was stained. He scrubbed and rinsed and scrubbed and dried and he thought it was all out. Getting it off the polished boards wasn't a problem, they were heavily lacquered and stains slid off. If only the wall behind had been one of the dark green ones. He'd probably have to repaint it; he'd still got a two-litre tin of the shade called Cumulus and he'd do it on Sunday.

By the time he'd finished, the fourth bucketful of reddened water down the sink and the cloths in the washing machine, he sat down with a stiff Bombay gin. It tasted wonderful, as if he hadn't had a drink for months. One thing was for sure: the body couldn't stay here. And if he tried to put it in Holland Park, for instance, he couldn't do it without someone seeing. The trouble was, the first and only time he and she went out together they might have been seen by any number of people in KPH. She said she'd told no one but how could he believe her? She'd admitted telling Madam Shoshana she had a boyfriend even if she hadn't said his name. Then there was the barmaid at KPH. She might remember. Miss Chawcer might not have answered the doorbell that evening but she'd remember it had rung if anyone asked. She might even have seen Danila through the window. No, he couldn't just dump the body.

His eye fell on *Christie's Victims* she or he had dropped on to the coffee table. Reggie, he thought, had faced the same difficulty. He'd been seen about with Ruth Fuerst, he'd eaten in the Ultra Works canteen with Muriel Eady and been out with her and her boyfriend. He dared not risk leaving their bodies to be found in case he was connected with their deaths. Something safer yet bolder had to be done. Mix referred to the book. Even though the neighbours saw what he was doing, even though they chatted to him and he to them, he had managed to dig a pit for Fuerst in his garden and put the body into it after dark. Muriel Eady he also buried a little way from the first grave.

Mix came upon a photograph of the garden in the next pages of illustrations. A white ring marked the spot where the leg bone had been found, a cross Muriel Eady's grave. If the marks hadn't been made there was nothing to show where the burial had been. Before interment, all the bodies of the women he had killed had been temporarily stowed under the floorboards or in the washhouse. Mix wondered if either would be available to him – was there a washhouse here? Certainly there was a cellar – but it might be possible, though difficult, to get into the garden. However, he lived in a house immeasurably larger than Reggie's half-house; well, half of a small terraced cottage, really.

He closed the book, put his keys into his pocket and let himself out of his front door, noticing on his way out that it was eleven-thirty. The old bat had amazing hearing for her age, but she would be asleep two floors below. Mix stood on the top landing, listening.

\*

121

He turned left and set off along the passage. Of course there was a possibility he would see the ghost but he was making resolute efforts not to accept that there was a ghost. He had imagined it. The cat had opened that door itself. To be on the safe side, he closed his hand over the cross in his jeans pocket. The light he had switched on quickly went out as it always did, but he had brought a torch with him. In the dark, he opened the first door on his left and found himself inside a room which must have been adjacent to his own living room. The gleam from the torch was rather feeble but because the window in here was uncurtained, it wasn't dark but dimly lit from still-lighted backs of houses and by the faint moonlight.

Just the same, he would have liked more. He couldn't see a switch on any of the walls and when he looked where the hanging cable and lamp-holder should have been, there hung only a strange object with two metal strings suspended from it. If anything could have distracted him from the matter in hand, this did. He directed the torch beam upwards. It took him a few moments to realise that what he was looking at was a gas mantle. He had once seen a television programme about the electrification of London replacing gas in the twenties and thirties. There were houses in Portland Road, not far from here, still lit by gas in the sixties.

The room contained a bedstead and a tall chest of drawers with a mirror on top. Anyone wanting to look in that mirror would have had to be nearly seven feet tall to reach it, Mix calculated. A stack of bookshelves, sagging under the weight of heavy tomes stuffed beside and on top of each other, nearly filled one wall. He went back into the passage and into the room opposite where the yellow light from St Blaise Avenue flowed in brightly, showing him that here too the system had never been replaced by electricity.

It made him feel as if he had strayed back in time, back beyond Reggie and all his works, back behind modern technology and everything that made life easy. He shuddered. Suppose he really had gone back in time and found it impossible to return? Suppose it was a dream, all of it was a dream, the killing, the blood, the gas and the darkness? But he had been through that one before and he knew it wasn't.

The air felt close. It had been another hot day. On this whole top floor only the windows in his own flat were ever opened. The closeness was dusty and although no fresh air came in, flies lived up here in swarms, crawling on the window glass in the dark. He turned round, passed his own front door and set off along the right-hand passage. Electric light was available in the first room on the right but there was no bulb in the fitment. Here the gleam of street lamps outside had curtains to penetrate. He pulled them back, too roughly, for fragments of cloth and dust fell off on to the sill. This room was partly furnished with an iron bedstead, a deckchair with no seat, a dressing table and an upright chair with a broken leg propped up on a jamjar. The deckchair again reminded him of Reggie. At least one of his later victims, Kathleen Maloney, he had put in a deckchair with a makeshift seat of woven string, in order to administer gas to her in his kitchen.

A folded newspaper lay on the floor. This copy of the *Sun* would be ages old, Mix thought, dropped there in the fifties probably. But when he picked it up and, in the yellow light, made out the date on it, he saw it was only from the previous October. More upsetting was the date, the thirteenth. The old bat must have been up here and left her paper behind. Who would have thought she'd read the *Sun*? She'd left this one with that date on it behind to frighten him, he thought. That must be it.

The room opposite, on the other side of the wall where Nerissa's picture hung and Danila had died, also had electricity, also lacked a light bulb and was just as stuffy. It was empty but for a bedstead without a mattress. He pulled back the thin curtains. Outside, he could just make out what he could only glimpse from his own windows, gables and annexe roofs of next-door, the pointed trees and squat bushes in pots the old man kept on the roof of a car port, a great chimney with a dozen flues spanning an expanse of tiles, the broken glass top of a derelict conservatory. All this would make access to the next room along easy, he thought. Anyone could climb up and get in. But when he tried the door, it was locked and no key was visible as he squatted down and tried to look through the keyhole. At least Chawcer had locked the door. She had taken that much precaution against burglars, though a flimsy one. A wonder the atmosphere didn't choke her.

One last room remained. It was quite empty, even to the extent of being stripped of what it might once have contained. There was a curtain rail but no curtains. Some sort of carpet there had been nailed, and in places glued, to the floor but it had been torn up, leaving nail holes and sticky-looking patches. She came up here sometimes, he could tell that, but not into the gas-lit rooms. The first one he had gone into, the room which had surprised him because of the means by which it had been lit, that would be Danila's resting place.

Christie had put Ruth Fuerst's body under the floorboards. Mix remembered how, years ago, when he was in his teens, one of the water pipes had frozen in the house where he lived with his mother in Coventry. She said she had a bad back and couldn't do anything, it was one of the times Javy had left her – he always came back again till the last time – so he went up into the icy-cold bathroom and, with her telling him how to do it, took up three of the floorboards. He'd had to prise up the tiles first. This would be much easier, nothing but the boards and these very old, to lift.

The only tools he had now were those he used in the maintenance of exercise machines. He let himself into his own flat, almost stumbling over the body he had laid in the little hallway, and searched through the bag that held his toolkit with fingers damp with sweat. Spanners, a hammer, screwdrivers . . . The biggest spanner would have to do and, if necessary, he'd ruin the screwdriver by using it to prise up the boards. He went back on to the landing and, leaving his door open, stood listening to the house. It seemed to him that, though it was always quiet, this silence was uncanny. Of course, at half-past midnight, the old bat had been asleep for hours, but where was the cat? It nearly always spent its nights somewhere on the staircase. And why hadn't Reggie appeared?

Because he'd protected himself with the cross or because he'd imagined it, he told himself sternly. But that maddening imagination was still functioning, creating now the figure in its shiny glasses standing beside him, watching what he did, until he shut his eyes against it. He plunged back into the lighted flat, breathing fast. Another drink. The door closing him inside, he poured his biggest gin of the night and, sitting on the floor beside the body, drank it down neat and ice-less. It filled him with fire and when he got to his feet, set him staggering.

But after another reconaissance and another listening at the top of the stairs, he dragged the body out. He pulled his red-wrapped bundle along the passage and into the first room on the left. Quietly he closed the door and switched on his torch. Someone had said it was never dark in London and more light came in – thank God for the guinea fowl man who seemed to keep lights on until the small hours – to show him the pins that held the floorboards in place. With the aid of the screwdriver and the flat shaft of the spanner, they came up quite easily. Beneath was a space between the joists, as far as he could see about a foot deep, though intersected with cables and old lead pipes. How dust could get in there was a mystery but when he brought his hands out they were furred with thick grey powder.

Torchlight wakened the flies and they began dancing round its beam. He had intended to take a last look at the body before he put it into the recess he had made but now he had forgotten why and he couldn't bring himself to unwrap that face and again see that wound. The featherlight body slid into the gap he had made with scarcely a sound. Its grave might have been measured to fit it so well. Replacing the boards took only a moment. A fly crawled across his hand and he swatted at it with disproportionate fury. He dared not hammer the pins in, not at this hour. He'd do it in the morning when she or anyone would expect him to be banging a bit, putting up a picture, say.

A shivery sensation made him feel that Reggie was behind him, watching his movements, perhaps bending close over his back, and this time he was afraid, rigid with fear. He liked Reggie, admired him really and felt sorry for him meeting such a dreadful fate, but he was terrified too. You were when the person you admired was the dead come back. If he turned now and saw Reggie, he would die of fright, his heart wouldn't be strong enough to stand the terror. Mix shut his eyes and rocked back and forth on his haunches, whimpering softly. If he had felt a hand on his shoulder, then he too would have died of fear; if the thing had breathed and its breathing been heard, his heart would have cracked and split.

He grasped the cross. There was nothing there. Of course not, there never had been. All the sounds, the single sighting, the opening door, everything was an illusion brought about by the horror film setting, the nasty creepiness of this house. Just getting back into his flat relieved him enormously. The silence now was welcome, the proper condition of this place at this hour. And the bodily sensations he had were a sour taste in his mouth, nausea rising and the start of a drumming in his head. He knew how unwise it would be to drink anything more but he did, filling the same glass which had held gin with the sweet cheap Riesling she had brought. As it hit him, he stumbled into the bedroom where her clothes lay as she had placed them, irritating him by arranging them neatly over a chair.

Reggie had wrapped Ruth Fuerst's body in her own coat and buried the rest of her clothes with her. He should have done the same. Collapsing on to the bed, noticing through glazed eyes that it was twenty to two, he knew he couldn't go back in there tonight, he couldn't take those boards up again, replace them again. In the morning he would take the clothes out of the house in a carrier bag and put them in a litter bin, or several litter bins. No, a better idea. He'd put them in one of the bins where the proceeds from their sale went to sufferers from cerebral palsy or some such thing.

And now he would sleep . . .

# Chapter 11

Today was the anniversary of the first time he had come into the drawing room to have tea with her. Half a century ago. She saw that she had made a ring in red round that date on the Beautiful Britain calendar that hung on the kitchen wall on top of last year's kitten calendar and the tropical flowers one from the year before. Gwendolen had kept all the calendars for every year back to 1945. They piled up on the kitchen hook and when there was room for no more, the bottom ones were all stuffed away in drawers somewhere. Somewhere. Among books or old clothes or on top of things or under things. The only ones whose whereabouts she was positive about were those from 1949 and 1953.

The 1953 calendar she had found and now kept in the drawing room for obvious reasons. It recorded all the dates on which she had had tea with Stephen Reeves. She had come upon it by chance last year while looking for the notice which had come from some Government department telling her about a £200 fuel payment due to be made to pensioners. And there, alongside it, was the Canaletto Venice calendar. Just seeing it again made her heart flutter. Of course she had never forgotten a single one of their times alone together but seeing it recorded – 'Dr Reeves to tea' –

somehow confirmed it, made it real, as if she might otherwise have dreamt it. Under the heading of a Wednesday in February she had written, in a rare comment, 'Sadly, no Bertha or any successor to bring our tea.'

Sheltered and quiet as Gwendolen's life had been, perhaps as unruffled as a life can be, it had included a very few peaks of excitement. All of these she thought about from time to time but none with such wonder as her visit to Christie's house. It too was more than fifty years ago now and she had been not much over thirty. The maid who carried up the hot water and perhaps even emptied the chamber pots had been with them for two years. She was seventeen and her name was Bertha. What else she was called Gwendolen couldn't remember, if she had ever known. The professor never noticed anything about people and Mrs Chawcer was too wrapped up in working for the Holy Catholic Apostolics to have time for a servant's troubles, but Gwendolen observed the change in the girl's figure. She was with her more than the other occupants of the house.

'You're beginning to get stout, Bertha,' she said, using a favourite word applied to others in the vocabulary of the skeletal Chawcers. Gwendolen was too innocent and ignorant to suspect the truth and when Bertha confessed it she was deeply shocked.

'But you can't be expecting, Bertha. You're only seventeen and you can't have . . .' Gwendolen couldn't bring herself to go on.

'As far as that goes, miss, I could have ever since I was eleven, but I never did and now I am. You won't tell the missus or your dad, will you?'

130

It was an easy promise for Gwendolen to make. She would have died before she mentioned such things to the professor. As for her mother, she couldn't forget how once, when she whispered to Mrs Chawcer, with much shame and diffidence, of an old man who had exposed himself to her, she had been told never to utter such words again and to wash her mouth out with soap.

'What will you do with the baby?'

'There won't be a baby, miss. I've got the name and address of someone who'll get rid of it for me.'

Gwendolen was not so much in deep waters as in an unknown country peopled with men and women who did forbidden things and spoke a language of words that should never be uttered, a land of mystery and discomfort and ugliness and danger. She wished very much that she hadn't asked Bertha why she was gaining weight. It never occurred to her to be sorry for this young girl who worked ten hours a day for them and was paid very little for performing tasks their own class would shudder to think of. It never entered her mind to put herself in Bertha's shoes and imagine the disgrace which would come to an unmarried mother or the horror of watching herself grow so large that further deception was impossible. She was curious rather against her will, but afraid and anxious to be uninvolved.

'You'll be all right then,' she said brightly.

'Miss, can I ask you something?'

'I expect so,' said Gwendolen with a smile.

'When I go to him, would you come with me?'

Gwendolen thought this an impertinence. She had been brought up to expect deference from servants and indeed everyone from a 'lower class'.

But her shyness and her fear of the different and of things she hadn't experienced wasn't absolute. Curiosity was a novelty for her but she felt it worm its way into her mind and wait there, trembling. She might see a little more of this new country which had unprecedently opened its borders to her. Instead of replying to Bertha with a sharp, 'Do you know whom you're speaking to?' she said, quite meekly but with an increased beating of the heart, 'Yes, if you like.'

The street was squalid, with the old chimney of an iron foundry at the far end of it, the Metropolitan Railway from Ladbroke Grove to Latimer Road running nearby and above ground. The man they had come to see lived at number 10. It smelt and it was dirty. The kitchen was furnished with two deckchairs. Christie might have been in his forties or past fifty, it was hard to tell. He was a tallish but slight man with a beaky face and thick glasses and he seemed dismayed to see Gwendolen. Later on she understood why. Of course she did. He wanted no one else to know Bertha had been there. She refused to sit down. Bertha took one of the chairs and Christie the other. Perhaps she had antagonised him or perhaps he only ever dealt with his clients tête-à-tête, but he immediately said he would want to see Bertha alone. For chaperonage, his wife would be present. Gwendolen never saw the wife nor heard anything of her. All they would do now, Christie said, was make an appointment for the examination and the 'treatment', but Miss Chawcer must go. Everything that passed between himself and his patient must be confidential.

'I won't be long, miss,' Bertha said. 'If you'd wait for me at the end of the street, I won't be a minute.'

Another impertinence, but Gwendolen did wait. Various passers-by stared at her with her carefully made-up face, hair permed into sausage curls and her full-skirted, tight-fitting blue dress. One man whistled at her and Gwendolen's discomfort showed in her darkly flushed cheeks. Eventually Bertha came. 'I won't be a minute,' was true. She had been at least ten. The appointment was for Bertha's next day off, a week ahead.

'I'm not to tell anyone, miss, and you mustn't.'

But Christie had frightened her. Although Mrs Christie wasn't there, he had done some strange intimate things, asked her to open her mouth so that he could look down her throat with a mirror on the end of a rod, and asked her to lift her skirt up to mid-thigh level.

'I've got to go back, miss, haven't I? I can't have a baby, not unless I'm married.'

Gwendolen felt she ought to have asked about the father of the child, who he was and where he was, did he know about the baby and was there a chance of his marrying Bertha if he did. It was too embarrassing, it was too sordid. At home, in the quiet and civilised atmosphere of St Blaise House, seated comfortably among cushions on the sofa, she was reading Proust, and had reached Volume 7. No one in Proust ever had babies. She retired into her cocooned world.

Bertha never went back to Christie. She was too frightened. By the time Gwendolen read about his murders in the papers, the young women who came to his house for abortions or cures for catarrh, his wife, perhaps too the woman and baby upstairs, it was 1953 and Bertha long gone. She left before the child was born, and someone married her,

133

though whether it was the father Gwendolen never knew. The whole thing was horribly sordid. But she never forgot her visit to Rillington Place and how Bertha too might so easily have been one of those women immured in cupboards or buried in the garden.

Bertha – she hadn't thought of her for years. The visit to Christie's house must have been three or four years before his trial and execution. It wasn't worth wasting time looking for the 1949 calendar but what else had she to do with her time? Read, of course. She had long finished *Middlemarch*, re-read Carlyle's *French Revolution* and completed some of the works of Arnold Bennett, though she considered them too light to spend much time on. Today she would start on Thomas Mann. She had never read him, a dreadful omission, though they had all his works somewhere in the many bookcases.

The British Fungi calendar for 1949 – what a ridiculous subject! – she found after searching for an hour, in a room on the top floor, next door to Mr Cellini's flat. In the night gone by, more the hour or so before dawn, she had been awakened by a scream and a thud she thought came from there but she was probably mistaken. This was one of the rooms which the professor had insisted it wasn't necessary to have wired for electricity. Gwendolen had been a child at the time but she remembered quite clearly the wiring of the lower floors, the men taking up floorboards and making great caves in the plaster of walls. This morning was bright and hot, light flooding in from the window on which the curtains had fallen into rags some time in the thirties and never been replaced. It was several years since she had been up here, she couldn't remember when had been the last time.

The bookcase, a store place for ancient, never very readable books there was no room for downstairs, novels by Sabine Baring-Gould and R.D. Blackmore among bound numbers of Victorian journals, *The Complete Works of Samuel Richardson* and Darwin's *The Origin of Species*. No Thomas Mann. Perhaps she would re-read Darwin instead. She looked in the drawers underneath the shelves. Blunt pencils and elastic bands and receipted bills filled them, along with pieces of broken china in labelled bags someone must have intended to repair but never had. The big chest of drawers was her last hope. Taking the few steps that would bring her to it, she tripped and would have fallen but for grabbing hold of the top of the chest. One of the floorboards stuck out perhaps half an inch above the rest.

Bending over as best she could, she peered at the floor. Her reading glasses were in one pocket of her cardigan and the magnifying glass in the other. She made use of them. The boards appeared not to be nailed down but they must be and the glasses weren't strong enough for her to see. How odd. Perhaps it was the damp making one of them protrude. There was a lot of it in this old house, rising damp and whatever the other kind was. With some difficulty, she got down on her knees, her joints cracking, and felt the surface of the protruding board. Quite dry. Odd, she thought. And all those little holes were odd too, dozens of them peppering the woodwork. But perhaps it was always like that and she had never noticed. On her feet again, she began to examine the chest. The fungi calendar came to light in the second drawer she looked through, and with it was one of those letters from a property developer, offering her huge sums to sell her house, this one dated 1998. Why on earth had she put it there five years before? She couldn't remember but she was sure the floorboard hadn't been that way then.

The calendar she took over to the window, the better to read her own handwriting. There it was, for 16 June, a Thursday. 'Accompanied B. to house in Rillington Place.' She recalled writing that but not the entry for the following day, 'Think I may have flu but new doctor says no, only a cold.' The rapid beating of her heart began again and she felt the need to put her hand over her ribs as if to hold it still. That was the first time she had met him. She had gone to the Ladbroke Grove surgery, waited in the waiting room for old Dr Smyth but the man who opened the door and smiled, ushering her in, was Stephen Reeves.

Gwendolen let the hand holding the calendar fall down to her side, and going back in time to her first sight of him in her youth and his, gazed almost unseeing out of the window. Otto lay sleeping on the wall, the crinolined birds pottered about in their wilderness as their owner in a white turban came down the path with corn to feed them. She saw Stephen, his bright smiling eyes, his dark hair, heard him say, 'Not many folks waiting this morning. And what can I do for you?'

The weekend would have passed with Danila's disappearance going unnoticed but for Kayleigh Rivers waking up with a bad cold. Danila had worked at Shoshana's Spa every weekday from

8 a.m. till 4 p.m. and Kayleigh worked there on Saturdays and Sunday mornings and every evening from four till eight. Kayleigh tried calling Danila on her mobile to ask her if she'd do her weekend and when she got no reply, called Madam Shoshana.

'She's still asleep, isn't she?' Shoshana said. 'Like I was. She's got her mobile switched off. Look at the time.'

She waited till eight. The spa didn't open till nine on Saturdays. When she rang Danila's mobile all she got was dead silence. It might be early, but it was too late to get a temp. She paid her girls – illegally – ten pounds a week below the minimum wage but Kayleigh needn't think she was paying her for pretending to be ill. As for Danila . . . Shoshana understood she was going to have to do it herself and she heaved herself unwillingly out of bed. In spite of owning and running a fashionable gym and beauty clinic with manicurist and pedicurist, waxing and electrolysis studio, aromatherapist and salt baths unit, Shoshana paid no personal attention to herself or any of these things and didn't wash much. When you got older you didn't need more than a once-weekly bath and an occasional dip for hands, face and feet. Patchouli, cedarwood, cardamom and nutmeg covered up any possible odours.

She visited the spa itself as little as possible. It interested her only insofar as it made money. Exercise and beauty treatments, keeping fit and retaining youth, bored her and when she sat downstairs at the receipt of custom, she tended to fall asleep. Her grandfather and then her mother had run hairdressing establishments, so it had seemed the natural thing to carry on, only on her own terms and with her own ideas in a contemporary form. She would really have liked to be a guru, founder of her own mystic cult, but had been obliged to compromise and settle for soothsaying.

In the underclothes she had taken off the night before with a baggy red velvet dress on top and a knitted shawl, she glanced into the mirror. Even to her uninterested eyes her hair looked in a bad state, dry and sprinkled white with dandruff. She tied it up in a red and purple scarf, rinsed her hands, splashed water on her face and stumped downstairs. Her temper, never sunny, was going from bad to worse. She had intended to spend the day at a field event organised by her water-divining teacher. A final attempt at getting hold of Danila failed and Shoshana perched herself reluctantly on the high stool behind the counter. The first client to arrive thought he recognised her as the old woman he had once seen in a Turkish village and from whom he had bought a carpet in the market square.

It had been the worst night of his life. He had slept fitfully, waking every hour with a raging thirst. The most horrible thing was opening his eyes for the final time at nine in the morning and, for a moment, forgetting entirely what had happened and what he had done. Memory returned almost at once and he groaned aloud.

There had been dreams and in one of them a creature had come across the roofs, climbed on drainpipes to his own window and tried to make its way in. At first he thought it was a cat but when he saw its human face, the staring eyes and the great gash in the forehead, he screamed aloud. After that he lay trembling, wondering if old Chawcer had heard.

It was only when he finally got up that the drink of the night before hit him. He poured water down his throat but it seemed to have no effect. His head felt sore all over as if it had been rubbed with sand-paper and an ache inside moved about, sometimes over his eyes, sometimes behind one ear or at the back of his neck. He remembered reading some-where, in one of those interviews she gave, that Nerissa never drank anything alcoholic but sub-sisted on sparkling water and vegetable juices. Having a bath helped him a little, he felt he wasn't strong enough to face the challenge of a shower, all that water drumming on to the top of his head. But he was almost too weak to get out of the bath and when he was standing on the bathmat, the towel round him, he staggered and almost fell.

Dressing was a long, slow process because movement made the pain in his head shift from front to back and ears to eyes. It was the worst hangover he had ever known. Not a heavy drinker in normal circumstances, he went straight to alcohol in moments of stress. I'm not used to it, that's the trouble, he said to himself. People who were always getting hungover recommended eating, or drinking milk, or the hair of the dog. The thought of any of it made him retch. Once he had been sick he felt slightly better, able to stand upright, drink more water and put her clothes into a carrier bag along with his own bloodstained underpants, a black Wonderbra and the hated tights, black leather miniskirt and boots, skimpy pink jumper and a cream-coloured faux fur jacket.

Cheap stuff, he judged it, accustomed as he was to the wardrobes of Colette Gilbert-Bamber and her friends, supermarket stuff, not even chain store. Her mobile was inside her pink plastic handbag along with her purse with five pounds fifty in it – he put that in his pocket – a Switch card, a compact of bronzing powder, a red lipstick, a hairbrush and her door keys.

He didn't want to think about what had happened but he couldn't help it: her blood running down his beautiful portrait, her eyes looking at him. Well, she had asked for it, she had only got what she asked for, talking about Nerissa like that, daring to find fault with her skin. Jealous, of course. Still, she should have known better than to have said those things to him. She should have recognised him as a dangerous man and should have . . .

His train of thought was abruptly cut off by the sound of the door to the next room closing. He put a hand up to his chest and clutched at the fabric of his sweatshirt, bunching it up in his fist, he didn't know why, perhaps to hold it against his heart. It was all he could do to stop himself letting out a moan of fear. Had whoever it was gone into that room or *been in there* and come out of it? He heard footsteps cross the floor, a noise as if someone had tripped over, and he held his breath. A drawer was opened, then another. The walls must be very thin up here. The old bat it was, of course. He knew her step, an old person's slow and heavy tread. But why was she in there? He couldn't remember a previous occasion. She must have heard something in the night, that girl crying out or falling to the floor or even his own movements with bucket and scrubbing brush. Suppose she wanted to come in here and saw that blood on the wall?

There's nothing for her to see in there, he said to himself, and repeated it, nothing for her to see, nothing. But he would have to know, he couldn't just leave it. Very carefully he opened the front door and put his head round it. The door to the bedroom where she lay under the floorboards was a little ajar. His head ached all over now, a vicious, squeezing, throbbing pain. But he came out, wearing his jacket, carrying the bag with her clothes in, the flat key in one pocket, car keys in another. He must have made some sort of sound, one of those involuntary moans or sighs he seemed to have been making all night, for suddenly, as he stood there, Miss Chawcer stumped out of the room and gave him a very unfriendly look.

'Oh, it's you, Mr Cellini.'

Who did you think it was, Christie? He'd have liked to say that but he was afraid, of her and of the Rillington Place killer too. Of his spirit or whatever it was he'd imagined haunted this place. She said, incomprehensibly, 'You look as if you have been frightened by a revenant.'

'Pardon?'

'A ghost, Mr Cellini, a phantom. "Revenant" means that which has come back.'

He couldn't stop her seeing the shiver that passed through him. Yet he was furious. Who did she think she was, a bloody schoolteacher and him in the first form? She gave a merrier laugh than he had ever heard come from her.

'Don't tell me you're superstitious.'

He wasn't going to tell her anything. He wanted to *ask* her what she had been into that room for but

141

he couldn't do that. It was her house, the rooms were all hers. Then he saw she was holding something, an old calendar, it looked like, and a book. Maybe she'd been in there to find those things. A load floated from his shoulders, hovered there, lifting the headache.

She took a step back, closed the door behind her. 'Someone should report that Indian man to the – the powers that be.'

He stared. 'What Indian man?'

'The one in the turban with the chickens or whatever they are.' She crossed ahead of him to the top of the stairs, turned her head. 'Are you going out?' She made it sound as if he were breaking the rules.

'After you,' he said.

He put the bag of clothes into the boot of the car, drove to a row of bins and, opening the clothes bank, dropped her skirt on to the tray. The bin was nearly full and it was with difficulty that he was able to make the tray swing and deposit its load. It wouldn't take any more. Maybe for the rest of the clothes he ought to go some distance away. He found himself driving towards Westbourne Grove and, reluctant to pass Shoshana's Spa, turned down Ladbroke Grove towards the Bayswater Road. Thinking of the spa brought into his mind something she had said to him he had forgotten until now. Nerissa wasn't a member. Going there, getting that contract together, chatting up Danila – all of it had been a waste of time. She ought to have told him Nerissa only went there to have her fortune told weeks before. That had been another nail in her coffin, he thought. If ever a woman had asked for what she got, she had.

Driving up the Edgware Road, he passed the

Age Concern charity shop but he dared not take clothes in there. Better the bin on the edge of Maida Vale and another in St John's Wood. While there he went down the steps in Aberdeen Place and making sure there was no one about, no boat coming, no watcher at one of the overlooking windows, he dropped her mobile and her keys into the canal. Returning the way he had come, he went up Campden Hill Square and parked a little way from Nerissa's house.

Perhaps it was because it comforted him. Just knowing that was her place and that she lived in it – with all her servants, no doubt, and maybe a good friend staying – made him feel he had something to look forward to. He could put the disposal of that girl behind him and move on. What better place to be in than here, thinking of new ways of getting to meet Nerissa? It was a pretty house with its white paint and blue front door, some kind of red flowering plant climbing across it. Her newspaper still lay on the step with a carton of milk beside it. Any minute now a servant would open the door and take in paper and milk. Nerissa would be still in bed. Alone, he was sure, for although he believed he had read everything written about her, there had been very little about boyfriends and no scandal, no shaming photographs of her behaving vulgarly with some man in a club. She was chaste and cool, he thought, waiting for the right man . . .

The door opened. It wasn't a servant but she herself. Mix could hardly believe his luck. Some of his adoration of her would have been lost if she had been wearing a dressing gown and slippers but she was in a white tracksuit and white trainers. He thought, what would happen if I went up to her and asked for her autograph? But he didn't want her autograph, he wanted *her*. She went indoors with the milk and the paper and the door closed.

Satisfied and tranquillised by the sight of her, he drove home, went upstairs and nailed down the floorboards in the room where he had put Danila. He'd have a rest and something to eat and then he'd start painting that wall.

In head office on Monday morning Ed was waiting for him and Ed was furious. 'I've been bombarded with calls from those two clients all weekend, I've been *persecuted*, thanks to you. One of them says she's buying a new elliptical but she won't get it through us and she'll be going elsewhere for her servicing.'

'I don't know what you're on about, mate,' said Mix.

'Don't you "mate" me. You never went near either of them, did you? You couldn't even call them and explain.'

Now Mix remembered Ed's Friday night call. It had come just after he had . . . Don't think of that. 'I forgot.'

'Is that all you've got to say? You forgot? I was very sick, I'll have you know. My temperature was up in the forties and my throat was killing me.'

'You've recovered very fast,' said Mix, unwilling to stand much more of this. 'You're looking pretty fit to me.'

'Fuck you,' said Ed.

He'd get over it. Things never lasted long with Ed, Mix thought. If only he could find out when Nerissa was likely to revisit Madam Shoshana. He was sure that if he met her on the stairs he'd be able to get a date with her. Driving to his first call, a work-out fanatic who had five machines in her private gym in Hampstead, he began a fantasy of that stairs meeting. He'd tell her he recognised her at once and now he'd met her he wouldn't go to Madam Shoshana, his fortune and his fate weren't important, but he had something special he wanted to say to her if she'd let him take her to a natural juice bar just a few steps down the street. Of course she would. Women loved that line about something special to tell them and whereas she wouldn't be interested in clubs or pubs, the idea of a natural juice bar would appeal to her. She'd be in her white tracksuit and when they entered the bar all eyes would be on her – and on him. He'd even drink carrot juice to please her. When they were seated he'd tell her he'd worshipped her for years, he'd say she was the most beautiful woman in the world and then he'd . . .

Mix found himself in Flask Walk almost before he knew it, and the exercise junkie waiting with the front door open. She wasn't much to look at, stringy and with a big nose, but flirtatious and with a lithe and lively air about her which led him to think that there might be something doing. She stayed, watching and admiring, while he adjusted the belt on the treadmill.

'It must be great to be so good with your hands,' she gushed.

He stayed much longer than he had expected, missing the call he had promised to make to a woman in Palmers Green but she was soft, a pushover, she wouldn't complain.

*

It wasn't until she had posted the letter to Dr Reeves in Woodstock that a very unpleasant thought came to Gwendolen. Suppose he had truly loved her and then he heard about her visit to Rillington Place. Not when she made that visit, of course, because that had taken place before Christie was even suspected of murdering anyone. Christie wasn't the infamous, appalling creature he had become when his crimes came to light and his trial began, but a nobody, an ordinary little man living in an insalubrious place. If Stephen Reeves had heard about the visit in those earlier days it would have had no effect on him.

Yet only suppose he had known of the visit at the time because, while making house calls, he had seen her go there. After all, on the very day after she and Bertha had gone to see Christie, she had consulted Dr Reeves for the first time, and what more likely than that he had recognised her as the woman he had seen in Rillington Place the day before? It would have meant nothing to him then but, at the start of Christie's trial, all of it would have come back to him, and as the vulgar people put it, he put two and two together. He had told her in the January that he was awfully fond of her and when Christie's trial began he had been on the point of proposing to her. Eileen Summers was to be told he no longer cared for her. Gwendolen Chawcer was his true love. But when he read in the newspaper that Christie had lured women to his house by claiming to carry out illegal operations he would naturally have thought Gwendolen had gone there for an abortion. Oh, the horror of it! The shame! Of course, no decent man would want to marry a woman who had had an abortion. And a doctor would be even more set against such a thing.

Gwendolen walked along Cambridge Gardens, thinking of all this and growing more and more dismayed. If only she hadn't posted the letter! She would write another, that was the only thing to do, and she wouldn't wait for a reply. Believing what he did about her, he very likely wouldn't deign to answer her at all. No wonder he hadn't been to her mother's funeral or come back to see her. No wonder he had married Eileen Summers after all. She was brooding along these lines when she came face to face with Olive Fordyce who was walking along with Queenie Winthrop. Queenie had a shopping trolley which she leant on as if it were a Zimmer frame, and Olive had Kylie on a lead.

'Goodness, Gwendolen, you were lost in a dream,' said Queenie. 'In another world. Who were you thinking about? Your fancy man?' She winked at Olive, who winked back.

It was too near the bone for Gwendolen. 'Don't be stupid.'

'I hope we can all take a joke,' Queenie said rather distantly.

Here Olive intervened. 'Let's not quarrel. After all, who have we got but each other?'

This went down badly with the other two. 'Thank you very much, Olive. I really appreciate that.' Queenie drew herself up to her full five feet one. 'I have two daughters, in case you've forgotten, and five grandchildren.'

'We can't all be so lucky,' said Olive peaceably. 'Now, Gwen, while I've got the opportunity, I want to ask you a very great favour. It's my niece. May I bring her to see you some time this week because she really is dying to see your house?'

'You say that.' Gwendolen spoke grumpily. 'But she won't come, she never does. I go to all that trouble and she can't put herself out to come.'

'She will this time. I promise. And you needn't bother with cakes. We're both on a diet.'

'Really? Well, I suppose she can come. You'll go on and on about it until I say yes.'

'Could we say Thursday? I promise I won't bring my little dog. That's a lovely ring you're wearing.'

'I wear it every day,' said Gwendolen distantly. 'I never go out without it.'

'Yes, I've noticed. Is that a ruby?'

'Of course.'

Gwendolen made her way home, cross and dismayed. Never mind about that silly Olive and the niece, they were just a minor nuisance like a mosquito buzzing round one's bedroom in the night. Nor did Olive's never before noticing the ring matter much. Her only true concern was with Stephen Reeves. The post would have been collected by now and that letter would be on its way to Woodstock. She must write again and put things straight. All these years he might have been thinking of her as a woman of low morals. He must be made to see her in her true light.

# Chapter 12

It was to be a long time before the disappearance of Danila Kovic was known to the police. She had been a solitary girl, come to London from Lincoln at Madam Shoshana's command, having no London friends but Mix Cellini. The room in Oxford Gardens had been found for her by a London acquaintance of her mother's. Danila had never met this woman or her husband, never been to her home in Ealing and heard nothing from her. As for her mother, she had come to Grimsby as a refugee from Bosnia, bringing her small daughter with her and, her husband having been killed in the war, had remarried. Danila sometimes said – when she had someone to say it to – that her mother was less interested in her than in her present husband and their two sons. Packing her off to London was a way of getting rid of her.

When she had been in London a month her mother died of cancer. Danila went home for the funeral but her stepfather made it plain he didn't want her staying with him. She went back to Notting Hill, virtually alone in the world, nineteen years old, not particularly attractive, without skills and, with one exception, without friends.

By the middle of the week, when she still hadn't

come to work, Madam Shoshana washed her hands of her and worried only about finding someone else to do her job. If she thought of Danila at all, it was to conclude that she had got fed up with the job or gone off with some man. In Shoshana's experience, there was always some man about for a girl to go off with. These days people seemed to wander about the country, and about Europe for that matter, whenever the fancy took them. Danila need not think she was keeping the job open for her.

Kayleigh Rivers hadn't been close to Danila. They had never been to each other's homes, but they had twice been for a meal together and once to the cinema. She was the nearest to a friend Danila had and the only person who knew her to worry about where she might now be.

Behind the counter in her Turkish carpet seller's costume, Shoshana phoned an agency she had used before, the Beauty Placement Centre, and was sent a temp. Just in time, as she had a new client coming to see her when she was wearing her soothsayer's hat.

A spiteful message left on his mobile warned Mix not to bother to come to Ed and Steph's engagement party. He wouldn't be welcome. The party, said Ed, was for *friends* and well-wishers, there would be no room at the Sun in Splendour for those who failed to keep their promises.

'What a carry-on over nothing,' said Mix aloud in the car.

On that terrible night when the girl had provoked him into beating her to death, when she had asked for it as plainly as if she'd said, 'Kill me', there had been moments of thinking his chances of meeting Nerissa for ever ruined. But as the days went by he began to feel better. He forced himself – he was proud of this – to phone the spa and ask for Danila. The reply he got hugely raised his spirits.

'Shoshana's Spa. Kayleigh speaking.'

'Can I speak to Danila?'

'Sorry, Danila's left. She doesn't work here any more.'

It wasn't difficult to interpret that as meaning they thought she'd given up her job. If they were worried, if they thought she might have been abducted or murdered or both, they wouldn't have said she'd left. They'd have said something about her being missing. Maybe, he thought, she'd never be missed, maybe there was no one to look for her or care what had happened to her. He'd read some-where that thousands of people disappear every year and are never found.

Almost as an afterthought, he asked to speak to Madam Shoshana.

'I'll see if she's free.'

She was and he made an appointment. On a Wednesday afternoon, going upstairs, Danila had met Nerissa coming down. Why shouldn't he meet her this Wednesday? Of course, it hadn't been a Wednesday afternoon but a morning on some other weekday when he'd seen her go into the spa. Still, he pinned his faith on her going to Shoshana tomorrow.

If that failed, he'd somehow sabotage her car and then be on hand to repair it for her or at least advise her. It was a bold stroke but it might really work, and with speed. He'd see her trying to start the car and failing and then he'd go over and very

151

politely offer his services. Mix lost himself in this new fantasy. She'd be so grateful when she heard the engine turn over that she'd invite him in for a drink. People like her never drank anything but champagne and she'd always have a bottle waiting on ice – but no, he remembered he'd read that she didn't drink at all. But she'd have champagne for visitors. They'd sit and talk and when he'd told her about his long devotion to her and about the scrapbook, she'd ask him if he'd like to come to a première with her that evening as her escort.

He had to get to know her first. Was there something he could do to run the battery down without her knowing? He'd find out, ask around, and then he'd do it. All he needed after that were jump leads. He pictured her struggling to make the engine fire. She'd look so beautiful, the exertion and the stress bringing a faint flush to her golden skin, her dainty foot wildly pressing, but in vain, on the accelerator. At this point he'd go over to her, say, 'Can I help, Miss Nash?'

She'd say, 'You know my name!'

The enigmatic smile he'd give would excite her curiosity. 'It's the battery, don't you think?'

It looked like it, he'd say, but luckily he happened to have jump leads with him. Once he'd recharged the battery, she ought to drive the car around a bit to stop it getting flat again. Would she like him to drive it? Of course she could sit beside him while he drove. Rather than her inviting him in that first time, this was a more realistic scenario. He'd take her down to Wimbledon Common or maybe Richmond Park and she'd be so thrilled by his driving and the masterful manner in which he'd taken over car and her, that she'd say yes immedi-

152

ately when he asked if he could see her again. No, he wouldn't ask if, but when.

He got to Shoshana's Spa half an hour earlier than the appointed time, so he managed to park the car on a meter – he'd feed that once the traffic warden had gone round the corner – then sat in the driving seat and read another chapter of *Christie's Victims*. Reggie hadn't seemed to think much about finding girls. If he wanted one girl he got her to come to his house, fixed up that gas arrangement ostensibly to cure her catarrh or abort her, and when she passed out he strangled her. Screwed her first, of course. Mix didn't fancy that part of it, he couldn't have had sex with a dead girl but to do that was Reggie's sole motive. And he killed how many? Mix had only got so far as the death of Hectorina McClennan and he thought there were more to come. Not old Chawcer, though, she was the one that got away. For his own part – and he considered this in a cool practical way of which he was proud – he probably wouldn't kill any more. It was a lot of trouble, especially covering one's tracks afterwards. Except Javy. Now he'd killed once, the idea of doing it again, and doing it when he really wanted to, seemed less formidable.

He read another couple of pages, saw rather ruefully that there were only three more chapters to go, put the marker in his book and, checking on the traffic warden, a further two pounds in the meter, and rang the bell at Shoshana's. She answered in a deep thrilling voice and he could tell she had someone with her. He heard her say, more briskly, 'I'll see you next week.' The door slid open when he pushed it. His throat dried and his heart beat faster at the prospect of meeting Nerissa on the stairs but the woman coming down was middle-aged and overweight. It couldn't be helped, he'd hear his fortune and try to find out the times she came; he'd ask if necessary.

The room where Shoshana sat was like nowhere he had ever seen before. It was very hot and, for the time of day, very dark. His sensitive nose smelt tobacco smoke. There seemed to him something not only eccentric but actively unpleasant in pinning the curtains together with those great clumsy brooches. He tried not to look at the owl and, with an even more deliberate turning aside, at the wizard in grey robes positioned behind Shoshana's chair. She herself he had expected to be a glamorous figure, skilfully made-up and svelte, as would befit the proprietor of a beauty spa. Little of her was visible but what he could see was enough: wizened face and sharp black eyes peering out of stormcloud-coloured draperies.

'Sit down,' she said. 'Will you have the stones or the cards?'

'Pardon?'

'Am I to look into your future by means of gem-stones or cards?' She frowned. 'I suppose you know what cards are.' She produced a greasy pack from a concealed pocket in her topmost layer. 'These things. Cards. Which is it to be?'

'I don't want my fortune told. I want your advice on – ghosts.'

'Fortune first,' she said. 'Take a card.'

Uncertain whether he would be allowed to dig into the pack, he took the top one. It was the Ace of Spades. She looked at it and then at him inscrutably. 'Take another.'

She had shuffled the first card he took back into the pack but still when he picked one it was the Ace of Spades. Even in the gloom he could see that her face had fallen. She looked like a woman who has just been told a dreadful piece of news, dismayed but still incredulous.

'What is it?' he said.

'Take another.'

This time it was the Queen of Hearts. A faint smile touched her lips. She took the card from him, set the pack face down on the table and, taking from a black velvet drawstring bag one piece of coloured crystal after another, black, translucent white, purple, pink, green and dark blue, arranged them in a circle round a white lace mat.

'Place your hands on the mandala.'

'What's that – what you said?'

'Place them inside the ring of stones. That's right. Now tell me which of the sacred stones you can feel drawn closer to your fingers. There will not be more than two. Which two are drawing gradually towards you?'

Mix could neither feel nor see any movement of the stones but he wasn't going to say so. He frowned and said in a very serious voice, 'The white one and the green one.'

Shoshana shook her head. She had never been known to tell clients they were right. In fact, her policy being to undermine them and make them feel ignorant, her popularity rested on the superior wisdom they saw in her, contrasted with their own inadequacy. 'You are wrong,' she said. 'The lapis and the amethyst are in your Ring of Fate today. Both are pushing hard but your fingers are putting up a stubborn resistance. You must slacken, cease to fight against them and bid them come.'

The stones failed to move for Mix but he fancied a slight shift in the stance of the grey-robed figure behind Shoshana's chair. The hand that held the staff of twisted snakes had seemed infinitesimally to rise. He meant not to speak of it but he was frightened now and the words came out.

'That thing – that man behind you – it moved.'

'So you do have something of the inner vision,' said Madam Shoshana, adding, 'Just a hint of it. The stones have retreated now. Leave them.'

Mix couldn't make out if she meant the wizard figure really had moved, due perhaps to some mechanism inside it, or that he was possessed of the same sort of imagination as hers. He clenched his fists to keep his hands from shaking.

'Your fateful balance is badly awry,' she began. 'The stones speak of self-doubt and suspicion, of fear that some sin will be discovered. Apart from that, they are silent, keeping their own counsel. Now to the cards. There is death in them.' She lifted her head and stared at him enigmatically. 'I would avoid telling you if I could, but you drew the Ace of Spades twice, and in the face of that I would fail in my duty if I did not warn you of the danger of death. You also drew the Queen of Hearts and she, as all must know, means love. I see a beautiful dark woman. She may be for you or not for you, that I cannot see, but you will meet her soon. That is all.'

Mix got up. 'That'll be forty-five pounds,' she said.

'Will you take a cheque?'

'I suppose so, but no credit cards.'

He had sat down again to write the cheque and had got as far as the date when the original purpose of his visit came back to him. 'I wanted to ask you about a ghost I may have seen.'

'What d'you mean "may"?'

'It's a murderer who used to live round where I live. He killed women and buried them in his garden. I've seen something – I think. I thought I saw his ghost in the house where I live.'

'That is where he killed these women?'

'Oh, no. But I reckon he used to go there sometimes. Would he – would he *come back*?'

Madam Shoshana sat quite still, apparently lost in thought. After a full minute, she spoke. 'Why not? You had better come and see me again in a week's time. By then I shall have decided what should be done. Remember, this will need the greatest care and spiritual protection. Meanwhile, if you see it again, hold up a cross towards it. There is no need to throw the cross, just hold it up.'

'All right,' said Mix, pleased he had the one Steph had given him. He felt much more secure and doubted that he'd go back.

'That'll be another ten pounds.'

Once he had gone, Shoshana lit a cigarette. Her next appointment wasn't for half an hour. She was used to the gullibility of clients and no longer marvelled or even sneered at it, as she had done in her early days. They would believe anything. She was herself a curious mixture of a ribald derision of all things occult and a certain credulousness. That small leaven of faith had to exist for her to follow her chosen path in life. For instance, she had no doubt about the efficacy of water-divining and the value of exorcism among other rituals. But she was fully in favour of helping things along with practical aids. For instance, the pack of cards she used consisted entirely of Aces of Spades and Queens of Hearts. She had bought it from a joke shop. The stones had belonged to her grandfather who had collected them on his Oriental travels, and the wizard figure was a reject from a junk shop in the Portobello Road. She had found it thrown in a skip on top of a nylon tiger skin and a portrait of Edward VII.

But yet . . . These 'but yets' were not insignificant in her interpretation of her vocation. The fortunes she told were based on nothing more than her imagination and her observation of human beings. What the stones did or the cards showed was irrelevant. Her ignorance of crystallomancy was profound and her knowledge of divination by cards non-existent. Yet it was strange, it was a little uncanny, how often her predictions came close to the truth. Very likely, that young man would die or bring death, or had already brought it, to someone else. As for the beautiful woman, the streets of Notting Hill were full of them, he might bump into one at any time. Another curious thing, though, was when she reached that point in his fortune, Nerissa Nash had come into her mind and given rise to that description, the beauty and the darkness. He had probably never set eyes on the girl, except in pictures. As for the ghost, all that stuff was rubbish but if it was also a source of money, she saw no reason why she shouldn't get her hands on it.

Writing that second letter to Dr Reeves was almost insurmountably difficult. Several times Gwendolen gave up and wandered about the house to stretch her legs and in a vain effort to clear her head. It would be absurd and inviting ridicule to write to a man that he had only dropped her because he thought she had had an abortion. She must attempt circumlocution. She must somehow get round it. Upstairs in her bedroom, gazing unseeing out of the window, she allowed herself to dream of what it would have been like to have shared a bedroom with him, to go to her wardrobe now and in the camphor odour which wafted out when she opened the door, see his suits and summer rain-coat hanging close beside her own dresses. It could still happen. He was a widower now.

She started up the stairs. All her life, since first she could walk she had climbed up and down them. The flight going up to the top floor hadn't then been tiled but plain wooden boards covered in drugget. Whatever had happened to drugget? You never saw it any more. Papa had had the tiles put down after the woodworm had been found and steps taken to eradicate it. Few builders, including plumbers and electricians, ever came to St Blaise House. Exterior painting hadn't been done since before the Second World War, no improvements to the electrical system since eleven or twelve years before that. But Papa had been fanatical about woodworm; worrying about it kept him awake at night.

She could write to Stephen Reeves that she remembered his seeing her in Rillington Place the day before they had met for the first time. Of course she couldn't really remember, she didn't even know for sure if he had seen her. If he hadn't he would think her very foolish, he might even think she had that illness – what was it called? Alzheimer's – yes, Alzheimer's disease.

Otto was sitting, sphinx-like, in the middle of the tiled flight.

'What are you doing there?'

She couldn't recall ever having addressed him before. Talking to animals was ridiculous, anyway. Otto got up, arched his back and stretched. He glared at her before leaping down one of the passages and crouching in the shadows at the end. Gwendolen unlocked the door of the flat and went inside. Everything was again depressingly neat. What kind of a fanatic plumped up the sofa cushions before he went out in the morning? The Psyche figurine on the coffee table she thought vulgar, the kind of thing that came from furniture stores which sold cream leather three-piece suites and moulded Perspex tables. She picked it up, finding it surprisingly heavy.

Its base was felted. It looked as if someone had put it down, surely by mistake, into a pool of coffee. What else could have caused the dark stain which covered half the base, turning the felt from emerald to maroon?

'The multitudinous seas incarnadine,' quoted Gwendolen aloud, 'making the green one red.'

She was rather pleased with the aptness of that. Macbeth, of course, had been talking about blood and Cellini's lump of marble had hardly stood in a pool of that. The paucity of the book collection in here made her shake her head. Nothing but works on that man Christie. Which reminded her she had that letter to write.

Still, she must first visit the room next door to this flat and take another look at that floor.

Contrary to the way she remembered it, the floor-board wasn't sticking up. Or not much. She must have imagined it, tripped over something else. She stood, staring down at the splintery old boards, and suddenly she knew what all the little holes were. They were woodworm. Papa used to say woodworm were as bad as termites, they could destroy a whole house. What was she to do?

Indecisively, she stood in the doorway, thinking once more of her letter. She would make one more attempt at it, perhaps telling him obliquely that no one should believe gossip – but surely she hadn't been the subject of gossip? She couldn't tell him not to believe his own eyes. There was a slight smell in the room she was sure hadn't been there when she last came in. She would have noticed it. Not a pleasant smell, far from it. Did woodworm smell? Perhaps. If it got worse, there was no doubt about it, she would have to get a man in, get those people who did something to floors and boards and furniture to banish the things.

When she had written her letter she would look them up in the phone book. There was something called the Yellow Pages and though she had never opened it since it was left on her doorstep, she would do so now.

# Chapter 13

'Newfangled' was a word that figured predominantly in Gwendolen's vocabulary. She applied it to most things which, in another favourite phrase, had 'arrived on the scene' since the sixties. Computers were newfangled, as were CDs and the means of playing them, mobiles, answerphones, parking meters and clamping (though she enjoyed seeing a clamp on an improperly parked car), colour photographs in newspapers, calories and diets, the disappearance of telegrams, and of course, the Internet. In respect of most innovations, she managed to ignore them. But the Yellow Pages was a book and with books of any sort she was familiar. Papa used to say that if he were in some isolated place with no company and only the telephone directory to read, he would read that. Gwendolen wouldn't go quite so far but she didn't find this directory of services as newfangled and incomprehensible as she had feared.

There were whole pages devoted to firms that treated woodworm. It was difficult to know which to select. Certainly not a facetiously named one, such as Zingy Zappers (Let Zingy Zappers zap your woodworm and dry rot) or anything commercial or industrial. Eventually she chose Woodrid, mainly because it was near at hand in

Kensal Green. This did nothing to mitigate the horror of failing to get through to a live human voice on the phone. She had to press key 1, then 2, did it wrong and had to begin all over again. After she'd got over these difficulties she was asked to press something called 'hache' and had to ask for an explanation. When there was no response from the automated voice to her inquiry she reasoned that since it wasn't a figure or a star it must be that thing that looked like a crooked portcullis. It was. She waited and waited while music was played, the kind of newfangled music which thumped out of cars being driven by young men down her street on Saturday nights. At last she was through but was told, to her dismay, that a 'representative will come and make a survey' two weeks and four 'working days' hence.

The phone call exhausted her and she had to lie down in the drawing room for a rest and half an hour's read of *The Origin of Species*. Olive was bringing her niece to tea. She had said both of them were on diets but Gwendolen knew how seriously she should take that. It just made things more difficult, for they wouldn't want simply to drink tea but would expect calorie-free crispbread, low-fat cake or other newfangled nonsense. Besides, Gwendolen, who never put on weight no matter what she ate, liked something substantial for her tea. These people never thought what a lot of trouble they were causing others.

She and Stephen Reeves had so much in common. There was no reason to believe his tastes had changed. Gwendolen believed that people changed very little, only pretended to as part of a showing-off campaign. Stephen had loved his teas, sandwiches and home-made cakes, especially her Victoria sponge. When they met again, would she be capable of making a Victoria sponge for him? But the letter still had to be written, if not today, tomorrow or the next day. The more she thought about disabusing his mind of the impression he must have got of her, the more awkward it seemed to have to explain to a man how she hadn't had an abortion but was accompanying someone else who nearly had. And that itself might appear reprehensible in his eyes.

Perhaps she could find a subtle way of doing it. She could begin practising now and once more she took pen and paper. *Dear Dr Reeves . . .* Why should the words 'illegal operation' even have to be used? *Dear Dr Reeves, I remembered something about our affection* – no, that wasn't right, it had been more what they called a 'relationship' today – *I remembered something about our relationship, yours and mine, after I had posted my previous letter*. That would do, that was quite good. And she hadn't called him Dr Reeves for a long time before they parted. *Dear Stephen, After I had posted my previous letter I remembered something about our relationship, yours and mine, which had slipped my mind. The day before we met in your surgery where I went to consult you about a minor ailment . . .* Should she put the date of that meeting? Perhaps not . . . *about a minor ailment I did not comment on the fact that we had seen each other the day before.* She couldn't know that he had seen her, any more than she had seen him, he might have been miles away and his desertion of her due to some quite other cause. But, no, that couldn't be. He had loved her, she knew he had, no doubt continued to love her but felt, in the circumstances, that she

164

would make an unsuitable wife for a medical practitioner. As indeed she would have if she had done what he thought she had.

She glanced up at the time and it gave her a shock. Olive, with or without her niece, would be here in an hour and she hadn't yet bought the cakes. She couldn't even be sure she had enough milk. This letter would have to wait till later or even until she had had a reply to the first one.

For all Olive had said about her niece's passion for old London buildings, Hazel Akwaa showed little interest in St Blaise House. She turned out to be a quiet well-mannered woman who drank her tea and ate a plain biscuit in silence while Olive chattered. Olive wore black trousers with bell bottoms and a red sweater patterned with fir trees and people skiing, more suitable for someone a third of her age, but her niece was in a grey wool dress with a valuable-looking gold necklace. When Olive introduced her Gwendolen had to ask her first to repeat the surname, then to spell it, it was so outlandish, it sounded African. Gwendolen knew her Rider Haggard from childhood and thought she remembered a character from *She* or *King Solomon's Mines* called Akwaa. Surely Hazel whatever-her-name-had-been hadn't married an African?

'Would you like to see over the house?' Gwendolen asked when tea was over. 'There are rather a lot of stairs.'

She expected the woman to say she wouldn't let a little obstacle like stairs put her off, but Mrs Akwaa looked far from enthusiastic. 'Not particularly, if you don't mind.'

'Oh, *I* don't mind. I can go up there whenever I

165

choose, of course. I was going for your sake, Mrs Akwaa.'

'Hazel, please. I can see this lovely room from where I'm sitting and I doubt if the rest of the house can be more beautiful than this.'

Gwendolen was mollified by this gracious remark. She decided to unbend a fraction. 'And where do you live?'

'Me? Oh, in Acton.'

'Really? I don't think I've ever been there. And how will you get home?' Gwendolen made it sound as if her guest lived in Cornwall and she wanted to get rid of her as soon as possible. 'Not in an underground train, I trust? You take your life in your hands using those.'

'My daughter said she would come and fetch us at five-thirty. We shall all go back to my home for supper.'

'How nice. And would that be the paragon your aunt is always telling me about?'

'I don't know about "paragon",' said Hazel Akwaa in nearly as cold a tone as Gwendolen's. 'I have only the one daughter. Her father and I think she's very special but we are her parents, after all. Would you mind telling me where your toilet is?'

Gwendolen smiled her tiny half-smile. 'The *lavatory* is on the first floor, the door facing you at the top of the first flight of stairs.'

She decided, in Hazel Akwaa's absence, to tell Olive about the woodworm. 'I have just been up there to examine it again. I've sent for Woodrid, but like all these firms today they mean to keep me waiting over a fortnight before they'll come. I don't suppose the floor will collapse in a fortnight.'

She gave a small humourless laugh. 'Do you happen to know if woodworm *smells*?'

'I really don't know, Gwen. I've never heard of it smelling.'

'Perhaps it was my imagination. I'd take you up and show you only that great-niece of yours is coming in five minutes.'

Hazel came back, followed by Otto. 'Your lovely cat rubbed himself against me and when I stroked him he followed me down.'

'Yes, it does seem to bestow its favours on some people,' said Gwendolen in the sort of voice which implied that there was no accounting for tastes.


Watching outside Nerissa's house in Campden Hill Square, Mix was rewarded by the sight of her coming out of her front door soon after half-past four and getting into her car. This time she was elegantly dressed in a honey-coloured trouser suit and a large golden hat which she took off and deposited on the passenger seat. She drove past him down the hill, slowing and turning her head briefly to stare at him. He was pleased. She'll know me again, he thought.

He had one more call to make before going home. This was at a house in Pembroke Villas, home of one of those rare clients who possessed a treadmill and actually used it, if not daily, three or four times a week. The belt on the machine had shifted on its rollers too far to the left and Mrs Plymdale wasn't strong enough, despite all her working out, to ply the spanner and fix it herself.

Her house had a drive on which he could park his car. He congratulated her on her adherence to exercise, adjusted the belt and oiled the machine.

But the belt really needed renewing and he advised her to order a replacement now. The visit was completed in fifteen minutes and he was free for the rest of the day. He drove home via the Portobello Road, Ladbroke Grove and Oxford Gardens, stopping on the way to buy a half-bottle of gin, a bottle of red wine and a frozen chicken masala.

The late afternoon was very hot and the wind had dropped. He thought, I wonder if they've started looking for that girl, that Danila, there's been nothing in the papers so no one's told the police. He was afraid to find out but at the same time he wanted to know. If Shoshana's Spa didn't care, surely the people she'd rented that room from, surely they'd be wondering. He turned into St Blaise Avenue. Outside the house where he lived, on a single yellow line, was parked a golden Jaguar. Funny, it looked a lot like Nerissa's from here. But, great cars as they were, one Jaguar was very much like another. That sharp-faced traffic warden he'd spotted round the corner would be down on its owner like a ton of bricks.

He couldn't help wishing he'd noted Nerissa's registration number but he never had. There had seemed no point. He put his own car on the residents' parking, locked it and went across the street to the Jaguar. Her large golden hat was lying on the passenger seat. So the car *was* hers. He lifted his eyes, turned round and came face to face with her. He couldn't be dreaming, it must be real . . .

'Nerissa,' he said, 'it's wonderful to get to talk to you at last.'

She raised her large black eyes to his but said nothing. She was standing quite still, as if in shock.

'You're parked on a yellow line, Nerissa,' he said.

'The traffic warden will catch you. Let me move the car for you, Nerissa.'

'Miss Nash to you,' said a voice from behind her. He had had eyes only for her, he hadn't seen either of the other two women. They were the kind who might have been invisible, he never noticed them. The one who had spoken said, 'My daughter will drive her own car, thank you. She is about to do so.'

Nerissa smiled at him. It was such a radiant smile, sweet, kindly and forbearing, that he almost fell on his knees at her feet. 'That was very thoughtful of you,' she said, got into the car and passed the hat to the women on the back seat. The window was wound down. 'Bye, now.'

The car disappeared round the corner just as the warden appeared, almost running, documentation in hand. Mix stood for a moment on the hallowed ground where the Jaguar had been, now occupied only by an empty beer can, a strip of oily rag and a Magnum wrapper.

The warden fancied himself as a wit. 'Stay there and you'll get clamped, sir.'

'Ha, ha,' said Mix.

He drifted towards the house. So much of what happened to him these days had this dream-like quality about it. The dreams were either glorious like the most recent, or nightmarish. What had become of reality? Well, it was real that he had spoken to Nerissa and – wonder of wonders! – she had spoken to him. And she had been so nice, so charming. She had called him thoughtful. If that old woman who said she was her mother hadn't interfered she'd probably have let him move the car, would even have got in beside him and let him drive her home. But the old woman *had* interfered.

Mix would have liked to knock her down and trample on her. How could she be Nerissa's mother with that reddish-grey hair and that pale dog-face?

The house was always quiet but this afternoon it seemed unusually silent. He began to climb the stairs. Nerissa would recognise him another time. She would come out and speak to him, maybe invite him in for a coffee. When that happened it would be his chance to ask her out. He'd take her to that double-barrelled Italian place with the funny name that won the Italian Restaurant of the Year award. Luckily, he'd been able to save a bit. He'd wanted it for one of those plasma-screen TVs but Nerissa was far more important.

As he reached the top flight thoughts of Reggie and his ghost invariably drove out everything else. Even Nerissa hadn't sufficient power over him to displace that. It was early, of course, but already dusk and the passages up here were always dark. Sometimes he thought of shutting his eyes when he got to the top and letting himself blind into his flat, but he feared a hand touching him on the shoulder if he did that or a voice whispering in his ear. Better to face up to it and look. No one was there, nothing was there. Everything was as it ought to be. Or was it? Mix stood still, trying to remember. He was almost positive he had shut the door to the room where Danila lay under the floor-boards. He *knew* he had because he always did. It had never been left ajar like that in all the time he'd been here.

Tiptoeing for some reason, he approached the door, thought that flinging it open would be the best way but opened it stealthily just the same. The room was empty and very hot. Sun blazed

170

down on the glass. A smell, not very strong but quite unpleasant, must be coming in through the open window, only the window wasn't open. He crossed to it and tried to raise the sash but found this impossible, the sashcords were broken, one of them dangling. Some of the smells you got in London were untraceable and seemed to make their way in through cracks in the fabric of a house. He looked out of the window. The Indian man's guinea fowl were huddled together on the roof of a low shed, watched by Otto on the wall.

Closing the door behind him, Mix put his key into his own lock. Not only a strange smell but strange music too. It must have started up while he was in that room, the sort of music he had never been able to follow or understand, while some people seemed to like it. He suspected they didn't really like it but pretended to because it made them seem clever. A piano, possibly two pianos, tinkled away while someone sawed at a violin. Where was it coming from? No doubt, the old bat's bedroom. He went into the flat, thinking about that girl under the floorboards.

Was he going to leave her there? He hadn't intended that at first. The room next door was just a temporary resting place. He'd meant to put the body in the boot of his car and dispose of it some-where. Reggie had never gone so far as that. His victims had all been buried inside the house or in the garden, but Reggie hadn't got a car, few had in those days. Of course his own experience was very different from Reggie's. The necrophile had killed all those women in order to have sex with them as they lay dying or were recently dead while he, Mix, had killed someone in self-defence

171

because she said such dreadful things to him. What he had done was no more than manslaughter.

In Reggie's day, forensics hadn't reached anywhere like the peak of expertise they had achieved now. Mix knew all about it, as anyone must who watched television. Now, with all the tests they did, they'd be able to tell if he'd carried a girl's body in his car, they'd know who she was by DNA testing. Reggie had to conceal those bodies from his wife until she became his victim too. He was forced to bury them. Surely things would be far safer for himself if he left Danila where she was, where no one would ever have reason to go. But who had been in that room today? Probably old Chawcer, hunting for more rubbish in the drawers of that cabinet.

Suppose it had been Reggie's ghost, fascinated by someone else's concealment of a body? Suppose Reggie, instead of haunting him with intent to frighten, was watching over him? He'd feel better about it when he'd been back to Madam Shoshana and heard what she had to say.

But a ghost was equally frightening, he thought, whether it was threatening you or protecting you. The fact that it was a ghost at all made you look at the world in a different way. He shivered, thinking that perhaps it wasn't too early to mix himself a Boot Camp.

# Chapter 14

Abbas Reza noticed Danila's absence only when she failed to pay her rent. He expected his rents to be paid in cash, preferably fifty and twenty pound notes, put in an envelope and pushed through the letterbox in his door. No cheques and no credit cards. Ms Kovic hadn't paid her rent last Saturday and now another week had gone by. He had already banged on her door to ask for it and got no answer, not even at half-past midnight. She had never seemed one of those stop-outs to him, not a night bird at all, but he had been mistaken. Now she'd been in London a few months she was finding her feet, changing her good ways for bad ones, as happened to them all. Such was the corruption and creeping evil of the western world where God was mocked and morals had flown out of the window. Sometimes he thought with nostalgia of Tehran, but not for long. On the whole it was better here.

The temp, who was still at Shoshana's Spa, was efficient, better-looking than the Bosnian girl and a good advertisement for the spa with that queenly figure, fine posture and face like a Nordic goddess. Pity she wasn't staying. Shoshana had had several replies to her ad and was interviewing applicants. Clients were coming thick and fast. That fool who thought he lived in a haunted house had been back and she'd had to stop herself laughing out loud at his face when she'd told him to avoid the number thirteen if he didn't want to see the ghost again. She had almost forgotten Danila's existence.

Kayleigh hadn't. Before she met Mix, Danila would have said Kayleigh was the only friend she had in London. Not that they had ever seen much of each other, Kayleigh coming on for her shift just as Danila was going off.

Danila hadn't a phone in her room in Oxford Gardens, so Kayleigh had made several attempts to call her on her mobile. It rang and rang but always in vain. Kayleigh wasn't worried yet. If anything had happened to Danila, like her being mugged or attacked, it would have been in the papers. She might be ill and not answering her mobile. Still, she wouldn't go on being ill for a fortnight and now it was over two weeks since Danila had failed to answer her phone when Shoshana called her. Kayleigh went round to the house in Oxford Gardens.

All the rooms and the two flats had entryphones. Abbas Reza was proud of organising things properly. Besides, he didn't want visitors waking him at all hours. Kayleigh rang and rang Danila's bell and when she got no answer, pressed the key above which was written rather mysteriously: *Mr Reza, Head of the House*, as if he were a top prefect in a school.

A slender, rather handsome man with a small moustache and hair so black and glossy it might have been painted on, answered the door. He looked in his late thirties. 'What can I do for you?'

He was polite because Kayleigh was a pretty

blonde of twenty-two. 'I'm looking for my friend Danila.'

'Ah, yes, Ms Kovic. Where is she? That's what I ask myself.'

'I ask myself too,' said Kayleigh. 'She doesn't answer my calls and now you say she's not here. Could we get into her room, d'you think?'

Mr Reza liked that 'we'. He smiled reassuringly. 'We try,' he said.

They knocked on her door first. Clearly, no one was inside. The landlord inserted his key, turned it and they were in. As he did so, the thought came to him that she might be lying in there dead. Such things happened, in Tehran as well as London, unfortunately. What a shock for this tender and surely uncorrupted young girl! But no, there was nothing. Nothing but the kind of untidiness they all seemed to live in, discarded clothes everywhere, an empty teacup with very old tea dregs in it and, in the sink, under cold water scummed with floating grease, a plate, a knife and a fork. The bed had been roughly made. Beside it, on top of a stack of magazines, was a copy of the Shoshana's Spa brochure, glossy turquoise and silver.

'She has done a moonshine flit,' said Abbas Reza, thinking of his rent. 'I have seen it before, many many times. They leave all like this, always it is the same.'

'I didn't think she was that sort of person. I'm really surprised.'

'Ah, you are innocent, Miss – ?'

'Call me Kayleigh.'

'You are innocent, Miss Kayleigh. At your young youth you have not seen the wicked world as I

175

have. Your purity is unsullied.' Mr Reza had left his wife behind in Iran years before and considered himself free in amative respects. 'There is nothing to be done. We cut our losses.'

'I haven't exactly got any losses,' Kayleigh said as they went down again. 'Unless you count losing a friend.'

'Of course. Naturally, I count.' Mr Reza was thinking that he could sell Danila's clothes, though they wouldn't be worth much. But while in the room he had spotted a watch that looked like gold and a new CD player. 'Come, I make you a cup of coffee.'

'Oh, thanks. I will.'

An hour had passed before Kayleigh emerged once more into Oxford Gardens, quite high on the strongest and thickest coffee she had ever tasted and a date for the following evening with the man she was already calling Abbas. Danila had gone out of her head but she came back into it now and she found she couldn't altogether agree with her new friend that his tenant had done a moonlight flit and simply vanished. She's a missing person, Kayleigh said to herself. The words sounded very serious to her. She's a missing person, she said again, and the police ought to know.

It was a cooler and duller morning than of late and Mix was once more sitting in his car at the top of Campden Hill Square. He should have been at Mrs Plymdale's. She had called him on his mobile to tell him, but very nicely, that the new belt he had fixed to her treadmill had come off the previous evening. Would he come and put things to rights as soon as possible? Mix had said he'd be with her by eleven in the morning but instead he was out-side Nerissa's house, desperate for a sight of her. It was as if she were his fix. He had made a call in Chelsea and another in West Kensington but a fur-ther shot of the drug was essential before he did any more work. Seeing her the week before, speaking to her and she speaking to him, hadn't improved things. It had made them worse. Before, he had wanted to get to know her for the fame being with her could confer on him. Now he was in love.

He waited and waited, reading the last chapter of *Christie's Victims*, but looking up every few sec-onds in case she appeared. It was half-past midday before she did, dressed in a white skirt suit, chic and very short, and incongruous white trainers. She was carrying a pair of white sandals with four-inch heels. Those shoes were for putting on, he supposed, when she got to wherever she was going and the trainers were for driving. He'd follow her. Having seen her, he couldn't bear her to be out of his sight.

She passed him but he wasn't sure if she saw him or not. He followed her car along Notting Hill Gate and down Kensington Church Street. For once, there wasn't much traffic and he kept behind her. From Kensington High Street she went east-wards and he did too. At a red light she turned round and he knew she had spotted him. He waved and she gave a small half-smile before driving on.

Before she went to the police, Kayleigh called Directory Enquiries and asked them for the number of a Mrs Kovic living somewhere in Grimsby. They found just one woman of that name. The first one Kayleigh phoned was English, a Yorkshirewoman who had married and divorced a man from Serbia. Danila's mother had been her sister-in-law. She gave her a phone number and Kayleigh spoke to Danila's stepfather, who seemed scared of being involved.

'If anything's happened to her,' he said, 'I don't want to know. We didn't get on. It's nothing to do with me.'

'She'd no one else,' Kayleigh said. 'I've been very worried.'

'Yes? I don't know what you think I can do. You want to look at it from my point of view. I've lost my wife, I've got two young boys to bring up. Me and Danny didn't never have a good relationship and when I saw her at the funeral I said I'd go my way and she'd go hers – right?'

It had begun to seem to Kayleigh that no one had cared very much about Danila. Madam Shoshana had quickly forgotten her existence. This indifference frightened her. It was very unlike the feelings in her own family where her parents took a keen interest in everything their three children did and worried themselves into small frenzies if one of them wasn't immediately available on the phone. Kayleigh went to the police in Ladbroke Grove and filled in a missing person form, saying nothing about the conversation she had had with Danila's stepfather.

Lunch with her agent was Nerissa's reason for going to the restaurant in St James's, and the request from a glossy magazine of international prestige to feature her on their front cover and run a four-page article about her, the reason for the lunch. She parked the Jaguar on a meter in St

James's Square and changed her trainers for the stilt-heeled white sandals. The lunch would have to be a short one or she'd get clamped. As she locked the car that man arrived, the one who had spoken to her on Thursday outside the old lady's house. This was the third time she had encountered him and she knew with a slightly sick feeling that he was following her.

He wasn't the first stalker in her life. There had been several, notably one who persistently called at her parents' house when she was very young and still lived at home, but her father, who was very large and very black, a formidable threat in the caller's eyes, had finally intimidated him. Darling Dad made a wonderful bodyguard. The other stalker had been rather like the present one, waiting outside her house and following her. It had been the police who had warned him off. The funny thing was, Nerissa thought, as she walked through into St James's Street, that they all looked very much alike. All were of middle height, in their early thirties, fair-haired with characterless faces and staring eyes. This one was following her along King Street now, probably fifty yards behind. She was a little early for her lunch and she wondered if she could make some move to shake him off.

The shops in St James's Street are not the sort a woman can go into and browse about, if necessary concealing herself behind racks of clothes or disappearing into the ladies' powder room. There was nowhere to hide. If she stopped to look into the hat shop window or crossed the street to linger outside the rather grand wine merchant's, would he take this as a reason to speak to her? The thing she mustn't do was look back. The strap above the high heel of her sandal had slipped down and the shoe flapped. She bent down to adjust it, felt the presence of someone standing close by her, unwillingly looked up – and into the face of Darel Jones.

She couldn't have been more delighted if it had been her father and said, almost involuntarily, 'Oh, I'm so pleased to see you!'

He seemed surprised. 'Are you?'

'There's a man stalking me. Look. No, he's gone. That's your doing, I'm sure. He saw you, thought you were a friend of mine and – and disappeared. How marvellous.'

If he minded being taken for a friend of hers he didn't show it. 'This stalker – that's very serious. You'll have to tell the police.'

'I can't keep telling them. He's not the first one, you see. Perhaps he'll give up now. I always hope they will. But what are you doing here?'

'I might say the same for you. I'm a banker.' He pointed to a Georgian edifice with a brass plate which said Laski Brothers, International Bankers since 1782. 'I work there.'

'Do you?' Nerissa had a very narrow idea of what a banker did. 'D'you mean that if I went in there and asked them to cash a cheque you'd be behind a glass thing and you'd give me a bunch of notes?'

He laughed. 'It's not quite like that. I've come out for my lunch. I don't suppose you – ?'

'I'm lunching with my agent,' she said. 'I've absolutely *got* to.' She looked at him with yearning love, thinking of Madam Shoshana's prediction. 'I wish I didn't but I *must*.'

'I'll say goodbye then.' Perhaps it was her imagination but she had never seen him look quite like

180

that before, *interested* in her, curious about her. 'You know,' he said, 'you're quite different from the – the – er, misconception I had of you,' and he was gone.

She went into the restaurant where she could already see her agent waiting at a table. What did he mean by 'misconception'? That he'd thought she was awful and had found out she wasn't? Or, more likely, in spite of that look which might have been mere sympathy, that he'd thought she was nice but now he knew she was horrid? Still, he'd been on the point of asking her out to lunch . . .

The urgent message summoned Mix to head office. His departmental manager, Mr Fleisch, had a few things to say to him. A call had come from Mrs Plymdale, no longer soft and easygoing, to complain that the new belt he had installed on her treadmill had come adrift and though he had promised to repair it at eleven, he hadn't turned up. She had to use her treadmill every day or she would get out of the rhythm. She really needed to exercise. Both her parents had died of heart disease and she was frantic with worry. Not only that but Mr Fleisch had heard from Ed West that Mix had failed to make two essential calls on his behalf that Ed was prevented from making by illness.

'I've been going through a bad patch,' Mix said without further explanation.

'What kind of a bad patch?'

'I've not been well. I've been depressed.'

'I see. I'll make a booking for you with the company's doctor.'

Mix would have liked to refuse this offer but he didn't know how. Matters would only be made worse by his failure to see the doctor, a dour elderly man, unpopular with the staff. Mix went home. It had been a bad day. All the time he was following Nerissa he had been planning what he would say to her when, having gained on her according to plan, she turned round and saw him. Remind her of last Thursday would be the first thing, then maybe put in a word about how sorry he was if he'd offended her mother. Would she show him there were no hard feelings by coming and having a coffee with him? She had been so sweet and gracious that previous time that he thought she would, she couldn't really refuse in the circumstances. And then that man had appeared, a young good-looking man who appeared to be a friend of hers. Just his luck. But he wouldn't let it put him off.

A message on his mobile summoned him to call on Colette Gilbert-Bamber the minute he finished work. It wouldn't be for something wrong with the equipment but what Mix called 'a bit of the other'. He'd still get forty pounds for the call-out . . . If he was so attractive to Colette, surely he should be to Nerissa? But he wouldn't go. It had been a bad day and he didn't fancy it.

It was oppressively hot again and the house would be hot and stuffy. How it could be so dark when the sun was shining brilliantly he didn't really know. Didn't she ever draw the curtains back? Did she never open a window? He stood for a moment where Nerissa had stood last week and spoken to him so sweetly – and her mother so nastily. But he wouldn't think of that. And he wouldn't hold his arms folded like that across his body so that he could feel the roll of flesh round his waist that sagged over the belt of his trousers. Walk, he said to himself, get into a walking routine tomorrow and do it every day.

The place might have been uninhabited for years, he thought, as he started up the stairs. Would it do any good if he complained to old Chawcer about the lighting system, the way the low wattage lamps went out before he reached the next switch? Probably not. People like her thrived on darkness. It was ridiculous, anyway, having to put lights on in summer in the afternoon.

No cat's eyes glowed from the tiled staircase and, thank God, there was no sign of Reggie. It was all in my mind, he thought, I was right about going through a bad patch, I must have begun to see things that weren't there. Whatever Shoshana said, ghosts were always hallucinations, the result of stress or pressure. The Isabella lights, dull red and green and purple, lay as still as if they were painted on the floor but bright golden sunshine streamed out of his hallway when he opened the door to his flat.

Perhaps, before he went in, he ought to go next door to the room where Danila was. He really ought to check on her every day until – well, until what? He got used to her being there? He'd moved her out and on to somewhere else? Leaving his own door wide open for the sake of the cheerful glow of light, he opened the bedroom door next to it.

The same sunshine was in here, or would have been if the window was ever cleaned. But he didn't think about that once he had smelt the smell. It forced him to take a step backwards. And now he knew what it was. For weeks the weather had been almost unnaturally hot, the temperature right up in the high twenties and low thirties until yesterday

183

had been almost unbelievably warm, and this smell was the result. He couldn't understand it; the body was wrapped and nailed down under floorboards. He braced himself to go in, closed the door behind him, no longer thinking of ghosts. This was real: that had been all in his mind. He had never smelt anything like it and, standing there, taking in a long inhalation, he shuddered. Why had he come in here this afternoon when he already felt so bad?

Would it go away? Eventually, perhaps. He found he had no idea whether decay continued for weeks, months, even years, or if it faded at last. Old Chawcer might come in here at any time. He couldn't risk it. He'd have to go to work and while he was out of the house he'd never have a quiet moment.

At present there was no point in staying here. After smelling that smell he felt he would never eat again. Those bodies in Reggie's house, especially the two he put in the recess in the kitchen wall, they must have smelt. Perhaps not, for it was December and cold and Reggie had been caught and arrested soon after he put them there. Mix stood at the top of the stairs and listened. Utter silence. He peered down the stairwell and began to move down. He was on the bottom step of the tiled flight when her bedroom door opened and she came out in a red silk dressing-gown and feathered mules. He was about to retreat but she spotted him.

'Is anything the matter, Mr Cellini?'

'Everything's fine,' he said.

She sniffed. 'I wish I could say the same. I believe I have the influenza.'

Mix had once before in his whole life heard flu

called that. His grandma had had a joke about it: 'I opened the window and in flew Enza.'

'Hard luck.' If she was ill she wouldn't be able to go into that room. If only she could be very ill and for a long time! 'You ought to be in bed,' he said.

'I need the bathroom. May I trouble you to do me a great favour and telephone my friend Mrs Fordyce – you met her outside my house last Thursday – and tell her of my – my plight? The number is in the directory by the phone. Fordyce. Can you remember that?'

'I'll try,' said Mix, putting a wealth of sarcasm into his tone. It passed unnoticed. He went downstairs, thinking it was typical of her to get flu on what was probably the hottest day of the year. He could barely see to find the Fordyce woman's number. Suppose she recognised his voice from Thursday? He put on an upper-class intonation. 'Miss Chawcer has a virus. She's very unwell. It would be an enormous help if you'd come to see her tomorrow and maybe her doctor would call, if you know who that is.'

'That's Mr Cellini, isn't it? Of course I'll come. First thing in the morning.'

In which case, he'd better be out of there before she appeared, but without him she wouldn't be able to get in. Well, old Chawcer would just have to get up and answer the door. He wandered about and saw she'd left the back door unlocked. He locked and bolted it. That would be a fine carry-on, in a rough area like this, any amount of lowlife coming in and helping themselves to whatever they fancied. He was in enough trouble without that.

He had never been in this huge living room before. Drawing room, she called it. He couldn't understand why unless it was because people used to draw pictures in it before the days of television and radio. The dust and the musty smell made him wrinkle his nose, but as smells went, compared to the stench upstairs it was nothing, nothing. Light shouldn't have been needed at this hour but it was always dusk in this house. The main light switch didn't work. He went about turning on table lamps, the last one on the desk beside several half-finished letters.

Who the hell was she writing to in this crazy way? One started, 'Dear Dr Reeves', another, 'My dear Doctor,' a third, 'Dear Stephen' and the last, 'My dear Stephen.' A lot of muddled stuff followed, all hard to read in her looped spidery hand, but the finest copperplate would be difficult in this twilight. Then a name caught his eye: Rillington Place. 'I know you saw me in Rillington Place one day in the summer a very long time ago. You were driving past, on your way to a call, I expect. On the following day I came to your surgery for the first time. As I am sure you recall, I and my parents had been patients of Dr Odess. I found out, when the trial of Christie took place, that he had been that dreadful man's medical attendant. Not that this, of course, had anything to do with our leaving him to come to . . .'

A few more words were heavily scored through. She had written no more. This proved she had been to Reggie for an abortion, Mix thought. Maybe she was writing to this doctor about it because he was going to do the job but Reggie would be cheaper. Reggie frightened her, so she found someone else to do the termination and this doctor was offended because he didn't get the money he'd expected.

That must be it. He'd taken Chawcer off his list as a result and refused to treat her any more. Now, after all these years, she was writing to explain.

The room wasn't simply dark as a place is before the lights go on. The lights were on, table lamps with cracked parchment or pleated silk shades, much frayed, but the effect of them was less to illuminate than to make shadows. Not one was in an alcove or beside a wall, so that the corners were in deep darkness. And it was so hot that the sweat began to stream from his face and trickle down his back. Mix thought it the most dreadful room he had ever been in. With that carved dragon snaking across the top of the vast sofa and that blotchy mirror in a black and gilt frame, it could be the setting for a horror film. She could make a bit of money like that, tell movie people about it and get a fat fee. They wouldn't have to change a thing.

Switching off the lamps was a creepy task. Darkness yawned behind him and after the last one was off he went to the french window and pulled back the long brown velvet curtains with violent jerks. Dust was shed in great clouds, making him cough. But light came in, plenty of light to dispel the worst of the horror. If downstairs had been nasty, holding God knew what secret things and hidden threats, upstairs loomed forbiddingly, with Reggie perhaps waiting for him and the body invisibly but surely decaying. It was almost as though it had a new life of its own, almost as if it were moving as it changed. Don't think of that, he muttered to himself. Forget what Shoshana said, it was all in your head.

He passed Chawcer's door. There was no sign of the cat and, of course, none of Reggie. As he'd used to do but hadn't done for a week now, he closed his eyes when halfway up the tiled flight, opening them at the top and looking down one passage after another cautiously and fearfully. Nothing there, not even Otto. Inside his own living room, sitting in a comfortable chair, a large gin and tonic at his elbow, he told himself all was well, he was lucky, he'd been reprieved for a while. She'd be too ill to go up there again and he must use that time, perhaps a week, somehow to remove the body from that room.

Was there a way of getting it into the garden? Not if that Fordyce woman was in and out. She might not suspect the truth, she certainly wouldn't, but she'd tell Chawcer she'd seen him out there, digging. And Chawcer herself might see him from her window. That bedroom of hers must occupy the same area as the living room, which meant it had windows facing both back and front. He dared not take the risk.

You'd better eat something, he told himself, but the thought of food made his throat close and rise. He was desperately tired. Once he'd had another gin or a Boot Camp maybe he'd go to bed, even though it was only six, go to bed and try to sleep. Two messages were on his mobile but he wouldn't bother with them now, he'd do that in the morning. In front of Nerissa's picture he paused and made his obeisances, saying, 'I love you. I adore you.'

How she'd smile when they were lovers and she saw her photo there and he told her how he'd worshipped it. Comforted, he wandered into the bedroom and at the window looked down into the garden, considering where it would be best to bury Danila's body. If he could get there, if he could get her downstairs and outside. Reggie had done it, and several times, though there was an old man living in the house on the middle floor and the Evanses at the top. The neighbours had seen him digging but thought nothing of it, exchanging with him the wartime catch-phrase about Digging for Victory.

There on the left, perhaps where the thick brambles could be held back and spread across the dug earth to conceal what he'd done. Or near the end by the wall, on the far side of which the guinea fowl man lived. But would he get the chance?

On the wall, stretched out to his formidable length, Otto lay luxuriating in the evening sun, his eyes closed but the tip of his tail giving an occasional flick.

# Chapter 15

Having been in the kitchen, put a blackened kettle on the gas and cast her eye round the drawing room, Olive was toiling upstairs with tea on a tray towards Gwendolen's bedroom. When she had arrived she had rung the bell and that man Cellini had come down, though with an ill grace, and been quite surly with her on the doorstep. Speaking to him on the phone, she had no idea this was the same man who had accosted darling Nerissa out on the pavement. It was quite a shock when he opened the door. Naturally, she wasn't very forthcoming either.

The heat in here was punishing. Like being in India at midsummer, stuck in some backstreet ghetto, dusty and smelling nasty. Somehow she must manage to get windows open. This one, here in the kitchen, refused to budge. When she'd seen to Gwen she must attempt those in the drawing room.

Gwen's door was ajar. Olive was concerned at her appearance, the wasted white face, the weak hands lying limp on the coverlet. When Gwen spoke in a cracked voice, she had to break off and cough breathily.

'You'll have to see the doctor, dear. No doubt about it.'

'Yes, I will. I must.' More coughing. 'Dr Reeves.

Dr Reeves will come if I send for him, he always does.'

'I don't know any Dr Reeves round here, Gwen. Is he new?'

'Papa said to leave Dr Odess and try the young doctor and we have.'

Olive thought it best to ask no more questions. Answering made poor Gwen cough so distressingly. 'You drink your tea, dear, and I'll find your doctor and phone the practice. I expect the number is in your phone directory, isn't it?'

She dragged the carpet sweeper downstairs with her. It had been in front of the fireplace so long that dust had settled thickly on its surfaces. A hunt for the telephone directory finally resulted in her finding it on top of an ancient copper in the washhouse. No Reeves in the directory but a Dr Margaret Smithers. Olive would never have expected Gwen to have a lady doctor but very likely, all the lists being over-full, she hadn't a choice. It was a scandal, and worse, Olive thought, when Dr Smithers's receptionist said she couldn't come today but would tomorrow when she was making her afternoon calls.

'Make sure she does,' said Olive sharply.

Gwendolen's coughing sounded all the way downstairs. Olive went up again, hanging on to the banister. How much more sensible it would be, at Gwen's age, to live in a flat. 'The doctor's coming tomorrow.'

'I'll wear my new blue dress.'

'No, you won't, Gwen. You'll stay in bed. I'm going to bring you a jug of water and a glass. You must drink plenty. It's better if you don't eat. I told Queenie you were ill and she'll be in at midday.

Where's your door key?' Gwendolen didn't answer. She was coughing too much. 'Never mind. I'll find it.' She did, after a ten-minute hunt.

One of the messages on Mix's mobile was from the departmental manager to tell him a doctor's appointment had been made for him for Wednesday, at 2 p.m. The other, from someone called Kayleigh Rivers, reminded him that he had a contract with the spa and would he come as soon as possible as a stationary bicycle and a cross-trainer had both ceased to function.

The spa was the last place he wanted to go near. One of the clients might remember seeing him chatting up Danila. Besides, he had a kind of general undefined aversion to the place. He knew he'd feel bad once he set foot inside. He'd let it go for now and then he'd try to terminate that stupid contract. The doctor he'd have to go to. He was bound to say there was something wrong with him, doctors always did, and this would be to his advantage, a ready-made excuse for forgetting calls and neglecting jobs. It wasn't that he wanted to skive off work permanently, it was just that at present he wasn't up to it, what with the body and the smell and women coming and going in the house at all hours – and Nerissa.

He was down the hill from her house now and had been since nine. It was therapy for the way he was feeling. At eleven, when she still hadn't emerged, he gave up for the day, drove himself to Pembridge Road and in the secondhand bookshop there, found a new book called *Crimes of the Forties* he'd never heard of before. He bought it because it had a chapter on Reggie.

Back once more in Campden Hill Square, he opened the book to find there was even less about the Rillington Place murders than he had thought at first. A bit of a waste of money. Still, the photographs were the best he had yet seen. The frontispiece, a large picture of Reggie driven to court, was particularly good. Mix gazed at the rather well sculpted face, the narrow mouth and large nose, the horn-rimmed glasses. What would you do in my position? he asked it. What would you do?

Nerissa saw him from an upstairs window and thought of some action she might take. Phoning the police, for instance. But he wasn't doing any harm. He would get tired of waiting, he must surely have work to do, and she wasn't going out till midday. She would like to have gone for a run first but that was impossible with him there.

Last evening she'd been sure Darel Jones would call her. He could easily get her phone number from his mother, who would get it from Nerissa's mother. She had stayed in all evening, waiting for him to phone. Actually sat by the phone in case it rang and she couldn't get to it in time. Like a teenager. Like she was aged fifteen, with her first boyfriend. When it had gone ten she knew it wasn't going to happen. Plenty of men would phone after ten, after eleven come to that, but not Darel. Somehow she knew that. Disappointed, she had gone to bed early.

Some women wouldn't wait, they'd phone a man themselves. Why couldn't she? She didn't know, something to do with the way Mum had brought her up, no doubt. Tomorrow they were going to start on the shots for that magazine cover and feature and soon after that the London Fashion Fair began. She and Naomi and Christy would be on the catwalk for that. These were her last days of freedom but instead of enjoying herself she was standing here at the window, watching a man watching her. The price of fame, her agent had told her, and then told her to tell the police. She flinched from doing that. Maybe she'd pluck up her nerve and get into the car, not looking in his direction, go over to her sister-in-law's, see the baby. Or perhaps she'd wait a while, give him half an hour. Madam Shoshana first, the stones or the cards and the latest instalment of her future foretold. If only that guy would give up and go.

She had a shower, sprayed herself with Jo Malone's Gardenia and accidentally dropping the cap of the bottle on the floor, put on combat trousers and a canary yellow sweatshirt. A difficult shade, her mother said, while acknowledging that, with her colouring, she could wear it. Letting fall the tracksuit she'd been wearing, leaving behind her a trail of tissues, cotton wool and orange sticks, she took another look out of her bedroom window. He was still there. If only this house had another way out, an escape route into a back lane as some Notting Hill houses had. She should have thought of that before she bought it.

If she didn't hurry she'd be late for her appointment. She went downstairs, deciding to risk it, run the gauntlet, whatever that meant, but when she took a final look he was gone. An overwhelming sense of relief flooded her. Perhaps he wouldn't come back, perhaps he'd had enough.

All the way to Shoshana's she half expected his car to appear suddenly from a side turning – blue,

a small Honda, index number starting LCO something – but he must have gone. Presumably he did
work somewhere. She was ten minutes late, thanks
to him. Mounting the stairs, she suddenly remembered once coming down them and meeting a
young girl coming up, a dark, sharp-featured girl
who reminded her of pictures she had seen of
women in that war in Bosnia. Funny I should think
of her, she thought. Shoshana had told her (when
she asked) that the girl worked at the spa and her
name was – was it Danielle?

The room was dark and incense-smelling as ever
but today Shoshana was in black silk with moons
and ringed planets embroidered on the bodice. A
veil covered her hair, secured in place by a kind of
tiara.

'I'll have the cards, not the stones,' Nerissa said
firmly.

Shoshana disliked being instructed but she liked
the money and Nerissa was a good client. 'Very
well.' Underlying her words was the implication:
on your own head be it. 'Take a card.'

The first one Nerissa took was the Queen of
Hearts, and the second and the third. 'You are
promised great good luck in love,' Shoshana said,
wondering how she had managed to allow three
queens to appear in sequence. The next one had
better be the Ace of Spades. But it wasn't. Nerissa
smiled happily.

'I have never seen such astonishing good fortune,' Shoshana said, hissing and cursing inwardly.
She much preferred doom-laden forecasts but she
could hardly invent a negative future when Nerissa
so obviously knew what the Queen of Hearts sig-
nified. 'Take a last card.'

It was bound to be the Ace this time and it was. Shoshana concealed her pleasure. 'A death, of course.' She put her hands into the bag of stones, took out the lapis and the rose quartz and rolled them between her palms. 'It's not you or anyone close to you. It's happened already.'

'Maybe it's my Great-aunt Laetitia. She died last week.'

Shoshana disliked clients coming up with their own interpretations. 'No. I think not. A young person, this is. A girl. I can see no more. The words were written but clouds have obscured them. That is all.'

The cards were put away, the stones replaced in their bag. Nerissa hated the way the wizard seemed to move when the candles flickered. The white owl had its amber eyes fixed on her. 'Forty-five pounds, please,' said Shoshana.

'That girl I met on the stairs once, she looked nice. Danielle, is she called?'

'What about her?'

'I don't know. I just thought of her.'

'She's left,' Shoshana said, opening the door to speed Nerissa on her way.

Two policemen called on Mr Reza and then at Shoshana's Spa. When they had been told at both places that Danila Kovic had left her work and her rented room without notice, without a word to employer or landlord, they began to take things seriously. Their press release was too late for the *Evening Standard* but in time for the BBC Early Evening News and the next day's papers, where it nearly, but not quite, took precedence over the 'hottest day since records began' story.

Nerissa heard it while baby-sitting for her brother but, in the absence of a photograph failed to identify her as the girl she'd seen on the stairs. Mix also saw the news. He thought he'd been quite worried enough but now he understood he had been living in a fool's paradise, continuing to believe that Danila's disappearance would never be noticed. He had had another bad day, beginning with his failure to see Nerissa, then a terrible row with Colette Gilbert-Bamber who threatened to report his lapses to the firm if there was ever another. Leaving her house without any lunch or even a glass of wine, he had had to go straight to the doctor.

Ever since he had known the appointment was to be made he had taken it for granted he was perfectly well, a young, fit healthy man. The doctor disagreed. He insisted on taking a blood sample to be checked for cholesterol. That was on account of Mix's blood pressure which ought to have been something like 130 over 40 and instead was an alarming 170 over 60.

'Smoke, do you?'

'No, I don't,' said Mix virtuously.

'Drink?'

'Not much. Maybe four or five units a week.'

That would have been little more than a single bottle of wine. The doctor looked at him suspiciously. Exercise, a fat-free diet, tablets were prescribed and no salt.

'Come back and see me in two weeks' time – you don't want to be a diabetic by the time you're forty, do you?'

Blood pressure could be raised by anxiety, Mix had read somewhere. Well, he'd had plenty of anxiety recently. The doctor's admonitions had brought on a headache and a queasy feeling. He'd call head office, tell them he wasn't well and go home. Maybe he'd got old Chawcer's flu. The sun was dazzlingly bright today, for once lighting up this gloomy house, showing up the dust that lay everywhere and the cobwebs dangling from defunct hanging lamps and begrimed mouldings on the ceilings. Someone had opened the downstairs windows and all the curtains were drawn back. He opened a door he had never touched before and found himself looking into a vast room with a dining table down the middle, twelve chairs arranged around it and oil paintings on the walls of dead deer and rabbits, ugly old women in crinolines and cows in fields.

On the first landing he met a woman he hadn't seen before and he immediately thought, she must be the one Reggie hadn't managed to destroy, old Chawcer's daughter. But she was too old for that and she introduced herself as Queenie Winthrop, smiling and for some reason fluttering her eyelashes.

'Poor darling Gwendolen is very poorly indeed, Mr Cellini. She has a temperature of over a hundred degrees. And that doctor won't come until tomorrow afternoon. I call it a disgrace.'

Mix, who had grown up measuring in Celsius, thought she had made a mistake. What could you expect at her age? 'Shame,' he said.

'A shame is just what it is. These doctors should be ashamed. Now, if you can just make her a cup of tea in the morning, I or Mrs Fordyce will be in by eight-thirty. We have a key.'

'Me?' said Mix feebly.

'That's right. If you'll be so kind. I don't know who will let that wretched doctor in but one of us will manage it somehow.'

'Well, I can't,' said Mix, escaping upstairs, and for once forgetting to look out for Reggie.

He sniffed. It seemed to him that he could smell it out here. That might be in his head too. How did you know which things were real and which your imagination? Still, he wouldn't go in there this evening. He'd think, make a plan. It was just after eight when Ed phoned. Mix wished he hadn't answered it because Ed would only start again on how he'd let him down. But instead he was asking for bygones to be bygones. He shouldn't have blown his top like that. His excuse was that he wasn't really over his flu and still feeling under the weather.

'There's a lot of it about,' Mix said, thinking of old Chawcer.

'Yeah, and it's not only that. Me and Steph are having problems getting a mortgage.'

He went on and on about this flat they were hoping to buy, calculating their joint incomes, Steph's chances of promotion and what would happen if she fell pregnant.

'You'll have to see she doesn't.' Mix had always found it difficult, practically impossible, to apologise. Admitting he was wrong seemed to him the ultimate humiliation. He couldn't say he was sorry but he had to say something. 'Feel like going for a drink?' he hazarded. 'Maybe tonight?'

'Yeah, well, I can't tonight. Sun in Splendour at eight tomorrow? And a word to the wise, Mix, eh? They're getting very hot under the collar about you at head office. I just thought I'd give you a hint.'

Mix nearly forgot about old Chawcer's tea in the morning. He hardly ever drank the stuff himself but he kept a packet of teabags next to the coffee jar and when he saw it he remembered. He'd have to take the sugar down too in case she took it.

She didn't. That was the first thing she said to him after he knocked and went in. 'You need not have brought that, Mr Cellini. I don't take sugar.' Nothing about how kind of him. No 'Good morning.' Her voice was weak and she kept coughing. As she struggled to sit up he could see great wet patches on her nightdress where she had sweated.'What day is it?'

Impatiently, he told her.

'Then it must be tomorrow the woodworm people will be here. They're coming to see about the woodworm in the room next to your flat. I can't remember what their name is but it doesn't matter.' Coughing shook her. 'Oh, dear, I can hardly speak. One of my friends will let them in. I expect they'll take up the floorboards, find out what that ghastly smell is . . .'

Old clothes lay all over the bedroom. Surely she could have cleared up the ashes in the fireplace. She hadn't always been ill. The air felt unbreathable and enormously, palpably, hot. Flies were everywhere, swarming in the dusty shaft of sunlight.

'Shall I open a window?'

She wasn't too ill to round on him. 'Please don't unless you want me to freeze to death. Just leave it.' Cough, cough, cough . . .

# Chapter 16

Nerissa recognised the girl from the photograph in the paper, Kayleigh cried when she saw it and Abbas Reza tried to comfort her by saying Danila would surely turn up safe and sound. Shoshana never read newspapers. The barmaid in the Kensington Park Hotel might have recognised her as Mix's companion but she didn't see the photograph. She had gone to Spain to work in a seafront bar on the Costa Blanca. Mix had no need to see it. It was enough for him to know that photograph or another would be there. The newspaper had got it from one of Danila's brothers who handed it over while his stepfather was out.

Mix sat downstairs in the drawing room, studying the Yellow Pages, though he should have been at work an hour before. There were so many messages on his mobile that he had erased the lot without looking at them. Ideally, he should phone all these woodworm specialists and check which one of them was coming, but there were dozens, if not hundreds. He'd made a tentative attempt at two of them and had had to hold on so long, pressing this key and that, listening to piped music, that he gave up. The only thing to do was take a day off, stay here and let the man in himself. Or, rather, not let him in, tell him his services weren't needed. If the Fordyce woman or the other one insisted on staying, they might have a tussle on the doorstep. He must somehow stop that happening.

He'd have to call head office and tell them he was ill. The doctor would come some time in the afternoon, the woodworm man at any time. This evening he was supposed to be going for a drink with Ed. Suppose he hadn't agreed to take old Chawcer her tea, he wouldn't have found out about the woodworm man – the outcome didn't bear thinking of. It drove him back into the room where Danila lay under the floorboards. The smell in this extreme heat was worse, awful, like things rotting in the back of a fridge someone had turned off. He felt like breaking a window to let some of it out but he thought of the noise it would make and the fuss it would cause.

As soon as possible he must move the body. Once the woodworm man had been got rid of, the doctor and those women had gone, he would move it and drag it down all fifty-two of those stairs. For the present, he couldn't stay in his own flat, it was too high up, too remote. He had to be sure he'd hear the doorbell when people came, preferably be stationed where he could see them coming. Halfway down the tiled flight he heard a key turn in the front door lock. Old Ma Fordyce or Ma Winthrop. It was Fordyce, the one with the long red fingernails. He heard her slowly stumping up the stairs below him and they met outside old Chawcer's bedroom door.

'Good morning. How are you today?'

'Fine,' Mix lied.

'Did you feed the cat?'

'Me?'

'Yes, you,' said Olive Fordyce. 'I don't see anyone else around, do you? Please give the poor thing some food at once.' She went into old Chawcer's bedroom.

Talking to me as if I was her servant, thought Mix. Why shouldn't she feed the bloody cat? He was rather afraid of Otto who gave him almost human stares of loathing but he went into the kitchen and looked about him for cans of catfood. His mother had been as messy as Chawcer, the reason he was such a fastidious housekeeper himself, so he had a good idea where to look. A tin decorated with a picture of a cat washing its paws came to light in the back of a cupboard full of sprouting potatoes and onions growing green shoots. He put half into a saucer and left it on the floor beside a large plastic bag stuffed full of mouldy loaf ends and bread rolls.

It didn't really matter when the doctor came or if he came at all, except that while he was there Chawcer wouldn't be able to get out of bed and wander about. The important caller was the woodworm man. Mix pushed a chair covered in fraying brown corduroy up close to the front window where he could sit and keep an eye on the street. He had left his mobile upstairs. Never mind, he could use her phone if he needed it. There Olive Fordyce found him half an hour later.

'I don't think Gwen's any better. That cough sounds like pleurisy. Imagine it, in this heat. What are you doing here?'

Mix made no reply. 'What's the name of the firm she's got coming to see to the woodworm?'

'Are you asking me? How should I know? Ask her.'

'She's forgotten.'

Olive sat down. For a ministering angel with stairs to climb, she was wearing highly unsuitable shoes, red, pointed and with two-inch heels. Even without looking she could feel her ankles swelling. 'She wanted me to go up into that room and see what I thought. She says there's a funny smell.'

If he hadn't been sitting down, Mix thought he would have fallen. His head swam. He managed to say, 'The woodworm people will see to that.'

'Well, I must say I don't really want to go up there now. My poor feet feel bad enough as it is, it's always the same in hot weather. Gwen really ought to have a stairlift.'

There was no answer to be made to this. She got up, having difficulty in balancing. 'You'll be here to let the doctor in, won't you?'

Mix wanted to shout something rude at her but he remembered that, improbable as it was, this woman must be Nerissa's great-aunt. 'I suppose so,' he said.

With scorn, he watched her totter down the street. If these old women knew what they looked like! It sounded as if neither she nor the other one would be back today, and that was to his advantage. He'd be in control of the house, who came and went. The woodworm man wouldn't force his way in, the doctor wouldn't want to go upstairs and find out where the smell was coming from. Hold on to that, he told himself, hold on to that. It's only a matter of waiting.

The call came for Nerissa as she was waiting for the taxi to arrive and take her to a shoot at the Dorchester. She had almost given up hope of hearing from him. If a man you've met (or re-met) doesn't phone you within forty-eight hours the chances are he won't phone at all. But the invitation he was extending to her was so unlike any she had ever previously received that she wondered for a moment if it was a joke.

'My parents and yours and your brother Andrew and his wife are coming to dinner on Saturday and I wondered if you'd like to join us.'

She couldn't ask him if he was serious. The temptation to say no was quite strong but warring with it was the lure of just seeing him, being with him, even if six others were there. She liked his parents and she and Andrew had always been close, he being three years the elder but still the nearest to her in age.

'Nerissa?' Darel said.

She spoke haltingly. 'Yes, thank you. I'd – I'd love to.'

He gave her the address, miles away in Docklands, somewhere near Old Crane Stairs. Wapping was the station on the East London Line.

'I expect I'll drive,' said Nerissa. 'Excuse me, I must go, my cab's come.'

What was the idea, she thought as she got into her taxi. Was he just very old-fashioned or was he afraid of being alone with her? He wasn't *gay*, was he? Her heart seemed to beat very slowly but loudly. No, he couldn't be. Sheila Jones had talked about some girlfriend he used to have. She considered. Perhaps he just wanted to test her, see if the way he'd used to think about her was right or if she really had turned out to be different, as he'd said.

\*

A client was with Shoshana, so Kayleigh talked to the police, though she had already told them all she knew. On that Friday Danila had worked at the spa as usual, Kayleigh herself had spoken to her on the phone at three-thirty, half an hour before she was due to take over from the Bosnian girl. She had seen her, exchanged a few words and Danila had gone off home to Oxford Gardens. Of the other tenants in the house, one, a man on the second floor, had seen her come in at four-thirty or thereabouts. He had been in the hallway, sorting out his letters from the rest of the post. Danila had said hi to him and gone off upstairs to her room on the first floor. Abbas Reza hadn't seen her, though he believed he had heard her leave the house at about seven-fifty that evening. If she had a boyfriend he knew nothing about it and nor did Kayleigh. No one had seen her since.

If she were dead, the police believed, her body would have been found by this time. They considered suggestions of a secret lover. But why should she keep a lover hidden? She had nothing to be ashamed of or even discreet about. The only clue, and that tenuous, was that the tenant on the second floor, a man of Chinese origin called Tony Li, had heard Danila and a man talking to each other outside her room one evening about three weeks before she disappeared. He hadn't seen the man, only heard his voice though not the words he spoke.

Waiting with nothing to do, no distractions, nothing to read or listen to or look at, is the slowest of all time-wasters. After two hours of it, Mix went upstairs and fetched *Crimes of the Forties*. Somehow he didn't want to read anything these days but books about Reggie, not magazines, not news-papers – definitely not newspapers. Coming back downstairs he heard old Chawcer coughing her lungs up. Otto was in the hallway, washing his face after eating the food Mix had put down. He behaved as if no one else was there or as if this human male was so insignificant as not to count and certainly not to be considered as interrupting his cleaning routine.

There seemed nothing new in the book, nothing he hadn't come across before. He knew all about Beresford Brown, an African Caribbean immigrant and new tenant of 10 Rillington Place, taking down a partition in the kitchen and finding two bodies pushed into an alcove. By then Reggie was far away, though not far enough to escape eventual arrest. All this was familiar stuff to Mix but he read this author's version with interest just the same, anxious for details of the process of decay in corpses. It had been December and cold. Fifty years ago, before this global warming, even March would have been freezing, and as for August . . . Just his luck that today it was hotter than Spain, according to the television, as hot as Dubai.

He had read about fifteen pages – there were only twenty-two on Reggie – when the phone rang. To answer it or not? Might as well. It would be something to do. A man's voice said, 'Is Miss Chawcer there, please?' He sounded quite elderly.

'She's not available now,' Mix said, and then quickly, 'You're not the woodworm people, are you?'

'I'm afraid not. My name is Stephen Reeves, Dr Reeves.'

This wasn't the doctor who was expected later

but the man old Chawcer had been writing all those letters to. Mix said, 'Oh, yes?'

'Would you give her a message? Would you say I'd like to drop in and see her when I'm next in London?'

He gave a phone number which Mix said he would write down but didn't. There was no paper or pen at hand. She probably knew the number anyway, she was bound to. 'I'll tell her,' he said.

Back to the book and the waiting. The illustrations horrified him but they drew his eyes as well. The bodies looked so squalid, like dirty bundles of rags instead of real dead people. Ethel Christie lay under the floorboards in front of the fireplace in the front room. Would Danila look like that when he lifted the boards? When *someone else* lifted them? Ghosts and those early fears seemed absurd, childish, now that he had real danger to worry about. The caption under another picture said Ruth Fuerst's leg bone had been driven into the ground to support a fence post. Reggie's callousness fascinated him. Not many people, surely, would have the willpower and the nerve to use a bit of a dead human being for such a purpose. He would think of that while he was disposing of Danila's body and it would bring him strength. He would think of Reggie's coolness and his nerve.

By now he was beginning to get hungry but he didn't fancy anything out of old Chawcer's kitchen. He ran up the stairs two at a time for the first one and a half flights. After that he was so breathless he had to rest, he had to sit down on one of the treads. Staggering up the rest, he went into his flat to hear his phone ringing and he stood still, wondering whether to answer it or not. The woodworm people wouldn't phone him and nor would the doctor. Might as well leave it. He made a couple of rough sandwiches by laying pre-sliced cheese between pieces of pre-sliced bread, found a packet of crisps and a muesli bar and went back down to his post at the window.

The two women arrived at the same time. Mix saw one of them step out of a car with a 'Doctor' label inside its windscreen and the other alight from a van with a woodgrain pattern all over, Woodrid printed in gold on its side. For some reason he knew plenty would call sexist, he hadn't expected either to be a woman. The doctor was the first to reach the doorstep, a few paces ahead of the van driver. She didn't bother much with Mix and spoke brusquely.

'Where is she?'

'In her bedroom,' he said with equal gruffness.

'And where might that be?'

'First floor. First door on the left.'

The doctor had gone past him and the wood-worm woman already had a foot over the threshold.

'We shan't need you after all,' Mix said.

'You what?' She was rather pretty, neatly dressed in a brown uniform with a W on the breast pocket.

'You're not needed. She's ill. Miss Chawcer, I mean. She's ill in bed. She can't talk to you.'

The woman stepped back outside but showed no inclination to go. 'I could still take a look. That's all I need to do for a start, take a look at the infestation.'

'There isn't an infestation,' Mix almost shouted. 'I told you, she doesn't want you. Not today. She's ill. Come back next week, if you want.'

She was saying she didn't want, not if she was going to be spoken to like that, when Mix shut the door in her face. After that he didn't look out of the window again until he heard the van start up, and when he did look out it was to see Ma Winthrop staggering up the path with carrier bags full of shopping.

She could let herself in, he wasn't going to. And if any of that stuff she was carrying was for old Chawcer's lunch, she could see to that too. How Queenie Winthrop guessed he was in the drawing room he didn't know, but she put her head round the door. She seemed unpleasantly surprised.

'What are you doing there?'

'Letting the doctor in.'

'Oh, yes, I saw her car. Isn't she a sweet woman?'

Mix didn't answer. It had suddenly come to him that he had forgotten to phone head office. 'I'm going up to my own place now,' he said. 'I fed the cat.'

Would she go into old Chawcer's bedroom while the doctor was there? Even if she did, even though the woodworm woman had come and gone, it was far too risky to attempt taking the body down all those flights of stairs. His only chance was in the night. He would have liked to get out into the garden and look round the place, find the best burial site, see if there was a shed or some sort of outbuilding in which to lay the body while he dug. Because of projecting roofs and bays, it was impossible to see more than the end of the garden from his flat.

Phone head office while they were all in that bedroom, get it over. Later on he could attempt going outside. The receptionist who answered didn't wait for him to say who he wanted to speak to.

'Jack wants to talk to you *now*.' Jack was Mr Fleisch, the departmental manager. 'He really wanted to talk to you like first thing this morning. I'll put him on.'

Mix scarcely had a chance to get a word in edge-ways. 'Are you ill? You must be seriously sick to miss four home visits, seven urgent phone calls and three text messages. Half west London is out gunning for you. Is it mental or physical? I'd say mental, wouldn't you? That's why sending you to the medic does fuck-all for you. You are up shit creek, my lad.'

'What can I say? Maybe it *is* mental. Maybe it's depression. I'll have to snap out of it, I know I will.'

'Too right. Spot on. Meantime, while you're doing your snapping-out, Mr Pearson wants to see you first thing tomorrow morning.'

'I'll be there,' said Mix.

'You'd better.'

Things must be serious if he was summoned to the Chief Executive's presence. A sacking matter, or at best a last chance matter. To hell with it, he couldn't worry about that now. If he got the body out from under the floor and out into the garden after dark, he would never manage to dig a deep grave and put her in it in a single night. Anyway, he'd be fit for nothing in the morning. He was once more in the room where she lay, nauseous from the strengthening stench but contemplating lifting the floorboard now, when he heard Queenie Winthrop's loud fluting voice yelling at him from the first floor.

'Mr Cellini, Mr Cellini, are you there? Can you hear me? Can you come down a minute?'

He'd have to or she'd come up. You could smell the smell at the top of the stairs now. 'OK, I'm coming.'

He shut the door and went down the tiled flight and the next one. Ma Winthrop looked flushed and excited. 'Gwendolen has pneumonia. I can't say I'm surprised. Dr Smithers is downstairs now, phoning for an ambulance to take her to hospital.'

Mix seemed to feel his heart leap in his chest. She was going away! He'd be alone in the house, maybe for a week. He had to ask.

'How long for?'

'Doctor doesn't know. A few days, certainly.' She addressed him as if he were fourteen years old. 'Now you'll be responsible for the place while she's away and we're relying on you. Don't disappoint us.'

# Chapter 17

Steph came too, of course. She always did. Those two were inseparable at the moment. That would last a couple of years, Mix thought, and after that, especially if there was a baby, Ed would start going out on his own again.

They were already in the Sun in Splendour when he arrived. He had come very close to forgetting their arrangement and it was a quarter to eight, while he was planning what to say and what excuses to make to Mr Pearson and Ed's name came into his calculations, that he remembered. If he failed to turn up Ed would definitely never speak to him again. Anyway, he wouldn't mind getting out, having some fresh air and talking to real people instead of those old women.

He ran down the stairs, feeling almost cheerful. The ambulance had taken her away at three-thirty and Queenie Winthrop had left with it. No need now to try going into the garden without being detected. No need to move the body yet. He'd lain down on the sofa with his feet up and read a Reggie book he'd had for a long time and read at least twice before, *Death in a Deckchair*, coming to the part that at present interested him most, how decay had proceeded in the bodies of those women, Ruth Fuerst, Muriel Eady, Hectorina

MacLennan, Kathleen Maloney, Rita Nelson and the murderer's own wife, Ethel.

It wasn't the best of the Reggie books he had read. The first prize had to go to *Killer Extraordinary* but he'd finish this one chapter. Funny, if anyone had told him six months before that he'd find a book, any book, more fascinating than TV or a game on line, he'd have laughed at them. He was still thinking about Reggie and the way he hid those bodies, only two of them buried in the ground, a couple of them partially burnt, when he walked into the pub.

Ed laughed when he saw him and said, 'Late as usual. Never mind, eh?'

Mix didn't much like that but he decided not to argue. Instead he admired Steph's engagement ring and asked when they were getting married.

'That's a long way off,' Ed said, fetching him a gin and tonic. 'Moved on to the hard stuff, I see.'

Mix thought this undeserving of a reply. He expected Ed to ask him to be his best man. Before their row he would have done; maybe he still would, if not tonight.

'You're up shit creek at head office,' said Ed. 'But I expect you know that by now.'

'You're the second person to say that to me today. I don't want to discuss it.'

'When Mr Pearson's the third person you'll have to.'

Steph giggled. But she wasn't an unkind girl and she changed the subject to weddings and houses and mortgages. They talked about that for a while and then she said what was very nearly the worst thing Mix wanted to hear.

'They've been looking for that missing girl in here.'

'What missing girl?' He had to pretend.

'Danila Kovic or however you pronounce it. Two policemen came in and talked to that guy Frank, the one who's the barman. I heard them say she'd applied for a job in here because what she was getting at some gym wasn't enough to live on.'

'She didn't get it,' said Ed. 'Didn't have the experience, Frank said after they'd gone. He knew all about it, he remembered her. Poor little kid, he called her, said she didn't look old enough to drink, let alone sell booze.'

'That wasn't much use to the police,' said Mix, rather relieved.

They were searching for her, but he already knew that. Thank God he'd never brought her in here. Talk about something else. 'When's the wedding to be?'

'You asked me that on the phone and you'll get the same answer. Not for a long time.'

'We want to get everything straight and everything paid for,' said Steph, 'before we actually get married. That gives the marriage a better chance, don't you think?'

Mix hadn't an opinion on this but he agreed and they talked about the new flat and the mortgage and building societies and interest rates until Ed suddenly said, 'Frank said he saw her again. Walking down Oxford Gardens with some guy.'

Mix spilt some of his drink. It made a small bubbly pool. He knew he should have said, 'Saw who?' but he didn't, he knew as soon as Ed spoke who 'her' was. In rather too loud a voice he said, 'Tell the police, did he?'

'He said he would. It had slipped his mind at the time he talked to them.'

This was the nearest they had got to finding a man in her life. Would this Frank be able to describe him? Would he recognise him?

'Is Frank on tonight?'

Mix fancied his voice hadn't been quite steady when he spoke and he thought Ed looked at him strangely. 'He'll be on later.'

Wait, don't say you're leaving now, they'll think it a bit dodgy if you do. He forced himself to remain in his chair, though it felt as if every nerve in his body was straining to push him out of it and drive him through the door. But he stayed, sweat breaking out on his forehead.

'Have another?' Ed was tired of waiting for Mix to offer. They could sit there all night before he did that. 'Same again?'

'I've got to go,' Mix said.

What did this Frank look like? He couldn't remember and he couldn't ask. Leaving, he might easily bump into him out in Pembridge Gardens without knowing who he was. But Frank would know him. He said an abrupt goodbye to Steph and 'See you' to Ed.

There were plenty of people about. There always were, these fine warm nights. Any of the youngish men might be Frank. The one coming up from Notting Hill Gate might be him or that one getting out of a car. At any rate neither of them seemed to recognise him. Mix could get the bus or walk but standing at the bus stop he'd be more easily spotted, while walking would get him away from the danger area and, besides, it was good for him.

Usually, when he came home to St Blaise House if it wasn't very late, a dim light showed in two or three windows. A greyish-yellow glow lit the glass half-moon over the front door, the drawing room casements and perhaps one in her bedroom. Tonight there was nothing, the house looked full of unrelieved darkness, a darkness strong enough and thick enough to push itself against the windows from inside. Stop imagining things, he told himself, you know it's all in your head. He unlocked the door and went into the silence he expected and wanted.

Ghosts don't exist, there are no such things. That Shoshana would say anything for a fast buck. Don't shut your eyes when you get to the top. Anything you think you see is only in your mind. He kept his eyes open, stared down the passages and saw nothing. And don't start drinking now you're home, keep a clear head.

On the way home he had made up his mind to get the body downstairs tonight. But why? There was no need to do it at once. Old Chawcer would be away for a week. Leave it till tomorrow, try and get home by four and do it then. Then you can dig the hole on Saturday in daylight. If any of the neighbours see you digging in the night they'll be suspicious.

He'd start it all tomorrow and meanwhile have a very small gin and go to bed. Once there, warm and comfortable, he began to worry about the interview with Mr Pearson in the morning. Suppose he said, 'We're going to have to let you go'? But he wouldn't, not for a few missed appointments. Would Frank bother to tell the police? And if he did, how could he tell who he'd seen with Danila? She might have had other boyfriends and any of them could have been walking her back to Oxford Gardens. He slept, woke, dozed, got up and put the light on, contemplated his reflection in the long mirror. How would he be described, anyway? He was just ordinary to look at, not as thin as he ought to be, pinkish face, blunt nose, eyes vaguely grey or hazel, hair fair going on brown. An identity parade would be another thing altogether but even Mix in his current state of nerves could see that once again he was letting his imagination run away with him.

Mr Pearson wasn't going to sack him, as he had half feared, but was giving him a last chance. He was given to delivering sententious little lectures to his staff when they were in trouble and he gave Mix one now.

'Exemplary behaviour isn't demanded of you simply on your own account or even on mine. It is for the benefit of the whole community of engineers in this company and for the reputation of the company itself. Think what it means to a client at present when you speak the firm's name on the phone. The client has a pleasant warm sensation of safety, of reassurance and satisfaction. It will be all right. It will be done, and promptly. No matter what the problem, this firm will solve it. And then think what it means when an engineer repeatedly lets the client down, fails to turn up as promised, neglects to call back. Doesn't he – or most probably she – begin to see the company as unreliable, untrustworthy, no longer first-class? And isn't she then likely to say to herself, "Maybe I should go through the Yellow Pages and find someone else"?'

In other words, thought Mix, he's saying I've let the firm down. Well, let him. It won't happen again, anyway.

'It won't happen again, Mr Pearson.'

Downstairs, in the reps' room where he had use of a desk, Mix phoned Shoshana's Spa. Shoshana herself answered, for the temp had left and no replacement had yet been found for Danila.

'I'll be along to look at those machines next week.'

'I suppose that means next Friday evening,' Shoshana said nastily.

'Not as long as that.' Mix tried to put the sound of a smile into his tone.

'It had better not be.' When he had put the receiver down she dialled the code that would tell her the number he had called from. She expected a negative result as supposedly he phoned from a mobile or else his home number but instead she got the London code and seven unfamiliar digits. Thoughtfully, she made a note of them.

Mix next called Colette Gilbert-Bamber and received a torrent of abuse. After all she'd done for him, as she put it, to be treated like some call girl to be picked up and dropped whenever he fancied. She'd found out the name of his company's chief executive and considered telling Mr Pearson what she'd almost told her husband, that Mix had tried to rape her.

'So what do you think of that?'

'I never heard such a load of bollocks.' He nearly said she'd never be raped because rape was only when the victim was unwilling, but he thought better of it and silently put the receiver down. After that he went into the stockroom where they kept a limited number of new machines for immediate delivery and found what he was looking for, a very large bag in thick but transparent light blue plastic of the kind used to protect stationary bikes and treadmills.

This packed safely in the boot of the car, he drove from client to client, enduring their reproaches and promising prompt follow-up visits. At two, with a Pret-a-Manger sandwich and a can of Coke (the Diet kind because he was slimming) he gave himself the treat of a sojourn outside Nerissa's house.

It was his first visit for days but, though he stayed for over an hour, she didn't appear. Once he'd dealt with that body he'd have to make himself a new strategy, a real campaign plan, for at present, as he reminded himself, he'd only spoken to her on one single occasion. Just after three-thirty he made a last call, this time at a big place facing Holland Park, and by four-fifteen, carrying the plastic bag, he was in St Blaise House.

So was Queenie Winthrop, though he didn't know it until he had been all the way upstairs and into his flat and down again to check that he'd be able to get the body into the garden by way of the kitchen and the two poky little rooms beyond it. She was in the kitchen, an apron over her red floral dress, tidying up and wiping down surfaces.

'Did you remember to feed the cat?' she said.

'I'll do it now.'

Ma Winthrop spoke in the triumphant tone of someone who has accomplished a challenging task with finesse and expects to be congratulated. 'Don't trouble. I have done it myself,' she said and added 'Though I must say he didn't seem hungry.'

Mix said nothing. How long was she going to be here? She answered him, though he hadn't asked. 'I shall be at it for another couple of hours. I've tidied up the boot room and the washhouse and now I've started on the kitchen. What a glory hole this place is!'

The word she used for one of those little back rooms made him start. 'Washhouse? Is there one?'

'Out here. Look.'

He followed her into a room that was more like a shed with walls of unplastered brick. A bulging thing like some sort of ancient oven filled one corner.

'What's that?'

'It's a copper. I don't suppose you've ever seen anything like it before, have you? My mother had one and did her washing in it. Ghastly. Women used a dolly and a washboard. Frightfully bad for their insides.'

Mix registered this as best he could. The words 'dolly' and 'washboard' meant nothing but 'washhouse' did. Christie had put each body in the one at 10 Rillington Place while they awaited burial. He'd do the same thing here if only that bloody woman would go. He should have had the sense to get the key back. Yesterday, while she was talking about him feeding the cat he should have asked for the key. But if she said no?

'I'd better have Miss Chawcer's key off you.'

'Oh, why?' she said, returning to the kitchen and vigorously spraying scented blue cleanser all over the sink. 'I told Gwendolen I'd hang on to it. I may need to be in and out. I'll certainly keep it if you don't mind. Olive and I may decide to spring-clean the whole place as a surprise for her when she comes back. Poor Gwendolen is no housekeeper, I'm afraid.'

There was no more to be said. He went back to his flat, wondering if she'd been up on this top floor. If she had she'd have smelt the smell and wouldn't she have said something to him? It was no good sitting down, trying to watch TV or even read the Christie book. He'd have to do something, make the preliminary moves. Cautiously, carrying his toolbag and the plastic bag, he went out on to the landing and listened. There was no sound from down there. He opened the door to the bedroom next door. He'd brought a scarf with him and this he tied round his head, covering his nose. The smell was still there, though muffled. It worsened beyond belief when he'd got the floorboards up but he told himself he had to get on with it, keep on, don't think about it, breathe through your mouth.

It looked just as it had when he put it in there, small, slight, wrapped in its shroud of red sheets. In order to lift it out he had to get his head and face very near it and twice he gagged. But he succeeded in lifting it on to the floor. If it hadn't changed in appearance it seemed to have gained in weight. Lying where it had been, on the dusty joists, was the thong, scarlet and black, a frivolous thing of elastic and lace. How had he failed to notice its absence when he dumped the rest of her clothes? He picked it up and put it in his pocket. The easiest part was getting her body into the bag. When it was inside he felt better and once the mouth of the bag was fastened with a length of wire wound round it, a huge relief came. Suppose that old woman was waiting outside the door or coming up the tiled stairs? She wasn't and he managed to drag the bag and body into his own flat. Once he had it inside he had to go back, replace the floorboards and check on that smell. If any of it still lingered.

Of course it did. Far less powerful but bad enough. Perhaps it would be better once he'd got the boards back. He couldn't tell if it was or not but time would surely fade it. On his way home he should have picked up another bottle of gin. Very little of what he'd had was left. Probably just as well. He drank it, waiting for Queenie Winthrop to leave.

She finally did at half-past six. From the top of the stairs Mix heard her go. He should have asked when she'd be back again, though asking might look strange. While he was in the house but of course not when he was out of it, he could bolt the front door top and bottom, and that was what he'd do while he took the body down. A procrastinator, he would never normally have said there was no time like the present but he said it now. First he went down and bolted the front door. That was nearly as good as having the key back. Going up and down these stairs must be doing him good even if it didn't feel like it. Remembering to take his keys with him, he pulled the body out of his flat and to the top of the stairs, kicking the door shut behind him.

If she had been any heavier he doubted that he could have done it. On the first-floor landing he encountered Otto, mewing at old Chawcer's bedroom door. Mix didn't know why he opened the door to let him in but he did. Perhaps it was just for the sake of having a rest from lugging this heavy bag down. When he got to the bottom he thought he couldn't take it another step but he braced himself to drag it along the passage towards the breakfast room and kitchen. He had almost reached the breakfast room door when he heard the grating sound of a key turning in the front door. He froze but his heart raced. The door was bolted, no one could get in, he didn't have to worry.

The key turned again, the letterbox flapped open and Olive Fordyce's voice called out, 'Mr Cellini, Mr Cellini, are you there?'

He was almost afraid to breathe. She called him again, then, 'Let me in! What are you doing, bolting the door? Mr Cellini!'

Hours seemed to pass as she shouted, tried the door again, rang the bell, flapped the letterbox. It was no more than three minutes as he discovered, looking at his watch once he heard her feet clacking down the path towards the gate. It had frightened him too much for him to think of digging now. He felt weak and almost faint. But he summoned up the strength to drag the plastic-wrapped bundle through the kitchen into the place she had called the washhouse. The huge old copper dominated one corner of the room, an excrescence of bricks and mortar about four feet high with a wooden lid at the top. Lifting the lid disclosed an earthenware tub, quite dry and evidently unused for years. He lifted the body, puffing and gasping, and placing his hand on his lower back felt a bulge in his pocket. It was the thong. Before closing the lid he dropped it inside. He'd retrieve it later and bury it with the body. No one, certainly not one of those nosy old women, would have reason to look inside the copper. Old Chawcer had a usable if antiquated washing machine, an advance, in spite of its short-comings, on this antique.

Going into the garden felt restful, almost restora-tive. The heat of the day had given place to a mild still evening. The unmown grass was the colour of blond hair and dry as a hayfield. In the garden beyond the rear wall the Indian man was trying to cut his lawn with an old hand mower and making little impression on it. The guinea fowl padded about and clucked.

There wasn't a bare piece of ground where digging would be easy. Every inch was overgrown with grass and weeds. Mix had never in his whole life dug into soil of any kind and this, what he could see of it between sturdy thrusting thistles and aggressive things he didn't know the name of, looked as heavy as concrete but a muddy yellow colour. Inside the semi-derelict shed he found rusty tools: a spade, a fork, a pick. Tomorrow he'd do it and that would be the end.

Tell yourself that, he whispered, tell yourself that by the time it's done all the worry will be over. He went into the house and drew back the bolts, top and bottom. Old Chawcer made no noise when she was at home. Reading is a silent occupation. Yet the house seemed quieter without her. An oppressive silence filled its spaces. His shoes were dusty from his exploration of the garden. Unwilling to leave behind any evidence of his visit to a place where he shouldn't have been, he took them off and carried them up the stairs, thinking of the task awaiting him on the next day. Perhaps he should have tried the soil to see how hard it was and how heavy. But what would be the use of that? He would have to do it, however difficult the job. A final visit should be paid to the bedroom where she had lain. It would cheer him up if the smell was fading and everything in there returned to normal.

He reached the top and opened the door. Whether the smell had gone he never knew, he was in there too short a time to tell. The ghost stood in the middle of the room under the gas lamp, gazing down at the floorboards below which had been

Danila's resting place. Mix fled. He scrabbled at his front door, his hand shaking and rattling the key against the woodwork. Gibbering sobs rose in his throat. He wanted somewhere safe to hide and there was nowhere if he couldn't get inside. The key shook in the lock, stuck, came out. He managed to push it in again and the door opened. He fell on to the floor and kicked the door shut behind him, his eyes squeezed shut and his hands drumming on the carpet. Shoshana had been right. After a moment or two he had recovered enough to feel for the cross in his pocket but by then it was too late to use it.

# Chapter 18

'She was only a kid,' said Frank McQuaid.

He had heard this phrase many times in detective series on television and always hoped for the chance to use it. The policeman interviewing him said, 'Yes? And you saw her walking along Oxford Gardens with a man. Can you describe him?'

'Just ordinary,' said Frank who might have been reading from a script. Sitting opposite the detective sergeant in a room behind the bar, he assumed a grave and thoughtful expression as if millions were watching him. 'Nondescript – know what I mean? Brownish hair, brownish eyes, I reckon. It was dark.'

'It's never dark in London.'

Frank considered this statement. It had an originality about it which made him suspicious. He decided to ignore it. 'Middle height or a bit less – know what I mean?'

'I suppose you mean a bit below middle height, Mr McQuaid.'

'That's what I said. She was just a kid.' Frank looked mournfully at an invisible camera. 'Came from some foreign place. Albania? Maybe she was an asylum seeker.'

'Yes, thank you, Mr McQuaid. You've been,' the policeman lied, 'very helpful.'

*

That night there was a storm at sea. That was what it sounded like, the waves pounding on the shore. Why the Westway should have been so much louder than usual Mix didn't know. Perhaps the wind was coming from a different direction. He should have asked that doctor for sleeping pills. As it was, he had no sleep until about four when he fell into a troubled doze. The brightness of the morning did something to reduce his terror to simple fear when he awoke at eight. His first thought was that he must move out, get away from this haunted house, his second that moving was impossible while that body remained downstairs in the washhouse. What he had seen the evening before so concentrated his mind that he barely reacted when he went downstairs and picked up from the doormat the letter from the blood-testing lab via the company's doctor and saw that his cholesterol level at 8.8 was alarmingly high. So what? He could get pills for it, statins or something. How would he dare go upstairs when he came home from work?

Mix dared not miss any more calls or leave one other message unanswered. Colette Gilbert-Bamber was lost but he had no regrets about her. Reluctant as he was to go near the place, he drove over to Westbourne Grove and Shoshana's Spa. It was ten o'clock in the morning.

He rang the bell and an unknown voice answered in an affected drawl of the kind he called 'Sloaney'. 'Mix Cellini to repair the equipment,' he said.

No reply but the door growled ajar. He walked in, lifted his head and came face to face with Nerissa descending the stairs. For a moment he thought he must be hallucinating, he couldn't believe his luck. It was as if fate was compensating him for his terrible experience of last evening. He found a voice that came out rather shrilly.

'Good morning, Miss Nash.'

She looked at him without smiling. 'Hi,' she said and she sounded frightened.

'Please don't be nervous,' he said. 'It's just – just that I'm always happy to see you.'

She looked very beautiful – she couldn't help that – in jeans and a cotton top with a red poncho over it. Halfway down the stairs, she had stopped and stood there, as if a bit scared to pass him. 'Did you follow me here?'

'Oh, no,' he said in a tone intended to reassure. 'No, no, no. I work here, servicing the equipment.' He walked away from the foot of the stairs and waited by the lift. 'Please come down. I won't harm you.'

That old bitch of a mother of hers and the great-aunt too must have been working on her, turning her against him. He'd like to kill that old Fordyce woman. Nerissa came slowly down the stairs, hesitated at the foot before saying, 'Well, goodbye. Please don't . . .' She had slipped out of the door before ending her sentence.

She was going to say, please don't think me rude, I didn't understand, Mix thought. Or, please don't think I meant you'd harm me. Something like that. She was as *nice* as she was beautiful, kind and sweet. It would be her nasty old mother who'd taught her to ask him if he was following her, not the kind of thing she'd say naturally. Mothers could be their children's enemies. Look at his own, marrying Javy and after he'd gone, bringing all those men back when she'd got three growing kids at home, learning her loose behaviour. Nerissa's mum ought to be thankful her daughter had someone to adore her and, more than that, respect her in an old-fashioned way.

By this time the lift had taken him up to the spa floor. Where Danila had presided the first time he came there, stood a woman almost as gorgeous as Nerissa, though an arctic blonde where she was dark, snow-white skin, a glacier-pale torrent of hair, long fingers tipped in silver. She must be the one who had answered his ring. 'I'll just let Madam Shoshana know you're here,' she said in the same débutante's voice.

Mix would very much rather she didn't. The chances were the crazy old soothsayer wouldn't remember him from the session in that upstairs room but she might. And if she did, would she think it funny him also being the one she had a service contract with? Did that matter? Mix would prefer no one to find anything funny about his behaviour. He didn't want attention drawn to himself. Anyway, she wouldn't come up herself, she'd send a message by this amazing-looking girl. Once more he gazed at her.

In the tones of Eliza Doolittle after her transformation, she said, 'Who do you think you're looking at?'

Mix walked a few paces away, 'Which machines want seeing to?'

'Madam will show you. I'm new here.'

Before he could answer, Shoshana came out of the lift, draped in black robes, hung with ropes of jet and looking like a female druid in mourning. Mix knew by her eyes that she recognised him before she spoke and when she did it was in a completely different voice from the one he had heard predicting his future, a shrill, sharp north London tone. 'You've taken your time about coming. If reading the cards means more to you than work, you're not going to get very far. The ones you've got to mend are two bikes, four and seven. Right?'

'Right,' said Mix through gritted teeth.

He had to stop his mouth falling open when she said, 'You fancied that girl who worked here. The skinny little one that left without a word. Didn't run off with you, did she?'

Mix managed a derisive smile. It was one of the hardest things he'd ever achieved. 'What, me? I hardly knew her.'

'That's what you men always say. I don't like men. Now you'd better get on with what you've come about.'

What an old horror! He'd never come across a female of her age quite so horrible, she put Chawcer, Fordyce and Winthrop in the shade. He shuddered and turned his attention to the two stationary bicycles. Both needed a new part but different parts in each case. He didn't carry spares with him and, since he was working freelance at Shoshana's, if he was to get them he'd have to pinch them from the warehouse. Nothing to be done now. He told the icy beauty he'd order the necessary parts and come back when he'd got them.

'When will that be?'

'A few days? Not more than a week.'

'It had better not be. Madam will do her nut if you keep her waiting any longer.'

He had more calls to make. One was a new customer who had never sent for him before and wanted to order a skier. She lived in a place called St Catherine's Mews on the border of Knightsbridge and Chelsea but though he drove twice up and down Milner Street he couldn't find it. Leave it, he said to himself, call her and ask her for directions. One of the few men who kept exercise equipment in his home had sent for him to Lady Somerset Road in Kentish Town but when he got there, perilously parked and afraid of being clamped, Mr Holland-Bridgeman wasn't at home. Mix decided to go back briefly to St Blaise House and check on that copper in the washhouse.

Approaching from Oxford Gardens, he wondered what he'd do if police cars were outside and policemen pacing about and blue and white crime tape stretched across the front garden. Turn round and hide somewhere, he thought, maybe go up north and home but not to his mother who'd either have some new lover living with her or be back in the bin. His brother? They'd never got on well. Shannon was the only one in the family he'd had any sort of relationship with . . . St Blaise Avenue was empty of people, relatively silent, the usual cars parked nose to tail along both sides. One space was left for Mix. He let himself into the house and stood listening, prepared for Ma Fordyce or Ma Winthrop to appear from the kitchen regions, waving a duster.

Unconvinced one or other of them wasn't in the house, he walked carefully through the breakfast room to the kitchen, a transformed place since cleaning operations conducted by those two, and into the washhouse. He sniffed, waited, sniffed again. No smell. His wrapping had been effective. Maybe Christie had also dealt with that particular problem in the same way – did they have plastic all that time ago? He found himself reluctant to lift the lid off the copper but he did it. There was no point in coming home at all at this hour and not doing that. The well-sealed, well-wrapped package she and the bag made was just as he had left it and, even with the lid up, he could smell nothing at all.

Then Mix made another discovery. If you didn't know what the package in the copper was you'd think it was just a big plastic sack full of old clothes someone had stuffed in there for a place to put it. You wouldn't investigate any further. If it didn't smell and looked like the kind of bag people took to a launderette, wasn't it perfectly safe where it was? The situation was quite different for that man Beresford Brown, who began putting up brackets for a radio, and behind a partition in Rillington Place found a woman's naked body. There was no smell because it was midwinter and cold. In his own case there'd be no smell because of the way he'd wrapped it. Why shouldn't it stay where it was? The idea seemed too daring and bold to be feasible, but why not? Wouldn't he worry about it all the time it was there?

Old Chawcer was no careful housewife. You could see that from the way Fordyce and Winthrop had had to work to get the place straight. She'd never go near that copper, she had a washing machine, and though it was old-fashioned it was still usable. In the unlikely event of her looking inside the copper, all she'd see was old clothes in a plastic bag. So why not leave it there? Mix closed the lid, wandered slowly back into the kitchen, thinking of this new and simpler plan, and came face to face with Olive Fordyce. Because of his stealthy entry he had the satisfaction of making her jump, as the ghost had made him, though he had been as alarmed as she and with more cause. She had a small white dog with her, about half the size of Otto.

'What are you doing out there?'

'I was in the hallway,' Mix said, 'and I heard a noise.'

'What noise?' She was very sharp with him.

'I don't know. That's why I went to see.'

The look she gave him was suspicious and searching. 'Where's the cat?'

'How should I know? I haven't seen him for days.'

The dog began sniffing the hems of his jeans. 'He'll run away if you don't feed him and find someone who will. Don't do that, Kylie, there's a good girl. You'll be pleased,' she said, pausing, 'to hear Gwen will be home in a day or two.'

She gave him a broad malicious smile. It was as if she knew what was going on in his head. He held on to the edge of the newly cleaned counter, afraid he might fall. All ideas of leaving the body where it was vanished and to get it out of the house, out of any possible sighting, became imperative.

'Naturally, I've been into the hospital to see her, as I always do every morning, and that's what she told me. The sister confirmed it. Tomorrow, she said.' She picked up the dog and cuddled it like a child with a toy. 'If not it'll be the day after. They don't keep patients in like they used to. Well, nothing's like it used to be, is it?'

He said nothing. He was aware of what she would have expected him to say – if he were a 'nice young man' that is. 'It'll be good to have her back,' for instance, or, 'She'll be pleased to have her kitchen all neat and tidy.' He couldn't find the words, any words.

'I'm going out again now to do a bit of shopping for her. She'll need a good deal of looking after.' She fluttered her free hand and he saw her nails were orchid pink today, like a young girl, pointed and glossy and sharp. With no inhibitions about looking someone straight in the eye and holding the gaze, she fixed him with a penetrating gaze, at the same time craning her neck forward and holding her head slightly on one side. 'You'll have to pull your socks up, make her cups of tea and fetch her bits and pieces. That won't do you any harm. She won't be able to get about much yet.'

'When are you coming back?' he said.

'What, today? I don't know. When I've done the shopping. Does it bother you?'

'Give me the list and I'll do the shopping,' he said.

It was evidently the best thing he could have said. For the first time since they had encountered each other in the kitchen doorway, she spoke pleasantly to him. 'That's very good of you. I won't say no. It'll save my legs. I'll give you some money.' She began rummaging in her bag, found the list and handed it to him.

'You can give me the money after I've done it,' he said, mollifying her further.

'It'll have to be a couple of days then. I'm not coming in again till then if I can help it. Queenie's taking over, she'll be in tomorrow, so I'll pass the key on to her. Now say goodbye to Kylie.'

The hell he would. Hadn't he done enough for her, offering to do the shopping? The two afternoon calls he was due to make, the expenses form to fill in, the meeting with Jack Fleisch, the other engineers and the reps went out of his head. Or, rather, were dismissed as of no importance compared with the urgency of hiding that body, not temporarily, not as an interim move, but for ever.

He need not go upstairs, not now, not till later. He'd have a drink in a pub or bar somewhere so that he could face going up there, have the strength to face what might be at the top.

A principle of Shoshana's was: never bother the police unless they bother you. She sat up in the soothsaying room above the spa, a client due in ten minutes, thinking about Danila Kovic, not with any anxiety as to her whereabouts nor fear that she might be dead, not with any sympathy for her friends or relations who could be missing her, not with any regrets that she no longer worked at the spa now that she had beautiful efficient Julia, but entirely from the point of mischief-making.

The idea had never crossed her mind that Mix Cellini might have made away with Danila. Why should he? As far as Shoshana knew, the two had been acquainted for perhaps two or three weeks and might never have gone out together. But a deep resentment of Mix was curdling and fermenting and bubbling inside her. The contract he had signed meant nothing to him; once Danila had disappeared he never came near the place. As for repairing equipment, he had told her he'd ordered those parts for the bicycles but she'd be a fool to believe him. He was putting her through the time-consuming process of finding new engineers, as if she hadn't had enough difficulties getting a replacement for Danila.

Until that morning, she had believed that her hope of retaliation lay in the number she had noted down when he called her and she found he wasn't on his mobile. She more than suspected that he worked for a company which had a rule forbidding operatives to engage in outside work. A call to a chief executive or managing director, whatever you liked to call it, might well lose him his job. This was the revenge she was saving up unless his behaviour changed radically. But might not a fitter retribution be to tell the police he was Danila's elusive boyfriend?

She didn't want them coming to the spa. There were things she would prefer them not to see – that security arrangements were far from adequate, that there was no fire escape from any of the upper floors and no safety measures were in place. But she could go to them. Perhaps there was no great hurry. Do nothing on impulse, was another of her rules. Think it through. She began taking the pieces of quartz and lapis and jade from their velvet bag and examining the cards to make sure they were suitably arranged.

The client, a new one, very young and obviously overawed by the room, its ambience and by Madam Shoshana herself, tapped on the door and came in rather fearfully. She crept to the chair which was waiting for her and lifted her eyes to the soothsayer's half-veiled face.

'Place your hands on the mandala within the stones, breathe deeply and I will begin,' said Shoshana in the mystical and occult voice she kept for forecasting the future.

Half a litre of milk, 200 grams of butter, cheese, sliced bread, a lamb chop and a chicken breast, frozen peas, a carton of soup and a great deal more. Mix put it away in the now wholesome and inviting fridge. He had done old Chawcer's shopping mechanically, buying what was on the list but still hardly noticing what he bought, losing the supermarket receipt so he had no idea what accounts to render to Ma Fordyce. A couple of gins in KPH had given him courage and a photograph in the *Evening Standard* of Nerissa modelling an Alexander McQueen gown cheered him up. She'd wear something like that at their wedding and carry a huge bouquet of white orchids.

Ma Fordyce wouldn't come back that afternoon and Ma Winthrop wasn't due till some time tomorrow. It was half-past two. He mustn't wait till tomorrow, he must get started now. He forced himself to go upstairs, glad of the bright sunlight penetrating the Isabella window. Because a little breeze was blowing the colours danced like strobe lights. Nothing there. Everything quiet and still – and unoccupied. He sighed and let himself in. Mix had no shoes suitable for heavy digging but he put on his thick-soled trainers and a pair of old jeans. A faint smell still hung about his flat and it was stronger in the room where she had been under the floorboards. That would fade in time. He bolted the front door top and bottom just in case Ma Winthrop decided to look in, and went outside into the garden.

The weather was still what people called glorious. He would rather it had been cold and grey, for this warmth and sunshine brought the neighbours out into their gardens. The people who kept theirs perfect were having a drink at a white metal table under a striped umbrella. Some of them could easily see what he was doing from where they sat. He took the spade and fork from the shed and found a place where the soil showing between the sturdy weeds looked softer than the rock-hard clayey areas. Digging was unskilled labour, so anyone could do it, he'd probably find it a breeze. But at first the spade simply refused to go in. By making an extreme effort he could just penetrate the top layer of earth down to about two inches. After that it might as well be rock he was encountering, it was so hard and apparently impenetrable. The pick might be the answer, though he was as wary of using it as he would be of plying a scythe. He fetched it from the shed, noticing with more misgivings that it was corroded, eaten into with rust. A patch of rot showed on its handle.

He tried to swing the pick the way he had seen labourers in the road do it but after three failed attempts was afraid of doing himself an injury. It came as a surprise to him that you had to be fitter than he was to use an instrument like this. Maybe he had been wrong about the quality of the soil here. He moved further away from the wall and nearer to the house, taking the pick and fork with him, his shoulders already stiffening. From here he could see over the end wall into the garden beyond where, instead of the guinea fowl, two large Canada geese strutted among the weeds. In deckchairs, a man in a turban and a woman in a sari sat reading, he the evening paper, she a magazine. Though he could see them he couldn't tell if they could see him. Perhaps it wouldn't matter. The deckchairs were the first he had seen since the one his grandma had sat in when he was a small boy. But instead of her and her peculiarities, they brought to mind Reggie who had furnished his kitchen with such makeshift chairs after selling his furniture.

Once more he began to dig, but this time using the fork. That was better. Its prongs were sharp enough to push through the top layer and gradually he developed a technique of digging the fork in perpendicularly instead of at an angle and this was more effective. He even learnt how to thrust his tool in lower down and attack the harder level of ground. He had to. Though despairing of digging down six feet, which he'd heard was the depth a grave should be, he knew he'd have to manage at least four.

After about an hour he rested. The front of his T-shirt was wet with sweat. A drink of something was what he needed, even tea, but he was afraid that if he went indoors he might not bring himself to come out again. A rather optimistic idea that perseverance might get his muscles used to the work so that they would stop hurting hadn't been justified. When he straightened up a burning pain ran down his back and his right thigh. His shoulders wanted to tense and bunch themselves round his neck. As he tried circling them in a clockwise and then an anticlockwise direction, turning his head from left to right and left again, he saw Otto watching him from his customary seat on the opposite wall. The cat was as still as a carving in a museum, its round green eyes fixed on him, its face composed into its usual expression of malevolent scorn. The Asian couple had gone indoors, leaving their deckchairs behind.

Mix began digging deeper with the fork but he had started to understand he would have to use the spade, however difficult this might be. He went back to where he had left it and, picking it up, saw something he hadn't noticed before, a heap of grey and black speckled feathers. No doubt it was his imagination that made him see smug satisfaction in the cat's face when he glanced at him again. Still, look what happened before when he called something his imagination.

Using the spade was heavy work. Each spadeful he dislodged brought sharp needles digging into the small of his back. You've got to, you've got to, you've no choice, he muttered to himself as he kept on. He saw that blisters were coming up on the palms of his hands. Still, he must do at least half an hour more.

The sun still blazed down, though it was nearly six. A sharp cackle which sounded as if uttered in his ear made him jump. He looked up, afraid it was human, and saw the man in the turban throwing handfuls of corn down for the geese. They jostled and shoved each other, making their harsh cries. To his surprise, the Asian man waved cheerfully at him, so he had to wave back. He dug for another ten minutes and knew he'd have to give up for the day. Back again in the morning. Not bad, anyway. He must have dug down a foot.

The tools put away, he returned by way of the washhouse where he checked on the copper and its contents. He dragged himself up the stairs, clinging to the banisters, pausing often. Again, he reminded himself, he'd forgotten to feed the cat. Still, it looked as if it ate well enough when left to its own devices. How had Reggie, years older than he was, managed to dig those graves in his garden? From the pictures he'd seen, it looked as neglected and overgrown as this one, the soil as unyielding. Of course, he'd claimed to have a bad back, the reason he'd given at the trial of Timothy Evans for being incapable of moving Beryl Evans's body. Perhaps his grave-digging had done him a permanent injury.

Mix hardly knew how he'd managed to get up the tiled flight. Pain dispelled all thoughts of the ghost. He staggered into his flat, poured himself a stiff gin and tonic and fell down on the sofa. Half an hour later he picked up the remote and put the television on, closing his eyes and falling immediately asleep in spite of the rock music pounding out of the set.

A louder noise woke him. The front door bell was ringing, and someone was clattering the letterbox and hammering on the front door with their fists. Mix crept to his door and came out on to the landing at the top of the tiled flight. His first thought was that it was the police. The Asian man had told them someone was digging a grave in Miss Chawcer's garden and they had come to check. They had targets to meet these days and they'd jump at the chance of discovering a crime. Mix couldn't see the front garden or the street from his flat. He went down a flight, then another, into old Chawcer's bedroom and looked out of the window.

By now it was getting dark. By the light of street lamps he saw there were no police cars, none of that crime tape he had so much feared earlier. Abruptly the noise ceased. A beam of light appeared on the path, followed by Queenie Winthrop holding a torch in her hand. Mix ducked down as she turned round and looked up at the windows. Checking up on him, he supposed, making sure he'd done the shopping. Well, she'd have to remain in ignorance. He wasn't unbolting that front door for anyone or anything until he'd completed the burial. He began the weary climb back.

Last night he had seen the ghost up there, in that bedroom, really seen it. There was no longer any question of its existing only in his imagination. Steph and Shoshana were right. It wasn't just that he had been in a bad nervous state, the stresses of the job had got to him, all the pressures of Ed, his worry over and longing for Nerissa, childhood memories. He had really seen the ghost.

# Chapter 19

The pain in his back kept Mix awake. If he hadn't been so frightened of Christie's ghost he'd have gone down to old Chawcer's bathroom and looked to see if she had any sleeping pills. She was bound to, those old women always did. But the thought of opening his front door and seeing that sharp-featured though blank face, those eyes behind the glasses staring at him, was a dreadful deterrent. He took painkillers instead, the 500 milligram ones the pharmacist said were the strongest you could buy over the counter. They weren't strong enough and the burning and stabbing went on. The last time he had known pain like this was when Javy had beaten him up after what he said he'd tried to do to Shannon.

At five in the morning, after a cup of coffee and a bit of toast, he made himself start again. It was beginning to get light, the sky red and grey with sunrise, a white frost on the grass but not enough to harden the ground further. There was nothing, he had discovered, like knowing you've got to do something, you've no choice, to make you get on and do it. They surely couldn't bring old Chawcer back home before midday, could they? At any rate, they couldn't get in if they did. He already knew he was physically incapable of digging to a depth of six feet – inches more than his own height. It was impossible. Four feet would be enough, it would have to be enough.

The geese had been shut up for the night but now, when the Indian man in turban and camel-hair dressing-gown opened their door, they came out, cackling. Mix had seen or read somewhere that geese make good watchdogs. He didn't want them watching him. Otto was nowhere to be seen. He dug on, accepting the pain, knowing he must, but still wondering from time to time if he was per-manently injuring his back, if he was making him-self an invalid for life. Again he asked himself how Reggie had done it, how, come to that, he had stayed so calm and steady, nerveless, when sur-prised by people arriving, by questioners, by his own wife. Maybe he was mad and I'm not, Mix thought. Or maybe I'm mad and he was sane, a brave strong man. At almost ten, he lifted out the last spadeful of earth and sat down on the cold damp stony ground to rest.

'I wish to go home,' said Gwendolen. 'Now.'

'I suppose I could get you a taxi.'

Queenie Winthrop had been told by the ward sister that an ambulance would take Gwendolen home at four o'clock that afternoon. 'At the ear-liest.'

'Taxis are a wicked price,' said Gwendolen. 'They cost more at weekends.'

'I'll pay for it.'

Gwendolen gave the humourless little laugh which was characteristic of her but which no one had heard for the past few days. 'I've never taken charity from anyone and I'm not going to start now. Surely you know someone with a car.'

245

'Olive used to drive but she's let her licence lapse.'

'Yes, very useful. What about her niece, Mrs some-African-name?'

'Oh, I couldn't ask her, Gwendolen.'

'Why on earth not? She can only say no but she'll be very rude if she does.'

Hazel Akwaa and her daughter were drinking coffee in Hazel's house in Acton. Or, rather, Hazel was drinking coffee and Nerissa was drinking sparkling water with ice and a slice of lemon. Before the phone rang they had been discussing what Hazel was to wear to dinner at Darel Jones's that evening and Nerissa was offering to lend her the only garment she possessed which her mother could get into, a heavy silk embroidered caftan.

'Fetch Gwendolen Chawcer from the hospital?' Nerissa heard her mother say. 'I couldn't before late this afternoon. My husband's got the car.'

'Tell her I'll drive her,' said Nerissa.

So they went to Paddington together, the caftan fetched from Campden Hill Square and hanging in a garment bag across the back seat. Even Gwendolen could melt when confronted by true kindness and when she realised what was being done to save her from staying longer than she need in hospital, she was very gracious to Nerissa. For once, in the company of a young woman, she refrained from remarking on the tightness of her jeans, the colour and length of her fingernails, the décolletage of her shirt and the height of her heels, but smiled and said how very thoughtful Nerissa was in giving up her Saturday morning to 'transport an ancient creature like me'.

They reached St Blaise House at exactly noon.

Queenie Winthrop, who hadn't been invited to accompany them but had done so just the same, gave Gwendolen a very acerbic account, lasting for the entire journey, of how she had tried to get into the house to make final preparations for its owner's return.

'I had a key of course. Extraordinary as it seems, I found the front door *bolted* against me. Yes, bolted. You wouldn't believe it, would you? Perhaps that Mr Cellini is nervous of being in the place alone. I'm sure I don't know but it was bolted top and bottom. I rang and rang and banged on the door and the letterbox. When it was all to no avail I looked up and caught a glimpse of him diving down out of sight. And which window do you think he was at, Gwendolen? The one that faces the street in the middle on the first floor. Your bedroom window. I'm almost positive. What do you think of that?'

'I might think something if you were *absolutely* positive. But you're not, are you?'

Queenie didn't answer. Gwendolen was a bit much sometimes. Looking cool and offended, she helped her out of the car but she wasn't surprised when Gwendolen shook off her arm as they approached the front door and inserted her key in the lock. In spite of treating Queenie's account of Mix Cellini's behaviour with derision, she had quite expected to find her own front door bolted against her and, as the key turned, she was thinking of the vituperative invective she would direct against him, culminating in notice to quit. But the door slid open easily.

They all went in and took off their coats. As they walked across the hallway towards the drawing room door, Mix came out from the direction of the kitchen. He was very disconcerted to see them so early, and both overjoyed and alarmed to see Nerissa, though he had completed his task half an hour before and had been back only to check that he had left no incriminating evidence behind. It was the sight of Nerissa which brought him to a standstill in front of Gwendolen. But for her, he would have made some perfunctory greeting, passed them and struggled upstairs, hand pressed to aching back.

He was about to ignore the rest of them and find the most gracious words he could think of for Nerissa when Gwendolen spoke.

'What have you been doing in my kitchen?'

Mix had been using lies and subterfuge to get him out of trouble almost since he was a baby and he always had some defensive excuse ready. 'I knew you'd be coming home today. I thought I'd make you a cup of tea so I went to check on the kettle and the teacups.'

'Very thoughtful,' said Gwendolen who didn't believe him. 'One of my friends will do that.'

This was dismissal and Mix recognised it as such. He had to speak to Nerissa before he went back upstairs. She was looking at him, smiling a half-smile. 'That was a great shot of you in last night's *Standard*, Miss Nash,' he said. 'You wouldn't have a copy you could sign and let me have, would you?'

'It was a press photo,' she said and her voice sounded smaller than it had before. 'They just took it. They don't give you copies.'

'Pity.' Mix was determined to say his piece before parting from her. He had rehearsed it for just such an occasion. 'Miss Nash, you're the most beautiful woman I've ever seen. You're just as beautiful in close-up as from far away.' He brought his face near hers. 'More beautiful,' he said and he staggered upstairs, desperate not to show the pain he was in.

Unwilling to listen to all this, Gwendolen had gone into the drawing room, attended but no longer physically supported by Queenie Winthrop. Hazel Akwaa was furiously angry. She wanted to run after Mix and berate him but Nerissa held her arm and said, 'No, Mum, don't. Leave it.'

'How dare he say things like that to you?' Hazel spoke loudly enough for Mix, by now on the first floor, to hear.

'I'm not the Queen, Mum. He doesn't have to get permission. I must be really stupid, I didn't realise he actually lived here. I mean, I know we met him outside that time but it never registered that he lived in this house.'

'I'm sorry you had to endure all that under my roof,' said Gwendolen as they went into the drawing room. Her tone was no longer kindly towards Nerissa, whom she blamed as much as Mix for his outburst.

Now she was home she wanted all these people to go. In an impatient way, she acknowledged Nerissa's kindness in fetching her from the hospital but there was nothing to stay for. She had her prescribed medicaments and vitamins, she wasn't hungry and her paramount desire was to lie on the sofa and open the post which Queenie had brought in from the hallway. There was bound to be a letter from Stephen Reeves. She was very tired and she wanted to read it before sleep overtook her. It was

249

Nerissa who recognised how weary she was and took her mother and Queenie away, Queenie calling over her shoulder that Gwendolen must waste no time in seeing what she thought of the spring-cleaning she and Olive had done in the kitchen.

Before opening her book, Gwendolen reflected that today was the anniversary of the first time Stephen Reeves came to the house to attend her mother. He had come downstairs and said, 'It's a sad sight to see the old folks come to this.'

She had offered him tea and because he looked hungry, that day's batch of home-made cakes.

The compliments Mix had offered to Nerissa and the proximity of his face to hers had upset her more than she had showed at the time. She had made a great effort at self-control in order not to cause trouble the moment poor Miss Chawcer came home after her stay in hospital, but once she had taken her mother and Mrs Winthrop home and was in her own house, she began to cry. All the telling of herself that the man had only said she was beautiful and come rather too close to her, that he was a harmless fool, had no effect and she gave way to a storm of tears.

Crying was a release, more salutary than attempting to pull herself together, and she was too young to be afraid of lasting marks to her face. She phoned the beauty salon she used and booked to have her hair done, a face massage and a manicure. About to leave the house, she thought of him again and she looked out of a front window to see if the blue car was parked down the hill. She knew the number by heart, had never had to write it down, but there was no sign of him. Still, she went nervously to her car and remained jumpy and alert until she was in the salon and her hair was being washed. Speculation about him went round and round the inside of her head as warm water splashed on its outside. What did he want of her? That she should *go out with him*?

She told herself not to be elitist, nearly sure she'd got the difficult word right. Perhaps not to be a snob. God knows, she had no right to be snobbish about anyone, her family weren't anything much, even though Grandma claimed to be the daughter of a chief. He – she realised she didn't know his name – was probably better educated than her and had a real job. He hadn't done her any harm, so why was she so afraid of him? A man had once told her she had a true woman's intuitive powers and perhaps she had, for she sensed something ugly about him, something almost evil. This had been particularly apparent when he brought his face close to hers. His eyes had seemed dead and his expression utterly blank, even while he was saying those things about her being beautiful. If only she could think of a way to get rid of him, make sure he never came near her again.

Nico was approaching her with his drier and his brush. She turned her head and gave him her glorious heart-melting smile.

Mix sat in his flat reading *Killer Extraordinary*. He quickly came upon an illustration, a full-face photograph, and that reminded him of the ghost. He laid the book down. Before he started reading he had heard the departure of Nerissa – how nice she had been, how gentle and sweet – with Ma

Winthrop and that old bitch of a mother. How did a woman like that come to have such a wonderful daughter? It was unimaginable. The way she'd spoken about him when he went upstairs! Once he and Nerissa were going out together, better than that, once they were married, he'd have his revenge. He'd make his wife forbid her the house. And their marriage would happen. He was sure of it now. He'd brought his face up to hers near enough to kiss her and she hadn't moved away. She liked being told she was beautiful, of course she did. Tomorrow he'd go up there on foot and stand outside and wait for her. If only he could sing he'd serenade her.

Mix recognised how much his self-confidence had improved since he had so successfully disposed of that girl's body. It was as if, having done that in the face of such difficulty, he could do anything. Of course he hadn't committed deliberate murder, it wasn't murder or even manslaughter at all but 'unlawful killing'. They called it that when they realised you couldn't help it. But if he had to he'd kill again. It wasn't that much of a big deal. He knew he'd have a really good night's sleep tonight. His worries were over and now, looking back, he wondered why they had seemed so overwhelming. *He* had surmounted them, *he* had dealt with them and they had dissolved like smoke.

His back was better. Two more ibuprofen and putting his feet up helped enormously. As for the ghost, it never came in here. If he was careful never to look down those passages or go into that room the chances were he wouldn't see it again. Of course he must move. It was a pity after what he had spent on the flat, he would simply be making a present of a nice little earner to old Chawcer, but there was no help for it. She might not find it so profitable when the next tenant saw things up here he or she didn't expect.

The water diviners, filing down a side street in Kilburn towards a mews under which they were told an ancient stream still flowed, chatted pleasantly to each other on such familiar subjects as astrology, cartomancy, exorcism, numerology, the Tarot, ailurophilia, hypnotism, the cult of Ashtaroth and leprechauns. It was too early to get out their divining rods. Shoshana usually secured for herself a female companion on these walks, a witch or a fortune-teller, but today she walked alone, thinking of the Mix Cellini dilemma. After about ten minutes of this she decided she needed advice and she lingered until the end of the crocodile where the witch caught up with her.

The witch was an old crony and Shoshana, while naming no names, had no hesitation in presenting the problem to her.

'What do you think I should do, Hecate?'

The witch wasn't really called Hecate. The name in which her Catholic parents had had her baptised was Helena. But Hecate had a more magical and sinister sound and it always impressed her better-educated clients who understood its derivations.

'I could make you up a spell,' she said, 'at a discount, of course. I've got a new one that gives the object psoriasis.'

'That sounds nice but since I've got these two leads sort of ready-made I don't like to waste them. I mean, I don't like to waste both of them.'

'I see what you mean,' said Hecate. 'Look, we'll

be over the underground stream in a minute. Why don't you leave it with me and I'll give you my answer by Monday.'

'Well, don't be any longer than you can help. I don't want the trail going cold.'

'I'll e-mail it by Monday morning without fail,' said Hecate.

The flat was bigger than Nerissa had expected and very tidy. Her own house could sometimes look like those interiors pictured in the magazines she read at the dentist's, but only after Lynette had been there for three or four hours and then not for long. Through the open dining room door she glimpsed a carefully laid table, set with eight places of course but with flowers too and candles. No boyfriend of hers had ever entertained in his own home in this fashion. They had all been well-off, some of them very rich, but when she had gone back with them their houses or flats had been as messy as hers and though there was an abundance of drink, cigarettes and other aids to changing consciousness, she had never seen a laid table or even food on a tray. But Darel, she reminded herself sadly, wasn't her boyfriend or likely to be.

He was a gracious host. Nerissa was used to men singling her out and being particularly nice to her but she had always wondered about this, knowing that if she had been plain and unknown she would have been largely ignored. And the fact that Darel treated her and her mother and his mother and Andrew's wife in exactly the same way, politely and attentively, far from irritating her made her feel that this was how things ought to be in society in general. But she did notice that when he was on the other side of the room, replenishing drinks or checking on the dinner it appeared he was cooking himself, he caught her eye rather often and always smiled at her. When she arrived too, although he had paid her no compliments, she was conscious as he took her coat that the look he gave her was unmistakably admiring of her appearance, her piled-up hair and the sleek red-gold dress she wore. She resolved that tonight she would forget her stringent discipline in the matter of diet and eat everything she was offered. She would do justice to his cooking.

Music was playing, but very softly. It was the classical kind which she always said she didn't understand, but she liked this. It was gentle and sweet with no underlying harsh beat. Apart from gatherings at her parents' house, this was the first party she had ever been to where no one drank too much, no one disappeared into a bedroom with a stranger, the conversation wasn't smart and malicious and the language never degenerated into obscenity. It should therefore have been dull but it wasn't. Nor did the subjects discussed centre on domesticity and the property market. Her brother and sister-in-law were both lawyers and they talked about cases which had recently come up in court. They moved on to the stock market, which Darel was as happy to talk about as he was about politics. Everyone had varying, but not ill-tempered, views on the Iraq war. Mr Jones was a head teacher with informed radical opinions on education. If Nerissa missed the gossip, she liked being asked what she thought, and she very much liked not being treated as the empty-headed model with only her looks and her money to recommend her. Just once she felt awkward and that was when Andrew mentioned a case in which he had been prosecuting and the defendant was a fortune-teller. Everyone present, though in a measured and civilised fashion, condemned fortune-telling as rubbish and astrology along with it. Darel was particularly scathing. Nerissa said nothing, unwilling to appear as the only one there who knew the names of the cards in the Tarot and had actually had her future told.

But she was puzzled as to why Darel had invited her. She couldn't think of a reason but she could see her visit as a prelude to something else. At the end of the evening there would surely be a follow-up. And then she'd try to make herself more into the sort of woman he'd like. She'd learn to be tidier and more methodical, she'd read more so that she could better understand what people like the Joneses were talking about and talk like they did herself. She'd buy some classical CDs and stop playing hip-hop and that song about the prettiest girl in town.

Her parents were the first to leave and Darel accompanied them to the front door. Nerissa had noticed that when the door was shut, nothing of what was said in the hallway could be heard by those in the living room. Only the sounds of Darel's calling goodbye and the closing of the front door were audible.

She let her brother and sister-in-law go, knowing she mustn't be the last to leave. Yet, oh how much she would have liked to be! She was in love with Darel Jones, knowing this quite clearly because she had never been in love before. He had never kissed her, never done more than shake hands with her, but she knew she wanted to spend the rest of her life with him. She was doomed, she thought, to thinking about him at every waking moment with no hope of her love being returned. But surely a little hope still remained?

Five minutes after her brother's departure, she got up to go, said a polite but not at all obsequious goodbye to Mr and Mrs Jones, and preceded Darel out of the room. His closing of the living room door behind him sent a shiver of anticipation down her spine. He fetched her coat, held it up for her, said, when she thought utter silence was to be maintained until their farewells, 'Have you had any more trouble from that guy who was following you?'

'Not really,' she said, and thought, why lie to him of all people? 'Well, yes, I have. Today. I won't go into it, it's a long story, but he spoke to me. Put his face up to mine actually, right up, and said things. Oh, nothing horrible, just compliments.'

'I see.' He was silent, thoughtful. 'Next time that happens, next time *anything* happens, will you call me? Here's my card with my mobile number. Will you do that?'

'But you're such a long way away.'

'Not that far and I'm a fast driver. Just call me. Especially at night. Don't hesitate after dark.'

'All right,' she said. 'Goodbye. Thank you for asking me, I've had a nice time.You're a very good cook.'

'Good-night, Nerissa.'

Shoshana looked at her e-mails before going to bed on Sunday night. Only one had come. It read:

Shoshana: On mature consideration I have decided phoning his Chief Executive your

257

wisest course. Teratomancy has revealed to me that this individual's name is Desmond Pearson. I have also made you up a spell which I am not risking on-line but sending by snail mail. It is a very effective one which cramps the object's spinal column and lasts up to one week, though it is renewable. Yours, in the shadows, Hecate.

Very satisfactory. First thing tomorrow morning – that is, at ten, the late hour at which these sort of people got in to work – she would phone Desmond Pearson and tell him Mix Cellini was breaking the rules by instituting a private contract with her and as soon as the spell arrived she would think of ways of administering it. She could always think of something, it was a gift she had.

# Chapter 20

The lodger might be in or he might be out. For once Gwendolen had no idea. She was too weak to bother, too sleepy to listen for his comings and goings. That nonsense this morning, young people behaving in an ungoverned way, as she never had, had taken it out of her. If they had all gone as soon as she was home, she was convinced she would by now have been feeling much better instead of as weak as a kitten. Talking of kittens, there had been a letter from Mr Singh among the few which had come for her, complaining that Otto had killed and eaten both his guinea fowl. Being a peaceable man, he wrote, he didn't intend to 'take the matter further'. He just wanted her to be aware of the 'predatory instincts and achievements' of her 'savage pet'. Meanwhile, he had purchased two geese which would be more than a match for the 'ornithophagous beast'. Gwendolen cared very little about guinea fowl or, come to that, Otto, but she grimly contrasted this excellently educated 'native', his use of polysyllabic words and his perfect spelling, with the illiterate English of the present generation. Even she wasn't entirely sure if 'ornithophagous' meant 'bird-eating'.

The rest of the post had been the electricity bill, the menu from a Vietnamese takeaway and an invitation to the opening of a new Bond Street store. Nothing from Stephen Reeves. Perhaps he was away on holiday. He had always gone away a lot and no doubt he hadn't changed. She would never forget, even after they were ultimately reunited she wouldn't forget, how he had been on his honeymoon while she waited and waited for him to come. Wherever he was now, he'd probably be coming back today or tomorrow.

The new orderliness in the kitchen, which she surveyed after she had had a sleep, made her cross. What business had those two to go about tidying her home? Now she wouldn't be able to find anything. All the tinned food was in one cupboard, all the brushes and dusters in another. Someone had washed the dusters, removing the encrusted grime of years which had comfortably transformed them from yellow to grey, grey to dark brown. Now they were more or less yellow again. She slammed the cupboard door in disgust. And what had become of all the things she kept in the washhouse?

The bulb in the overhead lamp had gone out. She wasn't climbing up to change that now, not in her state of health. Olive or Queenie could do it tomorrow. She looked for her torch which should have been in the fridge so that she could see it when she opened the fridge door and the light came on. The torch wasn't there and she had to hunt for it, finally discovering it on a cupboard shelf along with some can openers, a screwdriver and a box of shoe-cleaning equipment. Olive and Queenie and their tidiness mania again. In the half-dark she lifted the lid of the copper. It had formerly held a lot of clothes. Although just about past wearing, these would have come in useful for tearing up for washrags and plugging the sink, its original plug having perished years before. Olive and Queenie had very high-handedly disposed of the lot. She shone the beam of the torch inside, illuminating the depths.

What was that lying in the bottom? A mysterious object to Gwendolen's eyes. At first she saw it as a sling, the kind of weapon she remembered being taught in Sunday school that David had employed against Goliath, then surely as a garment. A kind of truss? It looked hardly strong enough to contain a hernia. Perhaps it was a body belt but if it was, it lacked anything in the nature of a purse. After several attempts, she succeeded in fishing it out by means of a pole with a hook on the end of it, originally intended for opening a skylight. She would show it to Olive or Queenie. The thing must belong to one of them.

Exhausted from her explorations, she went to bed and slept heavily till morning.

Off to spend Sunday with friends who had a house with a river frontage at Marlow, Nerissa left her house in Rodney's car ten minutes before Mix arrived on foot. He had read in a magazine that the thirties film star Ramon Novarro had kept his figure by walking a mile round Hollywood every day, holding his navel pressed as near as he could to his spine. Emulating him on the fairly long walk, surely a mile, from St Blaise Avenue down Ladbroke Grove and along Holland Park Avenue to Campden Hill Square, Mix was conscious of twinges in his back. They were nothing like the agony he had suffered the other night and he tried to ignore them.

Her car was parked outside. Good. He had been afraid he had started out too late and she'd have gone out. For about half an hour he hung about in the square, walking down and back again. The milk arrived and sat on the doorstep in the full sun. She must be counting on the breeze keeping the temperature down. He was wondering if she had already taken the newspaper in when it came and was deposited on the doormat beside the milk.

Someone would steal it and the milk as well. She'd thank him for ringing the doorbell and handing in the cartons and the enormous Sunday paper. It might even be possible for him not to hand but to carry them in for her. If he did that she'd be bound to ask him to stay for coffee. She'd probably be only half-dressed, in *déshabillé* as they said. He imagined her in a baby doll nightdress, barely covered by a diaphanous robe, and he marched up to the door and rang the bell.

No reply. He put his ear to the grille of the entryphone. Silence. He rang again. She wasn't in. She must have gone out on foot, running perhaps, or caught a train somewhere. He was bitterly disappointed. So near and yet so far, he said to himself, going back down the steps but still lingering in case she came back from her run.

No one went jogging for as long as two hours. He'd try again tomorrow. Then, walking back, he remembered that he'd better go in to work tomorrow and he remembered too that he'd never phoned head office to say he was ill on Friday, he hadn't phoned them at all. And he hadn't looked for messages on his mobile or checked his answerphone. Of course it wasn't important. If he couldn't take an afternoon off without crawling to management like a trainee after all the years of service, who could? He expected messages from at least one of the three clients he'd let down on Friday but, as it turned out, all three had phoned him, one disappointed and pleading, another furious and the third threatening to take her business else-where. Nothing from head office. Nothing from Jack Fleisch. He'd have been amazed if Mr Pearson bothered with him and there was nothing from him either. No doubt he had thought better of further reproaching such an asset to the firm as Mix was with his experience and his efficiency.

The day had as usual become very fine and warm. The Indian man's geese were grooming each other under a palm tree in the sunshine. It was the only tree in the garden Mix was able to identify and he recognised it from an illustration in his grandmother's bible. What had become of that bible he had no idea. But he remembered the pic-ture. The Indian man's palm looked as if it had been there for years and years, long before he and his wife came. Mix was surprised that it survived the winters, Notting Hill being a lot colder than Jerusalem. He had never noticed it till this morning. But he had never spent so much time watching the garden as he did now.

The two patches of freshly dug earth looked very obvious to him, the one where he had dug at first and where the heaviness of the soil defeated him, and the other that he had chosen for Danila's resting place. There was nothing to be done about it. He must wait for the weeds to grow back and he had no idea how long this would take. If only he'd had more time he would have dug deeper. It troubled him a little that her body lay only three feet down, less than three feet really, because although she was thin, a section through her at the ribcage would be several inches. Still, who was going to look?

Old Chawcer never went out there, or never had to his knowledge, and was even less likely to do so now. He had never seen Ma Winthrop or Ma Fordyce venture into the garden. The old man on the side with the conservatory never looked over the wall, as far as he could tell. The house on the other side was all flats but the basement or 'garden flat' had been empty all the time Mix had been there and he had heard that the damp made it impossible to live in. No one would be interested in two rectangular dug-over plots. Bodies buried in the earth, according to Dr Camps in *Medical and Scientific Investigations in the Christie Case*, became skeletons after a few months. Not that long. By next spring she would be just bones.

He had left her just as she was, naked and wrapped in the red sheet. The plastic bag he had slid off her, brought it back upstairs and carefully cut it up, depositing the small pieces in his rubbish sack for collection. Twice he had checked the copper to be sure nothing was left behind. It was dark in the washhouse and impossible to see to the bottom of the copper but he could tell there was no room for anything to be left behind . . .

A cold tremor passed through him. The thong. What had become of the thong? Now he remembered clearly feeling the bulge of it in his pocket and dropping it into the copper after he had heaved the body in. He had never retrieved it, of that he was sure. It must still be there. What does it matter, he thought, no one will look in there, she hadn't lifted that lid for years, probably never will again. Besides, he could go down and get it, almost whenever he liked. Now if he wanted. He was nearly certain she had still been in bed when he came back from his walk to Campden Hill and even when she got up, she'd take herself straight to that sofa in the drawing room.

He pocketed his keys and came out on to the landing. Bright sunshine streamed through the window above the stairs, so of course Reggie's ghost was hiding itself away in some dark corner. As he started down the tiled staircase he heard the front door open and close and a voice, unmistakably belonging to Ma Fordyce, called out, 'Hiya, Gwen! You still in the land of the living?'

Old fool. Now he'd have to wait for her to leave again and that might not be for hours.

Hoping she wouldn't have to climb all those stairs, Olive went straight into the drawing room, still carrying the two bags of food she had bought on the way. She was wearing her new black trousers and a lemon-coloured linen jacket which matched her new hair tint. To her relief Gwendolen was up, though still in her nightclothes and lying on the sofa.

'I've brought you some goodies, dear.'

'*Timeo Danaos et dona ferentes,*' said Gwendolen.

'I don't know any Tim, Gwen,' said Olive with a hearty laugh, 'and I can't understand a word of that lingo. How are you?'

'As well as can be expected. I've no appetite so you needn't have bothered with goodies, as you call them.'

'Don't be such an old curmudgeon. I'm trying

265

to help. I'm going to make us a coffee each, won't be long.'

While she was gone Gwendolen investigated the carrier bags. Chocolate – well, she could eat that – biscuits, marzipan fruits, a nasty sponge cake with mock cream. Still, Olive hadn't done badly. At least there wasn't a lot of salad stuff and green apples with no taste to them.

Olive reappeared with milky coffee and ginger nuts on a plate. 'You're so thin you can eat as much as you like. Aren't you lucky?'

'You don't mean you're dieting. At your age?'

'I always say you're never too old to take pride in your appearance.'

'On the subject of appearance, is this yours?'

The object that was put into Olive's hands made her giggle. 'Are you joking, Gwen? Is this some sort of game?'

'I found it in the bottom of *my* copper, in *my* washhouse. Is it yours and what is it?'

'Well, Gwen, you've never been married and I knew you were innocent about a lot of things but I didn't know it went that far.' So Olive took her revenge for years of rudeness and ingratitude. 'Even a child would know what that is.'

'Thank you. You've said quite enough. Now perhaps you'll tell me what it is.'

This caused Olive some embarrassment which she tried not to show. 'Well, it's a – it's a kind of pair of – well, knickers. Girls wear them. Once I'd have said only that sort of girl but things have changed, haven't they? Now even nice girls, I mean, not actresses or – well, stripteasers, if you know what I mean.'

'Oh, I know what you mean. In spite of my

profound naïvety and resemblance to a retarded child . . .'

'I didn't say that, Gwen.' Though not a slave to political correctness, Olive shuddered at some of the things that snapped off Gwendolen's tongue.

'No? I think you did. In spite of all my cerebral deficiencies, I do just about know what you mean. Don't, please don't, tell me it's yours.'

Olive was really incensed by now. 'Of course it isn't mine. Do you suppose that would go round my hips even if I was so – so . . .'

'Meretricious? Licentious? Concupiscent? Vain?'

'Oh, I've no patience. If you weren't unwell and didn't know what you're saying I'd be really cross.'

At last Gwendolen saw that she had gone too far. Sustaining this kind of altercation took more energy than she was capable of today. She drank her coffee which, she had to admit (though not aloud), was very good. 'Do you suppose it could be Queenie's?'

'Of course not. This has been worn by some *young* woman. A girl of twenty.'

Nerissa immediately came into Gwendolen's mind and along with her, the lodger, Cellini. The minute she arrived home, he had been coming out of her kitchen. Why? He had a kitchen of his own. 'Did you or Queenie put my bag of old clothes on top of the copper?'

'Certainly not. I found a bag of clothes in the washhouse and I left them there. Very musty and smelly they were, but there – it's not my business.'

'No, indeed.' After that, Gwendolen decided to be gracious. 'It was very kind of you to buy me the chocolate and those other things. What do I owe you?'

'Nothing, Gwen. Don't be absurd. If you want my opinion and I dare say you don't, that Mr Cellini had a girl here while you were in hospital and they were larking about where they shouldn't have been. People these days – well, I don't like talking about these things – but they do – well, have baths together, and it's just possible . . . You see, you could *stand up* in a copper which you can't in an ordinary bath.'

'I've no idea what you mean,' said Gwendolen. 'I need something lighter than Darwin to read. Before you go, would you see if you can find *The Golden Bowl*? Henry James, you know.'

He watched Ma Fordyce leave and once he had seen her disappear round the corner, he went downstairs, careful to tread softly. The drawing room door was open and on the sofa he saw old Chawcer lying on her back, asleep with her mouth open. Always one to notice domestic order and its reverse, he observed that the kitchen was fast reverting to its normal chaos. The old girl had only been home twenty-four hours.

Confident he would find the thong where he had left it, he tiptoed into the washhouse and lifted the lid of the copper. Of course it was impossible to see down to the bottom of it. How did women ever get the water out of there? Perhaps they didn't. Perhaps there was always some lingering, stagnant and smelly, in the depths. There must be a torch somewhere. Nearly sure he'd once seen her with a torch in her hand, he padded round the kitchen, looking into cupboards and opening drawers. No torch but he did find a candle and a box of matches. Afraid she'd hear the match striking, he waited and listened, holding the lit candle in his hand. Once he was sure she wasn't dragging herself off the sofa to come and find him, he put the hand holding the candle as far as he could down the deep well of the copper. The light was quite adequate to show him walls and a base apparently made of some sort of bluish pottery – and nothing else. Nothing. No thong. The copper was empty.

Still he held the candle there as if continuing to light the hollow space would ultimately reveal that it wasn't as empty as he'd thought at first. He stared down, closing his eyes and opening them again until a drop of boiling wax fell on his thumb, making him jump back and very nearly cry out. Instead he cursed under his breath, pinched out the flame and put candle and matches back where he had found them. He walked back slowly, passing the drawing room door. Old Chawcer was still asleep. Had she found the thong? Or was it one of the other two? It seemed to him that they must immediately have known it had belonged to the missing girl whose picture appeared almost daily in the papers. Only today there had been a bold headline: HAVE YOU SEEN DANILA?

Upstairs in his own flat, he asked himself if he should do anything. Ask old Chawcer or ask one of the others? But he was very alive to the awkwardness of it. How to explain what he was doing in the washhouse, why he was even touching the copper? They would want to know who the thong belonged to. He couldn't think of any explanation except the true one for how the thong got where it was. Perhaps they wouldn't ask. Mix had very little idea of how other people might react to his own activities or whether they might think things he regarded as normal and ordinary as quite different from that. But he had some small inkling through remarks made by the three elderly women that an older, a much older, generation than his own might be embarrassed by a garment so blatantly sexual as a G-string. If only they were, they might not mention it, they might prefer to pretend they had never found it, might throw it away in disgust or shock. You wish, he said to himself, but he began to think there was a possibility of this.

While she was still asleep, he went into her bedroom and examined the bottles and packets she had brought back from the hospital and left on her bedside table. Among them was a jar with a label on its side which said: *Two to be taken at night to promote sleep.* Certain she wouldn't have counted them, he helped himself to eight. If he needed more after four nights he could always come back. Instead of two, he took three and slept heavily for three hours. After that he was wide awake and passed the rest of the night uneasily.

He kept thinking of arguments against his optimistic theory of the three (or one or two) of the old women disposing of the thong. Suppose Ma Fordyce, say, had read all that stuff about Danila working in what the papers called a 'beauty salon and gym', suppose she knew very well what the thong was and decided a girl from a place like that would be more than likely to wear a thong – suppose all that and then would she go to the police? Easy to say, as he had in the bright light of afternoon, that this was a crazy far-fetched idea. In the small hours it seemed reasonable.

He had to see the Holland Park woman at nine-thirty and he was twenty minutes late. She was too pleased he had come at all to reproach him for failing to be there on time. On his way down to Chelsea he checked his calls and was quite surprised to see a message from Mr Pearson's PA. Would he call to arrange an urgent meeting with the Chief Executive? This gave Mix a cold feeling but one quite unlike the tremor that had lurched through him when he remembered the missing thong. Surely Pearson wasn't all that concerned about a few missed appointments. He was very polite to the man in Chelsea and showed him how to adjust the belt on his treadmill himself, providing the weakling was strong enough to wield a spanner. For all his working out, he still had the muscle development of an anorexic girl. Since his exploits with pick and spade, Mix had begun to pride himself on his physical strength.

Not anxious to appear in too much of a hurry, he fitted a new belt to a machine in Primrose Hill before phoning Mr Pearson's PA. She was a chilly young woman with an inflated idea of her own importance.

'You took your time,' she said. 'There's not much point in leaving you people messages if you never check them.'

'What time does he want to see me?'

'Immediately. Like twelve-thirty.'

'For God's sake, it's a quarter-past now.'

'Then you'd better get on your bike, hadn't you?' She suddenly became almost human, if in a nasty way. 'He's livid, incandescent. I wouldn't want to be in your shoes.'

Mix got on his bike, or rather, drove as fast as

the traffic allowed down the Outer Circle and Baker Street. It was still nearly twelve-forty-five when the PA showed him into Mr Pearson's office. Pearson was the only person Mix had ever come across who called people, in this case his staff, by their surnames alone. He associated such usage with what he knew of the army, men in prison or up in court, and he didn't like it.

'Well, Cellini?'

What kind of response was he supposed to make to that?

'No answer was the stern reply,' said Pearson, laughing at his feeble joke. He added as if it were an afterthought, 'We're going to have to let you go.'

# Chapter 21

From her sofa in the drawing room Gwendolen saw the postman come. She saw him walking up the path and heard the clatter of the letterbox as he dropped Stephen Reeves's letter on the mat. Already feeling stronger, she got herself off the sofa without too much strain and went to the front door for the letter. It wasn't from Stephen but from a charity appealing for funds to research cystic fibrosis. Her disappointment quickly gave way to reason. If he was away on holiday he wouldn't have come back until Saturday or Sunday, so could hardly have got a letter to her by today.

She was hardly back on the sofa, thinking that in an hour or so she would go upstairs and have a bath, when Queenie arrived. Queenie refused to burden herself with bags and had brought her offerings in a shopping trolley.

'What an enormous appetite you and Olive must think I have,' said Gwendolen. She examined the packet of Duchy Originals, the bag of marshmallows, the two tubes of Rolos, the dairy-free yoghurts and the pack of couscous salad without enthusiasm. 'Perhaps you'll put it all in the fridge. Oh, and –' as Queenie went '– please don't mislay the torch *again*.'

Queenie wondered what eccentric quirk or

whim would make anyone keep a torch in a fridge but she didn't move it and, coming back, sat meekly in a chair opposite Gwendolen. The weather being so unseasonably warm, she had put on her new pink suit and though she knew such a happening unlikely, she had been hoping for her friend to compliment her on her appearance. Instead she was shown a red and black pouch thing on a kind of narrow belt which, without ever having seen anything like it before, she immediately knew to be part of the costume (if you could call it that) of a certain kind of dancer. The realisation made her flush darkly.

'I suppose you know what it is and that's what you're blushing about.'

'Of course I know what it is, Gwen.'

She had spoken as she always did, very mildly, but Gwendolen chose to see it as recalcitrance. 'All right, no need to bite my head off. Olive thinks it may be the property of a – er, paramour of Mr Cellini's.'

'Does it matter, dear? It doesn't look as if it cost very much.'

'I don't like these mysteries,' said Gwendolen. 'It means he or she or both of them have been in my washhouse.'

'You could ask him.'

'I intend to. Of course he's out at present, doing whatever it is he does.' Gwendolen sighed. 'I think I shall have a bath in a minute.'

This was a hint to her friend to leave but Queenie took it differently. 'Would you like me to help you, dear? I shouldn't mind at all. I bathed my dear husband every day when he was so ill.'

Gwendolen contrived a stagy shudder. 'No,

thank you very much. I can manage perfectly. By the way,' she said, though it wasn't by any way, 'that Indian has written to me that Otto has eaten his guinea fowl.' Temporarily forgetting Mr Singh's prose prowess, she said, 'Of course no decent English person would break the law by keeping what amounts to chickens in urban surroundings, virtually in the middle of London.'

Very little roused Queenie, but as a voluntary worker for the Commission for Racial Equality, she could become irate when discriminatory remarks were made. 'You know, Gwendolen, or perhaps you don't know, that if you said something like that in public you could be prosecuted. You're actually committing an offence.' She added in a less haughty tone, 'Mr Singh is a lovely man. He's very clever, he was a professor in the Punjab.'

Gwendolen burst out laughing. 'How ridiculous you are, Queenie. You should hear yourself. And now I'm going to have my bath, so you'd better run away.'

On the way out Queenie met Otto in the hallway. He was sitting on the stairs near the bottom, part of a mouse gripped in his jaws, its head lying beside him on the worn carpet. 'Go away, you horror,' she said to him.

Otto gave her the sort of look that made Queenie very glad she was quite a large human being instead of small, four-legged and covered in fur. He managed to pick up the mouse's head as well as its hind quarters and streaked towards the first floor with his burden. Mix coming in the front door at that moment muttered something incomprehensible to Queenie and followed the cat upstairs.

Mr Pearson had insisted he continue working

through the week, though Mix would have liked to leave then and there. As for working out four weeks' notice . . . ! They'd pay him till the end of next month, that was something. Of course it hadn't been the missed appointments and failed calls which had made Pearson sack him but a call he'd had only that morning from that old bitch Shoshana. Mounting the tiled flight, Mix thought self-pityingly that nothing but trouble had come to him from his association with Shoshana's Spa. He had gone there in the first place only in the hope it would introduce him to Nerissa but he had got to know her anyway, she was almost his friend now, and through his own determination not through any help from the spa. That had simply brought him an association with Danila, who had so insulted and provoked him that he'd had to react violently against her. Frankly, she'd forced him to kill her. He'd agreed to produce and sign that contract, again because of Danila, and now the result of it was that Shoshana had called Pearson and told him about it and then had the nerve to allege he'd never carried out his part of it. The spite, the malevolence, took his breath away. What had he ever done to her? Nothing but fail to restore two pieces of equipment, not because he hadn't seen to them and told her what was wrong but because he hadn't yet been able to get the parts. He went into the flat and took a Diet Coke out of the fridge. When he had peeled back the cover and opened the hole in the lid, he drank about an inch of it and filled the can up with gin. That was better. Of course he'd have to get another job. That meant the Job Centre and probably drawing benefit for a while. The DSS would pay his rent, thank God. It was time he got something out of the Government, it was his right, he'd paid enough in. Of course it wasn't just Shoshana's treachery that had stitched him up, it was Ed too, going to head office instead of keeping quiet for a few days when Mix hadn't made those two calls for him. That was what started it.

One thing Pearson could be sure of. He'd take with him as many of his clients as he could persuade to come. He'd undercut his old firm – why shouldn't he set up in business on his own? This might be the making of him. He drank some more of the gin and Coke mixture. Everyone knew how much better it was to be self-employed than an employee. A fantasy began forming in Mix's mind of himself as founder and boss of the largest exercise equipment and gym fittings company in the country, a mega-conglomerate which took over Tunturi and PJ Fitness and of course Multifit. He pictured the joy of sitting at his huge ebony desk in his glass-walled thirtieth-floor office, two glamorous secretaries in micro-skirts in the anteroom, and Pearson coming to him cap in hand to beg a small pension for his enforced early retirement . . .

Meanwhile, freedom lay before him. He'd use the time in cementing his friendship with Nerissa. Maybe think of some other reason to call on her and get inside the house. Suppose he delivered a parcel to her? It wouldn't have to be real, it wouldn't have had to come from a mail order company or be something she'd ordered from a shop, it could be just old magazines wrapped up in brown paper. She'd understand once it had got him inside and she'd talked to him properly. Or he could pretend to be peddling election campaign literature, take her some candidate's manifesto that had been delivered first to him. There must be a local election coming up next month, there always was, wasn't there? Anyway, she wouldn't know any more than he did.

Once he was taking her about, getting in the public eye, the offers from TV and newspaper editors and fashion mags would start coming in. He might not even need to set up in business on his own. Or if he did, the money he got from being Nerissa's squeeze would get him off to a flying start. Dreaming on, he paused to congratulate himself on his resilience, how rapidly he was recovering from losing his job, what those supposed to know called one of life's major setbacks, comparable to bereavement.

Next day, though, he had to work. His head was banging from the gin and sometimes it swam so that he nearly fell, but he had to work. Every call he made he told the client he had resigned and would be setting up in business on his own. If they would consider staying with him he would make a special charge for them, less than they had been paying, and they would be assured of top-quality service. Three said they would remain where they were but the fourth agreed to come with him, after telling him he looked pale and asking him if he was all right. At head office he ran into Ed who told him Steph was pregnant, so they had decided to postpone the wedding until after the baby was born.

'Steph says she doesn't fancy looking fat on her wedding day. Her mum thinks people will say we only got married because she was pregnant.'

'I've resigned,' said Mix.

'So I heard.'

Ed's expression told him that what he'd heard was a different version of events. 'You telling management I'd let you down, which was an exaggeration to say the least, made it impossible for me to stay.'

'Oh, yes? What do you reckon you did then? Acted like a mate? Stood in for me when I was sick?'

'Why don't you fuck off?' said Mix.

That was the end of a beautiful friendship. He couldn't care less. He thought of driving up to the spa and having it out with Shoshana. But he ought to remember the spa was number thirteen, a fact which might be at the root of all his troubles. And when he thought about it, about that darkened room with the draperies and the figures, the wizard and the owl, and above all of Shoshana herself, dealing as it seemed to him in love and death, he realised he was afraid of her. Not that he put it like that even in that part of his mind which talked to itself, advising, warning and resolving. There, he said he should be cautious. It was one thing her getting on the phone and spreading slanders about him; he was more wary of darker deeds, the kind of thing witches used to do – spells cast, demons raised. All rubbish of course, but he'd once thought ghosts rubbish and now he lived with one.

By Saturday he'd have more time, all the time in the world, and that was when he'd begin his real efforts to see Nerissa. Meanwhile he'd plan what his campaign was going to be.

A cosmetic company with a fast-expanding line in make-up for black women had asked Nerissa to be their 'Face of 2004'. This year they had used a famous white model and Nerissa would be the first black woman for this sort of role. The money was mind-blowing, the work minimal. Visiting their

Mayfair salon for preliminary tests, she wondered why she wasn't feeling a greater thrill. But she didn't wonder for long. She knew.

Darel Jones had made it plain he wanted her for a friend only, someone to protect perhaps, a mate, a standby to make up the numbers at dinner. Her mother said a man and a woman can't be friends, they have to be lovers or nothing. Nerissa knew differently. Perhaps what her mother said had been true when she was young. It wasn't true now that women had careers and approached nearer to equality. She knew men who weren't gay but who had a woman friend they were at school or university with and were close to for years without ever even exchanging a kiss. Was that how it was going to be for her and Darel?

Not if she could help it. Sometimes she felt positive, at other times like she did now, rather despondent, with nothing to distract her from the certainty that what she wanted more than anything in the world, that he should fall in love with her, would never happen. The man Cellini hadn't shown himself outside her house since she had seen him on Saturday. Seeing him was the last thing she wanted but, on the other hand, if he showed up in his car and waited for her to appear, it would be an excuse for calling Darel.

She wandered about her house, newly cleaned and tidied by Lynette, and resolved to try and keep it that way. She ought not to be so messy, Mum was always saying so, saying she had been brought up to be neat and this was the result of too much money too soon. Darel's flat was a miracle of order. It wouldn't always be like that, she thought, picking up a tissue she had dropped on the bathroom floor, no doubt he had made it specially tidy for his guests but he was obviously a well-disciplined man. In the unlikely event of his coming here – and with each day that passed it seemed to become less probable – he would be put off her by all the cups and glasses which habitually stood around, the magazines dumped on the floor and absurd combinations like a bottle of nail varnish in the fruit bowl. She was as bad as old Miss Chawcer who, Aunty Olive said, kept a torch in the fridge and bread in a bag on the floor.

On Friday afternoon, Dad once more having the Akwaas' car, she had promised to drive her mother to St Blaise House. Hazel said it would be polite for her to call on Miss Chawcer, ask how she was and if there was anything she could do. Miss Chawcer was so very old and frail, she had been ill and must really be quite helpless.

'Oh, Mum, don't ask me. *He* lives there. Can't Andrew do it?'

'Andrew will be in court in Cambridge. You needn't come in, Nerissa, just drop me.'

So Nerissa had said she would. She'd drop her mother and come back for her after an hour. After all, if she did see the man, or the man saw her and came out to speak to her, she could call Darel on her car-phone. She dressed carefully, mistress as she was of the smart-casual look, in new olive drab combat trousers, a low-cut top and satin jacket. But when she was ready she realised that the clothes designed to attract Darel would also be attractive to the man, so she took them all off and got back into her jeans and T-shirt. Besides, though this was inimical to everything she worked to attain and to everything those she worked for took as gospel, she believed men never noticed what a woman wore, only that she 'looked good' or did not.

It would be just her luck when she had no time to spare to find the man waiting outside, but no one was there. Campden Hill Square lay deserted and silent, sizzling in the heat which continued into September. Her car had been standing in the sun and the driver's seat was almost hot enough to burn her. She picked up her mother from Acton and drove down to St Blaise Avenue, dropping her off outside Miss Chawcer's house. There was no sign of the man, nor did she meet him driving to Tesco in West Kensington where she did her week's shopping, buying as well as a quantity of sparkling water, a lot of salad stuff and some fish, two bottles of a very good Pinot Grigio because she had noticed that this was what Darel drank.

The spell which disabled its victim's spinal column came by second-class post. Hecate had always been as mean as hell. Shoshana had expected some potion or powder, which would have meant she had to think up a way of administering it and virtually eliminated anyone she had no easy access to, but this was only incantations over a smoking mixture in a crucible. As far as Shoshana could see, the spell might as well have been sent by e-mail. On the other hand, it was miles long and Hecate was too cheeseparing to get herself a scanner.

'I may as well give it a go,' Shoshana said to the wizard and the owl. Who better to try it out on than Mix Cellini?

Gwendolen had graduated from the sofa and was sitting in an armchair, well into the last chapter of

*The Golden Bowl*, the thong in a brown paper bag on her lap, ready to show to the lodger. Hazel had let herself in with her aunt's key and though Gwendolen didn't jump or look as if she was about to have a heart attack, she seemed less than pleased to see her.

She didn't quite ask her visitor what she was doing here. 'I must get those keys back. I suppose your aunt had another one cut. Without asking me of course.'

'How are you?'

'Oh, I'm much better, my dear.' Gwendolen was softening. She put the book down with the letter from the cystic fibrosis charity to mark the place. 'What have you got there?' Seedless white grapes, William pears, Ferrero-Rocher chocolates and a bottle of Merlot. Gwendolen was less disapproving than usual. She never ate any fruit except stewed apples but she would enjoy the chocolates and the wine. 'I see you're more discerning than your aunt and her friend.'

Hazel didn't know what to say. She had realised she was going to find conversation difficult with this elderly lady whom once, long ago, her own father would have called a bluestocking. Hazel didn't read much and was aware she couldn't talk about books or any of the things that probably interested Miss Chawcer. She was struggling to comment on the weather, the improvement in Miss Chawcer's health and the beauty of her house when the doorbell rang.

'Who on earth can that be?'

'Do you want to see anyone or shall I say to come back another time?'

'Just get rid of them,' said Gwendolen. 'Say what you like.'

It might be a letter from Stephen Reeves come by special delivery. Gwendolen hadn't yet heard from him and she was growing quite anxious. Suppose the letter had gone astray? Hazel went to the door. A man of about sixty, tall and handsome and wearing a turban, stood on the doorstep. To Hazel's eyes he looked very like a Pathan warrior she had once seen in a film about the North-West Frontier.

'Good afternoon, madam. Mr Singh from St Mark's Road to see Miss Chawcer, please.'

'I'm afraid Miss Chawcer hasn't been well. She's been in hospital. Could you possibly come back tomorrow? Well, not tomorrow. Say Sunday?'

'Certainly I say Sunday, madam. I return 11 a.m.'

'What did he want?' Gwendolen asked.

'I didn't ask. Should I have?'

'It doesn't matter. I know, anyway. It's about his wretched guinea fowl. Otto must have eaten them. I found feathers on the stairs. Now I expect this man wants compensation.'

Hazel was beginning to think this a very strange household, what with this old bluestocking and the stalker upstairs and now a person with a German name who ate the neighbours' poultry. She began to look forward to Nerissa's return and was relieved when the doorbell rang.

'Who is it this time? I can't think why I've suddenly become so popular.'

'It's my daughter.'

'Ah.' Gwendolen inevitably associated the daughter, and would associate her for the rest of the life which remained to her, with uncontrolled amorous behaviour in her hallway. 'I don't suppose she will want to come in.'

Hazel saw this as an unprovoked put-down and

was very glad to be leaving. Why had Aunty Olive never told her what an old horror Miss Chawcer was? She said a cool goodbye and rushed out to Nerissa, who was waiting on the doorstep in a fever of nerves in case the man suddenly appeared.

Gwendolen fell asleep as soon as she was gone. Since her illness she was finding a rest in the afternoon wasn't good enough; she needed to sleep. Dreaming she didn't need but the dream came to her, sharper and more vivid than any night-time episode, apparently real and happening in the present. She was young, as she always was in dreams, and visiting Christie in Rillington Place. The war was on, the only one she ever thought of as 'the war', discounting conflicts in Korea and Suez and the Falklands and Bosnia and the Persian Gulf. Sirens were sounding as she knocked on Christie's door, for in the dream which seemed real it was she who was pregnant and she who was going to him for an abortion. Only, like Bertha, but there was no Bertha in this reality, she was afraid of the man and his instructions and she fled, determined not to go back. When she came out, as is the way with dreams, instead of in Rillington Place she was with Stephen Reeves in the drawing room at St Blaise House and he was telling her he was the father of her child. It was a shock to her, a surprise and a relief. She thought then he would ask her to marry him but the scene shifted again. She was alone in Ladbroke Grove, standing outside his surgery in the sudden dusk, and he was nowhere to be seen. She was running this way and that, looking for him, when she fell over, banged her head and woke up.

Such daylight dreams take longer to recover

from than any nightmare met with in the hours of darkness. For a moment or two she lay in the armchair, wondering where he was and when he would come back. She even looked at her hands and marvelled that at her young age they were so wrinkled, the branching veins standing out like tree roots in dry soil. Gradually, a reality which was welcome yet unwelcome came back and she sat up.

While she slept and perhaps while she was talking to Hazel Akwaa, the brown paper bag containing the thong had slipped down between the seat cushion and the arm of the armchair. Wide awake now, she had forgotten it was there.

# Chapter 22

Mix left the company for which he had worked for nine years more with a whimper than a bang. He felt very sore because no one had suggested buying him a drink, still less had anyone presented him with a clock or a dinner service and no noises had been made about redundancy money. Worst of all he had to hand over the keys to the car which he had left in the firm's underground car park.

But he comforted himself with the thought that he had secured undertakings from five of his clients that they would continue using him to service and repair their machines. Inquiring of a cash dispenser as to the state of his bank balance, he had been informed he was nearly five hundred pounds in credit. And that was before the sum went in which the firm owed him for the three weeks they didn't want him to work. Still he lacked the heart to go back to Campden Hill Square. When he did make it down there he'd have no choice but to go on foot. At any rate, the walk would do him good.

On the Friday he went to the cinema on his own, passing on the way home pubs whose clientele spilled out on to the pavements and cafés where diners sat at tables outside. He bought Chinese takeaway for his supper, two bottles of wine and a bottle of Cointreau for the making of Boot Camps.

The weather was as hot as it had been in July and as dry. One afternoon it had rained heavily, the first rain for weeks, and while he watched it he relished the thought of all that water encouraging weeds to grow on the garden grave.

Going home was always an ordeal but less so if he could organise things so as to get back in daylight. That would soon be difficult with darkness coming earlier and earlier. Carrying his heavy bags, he kept his eyes fixed straight ahead as he climbed the last flight of stairs, gazing hypnotically at his own front door. Something had gone wrong with the street lamp immediately outside the house so that no light fell through the Isabella window. The top landing was pitch dark but once inside his flat he was all right. He was safe. And his back didn't hurt any more. He must be pretty fit to have got over a back injury so fast.

He read *Killer Extraordinary*, watched television to the accompaniment of a Boot Camp, ate his takeaway and listened to the singing and sighing of the Westway. If the police were going to question him about Danila they would have done it by now. Possibly, after years, after old Chawcer was dead which might be ages away, someone would buy the house and dig up the garden. They wouldn't dig down four feet, would they? By then he'd be long gone and far away from this haunted house. Living with Nerissa, married to Nerissa, and maybe they'd buy a place in France or even Greece. Even if they found Danila's body they'd never connect it with Nerissa Nash's husband, the famous criminologist.

Backache woke him in the small hours. It was so bad that he groaned aloud, put the light on and saw it was ten past three. Just his luck when he'd been congratulating himself on his total recovery. This felt the way they said it did when you slipped a disc. Four ibuprofen and a cup of neat gin sent him off to sleep again but he woke at seven. No chance of beginning on his exercise regimen, as he had intended to do today. The backache felt as if it was there to stay and it was far worse than the last time. It seemed to affect the whole length of his spine.

A hot bath and two more ibuprofen helped, though he was left feeling rather dizzy. He took the bus along Westbourne Grove and got off at the Portobello Market, for food had to be bought. The market was always crowded, particularly around the stalls, but Saturdays you could only move by becoming part of the throng and going where it took you. He bought takeaway and a roast chicken, bread and cakes, his only concession to what the papers called 'healthy food' a bunch of bananas. Any more and he wouldn't be able to carry it, not with his back in agony like this.

In a half-hearted attempt to scan the ads for a job to tide him over until he'd established his own business, he bought an *Evening Standard* and walked down to Notting Hill high street to find a pharmacist. More ibuprofen was needed if sleep were not to be a problem and he'd better get something to rub on his back. Outside the big Boots a man was begging. He was sitting on the pavement with an open biscuit tin in front of him, but no dog to win sentimental hearts and no sign proclaiming that he was blind or homeless or had five children. Mix never gave money to beggars and there were already twenty or so coins in the box but something made him look at the man, a sense of familiarity, perhaps a kind of chemistry between them. He found himself staring into the face of Reggie Christie. It was him to the life, the clear-cut jaw, the narrow lips, the big nose and the glasses over cold eyes.

Mix went quickly into Boots and bought his analgesic. If there had been another way out he would have taken it but he had to go back into the high street. The beggar had gone. Mix crossed the road to wait for a bus that would take him home. There was no sign anywhere of Reggie. Had he really been there? Had his own mind invented him as a result of thinking of him so much and of looking at those pictures? And was it the result of stress? The horrible idea that Reggie's ghost had followed him down here or had come down, expecting to see him, was too frightening to think of.

Gwendolen had looked everywhere for the object she had come to call 'the thing', 'thong' being a word she associated with sandals. Supposing she must have put it in 'a safe place', she investigated, among many other possibilities, the oven and the space behind the dictionaries in one of the numerous bookcases. She even unzipped the stomach of the toy spaniel nightdress case her mother had given her for her twenty-fifth birthday. It wasn't in any of these potential hiding places. She was irritable with frustration. How could she take the lodger to task without the thing to prove her case?

No letter had come from Stephen Reeves. She was sure now that he had written to her but the letter had gone astray. It was the only explanation. Before she wrote again she would talk to the lodger. What more likely than that he had taken her letter, either by mistake or with malice? She was beginning to think that many of her present problems stemmed from Cellini. Mysteries and misfortunes had seldom come her way before he moved in. He had probably infected her with the germ which brought on her pneumonia

She meant to catch him when she heard him come down the stairs preparatory to going out. Or when he entered the house. Her difficulty was that since her illness she fell asleep far more easily than she used to do and she was afraid she must have dozed off when last he came in or left the house. Climbing all fifty-two stairs to his flat was too much for her at present, though she would have admitted this to no one. Nor would she have told Olive or Queenie that making her way up to her bedroom and getting ready for bed exhausted her so enormously that she barely had the strength to wash her face and hands.

No doubt the lodger did enter the house at some time in the late morning. She was almost sure she heard his footsteps mounting the stairs. Would he come down again? She doubted she could tell for she fell into catnaps throughout the afternoon. Olive came in at about five but she didn't offer to go up and see if he was at home. She wasn't weak from illness, Gwendolen thought scornfully, but far too fat.

'You could phone him.'

Gwendolen was shocked. 'Make a telephone call to someone living in the same house! *O tempora, o mores.*'

'I don't know what that means, dear. You'll have to speak English.'

'It means, O times, O customs. That was my

reaction when you suggested phoning an individual who lives upstairs.'

Olive decided Gwendolen must be exhausted to speak in that ridiculous way, and offered to make 'your evening meal, Gwen'. Her friend's adamant refusal had no effect. She had brought all the materials for a meal with her.

'Not "meal", Olive,' Gwendolen said feebly. 'Please not "meal". Dinner – or supper if you must.'

The moment Olive had gone she prepared to go to bed. It took her an hour to get up there and into her nightgown. The house was silent, more silent than usual it seemed to her, and not at all warm. The forecast on her wireless had said it would be a fine day, the temperature in the high twenties, whatever that meant, and the night exceptionally mild for the time of year. The wind was supposed to be westerly and therefore warm, but it felt cold to her as it penetrated ill-fitting windows and plaster cracks. There were two windows in her bedroom, but from the front one she could see nothing but darkness and grey branches. The street lamp had gone out, its glass broken, probably by the thugs with bottles who roamed the street. Down in the garden, seen from the other window, the shrubs bent and twisted in the wind and the tree branches swayed this way and that.

Earlier she had heard Mr Singh's geese cackling but now they were quiet, shut up for the night. There was nothing alive in the windswept garden but Otto sitting on the wall, eating something he had caught himself. From the window in the darkness, glazed by yellow light, Gwendolen could just see or divine that he was making his supper off the pigeon which roosted in the sycamore. She wrapped a thick wool cardigan about her shoulders, went to bed and fell asleep before she had pulled the bedclothes up to cover her.

Sunday had meant nothing to Mix since the death of his grandmother. Now it was just a pallid version of Saturday, rather unpleasant and irritating because some of the shops were shut, streets were empty and men who had girlfriends or wives or families took them out in cars. Still, it was also the day he had resolved to renew his campaign of really getting to know Nerissa. He hadn't yet got used to being without a car and, as he had yesterday, he went downstairs at nine-thirty and sauntered outside to begin the drive to Campden Hill Square. No car, and then he remembered what had happened to it, cursing roundly. Heavy doses of ibuprofen had numbed his back and he set off to walk.

The wind was cooler this morning. Autumn was coming. Being used to the warm interior of a vehicle, he was inadequately dressed in a T-shirt and he shivered as he walked. As he approached her house he saw that the Jaguar was on the front drive and his spirits rose. He had forgotten to supply himself with something to take to her door, a campaign leaflet or an envelope to be filled for a children's charity, so all he could do was wait and trust to the inspiration of the moment.

He began to shiver and goose pimples came up on his arms. To warm himself up, he marched to the bottom of the hill, along Holland Park Avenue and up the other side of the square. He was breathless when he got back to the top but no warmer. To his horror, he saw the Jaguar reversing out of the drive. He had missed her.

She drove past him down the hill and though he waved, she couldn't have seen him. She kept looking straight ahead and gave him no answering smile. There was nothing for it but to make his way back home and nothing to do when he got there but rub the stuff he had bought on his back and write applications to the two jobs he had seen in the *Evening Standard*, both of which looked likelier than the others.

The lodger had lived in her house for nearly four months now and sometimes weeks had passed without her seeing him or wanting to see him. They had spoken only when they encountered each other by chance and then not for long. He was not her kind of person, she had told herself, and no doubt she was not his. Therefore she found it strange how much she now needed to see him. It seemed to her essential that at some point during this Sunday she should confront him and have out with him this business of the thing and the missing letter. There was also the matter of his failure, according to Queenie and Olive, to feed Otto in her absence. Her own indifference to Otto was not the question. It had been Cellini's *duty* to feed the cat, he had promised. Besides, she was sure Otto would never have killed and eaten those guinea fowl and that pigeon if he had been properly fed.

Thinking of the guinea fowl reminded her that Mr Singh was due to call on her at 11 a.m. She was so sure he would be late, everyone always was these days, that she was astonished and nearly disbelieving when the doorbell rang promptly on the hour. When she got to her feet she felt so dizzy she had to grab hold of the back of the sofa so it took her a few minutes to get to the door; he rang again, which gave her an excuse to be irritable.

'All right, all right, I'm coming,' she said to the empty hallway.

He was a handsome man, taller and paler than she had expected, with a small iron-grey moustache and instead of the anticipated nightshirt-like garment, he wore grey flannel trousers, a sports jacket and a pink shirt with a grey and pink tie. The only incongruous note (to Gwendolen's eyes) was his snow-white, intricately wound turban.

He followed her into the drawing room, patiently walking at her own slow pace. 'It is a fine place you have here,' he said.

Gwendolen nodded. She knew it. That was why she stayed. She sat down and motioned to him to do the same. Siddhartha Singh did so, but slowly. He was looking round, carefully taking in the spaces and corners, the peeling walls and cracked ceiling, the shaky and splintered window frames, the prototype radiators dating from the twenties and the carpets, one piled on another, all eaten by moths and apparently chewed by small mammals. Only in the slums of Calcutta, years ago, had he seen such a degree of disintegration.

'If it is about your birds,' Gwendolen began, 'I really don't know what I'm supposed . . .'

'Excuse me, madam.' Mr Singh spoke very politely. 'Excuse me, but the bird episode is a thing of the past. History, if I may so put it. I cut my losses and turn over a new leaf. And on this subject, perhaps you, obviously an English lady, can tell me why "leaf". Is it perhaps that we go out into the woods and turn over a leaf to discover a secret beneath?'

Gwendolen would, in normal circumstances, have made a withering rejoinder but this man was so good-looking (and not just for an Oriental) and so charming that she felt quite weak in his presence. Like the Queen of Sheba when confronted by Solomon, there was no more spirit in her.

' "Leaf" means a page,' she said unsteadily. 'A page in the – well, the book of life, I suppose.'

Mr Singh smiled. It was just such a smile as the sun god might bestow, broad, benign, lighting his whole handsome face and displaying the kind of teeth possessed by American adolescents, shiny, white and even. 'Thank you. Sometimes, although I have been in this country for thirty years, I feel I dwell in a new age of enlightenment.'

Gwendolen smiled back helplessly. She made an offer the like of which she hadn't extended to a casual visitor since Stephen Reeves disappeared from her life. 'Would you like some tea?'

'Oh, no, thank you. I am here only for a jiffy. Let me come to the point. While you were unwell and not in residence, I see your gardener working away, a most industrious young man, and I say to Mrs Singh, look, this young man is just what we need to set things to rights here. And that is why I come to you. For the name and, please, the telephone number of your gardener, in the hope that he requires more work.'

Various emotions fought each other in Gwendolen's head. She hardly knew why she had felt a sinking of the heart when a Mrs Singh was mentioned, though she could understand the astonishment and incipient anger which rose in her at the same time. She sat up straighter, wondering fleetingly if he might take her for ten years younger than she actually was and said, 'I haven't got a gardener.'

'Oh, yes, indeed, madam. You have. Perhaps it has slipped your mind. I understand you have been indisposed and in a hospital. That was when he was here. No doubt you engaged him and he came to begin the work in your absence.'

'I did not engage him. I know nothing about it.' Impossible to delude herself. He was looking at her pityingly as if he saw her not as ten years her own junior but as an old woman suffering from senile dementia. 'What did he look like?' she asked him.

'Let me see. About thirty years old, fairish hair, a British face, blue eyes, I think, and handsome. Not as tall as I or – ' he sized her up critically – 'as you, I would respectfully say, madam.'

'What exactly was he doing?'

'Digging the garden,' said Mr Singh simply. 'He dug in two places. The ground, you know, is very heavy, like rock, like –' he ventured a flight of fancy '– adamantine stone.'

He even spoke, she thought, the same language as she did. If she had known him sooner, would he have replaced Stephen Reeves in her affections? 'The man you're talking about,' she said, her anger surfacing again, 'is my lodger. He lives upstairs, on the top floor.'

'Then I apologise for troubling you.'

Mr Singh got to his feet, affording Gwendolen another sight of his tall soldierly figure, his height and the board-like flatness of his stomach. She wanted to cry, 'Don't go!' Instead she said, 'His name is Cellini and he is not permitted access to *my* garden.'

Another smile, but sad this time. 'I won't say I'm not disappointed. No, please don't get up. You are a convalescent lady and not, if I may say so, quite in the first youth.' He caught sight of himself in one of Gwendolen's many fly-spotted, desilvered mirrors. 'Who is?' he said more tactfully. 'Now I say good morning, thank you for your trouble and I let myself out.'

With his departure the sun went in. Anger remained, hotter than before. She would lie in wait for Cellini now, drink black coffee, do anything to stay awake until she heard him come in. The thing, the letter, and now this, she thought. She'd get rid of him and find a nice quiet lady, not in her first youth. Oh, the hurt the phrase had done her! Even though he bracketed himself with her in that category. But Cellini. She would evict Cellini just as soon as she could.

# Chapter 23

He had begun to walk home but when he was
passing a bus stop and a bus came, he got on it. It
was too wild a day for a walk to be enjoyable. A few
yellow leaves were already falling from the plane
trees, whirling past the windows of the bus.
Something seemed to be pinching his spine with iron
fingers and whatever it was stabbed his lumbar
region as he was getting off on the corner of St Mark's
Road. The rest of the way he had to go on foot, the
pain subsiding a little with enforced movement.

Cars were as usual parked nose to tail all along
the residents' parking in St Blaise Avenue and he
noticed what he had had no need to notice before.
One of them, an ancient Volvo, had a For Sale sign
in its windscreen and underneath, the price: £300.
Volvos were good cars, supposed to last for years,
and this one appeared quite well cared for. He was
walking round it, looking in the windows, when a
woman emerged from one of the houses on the St
Blaise House side and came up to him.

'Are you interested?'

Mix said he didn't know, he might be. Though
no longer young, she was quite good-looking with
the kind of hour-glass figure he liked.

'It's my husband's. We're called Brunswick –
Brian and Sue Brunswick. Brian's away but he'll

be back on Wednesday. He'd go with you on a trial run if you'd like to.'

'You're not a driver yourself?' He wouldn't have minded going on any sort of trial run with her.

'I'm afraid it's years since I was at the wheel of a car.'

'Shame,' said Mix. 'I'll think about it.'

Padding across the hallway in St Blaise House, his hand pressed to the small of his back, he noticed that the drawing room door was ajar and he peered in. Old Chawcer was lying on the sofa fast asleep. He began to climb the stairs. Though cold in comparison to what it had been, the weather was brighter and the sun had come out. Sunbeams striking the walls of the stairwell showed up every crack, hairline as well as wide, the fly spots on the crookedly hung pictures and the flies that had got in between the print and the glass and died there, the cobwebs that clung to frames and cords and light fittings. He wondered where Reggie's ghost went in the daytime and told himself not to think about it unless he had to. The pain in his lumbar region sharpened. If it didn't improve he'd have to go to the doctor.

The first thing Gwendolen thought of when she woke up was Mr Singh's revelation. Mr Singh himself was not for her and she knew it, while Stephen Reeves was. Momentarily she had been carried away by his looks and his charm but, anyway, she didn't approve of cross-cultural marriages – miscegenation, they had called it when she was young – and the wife was a considerable stumbling block. The unknown and unseen Mrs Singh she dismissed as a 'tottering native woman in a veil'. What Mr

Singh had told her now excluded almost everything else from her mind.

While she was absent, and not only absent but ill in hospital, that man, that lodger, had been in her garden, twice been there, and dug holes in the flowerbeds. Once upon a time, in the days of Chawcer prosperity, a real gardener had attended to horticultural matters, the beds had blossomed with lupins and delphiniums, zinnias and dahlias, the shrubs had been trimmed and the lawn mown to a velvet carpet-like texture. To some extent Gwendolen saw it like that still, or she saw it as allowed to grow a little shabby, but nothing that a handyman and a lawn mower wouldn't set to rights in an hour or so. And into this small paradise the lodger had ventured with a spade – almost certainly *her* spade – and dug holes. He had gone into the garden and dug holes without her permission, without even attempting to get her permission, and in order to do so must have passed through her kitchen, her washhouse, probably depositing the thing in the copper on his way. Why had he? To bury something, of course. Possibly, no, *probably*, he had stolen something of hers, something valuable, and buried it out there until he could find a receiver of stolen goods. She would have to go all over the house, finding out what was missing. Rage returned, banging in her blood vessels. It was no wonder that, now she was wide awake, she felt distinctly strange, her head swimming and her body very weak.

For all that, she would very likely have attempted the stairs, taking them slowly and with rests at every landing, but for Queenie Winthrop arriving as she was making up her mind. She heard the door open, hoped it might be the lodger to save her climbing fifty-two stairs, and had her hopes dashed by Queenie's voice calling, 'Yoo-hoo, it's only me.'

Gwendolen wondered how long they were going to keep this up, she and Olive, calling on her with presents every day. For weeks perhaps, for months. For *ever*? She didn't want any more chocolates, cereal bars, pears or grapes. The bottle of port Queenie took out of her shopping trolley was far more acceptable and Gwendolen, cheering up, actually thanked her friend.

'I hope I'm not becoming an alcoholic,' she said. 'I'm sure I would if you and Olive had your way. Of course it's my lodger who has driven me to it. I never used to drink anything stronger than orange juice.'

She had been going to tell Queenie about the encounter with Mr Singh and what he had unwittingly revealed to her. But somehow she didn't want to discuss her neighbour with Queenie or anyone else and she couldn't describe the lodger's crimes without involving Mr Singh. Instead she said, 'I really don't like to ask. It's something of an imposition. But could you bring yourself to go upstairs and knock on *his* door and tell him I would like to see him this evening at six? Please,' she said, though it went against the grain. 'I have several matters I must bring up with him.'

'Well, dear, I will if you don't mind waiting a bit. I've still got to catch my breath after walking all the way here. I waited and waited for a bus but it never came. I'll go up before I go. I promise. Now shall I get you something to eat?' Queenie looked longingly at the bottle. 'Or a drink?'

'We could both have a small glass of port.'

'We could, couldn't we? After all, it's Sunday.'

'Surely it's communion wine one drinks on a Sunday, not port.'

'Possibly, dear, but not being a churchgoer I wouldn't know. Shall I be mother?'

Gwendolen shuddered. 'It's fortified wine, Queenie, not tea.'

She thought this habit of bringing a present to a sick friend and then expecting to share it, deplorable. But even a lifetime of rudeness hadn't taught her to drink exclusively in front of someone else. She watched Queenie pouring measures she considered too liberal into the wrong sort of glasses, raised hers and said what the professor used to say in like circumstances, 'Your health!'

A snack of cheese and biscuits, fruit and a slice each of the carrot cake, an offering from Queenie's elder daughter, was eaten off trays laid with ancient yellowing lace-trimmed cloths found in a sideboard drawer. 'You look as if you might drop off to sleep at any moment,' Queenie said.

'The thing isn't the only matter I have to complain to the lodger about,' said Gwendolen as if she hadn't spoken. 'I was expecting a very important letter while I was in hospital. It should have come here and apparently it didn't.' She had no intention of disclosing much about the nature of this letter or its sender to Queenie. 'I suspect Cellini of tampering with it.' She had long dropped the 'Mr'. 'Unless you or Olive have been interfering with my post, which,' she added in a more conciliatory tone, 'seems unlikely.'

'Of course we didn't, dear. Where would this letter have come from?'

'The postmark would probably be Oxford. And now I really do want to sleep so perhaps you'd go upstairs to the lodger. Six o'clock he's to present himself.'

Queenie lumbered up the stairs, looking longingly at the telephone as she passed it. But she would only have had to lift the receiver for Gwendolen to hear it and be down upon her like a ton of bricks. For all her seniority, Gwendolen had better hearing than she had. On the first landing she removed her punishing high-heeled shoes and, taking deep breaths, struggled on, shoes in hand. If he wasn't in she'd have something to say to Gwendolen. Her friend needn't think she had a prerogative in rudeness. Two could play at that game.

He was in. He came to the door with a cardigan tied round his shoulders and his feet bare. 'Oh, hi. What is it?'

Ever since she was fifteen Queenie had believed, and acted according to her belief, that if you want anything out of a man, if you simply want to exist in his presence, you must be extravagantly polite, sweet, winning and even flirtatious. It hadn't contributed to her comfort, but to the happiness of her marriage it had. 'Oh, Mr Cellini, I'm so sorry to bother you and on a Sunday too, but Miss Chawcer says will you be an angel and give her just five minutes of your time at about six o'clock this evening. If you'd just pop down and have a word with her. I'm sure she won't keep you, so if you could . . .'

'What's it about?'

'She didn't say.' Queenie flashed him an enormous toothy smile of the kind some man had once told her lit up her whole face, and proceeded to run with the hare and hunt with the hounds. 'You know what she is, Mr Cellini,' she said, betraying Gwendolen without knowing she was doing so, 'awfully fussy about every little thing. Not that you'd think so, would you, from the state of this house?'

'Too right.' Mix wanted to get back to the video he'd made a couple of weeks back of Man U playing some Central European team. 'Tell her I'll be there around six. Cheers, then.'

When she got back to the drawing room Gwendolen was asleep. She wrote on a scrap of paper. *Mr Cellini will come at six. Love, Queenie.*

Up in the top flat the football remained unwatched. Taking the message without much thought, Mix had gone back inside and become an immediate prey to misgivings. She must have found the thong, he thought. Someone had and who more likely than old Chawcer? He must think up some reason for its being in the copper and the only one he could think of, that he had been doing a girlfriend's washing because her machine had broken down, was obviously not feasible. Who washed in antiquated *holes* like that any more? What was wrong with the launderette? Anyway, it wouldn't account for the fact that he shouldn't have been in her washhouse.

Perhaps he could deny all knowledge of it. That might be best. Even better, if he could manage it, would be to suggest Ma Fordyce or Ma Winthrop had something to do with it. He could even say he'd seen one of them with the thong in her hand. Don't worry about it, he said to himself, don't even think about it. Think about something else. Like what? That Frank from the Sun in Splendour might be with the police at this moment? That Nerissa was out with another bloke? No, think about the possibility of offering Brian Brunswick two-fifty for the Volvo. Why shouldn't he go back to the house tomorrow and ask Sue Brunswick to come out in the car with him? She didn't have to be a driver, she only had to sit beside him. That would be brilliant. He could drive her down to Holland Park or, better still, to Richmond and suggest they had lunch in one of those trendy pubs. She couldn't refuse, not if she wanted to sell her car. Then, afterwards, with the old man, this Brian, out of the way, when they got back to her place . . .

It would probably be a one-off and just as well. Once he'd got inside Nerissa's house and talked to her over coffee he wouldn't need second-rate women like Sue Brunswick or secondhand cars, he'd have the Jaguar and, above all, he'd have Nerissa. By next Sunday his whole circumstances could have changed. He wouldn't even be here in this flat, attractive as it was, he'd be moving into Campden Hill Square, he wouldn't need a job or a car or care about what a bunch of old women thought of him. There'd be no murderer's ghost in her house. He'd tell her about the thong and they'd have a good laugh over it together, especially the bit about when he'd told old Chawcer the thong belonged to Ma Winthrop. As if she could even begin to get it round her fat arse!

He took three 400 milligram strength ibuprofen, put socks and shoes on and his arms into the cardigan sleeves and went down at ten past six. Gwendolen wasn't lying down, she wasn't even sitting down, but pacing the room because the lodger was over ten minutes late. When he appeared she was so angry she couldn't control herself.

'You're late. Doesn't time mean anything to people any more?'

'What was it you wanted?'

'You'd better sit down,' said Gwendolen.

Was it a fact that anger made your blood pressure rise and that you could feel it rise, pounding in your head? Sometimes she thought about her arteries, lined as they must be by now with stuff like the plaque you got on your teeth. Her head swam. She had to sit down, though she would have preferred to stand and tower over him. But she was afraid of falling and thus making herself vulnerable in his presence.

'A very charming neighbour of mine called on me this morning,' she said, taking a deep breath. 'These immigrants to our shores could teach some people around here what good manners are. However, be that as it may, he had something to tell me. Possibly you can guess what it was.'

Mix could. Though he had been turning over in his mind possible reasons for old Chawcer wanting to see him, this wasn't one of them. He had no explanation to offer. With increasing dismay, he listened to her long account of Mr Singh's visit, his misapprehension as to Mix's presence in the garden and her own indignation.

'Now perhaps you'll tell me what you thought you were doing.'

'Digging the garden,' said Mix. 'You can't say it doesn't need it.'

'That's no business of yours. The garden has nothing to do with you.' Gwendolen had decided not to mention the thing. The letter was another matter.

'And I've reason to believe you've been tampering with my post.'

'That's a lie, for a start.'

'Don't speak to me like that, Mr Cellini. How dare you suggest I might be untruthful? You still haven't given me any reason for digging up my garden, not to mention going into my kitchen and my washhouse.'

There had been a teacher like her at his comprehensive school. He even remembered her name: Miss Forester. She'd taught his mum before him and his grandma too, for all he knew. But his generation of kids gave her a hard time and she'd had to leave before she had a nervous breakdown. He'd been one of them but in those days he'd had nothing to lose. This was different. He'd like to have said what he remembered saying to Miss Forester but somehow the words, 'Piss off, you old cow,' died on his lips.

'Either I get a satisfactory explanation of your conduct or I shall serve you notice to quit the premises.'

'You can't do that,' he said. 'It's an unfurnished flat. I've got a protected tenancy.'

Gwendolen knew that very well, iniquitous though it was, but she had still tried it on. 'What did you bury? Some piece of property of mine, I suppose. A valuable piece of jewellery? Or perhaps the silver? I shall check, have no fear, I shall make an inventory of missing things. Or maybe you murdered someone and buried the body. Is that it?'

The stain on the base of the Psyche notwithstanding, Gwendolen didn't for a moment believe this was what had happened. It was the stuff of fiction and as such something she had read of many times over the years. She said it, not because she gave it credence or even saw it as remotely likely, but to insult him. She even failed to notice that Mix had gone white, his expressionless face no longer blank. But he said nothing, only lowering the eyes which had been fixed on hers.

Triumphantly, she saw that she had utterly vanquished him and now she would finish the job. 'Tomorrow morning, without fail, I shall inform the police. When you come out of prison I doubt if you will wish to return here even if that be allowed.'

'Have you finished?' Mix asked.

'Almost,' said Gwendolen. 'I simply repeat that I shall inform the police of your activities tomorrow morning.'

When he had gone she had to lie down. Once she heard his door close – he slammed it and the whole house seemed to shake – she hauled herself off the sofa and began to crawl towards the stairs. Later on, she might lack the strength to manage them as she lacked it now to begin the climb. For about ten minutes she remained sitting on the floor and then she started to crawl up the stairs on hands and knees. It seemed like hours later that she reached her bedroom and got inside.

Heaven forbid that she should have her bed moved downstairs. Neither Queenie nor Olive had yet suggested it, but they would, they would. She would never submit to that, she thought, as she struggled, and failed, to remove her clothes and get into her nightgown. She did manage to take off the ruby ring and put it in the jewel box, thought of washing her hands but only thought of it. Reaching the bathroom seemed as impossible as, say, walking to Ladbroke Grove and back. She lay down and closed her eyes. Weakness enfeebled her whole body, but sleep which had come so easily and irresistibly during the past week, come when she didn't want it and even tried to fight against it, now backed away from her, banished by anger.

It wasn't only the wrath aroused by the lodger's behaviour, though that was bad enough, but the rage of a lifetime welling up and bubbling, churning through her veins. Rage at Mama who had taught her to be ladylike at the expense of freedom of speech, cultivation of the mind, liberty of movement, love, passion, adventure and the pursuit of happiness; rage at Papa who hid his denial to her of a real education under a cloak of protecting her from the wicked world and who kept her at home to be his nurse and amanuensis; rage at Stephen Reeves who had deceived her and married someone else and failed to answer her letters; rage at this enormous decaying house which had become her prison.

For a long while, she didn't know how long, she felt she had no physical existence and was only a mind which swirled with rage and thoughts of revenge. Then, at one moment she was in a fury of anger, at the next blank and still. It was like sleep and yet it was not. Her first thought when she emerged from it was that at least she could punish the lodger with the police. She struggled, and failed, to sit up. This wouldn't do for, tonight certainly, she must check on the rest of the jewellery in the box, see what, if anything, was missing and lying in a muddy hole in the garden. She must go down and look in the cabinet where the silver, untouched for many years, lay wrapped in green baize.

It seemed as if, for a few moments, she had lost

consciousness. She doubted if she could stand up. This time it wasn't a fear of dizziness which might cause her to fall but an apparent inability to move her left side. Cramp, of course. She occasionally suffered from cramp and usually in the night. She rubbed her left leg and then her left arm and though she fancied a little feeling returned she could only put her foot to the floor by a huge effort. Her arm hung useless. As she thought she must try to get to the light switch and the door, it opened slowly and Otto strolled in. His sleek chocolate form became black in the faint light from those street lamps still in working order, while his eyes glowed the colour of the limes for sale in the corner shop. She found herself thinking, incongruously, as she had never thought before, that his eyes were beautiful and that he, young and lithe, was the only perfect thing she ever saw. He took no notice of her but sat down in front of the empty grate and began picking pieces of twig and tiny stones out of his pads with sharp white teeth.

Gwendolen dragged her left leg back on to the bed, tugging it there with her right hand. The effort exhausted her. His manicure complete, Otto leapt gracefully on to the bed and curled up beside her feet.

# Chapter 24

From his bedroom window Mix watched Mr Singh pinning up fairy lights along the fronds of the palm tree. It wasn't Christmas or that festival Indians had about the same time, so what was he playing at? Maybe it's just as well we can't have handguns here like they do in the US. If I had a gun I'd shoot that guy here and now. Mr Singh climbed down the ladder, went into the house and switched the lights on, red and blue and yellow and green twinkling in the exotic tree. Then Mrs Singh came out in a pink sari and the two of them stood looking at the tree, admiring the effect.

Even at this hour, the places where Mix had dug the garden showed up quite clearly from a distance, a small patch of turned earth and a larger one. He should have done his digging under cover of darkness, he knew that now, but that would have meant after midnight. Lights were on in the houses along Mr Singh's road but on this side he couldn't see the backs of the terrace, only their gardens. One of them had outside lights along the wall and among the evergreens. A woman who had come out to take in a blanket and a pair of jeans from the washing line he recognised as Sue Brunswick. Thoughts of buying her husband's car now seemed like a half-forgotten dream, let alone the designs he had had on her. Even Nerissa, whom he often thought of romantically at this time of day like a song at twilight, faded from his mind. Nothing mattered, not jobs, nor livelihood, nor lack of a car, nor love, nothing but stopping old Chawcer phoning the police.

Yet ever since he had come upstairs he had been paralysed with fear. The ibuprofen he had taken, far in excess of the maximum recommended dose, made his head swim and hadn't done much for his backache. He hadn't even been able to pour himself a drink or think about food or sit down, but had stood here at the window, holding on to the sill for support and staring out. She would do it, he was sure of that. He hadn't tried to dissuade her because he knew for certain that she'd do it. She only put it off till tomorrow because she belonged to that generation who thought you didn't phone the police or a doctor or go to the shops on a Sunday. His gran was the same. They saw Monday as the day you got down to things so she'd tell them first thing in the morning.

The twin gleams of Otto's eyes were nowhere to be seen. Mix, who had never given Otto much thought before, now imagined how glorious it must be to be him, fed and housed for free, no job and none needed, insomnia unknown, freedom to wander a rich hunting ground all day and night if he wished. Free of pain, supple and fearless and free to murder anything that got in his way. No sex of course. Otto, he was sure, had been fixed. But sex was a nuisance anyway and what you'd never had you couldn't miss.

This small distraction from his troubles sent Mix into the living room where he mixed himself a Boot Camp with an extra shot of Cointreau. He should have had the sense to do this a couple of hours ago. Then maybe he wouldn't have felt so bad. The cocktail had its wondrous effect and almost instantly made him feel there was no problem he couldn't solve. You had to get things in perspective, you had to know your priorities. His priority, in the here and now, was to stop old Chawcer talking to the police. It was probable, he thought, that she didn't know the effect her words would have on them. He knew. Searching for Danila's body simultaneously with their hunt for her killer, they would immediately be alerted to the chance of discovering both and be round here in ten minutes. She had to be stopped.

He knew how to stop a woman's tongue. He had done it before.

How she got out of bed Gwendolen hardly knew. She crawled a few inches across the floor. In Mr Singh's garden a palm tree had turned into a chandelier of coloured lights. She must be imagining it, something had happened to her brain. To reach the door, let alone the stairs, the drawing room and the silver cabinet, was impossible. She would have liked to phone her doctor or even Queenie or Olive but she would have had to roll herself down the stairs to do so. But it was Sunday, still Sunday as far as she knew, and angry as she had been with her long-dead mother, Mrs Chawcer's principle of not making a phone call to anyone but members of one's family on a Sunday – and never, on any day, after nine at night – died very hard. So she crawled back without the strength to wash or what her mother had called 'relieve herself', saw that the

imaginary tree was still there, still bright with
twinkling coloured stars, and fell on the bed still
fully clothed, though she managed to pull off one
shoe and kick off the other.

Lying there on her back, she pulled the quilt over
her with her sound right hand. What was wrong
with her she guessed and had done so for the past
hour but only now could she put it into silent
words. She had had a stroke.

Mix had come out on to the landing because she
made such a noise getting out of bed. What was
wrong with her? Perhaps she always made that
much noise about going to bed. He wouldn't
know, he never remembered noticing her bedtime
before.

He asked himself if he'd be able to kill her in
cold blood. Danila had been different. Danila had
driven him into an uncontrollable rage with her
insults and her unprovoked attack on Nerissa. The
light on the landing went out and the Isabella lights
had disappeared while the street lamp was out of
order. Once I'm alone here, he thought, I'm going
to get all the lights in the place changed so that
they stay on longer and I'm going to buy normal-
size bulbs for them, hundreds or hundred and
fifties, not this rubbish. It won't be for long, I'll
soon be gone.

He looked across to the thin shaft of light coming
from his slightly open front door, then, his eyes
becoming used to the dark, along the left-hand passage. A figure was walking silently away with his
back to Mix, as if he had come out of the nearest
room. He turned as he reached the farthest door,
saw him and grew still. Mix saw the gleam on the

315

glasses on his beaky nose. Then the ghost lifted his shoulders in a small shrug. He put out his hands in the sort of gesture that indicates doubt or despair, and his lips parted. No sound came from them. Mix shut his eyes and when he opened them the ghost was gone.

The fear he usually felt seemed to have been partly banished by the greater terror of the police. He remained where he was, staring at the place where the ghost had been. The shrug had meant something. The ghost had been trying to tell him something. Perhaps it had been advising him to do what he had almost decided on. He, Reggie, had killed six women and been not much fazed by it. No one knew why he'd killed his own wife but opinion was that she had found out about his murders and not only refused to protect him but threatened to do just what old Chawcer was doing to him. So was that what his ghost had been saying? Kill her. I never thought twice about it. Kill her and do what I did with Ethel.

Thoughts had begun to run out of Gwendolen's head, leaving it almost empty. Stephen Reeves appeared fleetingly before vanishing down a long road where those thoughts ran and where in the distance, on the edge of something indefinable, she could make out misty shapes who might or might not be Papa and Mama. Gradually they too faded and slipped over that edge where Stephen had gone. She was alone in the world but there was nothing unusual in that. She had always been alone. And now, as something rumbled and murmured inside the place where thoughts had been, she knew she was going out of the world alone.

For no reason, with no particular desire, she told her hands and her arms to move, but they no longer obeyed her and she was too tired to tell them again. She breathed very slowly, in and out, in and after a long time out, in again very lightly and out on a long rattling sigh. If there had been watchers they would have waited for the next inhalation and when none came, have risen from their chairs, closed her eyes and drawn the sheet up over her face.

Bright moonlight poured into the bedroom. When she came to bed Gwendolen had been too ill and too tired to draw the curtains and in the four hours which had passed, an almost full moon had mounted into the clear sky. Because of the position of the large double bed and the height and width of the window, the moon between the half-open curtains spread a pale band across the bed-clothes, a stripe of whiteness, leaving her face in the dark. Earlier than usual, the lights in Mr Singh's house had gone out and the fairy light tree was also in darkness.

To his dismay Mix found himself trembling as he came into the bedroom, not from the temperature but from fear. Yet what was there to be afraid of? This time the ghost hadn't even made him shiver. All the doors downstairs were locked and, where this was possible, bolted. He and she were alone. The ghost was upstairs of course but Mix had felt and still felt that Reggie approved of what he was about to do. And, mystifyingly, the pain in his back had gone. He had taken no more ibuprofen, yet it was gone. He'd be all right now.

As he approached the bed a black shape uncurled itself and reared up, arching its back. The green eyes seemed larger and brighter than usual.

'I'll kill you too,' said Mix.

He made a lunge for Otto who eluded his grasp with ease, hissed like a snake and leapt for the open door and the stairs. The woman on the bed was perfectly still. Do it quickly, he said to himself, do it now. Don't look at her. Just do it. Her head was on one pillow and there was another beside her, a third up-ended against the bedhead. He took hold of the up-ended pillow in both trembling hands and turning his head away, pressed it down on her face as hard as he could.

She didn't move. There was to be no struggle. She remained utterly still. He held his hands there and they steadied while he counted to a hundred, two hundred . . . At five hundred he let his hands relax and as they did so his fingers touched the skin of her neck. It was icy cold. He had never before touched such an old person – his grand-mother had died at seventy – and he wondered if all of them were as cold as that, the heat in the blood, the warm life, cooling gradually with age.

He put the pillow back where he had found it and pulled the bedclothes off her body. It surprised him to see that she was fully dressed. Maybe she always went to bed like that, never took her clothes off. He stripped the top sheet out from under the coverlet and blanket and began to roll the body up in it. By now he had some experience of this sort of thing, he was less fearful and less clumsy. The trembling which he couldn't account for had entirely ceased. He felt very calm and resigned. He had had to do it. Before he wound the end of the sheet round her head and face he made himself look. Her wide-open eyes reminded him of Danila's. But Danila's had been young and clear, her body warm to touch.These eyes, rheumy, clouded, lay in a nest of wrinkles. And this old woman was ice-cold.

She was much heavier than Danila and it took him a long time to drag her up the stairs to the top, the body bumping on every step. He expected renewed back pain but there was none. Once the body was inside his flat and he had had a drink, a fairly stiff gin, he went back to her bedroom and tidied the bed, making it look as he thought she might have made it, in a rather slovenly way. Her shoes, which she must have kicked off before lying down, he put into the cupboard to join the jumble already there. He was going to tell those who inquired that she had decided to go away and convalesce, leaving everything the way she would if she had really gone.

All the time he was dragging her upstairs he was thinking he might injure his back again but he was quite free of pain. And somehow he knew he would continue to be unless it came on later, as it had done last time. At the trial of Timothy Evans, Reggie had made the court believe he couldn't have killed Evans's wife because his back was too bad for him to lift her. I won't be going near any court, Mix told himself resolutely. I got rid of her to keep myself out of court.

He went downstairs and drew back the bolts on the front door in case Ma Winthrop or Ma Fordyce decided to come very early in the morning and thought it was funny the door being bolted. He didn't want anyone thinking anything was funny.

This house was a dreadful place at night, such a place as shouldn't be allowed to exist, he thought. Living here for long would drive you mad. You'd feel it was mouldering away and slowly rotting around you, the wood and the hangings and the ancient carpets disintegrating hour by hour, minute by minute. If you stood still and listened you could almost hear it, tiny drippings and droppings, moths chewing, flakes falling, splinters, rust and mildew turning to dust. Why had he ever thought he wanted to live here? Why had he spent all that money on making a small part of the house fit to live in?

Returning to the stairs, he saw Otto above him sitting on the first landing. Had she fed the cat? She would always do that before she went to bed and would have done so before she left in the morning on this journey she was supposed to be going on. He went back to look in case one of those two old women checked and found it funny the cat's plate being empty. Either Otto had eaten it or none had been put down. Mix opened a can and filled the plate.

'I'd put poison in it if I'd got any,' he said aloud.

Otto came down the stairs, Mix aimed a kick at him and the cat sprang, raking claws down his bare ankle. Mix cried out, reached for his leg and brought his hand away covered in blood. He cursed, peering through the moonlit dark for that shape and those eyes but Otto had disappeared, leaving the food uneaten.

Mix followed, dripping blood. The moonlight came in everywhere it could find an uncurtained window or a crack between door and jamb, scattering spots and lines of white light. The landing

windows let it in and it seeped through her bedroom door which he had left ajar. Above him he
saw Otto padding up the tiled flight. At the top,
without hesitation, moving through a big square
of moonlight, the cat turned left along the passage.
When Mix got up there he was nowhere to be seen.
Like some witch's familiar, he had disappeared into
the ghost's abode. There Mix was too frightened to
follow him.

He thought of searching once more for
Gwendolen's sleeping pills but he was afraid. Such
fear was irrational, he knew, as was the horrible
fantasy he had of sleeping for too long and deeply
until he awoke blearily to find police in the flat,
the front door kicked in and Ma Fordyce unwrap-
ping the bundle in which was Gwendolen's body.
He must stay alert, lie down and rest but not sleep.
He had things to do in the morning which couldn't
wait.

Queenie had been invited to a Fordyce–Akwaa
family brunch. She thought it extraordinarily nice
of them to ask her because the company would
consist of Olive, her sister, her niece Hazel and
Hazel's two sons with their wives and two babies;
she would be the only outsider. Gwendolen also
had been invited but she had refused as Olive –
this was perhaps the reason she had been so anxious to ask her – had known she would.

Gwendolen was difficult. Everyone who came
into contact with her knew that but you had to
make allowances for her age, ten years older than
Queenie herself, and her single status. It was a well-
known fact that being single all those years made
you selfish. Queenie and Olive often discussed

Gwendolen's rudeness and 'contrariness' but agreed that they must put up with it and not consider withdrawing their friendship. They were also in agreement that it was unthinkable for her, in her present state, to be left alone for more than a few hours. Queenie should be the one to call at St Blaise House in the morning while Olive would try to look in later, as she would be busy before that with the brunch.

Nine o'clock was early but she couldn't help that. She had things to do before she went round to Olive's. Still outstanding was the vexed question of what she was going to wear. The pink dress or the new white trouser suit she had been lucky to get in a size 18?

Gwendolen was probably still in bed. Queenie let herself into the house, calling, 'Yoo-hoo' as she always did because she didn't want to startle her friend. She looked first of all into the drawing room. The bottle of port was still on the table and so were their two glasses with crimson dregs in the bottom of each one. In the kitchen was the customary mess. Nothing unusual in that. Queenie knew the tidiness and cleanliness achieved by herself and Olive was bound not to last. Otto's food bowl was half full. Without quite knowing why, Queenie felt relieved Gwendolen had been strong enough to feed him before she went to bed.

There was no help for it, she was going to have to climb those stairs. Twice, probably, because Gwendolen would be bound to want a cup of tea. Solve that problem by making it now. The old kettle, burn-encrusted on its outside and no doubt coated in limescale within, took ages to boil. Finally Queenie was able to make the tea, a cup for

Gwendolen and one for herself, liberally sugared with granulated for energy. She put both on a tray and began the climb.

Gwendolen's bed was empty and so was the room. The bed was made, not approaching Queenie's own standard with 'hospital corners' but exactly the way Gwendolen would think adequate. The curtains were drawn halfway across the windows and the place was as stuffy as usual. Queenie came out and a voice from above said, 'Hi, there.'

Very unlike him, she thought. Why was he being so pleasant? 'Is that you, Mr Cellini? Good morning. Do you happen to know where Miss Chawcer is?'

He came down. She thought he looked terrible, his round face gaunt and hollow-eyed, the skin with a clammy sheen to it. His belly bulged over his jeans and the laces on his trainers were undone. 'She's gone away,' he said. 'For convalescence, she said. Somewhere near Cambridge. She's got friends there.'

As far as Queenie knew she had no friends but her and Olive. Then she remembered Gwendolen had said she was expecting a letter from Cambridge – or had it been Oxford? – the one she had practically accused Mr Cellini of purloining. Had Gwendolen had a letter from these friends and said nothing about it to her or Olive? It was more than possible. It would be like her. Or these Cambridge people might have phoned last evening. Still, it was very short notice. And Gwendolen had hardly seemed fit enough . . .

'When did she go?'

'Must have been about eight. I went downstairs to get my mail and there she was in the hall with her bag packed waiting for a cab to come.'

Queenie couldn't imagine Gwendolen calling a cab, still less having an account with some taxi company, but what did she know? How would she know?

'I supposed she asked you to feed the cat?'

'Sure and I said I'd see to it.'

'Do you know when she'll be back?'

'She never said.'

'Well, there's no point in me staying, Mr Cellini. I've a brunch party to go to.' Queenie was proud of having been invited, as a widow of no particular importance, to what amounted to someone else's family gathering. 'It's a joint venture of Olive and her niece Mrs Akwaa.'

He stared. 'Will Miss Nash be there?'

Ridiculous man! She remembered the things he had said to Nerissa the day Gwendolen came out of hospital. He obviously had it bad, was quite smitten, as her late husband used to say. 'Sadly for us, she won't.' Queenie disliked a man showing a preference for any woman but herself. She took a certain malicious pleasure, quite unlike her, in denying Mr Cellini the chance of sending some lovey-dovey message. 'She always has a day out with her father about this time of year and they've fixed on today. It's become quite a tradition.'

She went downstairs and to her surprise he followed her. 'Did you drive here?' he asked when they were in the hallway.

'I haven't got a car. Why do you ask?'

'It doesn't matter. I just thought if you had you might take me up to the DIY place on the North Circular.'

Queenie, who generally lacked Olive's acerbity, for once forgetting to exercise her charm on a man, said sharply for her, 'I'm sure I'm sorry to disappoint you. You'll have to go on the bus.' At the front door she turned round. 'Olive and I will both be back. We'll want to get to the bottom of this mysterious trip of Gwendolen's.'

# Chapter 25

Buying a sufficiently large and sufficiently thick plastic bag was less easy than he had thought. There was nothing available as tough as the one he had taken from the firm's warehouse – why had he been such a fool as to cut it up and throw it out? – and he had to be satisfied with a cot mattress cover, designed to be urine-proof. All the way back on the bus he was thinking of the smell of Danila's body as it began to decay. The weather was warmer again. On some days it had been up in the twenties Celsius. Just the same, he knew that burying Gwendolen's body in the garden would be impossible. As he was walking round the DIY supermarket he had felt shooting pains begin, little stabs like tiny knives pricking his spine. He could disable himself for life, he thought, if he attempted putting a spade to that concrete-like clay.

The body he had wrapped in one of her own threadbare sheets. It lay in his little hallway. He took the mattress cover out of its packaging and saw at once it wouldn't do. It was too thin and – he shuddered – too transparent. If he used it he would be in the same mess as he'd been in last time – worse, because eventually there would be a search for old Chawcer. All he could do was wait until tomorrow and try to get a stronger, thicker bag.

The pain in his back had returned. He shouldn't have dragged that much heavier body up all those stairs. But what choice had he? And he was going to have to drag it further in case something happened to make it impossible for him to refuse entry to anyone who needed to come into the flat. As well as the pain he had a sore ankle where that cat had scratched him. The whole area was red and swollen and he wondered if Otto's claws were infected with nasty bacteria. But his life was more important than pain, he thought, and he lugged the body into the living room where he dropped it in a corner and pushed the cocktail cabinet across to hide it.

Its presence there haunted him and he had to move first into the kitchen, then the bedroom. How could you relax in a room with a body, however disguised, rolled up in one corner? In the bedroom it was better, a bit better. He lay on his bed and thought, tomorrow I'll find somewhere to buy a thicker stronger bag and then I'll put her in it and under the floorboards. After that, I'll put it out of my mind, I won't think about it any more.

Nerissa was out with her father. She was his only daughter and his youngest child and though he couldn't have said he loved her better than his sons, he loved her differently, partly because she was the girl he had longed for and partly because her skin was almost as dark as his. His sons had their mother's features and skin lighter than his own. They were tall and handsome and successful at what they did and he was proud of them but

327

they didn't look like members of his tribe – its women were famously beautiful – as Nerissa did and his old mother did. So, for no religious or ritualistic reason but just because they always did, he took the day off and he and Nerissa went to the sheltered housing in Greenford where his mother lived and, also for no particular reason except that they always did, took her a flowering plant from Africa and the best mangoes they could find (not, alas, sun-ripened and with juice-dripping golden flesh) and a bunch of pink and red and gold banksias from the Cape, though this was not her part of that continent but the best they could do.

In the car on the way Nerissa tied up her head in a wonderful white and pink and emerald turban because this was what, in Grandma's eyes, women who dressed properly went out in, and she wore an emerald green caftan with a ruby border and looked like a chief's wife. When they had made Tom's mother happy and in her company had eaten and drunk all sorts of things Nerissa knew she would have to compensate for by starving herself, they got back in the car and drove to wherever they were going for their day out. Somewhere different each year. Last time it had been the Thames Barrier and the Maritime Museum at Greenwich and this time it was Hampton Court Palace. Before they got there Nerissa unwound the turban, tied her hair back in a ponytail and put on big sunglasses so that she wouldn't be recognised. She kept the caftan on.

While they were walking round looking at things, the day having turned out to be warm and fine, Nerissa told her father, the words coming out in a rush, that she had fallen in love with Darel Jones.

'But you don't know him all that well, do you?' said Tom.

'I suppose not. I haven't seen him since we all went there for dinner. But I know. I know I've been in love with him for years and years. Ever since they came to live next door.'

'Is he in love with you, my darling?'

'I wouldn't think so, Dad. Not for a moment. If he was he'd do something about it. He wouldn't just ask me to dinner with all you lot there as well.'

They had lunch in an Italian restaurant in Hampton, discovered by Tom who was good on restaurants. While they were eating their zabaglione – or Tom was eating his and Nerissa was pretending she couldn't finish hers – he told her that as she was so beautiful and he, personally, thought she was pretty nice as well, neither her appearance nor her character could be responsible for Darel's indifference.

'I suppose it could just be a case of Dr Fell,' said Tom.

'Who's Dr Fell?'

> ' "I do not love thee, Dr Fell,
> The reason why I cannot tell,
> But this one thing I know full well,
> I do not love thee, Dr Fell." '

'I hope not,' said Nerissa, 'because if that's it there'll be no putting it to rights.'

'Love's a funny thing. Your mother was beautiful, still is in my opinion, but I don't know why I fell in love with her and God knows why she fell in love with me. Your grandma would say things were a lot easier when the suitor and the girl's parents arranged the match and the chap got a flock of goats and some bushels of corn with his bride.'

'Darel couldn't keep goats in Docklands,' said Nerissa, 'and I don't suppose he'd know what do with bushels of corn. He did say that if I got harassed by that man who's stalking me I was to call him and he'd come. Any time of the day or night, he said.'

'Are you being harassed?' Tom sounded anxious.

'Not really. I haven't seen him for a week.'

'Well, if you do, call Darel and kill two birds with one stone.'

Nerissa thought about it. 'I don't want to actually look forward to the guy coming back.'

'Think again,' said Tom. 'Maybe you do want to.'

Early next morning Queenie and Olive met at St Blaise House and held a two-woman conference. Both were indignant that Gwendolen had gone away without letting them know. They sat in the drawing room, having spread two clean table napkins across the seat of the sofa, drinking an instant coffee brew which Olive had made and eating pastries from the confectioner's box Queenie had brought with her, neither of them much fancying food which came out of Gwendolen's kitchen.

'This room is filthy,' said Olive. 'This whole house is filthy.' She had sterilised the cups with boiling water and Dettol before filling them with coffee.

'Well, dear, we *know* that but we don't have to live here, thank goodness, and if you're thinking of having a whole house clean-up while poor Gwendolen is away, I wouldn't. You know what she was like when we tackled her kitchen. I think we should mind our own business.'

'I can't understand her going away at all. In all the years I've known her she's never been away.'

'And she's never mentioned friends in Cambridge.'

'No, but the professor may have known people there. In fact, it's quite likely.'

'That may be,' said Queenie, 'but why has she never said? And, you know, dear, people of her age –' Gwendolen had been ten years older than she and twelve years older than Olive '– take absolute ages to prepare themselves for going away to stay anywhere. I remember my dear mother when she was in her eighties taking a good two weeks to get herself ready and she was only going to my brother. *And* she discussed the pros and cons every day before she finally went. Should she leave in the morning or the afternoon? Which train should she catch? Could she ask my brother to meet her or would he do that anyway? You know the sort of thing. And Gwendolen would be just the same. No, she'd be worse.'

'Well, I don't know. Drink your coffee before it gets cold.'

'I'm sorry, Olive, but I can't. It tastes of disinfectant. Do you think she's got an address book about anywhere? We could look in that. She must have somewhere she writes down people's addresses.'

They walked about the room, remarking on the grime and the cobwebs, and were pulling books out of the bookcase and blowing dust off their spines when Mix came down into the hallway. He had been on his way downstairs, starting once more on his quest to find a thick stout plastic bag, when he heard them come into the house. At first he had retreated into his own flat, then, later, decided it would be best to confront them and, most importantly, ask them to return the house key.

A few moments before he entered the drawing room, Olive had found Gwendolen's ancient address book in a drawer among scraps of paper, broken pencils, safety pins, elastic bands, antique 15 amp electric plugs and about fifty used cheque-books in which only the stubs remained. When Mix came in she looked up from the entries under B, which was as far as she had reached, and said, 'Oh, good morning, Mr Cellini,' in an unpleasant tone.

'Hiya,' said Mix.

'We were just wondering if you happened to know the name of the friends Miss Chawcer is staying with.'

'No, I don't. She didn't say.'

'We're very anxious to know,' said Queenie. 'It's so unlike her to go away without a word.' But she gave Mix one of the smiles which had been so winning when she was eighteen, and laid her hand on his arm. After all, he *was* a man. 'We thought she might have confided in you.'

He made no answer. 'Can I have the key back?'

'What key?' Olive said sharply.

'The key to this house. You won't need it now she's OK.'

'Yes, we will. We need to come in and see to the place while she's away. And another thing. I shall give this key up to Miss Chawcer and no one else. Is that understood?'

'OK, keep your cool.' Mix turned away, said over

his shoulder, 'You don't want to send your blood pressure up at your age.'

This was unwise of him, though Olive appeared to react not at all. She said nothing to him or to Queenie even when she heard the front door close behind him but sat down on the napkin-covered sofa by the table and continued to turn the pages of Gwendolen's address book.

'What a terribly rude person he is,' said Queenie.

'Yes. There's not a single Cambridge address in this book, Queenie.'

'Perhaps she knows it so well she doesn't need to write it down.'

'At her time of life you forget your own name if you don't write it down.'

Olive closed the book. 'What are we going to do? We can't just leave it. I thought Gwen was looking very unwell when I saw her on Sunday. She looked as if she ought to have been in bed. And the next thing we know is she's gone off first thing next morning to stay with people no one has ever heard of in Cambridge. In a taxi? When did Gwen ever go anywhere in a taxi, always supposing she knew how to order one.'

'Well, dear, I wouldn't trust that man Cellini an inch.'

'Then what were you doing smirking at him in that flirtatious way?'

He should have been out, calling at DIY places and hardware stores, but he was afraid to leave those two old hags at large in the house. They would be bound to search it. And what if old Chawcer had kept a key to his flat? He'd never inquired and, to his knowledge, she hadn't been in there while he was out. On the other hand, she had never told him she possessed a key to his place and he'd never asked. If she had one they would find it. He dared not take the risk of going out.

Outside his flat he sat on the top step of the tiled flight and listened. He heard them come out of the drawing room. He could hear their voices, twittering to each other shrilly. Like birds of prey, he thought, ravens or whatever those creatures were that you saw pecking at dead things on motorway verges. Dead things – his comparison reminded him of the body which lay, inadequately wrapped, behind the cocktail cabinet not many feet away from him. It was very warm in the flat. He remembered what had happened to Danila's body when it got warm and he went about, opening windows.

It seemed those two had gone into the kitchen. He crept down a floor, twinges running through his back. From there he could hear them banging about in the kitchen and washhouse. What were they looking for? They came back into the hall and he went back to halfway up the last flight. Not that there was much chance of their seeing or hearing him. Their lumbering progress up the stairs was too slow for that as they puffed and panted and took rests, clinging, he guessed, on to the banisters. Of course they were making for old Chawcer's bedroom and their presence there made him more uneasy than ever. From the top landing, through the banister rail, he watched them go into the room. To his relief they didn't close the door. He heard them walking about in there, moving small pieces of furniture, shifting ornaments about. One of them coughed, no doubt from dust released when a curtain was lifted or a shelf searched.

He didn't like them being in there. That was where he had killed her and he still wondered if he had left behind some evidence of his presence and his activities. Then he remembered he had taken the top sheet off her bed to wrap her in. A wash of heat flooded over him. Old women would be bound to spot that, it was the kind of thing they noticed. He found himself trembling all over, his hands shaking and out of control.

But they came out of the room after about ten minutes and he heard Ma Fordyce say as they went down the stairs, 'I feel sure there's something we've missed, Queenie. It's just a feeling I have.'

'So have I, dear. There's something in this house which if we could find it would tell us at once where she is and what she's up to.'

'I'm not so sure of that.'

The rest of what Ma Fordyce said he could no longer hear. By that time she was down in the hallway and all that was audible to him was the twitter of their voices. He listened for the front door to open and close.

Putting her coat on, Queenie said that the weather was getting hot again. There was something unnatural about it, didn't Olive think?

'Global warming,' said Olive. 'I expect the earth will burn up but at least we won't still be here to see it.'

'Now isn't that being a wee bit morbid, dear?'

'Just realistic. I've been thinking about that missing sheet. Gwen is such a peculiar woman, perhaps she never used a top sheet, just a blanket and an eiderdown.'

'Oh, no, dear. I don't mean she's not peculiar. I absolutely agree with you there. But as to not using

335

a top sheet, I know she did. I distinctly remember seeing one when we used to go into her bedroom before she went into hospital. Very grubby it was, too.'

'Then where is it?' said Olive as they closed the front door behind them and went down the path into St Blaise Avenue.

It was the middle of the afternoon before Mix succeeded in buying a sufficiently large and stout plastic bag. The pain in his back which had eased a little that morning now came back with stabbing shafts and a very unpleasant kind of prickling like red-hot needles being dragged up and down his vertebrae. Once the principal aim of his errand was satisfied, he had meant to go into the Job Centre but he was finding that he could scarcely walk upright and the negligible weight of the plastic bag was almost too much for him. If he went into the Job Centre like that they'd think he'd come in to apply for incapacity benefit. At this rate, maybe it would come to that . . .

Once he was home again, a little comforted by a large Boot Camp – he had run out of gin – he braced himself to take the body out of its sheet wrapping and transfer it to the bag. He crawled towards it on his hands and knees but, as he pulled himself up by holding on to the cocktail cabinet, he knew he would be unable to move even so relatively light a piece of furniture without injuring his back perhaps beyond cure, and there was no other way of getting the body out from behind it, for the two rear corners of the cabinet were close up against the walls which met at right angles.

Panic took hold of him. Tears started in his eyes and he drummed on the floor with his fists. After a while, doing his best to control himself, he crawled into the kitchen and, once more hauling himself up, took four strong ibuprofen and swallowed them down with the Boot Camp dregs.

Some hours later Olive came back to St Blaise House, bringing her niece Hazel Akwaa. She felt she needed the support of a sensible younger person.The sun was setting and crimson light lit up the sky over Shepherd's Bush and Acton when the two women went out into the garden. On the other side of the wall, where the fairy light palm tree rivalled the sunset, Mr Singh was throwing down handfuls of corn for his geese.

He said, 'Good evening, Mesdames,' with exquisite politeness.

'I love your tree,' said Hazel. 'It's gorgeous.'

'You are very kind. In the absence of a gardener, my wife and I felt the place needed a soupçon of beautifying. How is Miss Chawcer?'

'She seems to have gone away to convalesce with friends.'

'To the countryside, I hope? That will do her good.'

Olive was looking round for Otto. 'D'you know,' she said, 'I haven't set eyes on that cat since the day before yesterday.'

'Now you mention it,' said Mr Singh, 'nor have I. Not, I must say, that I find this a matter for regret. It is such a predator that I fear my poor geese may meet the same fate as my guinea fowl.'

Throwing a final handful of corn, he gave Olive and Hazel a kind of court bow and went off into his house. The geese cackled and gobbled.

'Have a look at that flowerbed,' said Hazel. 'Doesn't it look as if someone's been digging a grave?'

'You've got too active an imagination, Hazel.'

'If I have it's because when I'm round here I always think of the murderer Christie. He only lived a stone's throw away. I was a baby when it happened but when we were little kids we used to go round to Rillington Place and stare at his house.'

'I remember it well,' said Olive. 'First they renamed it, then they pulled it down. I don't remember that happening anywhere else a murderer lived.'

'Like what the Romans did to Carthage. They razed it to the ground, Tom told me, and ploughed over the site. Christie buried several of those women in his garden.'

'Well, no one's buried Gwendolen. That earth's been turned like that quite a while ago. Thistles are starting to grow on it. But I do wonder what's become of that cat. Whatever Gwendolen says, I'm sure she's quite fond of it and if it's missing when she gets back from wherever she's got to, no prizes for guessing who gets the blame.'

They passed through the house and walked slowly back through the unseasonably sunny morning to Olive's home, scanning the street in nervous anticipation of finding Otto's corpse in a gutter.

It may have been the effect of the pills or the strong spirit or both, but after Mix had slept for a while he awoke feeling dizzy, the pain still there but weak like the memory of a past backache or the antici- pation of one still to come. When he first lay down and closed his eyes, it was with an uneasy feeling that something had happened earlier which was vitally important but that for some reason he hadn't recognised for what it was. It nagged at his mind but drifted away when sleep came. Now, as his dizziness subsided, his mind seemed to clear. He knew what had happened earlier and understood perfectly what it would have said to him if he had been open to receive it.

Ma Winthrop had touched his arm, his bare arm, with one finger. It was when she was asking him if old Chawcer had confided in him. Her finger had touched him and it had been warm, as warm as the skin it touched. And that should have told him, but told him only now, that old people weren't cold to the touch, their temperature was the same as in young ones. So if old Chawcer was ice-cold it was because *she was dead already.*

She had been dead before he entered the room, before he looked at her, before he touched her. That was why her skin felt like ice and why she hadn't struggled when he held the pillow over her face. Sweat broke out across his face and the palms of his hands, yet a great chill passed through him. He had killed a dead woman. It seemed to him an awful thing to have done and a stupid thing. He had killed someone who was already dead.

In a way it was like what Reggie did. No wonder the ghost had seemed sympathetic to him. Of course he hadn't touched her like Reggie did – the horror of that brought him out in a fresh sweat. But there had been points of resemblance. Was he under Reggie's influence, then? Had the ghost directed him?

He got up and walked across the room to where the body was. He put his hands on the top of the cocktail cabinet and leant on it. Gradually it was coming to him that if he had known, if only he had realised, he could have simply looked at her, touched that cold skin and left her there. She couldn't have said anything to the police. She was dead. Instead, he had held a pillow over her face while counting to five hundred. He had pulled a sheet from her bed and wrapped up in it a woman who had been dead for hours. It must have been hours for the body to be so cold.

In doing so he had incriminated himself, for who would now believe she had died a natural death? He had taken away her body and hidden it, he had removed a sheet from her bed, perhaps left some of his DNA – he was vague about this – adhering to her skin, told those two old women she had gone away, said he had seen her waiting for a taxi. And now he had her body up here. Would the police be able to find out she died naturally? Would a coroner? It mustn't come to that.

Whatever it might do to his back, even if it crippled him for life, he had to get it into the bag tonight and stowed away under the floorboards. His ankle felt more painful than ever, a pulse throbbing under the stretched purplish skin.

# Chapter 26

When he first went into the room it looked pitch dark, dark as the inside of a black box, and he thought he might have to leave his task until it grew light at six-thirty in the morning. But gradually his eyes grew accustomed to this absence of light. The sky outside the window began to seem transparent and luminous and the moon was gone. He switched off the torch and still had enough light to see by. He closed the door. As he knelt down and got to work he told himself not to think about the ghost, to force himself to dismiss it from his mind in case fear paralysed his hands.

When it was done he made sure the boards were back exactly as they had been when the floor was first laid: dovetailed, parallel, and with no protruding edges. Gwendolen's body he had sealed up in the heavy plastic, first tying up the mouth of the bag with wire, then making his confidence in the security of this fastening absolutely sure with superglue. All the time he worked his back hurt him, the pain sometimes a steady ache but sometimes hammering instruments of torture into his spine. These totally incapacitated him for whole minutes at a time so that he had to bend forward until his chest was almost on his knees, and hold his hands pressed into the small of his back.

When he had finished and the body was gone, he felt more than relief. It was as if he or someone had utterly destroyed it, by burning perhaps or by some chemical process. Or as if she had never died, only been hidden away beyond talking to the police, beyond return to this house. In the gloom the bedroom looked the same as ever with all tools and glue and wire put away. There were the old gas lamp, the tall chest of drawers with the crazed mirror on its top, the naked bedstead, the window which refused to open. Cobwebs still hung from the ceiling and dust still lay on the windowsill. This was the Westway's quietest time, its breakers almost stilled and its sighings muted.

A great weight seemed to be lifted from him. His back still ached, his ankle was still throbbing and he was very tired, but he felt that his troubles would soon be over. All the time he was in there he had quite successfully kept away thoughts of the ghost but they returned when he was out on the landing. Inside the flat, he tried to relax, to read himself to sleep with the one Christie book he hadn't yet opened, though he'd had it for weeks. He lay on his bed and turned the pages of *The Man who made a Judge Cry* but every chapter heading he read and every illustration he looked at reawakened fears that he might have left some incriminating evidence behind. The book too reminded him of his fate if he were discovered, not the same as Christie's, for his killings had been in the time of capital punishment, but bad enough. It was at this point that he realised he had stopped calling the murderer Reggie and begun referring to him in his mind by his surname.

To stop himself repeating over and over, I killed

a dead woman, I killed a dead woman, he turned his thoughts to the problem of where Gwendolen was supposed to have gone. There was no way they could prove she hadn't gone, no way they could discover where she had or had not gone. Those two old women would soon grow tired of speculating about her. The house would remain empty for a while but for himself. He'd have no rent to pay in old Chawcer's absence and he'd stay where he was just until he'd become Nerissa's boyfriend.

There seemed no impediments now to getting to know her properly. She had always been so nice to him that she was probably waiting for him to come and see her, she might even be disappointed that he hadn't come yet and was thinking he'd let her down. He'd go over to Campden Hill today. Thus he reassured himself.

It was two in the morning now. He anointed his back with the anti-inflammatory preparation the pharmacist had recommended and felt the glowing warmth it produced spread through his muscles. He took two ibuprofen, stripped off his clothes and lay on his bed, thinking, I killed a woman who was already dead.

Although she had resolved on the night of Darel's party that she would never go near a fortune-teller again, that it was obvious nonsense and she should never have fallen for it, everyone said so, Nerissa was again consulting Madam Shoshana. It would be the last time, she was determined on that, but she had to have the soothsayer's opinion on whether or not she had a chance with him. Before she went out she tidied her bedroom, putting used tissues and scraps of cotton wool into the waste basket, picking up discarded garments and dropping them into the linen bin. She even pulled back the quilt to air sheet and mattress before Lynette came to make the bed. Downstairs everywhere was already tidy. It was a dreadful chore and it wore her out but as she took dirty glasses into the kitchen, she thought how approving Darel would be when at last he came here, that he'd think how suited she was to be his girlfriend and even what a wonderful wife she'd make.

Johnny Cash and the girl who loved the boy next door who worked at the candy store had been put away. The CD currently on the player was Dvořák. Two new books from Hatchard's, one on European politics in the post-Cold War period and the other called *The Case against the Occult*, lay on the coffee table, from which everything else had been cleared away. If only he would come and see the civilised, even intellectual, milieu in which she lived!

Fear of again meeting Mix Cellini on the stairs at the spa troubled her during her drive to Westbourne Grove. She had put on baggy jeans and a grey sweatshirt because she knew these clothes did nothing to flatter her, and she hadn't made up her face. Still, it hadn't escaped her notice that make-up does very little for a black woman who is already beautiful. Her dad even said – of course he *would* – that she looked better without it. She just had to hope it wouldn't be Cellini's day for doing whatever he did to the spa's machines. If she had to see him she wanted it to be in Campden Hill Square where she'd at least have a reason for phoning Darel.

In the event she got up those stairs without an

encounter of any kind. She knocked on the door and the unprecedented happened. Shoshana asked her to wait one minute. Take a seat and wait just a minute. She noticed from her watch that she was two minutes early. Learning to be punctual was also part of the Darel-pleasing drive. Unless she had sat on the floor there was nothing on that tiny landing to sit on, so Nerissa stood, thinking about Darel Jones and her new Face of 2004 job and a photoshoot for *Vogue* and Darel Jones and the books she meant to read to please him. Then Madam Shoshana called, 'Come,' in her low, thrilling voice.

She had asked Nerissa to wait because the girl was early for once and when she knocked on the door Shoshana had been busy with Hecate's spine-crippling spell. She had renewed it once and now decided it was time to call a halt. Not because she had any pity for Mix Cellini but through her own frugality. The spell could be re-used four times, she had only done the business twice and who knew when someone else would come along that Shoshana would think deserved a bad back? After all, she was going to have to pay for it. Just because no account had yet come in from Hecate, this didn't mean the witch wasn't going to charge her. Hecate was like those very up-market doctors or dentists who send in their accounts and give you a nasty shock months after their treatment has ended and you've forgotten all about it.

The table was still littered with the paraphernalia required by the spell. Not exactly eye of newt and toe of frog but several vessels of distilled water, a phial of sulphuric acid and one of pregnant woman's urine – difficult to get, that one, but Kayleigh, who was living with Abbas Reza and expecting his child, had happily produced it – a jar of bicarbonate of soda and a bottle of green ink. Not that she was going to use any of it, he had had his two weeks of pain, but she had to throw the urine away, restore the bicarb to the cupboard where it belonged and put the sulphuric acid back in its ribbed green bottle. All this must be put away before Nerissa came in and the gemstones were laid out instead.

Nerissa had always been in awe of Madam Shoshana. She was more than a little afraid of her and she disliked the wizard and the owl, the dirt (though not the untidiness) repelled her and Shoshana herself was possessed of an ugliness which made her shrink. Today the soothsayer had got herself up in a feather-trimmed robe, greyish and bluish, and she wore a crest of black feathers on her head so that, to Nerissa, she looked like some evil bird of prey. Her claw-like hands played mysteriously above the ring of stones.

'When we've done that,' Nerissa said tentatively, putting her hands inside the circle, 'may I ask you something?'

'Why not ask the stones? Which ones do you feel drawing towards your fingers?'

Knowing very well that whichever she said she felt moving towards her, Shoshana would say she had picked the wrong ones, Nerissa said the first colours that came into her head. 'The yellow one and the mauve one.'

'Really? I don't believe you are concentrating. Plainly, it's the blood-red carnelian and the pallid rose quartz which are drawn to you today. Make your request to the carnelian.'

'All right.' The guests at Darel's party might have

been gratified if they could have seen what a fool Nerissa thought she was, asking a piece of rock its opinion. But, blushing, she asked it. 'There's a man,' she began and faltered. She cleared her throat. 'There's a man that I want to know, I want to get some idea if he'll – well, if he'll ever love me.'

Not surprisingly, the dark red crystal remained silent. Nerissa, feeling better now the words were out, almost giggled at the idea of its finding a voice. I wouldn't feel like laughing if it did though, she thought. Shoshana appointed herself its interpreter and Nerissa felt very unlike laughing at what she said.

'You will have to summon him. Call him and he will come. And then, when he comes, all will depend on how you speak to him. What you say then will determine your fate – for the rest of your life.' Shoshana looked up and met Nerissa's eyes. 'That is all. The carnelian has spoken.'

The fifty pounds paid, for Madam Shoshana had put up her fee, Nerissa went back down the stairs, half afraid of encountering Mix Cellini. The only person she saw, waiting downstairs, the stairs being too narrow for two people to pass, was a woman and Madam Shoshana's next client.

The backache was still there when Mix woke up, but it had become subdued and dull, and the scratches on his ankle were healing. He had slept well but for one bad dream. He showered, washed his hair under the shower and dressed carefully, feeling much better, though unable to forget the dream. It had concerned his stepfather and his, Mix's, journey up to Norfolk to find Javy and kill him. This was something he had often fantasised about while still a child and hadn't thought of for years. Javy had walked out on Mix's mother when Mix was fourteen and gone to live with another woman in King's Lynn or near it. But the desire to kill him in a painful way and watch him die in agony came back in the dream and when wide awake, as he now was, Mix saw nothing irrational or impractical in it. After all, he had killed two people (or thought he had) and got away with it so there was no reason why he shouldn't kill a third. Christie would have thought nothing of it, it would have been all in the day's work to him. Javy had done more to deserve being his victim than either of those women, the young or the old.

There was little point in his going to Campden Hill Square before ten. The morning was fine, the sky clear and blue, and breakfast television told him it was going to be a warm and sunny day with the slight chance of a shower. The walk ahead of him seemed a pleasant prospect and what came at the end of it . . . He had a plan for getting into her house and to this end armed himself with an orange cardboard folder left over from his job with the firm, a couple of election pamphlets he'd kept for some forgotten reason and two ballpoint pens. At twenty past nine he was ready to leave when he heard the front door open and close and someone enter the hallway below.

Of course it was Ma Winthrop. It was bound to be one of them. They were like buses, another would be along in a minute. He should have got that key from them, by force if necessary. Imagine the fuss there'd have been as a result! At first he felt at her arrival that tautening of the muscles which is one of the signs of fear and then he reminded himself that he had nothing to be afraid of. Old Chawcer was as hidden and invisible as if she really was in Cambridge; more securely hidden, for no one could run her to earth where she was. So he said, 'Morning,' to Ma Winthrop as he passed her in the hallway, and 'Lovely day,' as he opened the front door. Ma Fordyce was turning in at the gate.

'Another meeting of the Women's Institute?' said Mix rudely. 'Must be great to have so much time on your hands.'

Olive walked past him with her nose in the air.

She and Queenie spent a while indignantly discussing his behaviour and tearing his character to bits. Then, with two milky coffees with grated chocolate on top, in cups which Queenie had brought with her, and a Danish pastry each, they sat by the open french windows in the drawing room, holding a council as to what should be done about Gwendolen. Opening those windows had not been easy. The bolts were stuck until Olive oiled them. Finally she managed to wrench the two glass doors apart. About fifty dead spiders and their accumulated webs of a quarter of a century fell down on to the floor and something that looked like a very old and long-deserted swallow's nest collapsed on the steps, scattering mud and sticks and shattered eggshells everywhere.

'How anyone can live like this!' exclaimed Olive, not for the first time.

Queenie gave an exaggerated shudder. 'It's quite awful. But you know, dear, we have to think what we're going to do about Gwen. If that man is to be believed she went to catch a train for Cambridge on Monday morning, two days ago. Suppose he made Cambridge and the train up? Suppose she was just going for a little walk and while she was out she collapsed and now she's in hospital somewhere? Who would know? Who would they tell?'

'Yes, but why would he?'

'Who knows what goes on in the mind of a man like that? He might be planning to get her out of this house so he can take it over. I've heard of unscrupulous tenants doing that to old people who are their landlords and he's exactly the type.'

The more practical Olive said they could try phoning hospitals.

'Yes, dear, but which hospitals? There must be hundreds in London. Well, dozens. Where do we start?'

'Round here. If she went for a little walk, like you said – though it seems very unlike Gwen to me – she wouldn't have got far before she collapsed. So it's going to be St Charles round the corner here or St Mary's Paddington, isn't it? I'll phone St Charles the minute I've finished my coffee. Oh, Queenie, look what I've found down the side of this chair! It's that thong thing poor Gwen went on and on about.'

'How very peculiar. I'm going to shut those doors, dear, or more flies will come in.'

Before leaving home, he had fortified himself with two strong vodkas. No tonic, just a couple of ice cubes. Not Dutch but Russian courage. He set off to walk along Oxford Gardens towards Ladbroke Grove. His backache had gone but for the occasional faint twinge to remind of what had been, and he felt charged with confidence. Passing the house where Danila had lived, he told himself how silly he'd been to worry about her. Nothing had come of it. Most of the things you have worried about have never happened. He had read that somewhere and it was true.

Above his head, Kayleigh was at one of the windows of the first-floor flat she now shared with Abbas Reza, looking down into the street. Trees, still in full leaf, grew on both sides along it but outside this house one had been cut down and removed so it was possible to get a clear view. They were going out for lunch which they planned to have in a pub on the river. Kayleigh wasn't due for work at the spa before four, and she was studying the pavements for evidence of raindrops. She never bothered with macs or umbrellas herself but Abbas, being older, took a serious view of these things.

She called to him, 'I don't know what those splashes on the window was, Abby, but it wasn't rain. Come and see.'

Abbas came over, put his arm round her waist and looked down. A man in the kind of clothes called 'smart casual' was walking past in the direction of Ladbroke Grove.

'It is he!'

Any student of such matters would have known Abbas was an incomer to the United Kingdom by the grammatical correctness of his English. Kayleigh set him right.

'What's him, Abby?'

'The person who has just passed by, it is he I passed on the stairs when he has been visiting Miss Kovic.'

'You're kidding.'

'Oh, no, I kid you not, Kayleigh. He is the boyfriend all search for.'

'Are you sure? Are you absolutely sure? 'Cos if you are, you'll have to tell the police. So are you positive?'

'Now you put it like this, no, I am not sure that I could swear in a court, this is he. I must think. If only it is possible for me to see him close. If I go after him, if I go now . . .'

'No, you don't, Abby. We're going out – remember? And if you get up close and personal it'll be you they're arresting, not him.'

No bus came so Mix walked all the way down Ladbroke Grove and crossed Holland Park Avenue to make his way up to Nerissa's house. Her car wasn't on the forecourt. Did that mean she had put it away in the garage or could she be out? Please don't let her be out, he prayed to a deity whom he didn't believe in and who he dimly knew wouldn't support him in escaping retribution but just might help him to become Nerissa's lover. The deity, or guardian angel, did. As he was walking up the path of a house next door but two, rather ostentatiously brandishing the orange folder, the Jaguar swept up the hill and swung into her driveway. She couldn't have seen him, he was concealed from view by a large bush covered in red berries. Mix rang the bell and when it was answered by a woman in large black-rimmed glasses and a pin-striped suit began earnestly outlining to her his own assessment of the virtues of Proportional Representation.

As always, Nerissa had scanned the street as she drove up it for the blue Honda. Once more it wasn't there. It hadn't been there for – well, it must be two weeks by now. He's given up, she thought, and this, though what she longed for, would leave her with no excuse for phoning Darel Jones.

352

Even though she had had a shower before she went out, she always felt soiled after she had been in Madam Shoshana's – well, 'den' was the word she always used for it. Anyway, she was going out to lunch with the *Vogue* woman and she might as well get ready now. So when Mix rang her door-bell half an hour later, she was dressed in a pale yellow suit, her hair up in a chignon and her legs encased in primrose yellow suede boots.

The woman in the severe suit and the glasses had given Mix a hard time. She told him she was a Member of Parliament, until recently a lecturer at the London School of Economics. What she didn't know about Proportional Representation, and indeed all psephological systems, plainly wasn't worth knowing, while he knew nothing but what he had read in a tabloid newspaper. He left, feeling unfairly punished for simply trying to find out if people really like voting for an individual instead of a political party. The man who answered the door at the next house wasn't interested and became plainly exasperated when Mix, in rather a muddled way, tried passing on to him some of the explanations put forward by the MP. No one was at home next door to Nerissa. He drew a deep breath, told himself not to be shy, she was just a woman like any other, and went to the door.

She was aghast to see him but where another woman in her position might have slammed the door in his face without waiting to hear what she had to say, she stood, holding it open. She had been brought up to be well-mannered.

Mix had rehearsed what he would say. 'Well, good morning, Miss Nash. We're not exactly strangers to each other, are we? If I remember rightly, the first time was at my friend Colette's home.'

'We've met before, yes,' she said.

She looked so beautiful he could hardly keep the yearning out of his eyes or the hope from his expression. Like a yellow rose, he thought, un-accustomed to lyrical comparison, like an African queen. 'I don't expect you knew,' he said, using the rehearsed words, 'that I do market research in my leisure time.'

'No,' she said. 'No, I didn't.'

'I'd like to talk to you today about elections. I expect you know what Proportional Representation is, don't you?'

She said nothing, her face puzzled and, in some way he recognised but couldn't have explained, helpless.

'May I come in?'

It was the last thing she wanted. If he had been a total stranger she would have been able to refuse him but they had spoken before, three times before. 'I'm going out.' She wasn't for an hour. 'Just for a minute, then.'

As soon as the words were out of her mouth she knew she shouldn't have uttered them. She should have been firm, strong, said what she'd have said and often had, to Jehovah's Witnesses and kitchen equipment salesmen, thank you very much but she just wasn't interested. Before she had thought this he was in the house, walking slowly through the hallway looking admiringly from side to side, nod-ding and smiling in a way that plainly indicated admiration of everything.

She would have kept him in the hall and as near to the front door as possible but he didn't give her the chance. He was in the living room before she could attempt to stop him. Today was the day the flowers came. Lynette had taken them in while she was at Madam Shoshana's and arranged them in the big cream pottery and etched glass bowls. For a moment she saw it with another's eyes, the eyes of someone not used to opulence garnished with lilac and lilies and gerberas, and she understood why he was so impressed.

'This is a very lovely home you have.'

'Thank you,' she said in rather a small voice.

'May I sit down, Miss Nash? And I have a second request. May I call you Nerissa?'

She didn't know how to say no to either. To refuse seemed churlish and somehow setting herself up as superior, and ever since she began to be known and sought-after she had resolved never to think herself better than anyone else and certainly not to show it. Helplessly, she watched him settle himself on one of the sofas, open the orange cardboard folder he was carrying and look up to give her a hugely wide and toothy grin.

Mix had had plenty of practice, if not quite at this sort of thing, at least in selling himself and his various products, being pleasant and mildly flirtatious with women. Any diffidence he might have had in other circumstances faded when he was talking to a woman and putting across a point. Besides, the vodka had begun to do its work before he rang the MP's bell.

He no longer saw any reason to beat about the bush and he said, 'I'm going to come out with the truth frankly, Nerissa, and tell you I'm not here to talk about politics or elections or boring stuff like that. I don't know much about it anyway as your smartass neighbour was kind enough to tell me to my face. No, I'm here to see you because what I said when we met in old Chawcer's house was all true, every single word of it. And I'd like to tell you again, choose my words a bit more carefully this time, but do you think you could rustle us up a coffee first, my love?'

Whether it was that 'my love' which did it or his calling her great-aunt's friend 'old Chawcer' or just his tone and look, she couldn't have said, but as for the coffee, she was glad of a chance to get out of the room and to her mobile. Not that she was going to call Darel Jones, much as she would have loved to see him. But she knew she couldn't summon him. It would be unfair on him to fetch him away from work and a nasty underhand trick to play on this awful man. All these weeks she had been longing for the chance to call him, even thinking of encouraging this man in order to have an excuse, but now she couldn't do it. It was her father she was going to phone. She put the coffee and the boiling water in the cafetière first. Then she dialled her dad at his office and when he answered, just said, 'Dad, he's here, in the house, that stalker I told you about.'

'Right,' he said. 'I'll handle it.'

Nerissa's agent and, come to that, her mother and father and her brothers and Rodney Devereux, would all have said if asked that Nerissa must be quite accustomed to dealing with men making unwelcome overtures to her but in fact very few had done so. There was something about her, something ice-maidenish yet warm and innocent, which put off any man even marginally more sensitive than Mix Cellini. Those whose approaches were

356

welcome had been few and all of them knew where they stood before the initial overture was made. Mix, on the other hand, was unable to tell the difference between a woman who agreed to give him coffee and a seat because she loathed the idea of being rude and one who did so because she shortly hoped to be in bed with him. He took the cup she handed him with a slight smile and a sexy look and said, 'Come and sit here by me.'

'I'll stay here if you don't mind.'

'Well, I do mind, I mind a lot.' Mix distorted his face into an ingratiating smile. 'But we'll let it pass for the time being. Now tell me, where did you get your lovely name, Nerissa? It really is a most beautiful name and, do you know, I don't think I've ever come across it before.'

'My mum got it out of a Shakespeare play.'

'Really? I see you come from educated people. I reckon these mixed partnerships are best, don't you? Mixed-up genes and all that. My grandad was Italian. I don't mind telling you, though I don't tell everyone, he was an Italian prisoner of war. Romantic, eh?'

She said helplessly, 'I don't know.'

'Maybe I'd best get down to the nitty-gritty. This is very good coffee, by the way. Very good. What I'm starting to say is, me and you, I guess we've a lot in common, same sort of background, same sort of age, both fitness freaks and both living in good old West Eleven. I don't mind telling you I've been in love with you for yonks and I flatter myself you don't exactly dislike me. So what say we put it to the test?'

She was on her feet now, seriously frightened and more so when he too got up. They stood no more than a yard apart and he took a step towards her.

'How about a little kiss for starters?'

She was preparing to fight him off, use her boot heels as weapons if necessary, but as she backed away the doorbell rang. It disconcerted him. He looked, not bewildered or disappointed, but furiously angry, a pinpoint of red light in each eye, his upper lip curling back.

'Excuse me,' she said, knowing these words were ridiculous in the circumstances. She almost ran to the door to let her father in.

It wasn't her father. It was Darel Jones.

# Chapter 27

'Your father called me.'

I'll kill Dad, was her first thought, and then love for her father overwhelmed her. 'He shouldn't have,' she said.

'That chap – has he gone?'

'He's still here. He's in there.'

Darel walked into the room where Mix, still on his feet, was examining a glass figurine very like the one he had been forced to use on Danila. Something else they had in common . . .

'Get out,' said Darel.

'Pardon me? I don't think we've met. Mix Cellini. I'm a friend of Miss Nash. In point of fact, we were just arranging how we were going to spend the evening till we were so rudely interrupted.'

'I said get out. Go. Unless you want me to put you out.'

'For Christ's sake!' Mix was mystified. 'What have I done, I'd like to know? Ask her if you don't believe me.'

'I really would like you to go,' Nerissa said. 'Please don't fight over it. Just go.'

'Because you ask me, I will,' said Mix. 'I know you don't mean it. You know and I know that I'll be back once your bully boy is out of the way.' He tried to move with dignity towards the door. But he was learning that though it is possible for a man with a protruding belly to be many things, dignified is not one of them. He turned in the doorway. 'I'll never let you go,' he said, more because it was the right thing to say than because he meant it. He opened the front door and closed it behind him.

'Thank you for that,' Nerissa said in a weak voice. 'Do you think he meant it, that he'd never let me go?'

'No. He probably thinks I live here, that I'm your significant other or partner or whatever.'

She wanted to say, I wish you were, and, will you be? But she could only look at him, at his beautifully chiselled Celtic face, the black hair, the pale skin with the faintest red bloom on the cheeks, at his lean, long-fingered hands, at the length of him.

'I've got something to say to you, Nerissa. I've been hoping for a chance to say it for weeks now.'

Impossible to resist a rejoinder to that. 'You could have called me.'

'I know. I wanted to think carefully about what I knew and what I wanted. I needed to be sure I'd be doing the right thing. I'm sure now.'

'Sure of what?'

He smiled. 'Come here. Sit beside me.'

Mix's invitation she had unhesitatingly refused but now the same request, uttered from the same place on the sofa, had come from Darel, she accepted it. He turned to face her and took both her hands in his. 'When we came to live next door I was a big teenager and you were a small one. I thought you beautiful even then – who wouldn't? – but I did nothing about it. I soon had a girlfriend, anyway. I was away at university – I was training for five years, one year in the United States – and when I came home again, you were a famous model.'

'I remember,' she said.

'I got it into my head you must be an empty-headed frivolous woman. I thought all models were. Capricious too and what my mother calls stuck-up, and – well, with an I-only-get-out-of-bed-for-ten-grand sort of attitude. Of course I couldn't help being attracted to you, but I got to think that if I was in your company the way you were bound to talk and act would just make me angry. So I didn't go with my parents when yours asked us next door for drinks. I knew you'd be there and that stopped me going with them the day before I moved.'

'So what happened?'

'Well, I knew that if I was ever alone with you I'd be bound to ask you out, I couldn't help myself. I kept thinking too how my mother once said your mother told her how messy you were about the house and how unpunctual and I knew I couldn't stand that. I've made a plan for my life, Nerissa, it's all worked out, where I'm going and how I'm going to get there. Among other things, I want a serious relationship. I'm nearly thirty-one and I'm looking to a long-term partnership, even marriage.'

She nodded, feeling his hands tighten over hers.

'Marriage and kids too. Why not? But I wasn't willing to travel that road, playing second fiddle to a woman everyone admired and adored. I didn't want to be with a woman who was care-less and – well, profligate and extravagant. And I can't stand people who are always late. Frankly, I wasn't prepared to be "Mr Nerissa Nash", arriving at your sort of party – or what I thought was your sort of party – an hour late and then have no one talk to me because you were the cynosure of all eyes.'

She didn't know what 'cynosure' meant and she wasn't too sure about 'profligate'. She listened.

'But that day we encountered each other in St James's Street,' he went on, 'that began to change me. I put you to the test in little ways. There was that dinner party, for instance. You were actually on time. And look at this place. I don't imagine you clean it yourself but you certainly keep it the way the daily has done it. At dinner you talked about politics and morality and – well, even economics. I thought, I'll leave it a while. If she phones me and starts being demanding or pulling her rank, if she thinks I'm hers for taking whenever she pleases, that'll be it. But you didn't.' He drew her a little towards him. 'You passed the test. With flying colours. I thought, yes, right, she's fit for what I want, she's really OK. So how about dinner tonight, Miss Nash?'

Her hands gently withdrawn from his, she moved a few inches back along the sofa. Her heart, which normally had the slow steady beat, a doctor had told her, of an athlete or a well-exercised young woman, now began to race and pound.

'I don't think so,' she said, and her voice, even to herself sounded remote. 'I didn't know I was taking part in a quiz, a competition, whatever. I wouldn't have if I'd known.'

'What are you talking about, sweetheart?'

'I'm not your sweetheart and I never will be. I don't do tests to see if I'm a – a suitable candidate.'

'Now, Nerissa, come on.'

'I'm what I am. And whoever does have a what-d'you-call-it, permanent relationship with me, he'll have to take me as I am. Thank you for coming here and getting rid of that man. I'm grateful but we won't meet again.'

He got up, his face registering a simple lack of comprehension.

'Goodbye, Darel,' she said.

As soon as he had gone she picked up the phone, dialled the restaurant where she was lunching with the *Vogue* woman and said she'd be half an hour late. Then she wept for a little. The phone rang while she was re-doing her make-up, repairing the damage tears had done. It was her father.

'Did he come?'

'Yes, he did. You shouldn't have, Dad. I know you meant well.'

'As long as I live I'm going to see my girl gets what she wants if it's in my power. When are you seeing him again?'

'Never. I'll call you later.'

She had one phone call to make before she went out. He picked up the phone after two rings.

'Rodney, will you take me out tonight? Somewhere awful. I fancy that Cockatoodle Club in Soho, I've never been there. We'll be late and get home late and have champagne. No, I know I don't drink but I'll break my rule tonight. Will you? You're a lamb. See you.'

She didn't have to have a partner, she didn't have to marry, she thought as she got into the taxi. She was young. Why not just enjoy herself? So long as she was nice to people and didn't get above herself or start thinking her looks were something she'd achieved and ought to be proud of. First of all, she'd go to her hairdresser and get him to do her hair in corn rows or maybe even dreadlocks. She badly needed a gesture of defiance . . .

I can't call my home my own these days, Mix thought, coming downstairs to pick up what post he had. It was the following day, midway through the morning, and standing in the hallway, he could hear the voices from the drawing room of three women. Ma Winthrop, Ma Fordyce and who was the third? He listened. *Her* mother of course, Mrs Mumbo-jumbo. What was the point of them coming back here day after day? Until he realised what he was doing, he felt indignant on old Chawcer's behalf, not allowed to go away to friends for a few days. What business was it of theirs? Then he remembered she was dead.

Mrs Mumbo-jumbo had probably heard all about his stand-off with bully boy the day before. On the other hand, Nerissa might not have told her. She might want to get rid of bully boy and establish a proper relationship with him before she said anything to her parents. He'd leave it a day or two and then he'd go back and hear what had happened after he'd decided the mature thing to do was leave. There was something about bully boy that reminded him of Javy, the look of him more than anything. Javy would be grey by now but before Mix left home he'd had that olive skin and pink cheeks and a lot of black hair. Women found him attractive, though Mix could never see why.

He'd been to the Benefit Office and signed on. They gave him some money and offered a whole lot of jobs he hadn't liked the look of. Time enough for that in a couple of weeks. Not wanting to encounter any of the three women, he picked up the Dig-it and the Wall mail order catalogues and took them upstairs, though being neither a gardener nor a woman, they weren't much use to him. Twenty-two stairs to the floor where she'd slept, seventeen up to where no one slept and no one ever went, thirteen more to the top. He didn't always count them, not when he was afraid, but he did now, as if he could make them fourteen.

The thong lying in her lap, Hazel Akwaa was asking her aunt and Queenie if they had thought of going through Gwendolen's clothes. They both shook their heads and Olive shrugged.

'It seems so intrusive, dear,' said Queenie, 'such an invasion of her privacy. I mean, how would you like it if you went away and your friends started rifling through your clothes? You'd feel *violated*.'

'Yes, I would if I'd told them where I was going and left the address of where I'd be. But if I'd disappeared and was missing I'd be glad. I'd want to be found.'

'On the whole, I think we should,' Olive said. They began climbing the stairs. 'I hope someone's feeding that cat.'

'Food has been put down for him every day but it's not been touched since Sunday. He's gone off somewhere.'

'It looks as if he went when Gwendolen went,' said Queenie. She told Hazel about the missing sheet.

'Are you quite sure?'

'She has such funny ways. I thought she could have just taken off the top sheet and left the bottom one and the blankets but I looked in the washing machine and even inside that awful old copper – you never *know* with Gwendolen. She might even have taken it with her.'

'What, the cat or the sheet?'

'Well, either. No one, but *no one*, no matter how eccentric, would take a soiled bedsheet away somewhere to stay with friends. You'd have to be seriously mad to do that. And how could she manage a cat?'

By now they were all in Gwendolen's bedroom and Olive had opened the window because the weather was still fine and the sun shining.

'It doesn't smell very nice,' said Hazel.

Her aunt shrugged. 'Places don't if you don't clean them.'

'You know, this carpet is actually blue but it's got such a mat of cat's hair covering it that it looks grey.'

Hazel opened the door of the wardrobe and was met by the powerful reek of camphor. Gwendolen's ancient dresses crowded together on hangers long ago covered in ruched silk and hung with lavender bags. Shoes were jumbled together underneath them, not placed in pairs. Olive began to count them.

'Seven,' she said. 'And that's significant. She told me not long ago she had seven pairs of shoes.'

'She must have bought some more.'

'I'm sure she didn't. She would have told me. I'm not saying she made a special confidante of me, only that Gwen couldn't buy anything, let alone a big item like that, without moaning about the cost of it to everyone she spoke to.'

'She couldn't have gone away without any shoes,' said Hazel.

'Nor without her ruby ring, dear.' Queenie had opened the jewel box and was looking inside. She held up a ring with a red stone. 'It was her mother's and she never went out without it.'

# Chapter 28

'You are saying I sit at this window all day every day in case this man comes by? You are not serious, Kaylee.'

'Yes, I am, Ab. If it's him and he's taken Danila hostage and got her shut up somewhere, handcuffed and tied up and all that, you won't be able to live with yourself if you don't go to the cops. I bet he comes down here a lot. I bet he lives round here.'

'Kaylee,' said Abbas in the voice of someone to whom a great revelation has been vouchsafed on the road to Damascus. 'Oh, Kaylee . . .'

'Whatever is it? You've got quite – well, pale, if you see what I mean.'

'Kaylee. That night, after I see him on the stairs, I pick up a card from the floor I see him drop. He is drunk, you understand, and it fall from his jacket. I bring it here, into my own flat and . . .'

'Where is it now, Ab?'

'Do you think I keep it? A strange man's visiting card?'

'But you read what was on it?'

Abbas sat down and pulled Kayleigh on to his knee. 'Sit with me, my flower, and help me to think. I think hard what was on it.'

'Yes, you do that, darling. If you let poor Danila

down now, what's our baby going to think of you?'

Their baby, as yet a very small foetus in its mother's womb, need know nothing about it, as far as Abbas could see, and would hardly be concerned with its father's memory processes for another fifteen years, if then. But he could understand that if it was in his power to help the police find the author of Danila's wrongs, whatever they might be, untimely death possibly, though he wasn't going to say that to Kayleigh who was in a fragile condition and might easily be upset, he was bound to do so. He thought.

'One word I remember from that card,' he said. 'Not a man's name or address . . .'

'Oh, Abby . . .'

'Wait. One word. It is Fiterama. Yes, Fiterama. What it means, I cannot tell. But this is on the card.'

Kayleigh jumped off his lap. She was very excited. 'I know what it means, Ab. It's the name of the firm the man works for as services the machines at the spa. Madam Shoshana told me. He didn't come back with the parts so she gave them a bell to slag him off.'


The secondhand crime bookstore wanted to charge Mix twenty-five pounds for a book on Christie, published forty years before. He had just happened to take it down from the shelf to look at an illustration, when the shop assistant pounced.

'It's daylight robbery,' he said. 'I hope you don't find a buyer.'

'There's no need to be abusive,' said the shop assistant.

Walking home from Shepherd's Bush, Mix told himself he would buy no more books on Christie, he would read nothing more about Christie, it was all over. He might even bring the books he had and see if that chap would buy them. But for Christie, Danila would be alive and he, Mix, would never have killed a dead woman. If he were being strictly honest, he'd say Christie had killed them both himself, bringing his total up to eight.

Before he set up his own business he'd have to get himself work and he certainly couldn't take any of the clerks' and janitors' and council drivers' jobs on offer. He'd be in Javy's class if he did that. Javy – ever since he'd had that confrontation with Nerissa's bully boy he'd been thinking of Javy, brooding on him, even dreaming of him. It was thirteen years since he'd seen the man but his hatred hadn't diminished. He'd thought it had, that it was in the past, but he'd been wrong. Javy had seemed an obstacle he could never surmount, but now he had dealt with those two women – 'dealt with' was a more realistic way of putting it than 'killed' – taking revenge on his stepfather presented itself as quite feasible.

Ahead of him, still parked at the kerb, he could see the Brunswicks' old Volvo. It would just be trouble, he thought, a car, however reputable, of that age, breaking down on longer journeys, requiring endless maintenance. While he stared at it, noticing that the £300 notice on its windscreen was now hanging lopsidedly, Sue Brunswick came out of her front door, carrying a large sooty-brown cat in her arms. In the events of last weekend, he had forgotten all about pursuing her.

'Have you thought any more about buying our car?'

'I don't reckon I want it,' he said.

The cat he recognised. If he hadn't known him by his colour and size he would have by the look of contemptuous hatred Otto turned on him. The eyes of imperial jade lingered coldly and then, snuggling against Sue Brunswick's full bosom, Otto buried his face lovingly in her neck.

'I see you're admiring my cat. Gorgeous, isn't he? He just walked in on Monday and we've adopted him. We're calling him Chockie on account of his colour. I don't know where he came from but he's so affectionate and sweet, I just adore him.'

It sounded very unlike the Otto he knew. A faint throbbing in his ankle reminded Mix of their last encounter. 'Well, cheers,' he said and passed on. Back at home, he went into the bedroom where she lay under the floorboards. None of the books, none of the court proceedings, told him whether Christie had sometimes checked the hidden places to which he had consigned his dead wife and those others. Did he sniff the air as Mix was doing now? Did he stand at a rear window and contemplate the garden of 10 Rillington Place, assuring himself that the graves of Ruth Fuerst and Muriel Eady were undisturbed?

He could smell nothing beyond the usual odour of this house outside the confines of his own flat, a smell of dust and dead insects and aged never-cleaned fibres. The scent of an old person, but not a dead one. His next natural move was to the window that overlooked the garden. In spite of the lack of rain, weeds were growing, green and vigorous, over the slight hump of Danila's grave. To everyone but him it would soon be undetectable.

Why not go away for a bit? Use up the time

between now and the day he'd fix on for seeing Nerissa again. He couldn't remember when he'd last had a holiday. Of course, going to Colchester to stay with one's sister wasn't what most people would call a holiday but this trip would have another purpose. He'd find out from Shannon where Javy was now. Not still with the woman who had succeeded their mother, he was sure. Javy would have moved on, to a new life, a new girl-friend, a new benefit office.

It was funny, what you'd call ironical, that the member of his family he got on with best, the only one really he got on with at all, was the sister Javy said he'd tried to kill. And it wasn't as if she didn't know about it. Javy had taken care to tell her. Mix could hear his words now.

'You wouldn't let him handle your dolls if you knew what he'd done. Tried to kill you, he did. Would have bashed your brains out if I hadn't got there in time.'

They went to the police station in Ladbroke Grove together on Friday morning. Hazel said they didn't need her, she had to get home, but they were to tell her what the police said and every-thing that happened. A Middle Eastern man was coming out with a pretty young blonde woman as they went in.

'I wonder what they were in there for,' said Queenie. 'Perhaps he's an asylum seeker and she's going to marry him to make him a British citizen.'

'It doesn't work like that any more.' Olive stared after the couple. 'It's a much more complicated business.'

They were given a Missing Persons form, which

Olive filled in as best she could. 'Is that it?' she said to the young detective constable.

'What do you want "it" to be?'

'You could look for her, for a start.'

He went away, was away for ten minutes, then came back with another officer, the one who had seen Abbas and Kayleigh. The other officer said, 'Is there a youngish guy called Michael Cellini, formerly of the Fiterama Gym Equipment Company, living on the premises?'

'I don't know about any gym equipment,' said Olive in a voice full of scorn, 'but his name's Cellini all right. Why?'

If she had been less innocent or had watched more television she would have known better than to ask that question. Naturally, it remained unanswered.

'If we call at the address will there be anyone to let us in?'

'Cellini, I suppose,' said Queenie, who had dropped the 'Mr' after Mix's remark about the Women's Institute. 'No, you can't rely on him. One of us will take care to be there.'

'We would anyway.' Olive spoke grimly. 'Leave the place empty and he's capable of setting fire to it.'

They returned to St Blaise House in a taxi after Queenie had bought two slices of lemon cheesecake and two cream horns for their tea at a pâtisserie in Holland Park Avenue.

'I wonder if he's up there,' Queenie said at the foot of the stairs.

Mix was. He'd spent most of the day phoning those of his old clients he hadn't already targeted but at the final count only six had agreed to transfer their business to him and one of those was hesitant. In the early evening he phoned his sister to ask if he could come and stay for a few days. Shannon, who couldn't understand why anyone who didn't have to would want to spend even a single day in a house on a council estate outside Colchester with an exhausted woman, her boyfriend, her three children and his two, asked him why.

'Do I have to have a reason? I reckoned it'd be nice to see you and Markie and the kids, that's all.'

'It's not that I mind, Mix, only you'll have to bunk in with the boys. There's only three bedrooms.'

'I haven't seen you for I don't know how long, Shan. Must be all of five years.'

'More like seven,' said Shannon. 'Lee was just a baby. Look, I've got to go. When was you thinking of coming?'

Tomorrow, Mix said, some time tomorrow morning. He'd have to come on the train. 'My car's in dock. Having a new sump fitted. I'll get a taxi from the station.' He'd get the bus but there was no need to tell her that.

Downstairs, Queenie and Olive waited for the police to come. Although they had asked if anyone would be in later no police had appeared, it was eight o'clock and beginning to get dark.

Queenie stood at the french windows, looking out into the twilit garden. She had watched Mr Singh calling to his geese to shut them up for the night and now he had gone in and there was no one to be seen. The coloured lights on the palm tree came on, went off and came again, twinkling brightly.

'He really is a very handsome man, you know, dear. Quite distinguished-looking. He has the backbone of a high-ranking army officer.'

'Don't be absurd, Queenie.' These days, listening to herself speak, Olive was conscious that the mantle of Gwendolen's mannerisms and speech patterns was descending on to her shoulders. She must watch herself. 'It has occurred to me that perhaps one of us should stay the night.'

'Well, don't look at me. I should be frightened out of my wits staying in this place. Have you noticed how dark it is? And it's not possible to make it any lighter. The wattage of the bulbs is too low. We should have bought some hundred-watt bulbs.'

'Why don't you just pop home and fetch some. I'll stay here till you get back. I shan't mind,' said Olive, who would mind very much but was putting a brave face on it. 'I shall phone my niece and see if she can persuade her husband to come and stay. He's a lovely man but he's very big and he looks quite alarming.'

Queenie went off to fetch the light bulbs and Olive remained where she was in the drawing room. They had cooked themselves scrambled eggs on toast for their supper and had tinned peaches afterwards. The peaches came out of Gwendolen's cupboard but had a sell-by date of 30 November 2003 on the can, so Queenie thought they couldn't do them much harm. After a while Olive phoned the Akwaas and Tom said he'd come over about nine-thirty. Staying in that crazy place would be a lark, he said.

Sleeping arrangements would have to be made for herself and Tom. Olive hated the thought but it was no good postponing it. She toiled upstairs to the first floor. Gwendolen's bedroom and dressing room and the bathroom occupied most of it but two other rooms had bedsteads and mattresses. They seemed rather less damp than the rest of the house and the curtains at the windows neither resisted drawing nor hung in rags. In a cupboard in one of these rooms she found sheets and pillowcases and blankets. The blankets were far from clean and the sheets, though washed, had never been ironed, but they would do. For one night they would do. Making up the bed in the room nearer to the head of the stairs, Olive asked herself if she were mad, electing to stay overnight in this house. And then she heard Mix Cellini's footsteps overhead and she understood that she was right. In the morning she would phone the police and ask them if they meant to come.

Mix heard her too and wondered what was going on. Probably nothing. It was very likely no more than those two old vultures deciding to help themselves to whatever they could find before old Chawcer came back. That would be typical. She had probably possessed some valuable jewellery, those old girls always did. He congratulated himself. Most guys in his position would have been into her things once they'd found her dead and he felt quite smug because he hadn't touched a single one.

He heard the front door open and close, Ma Winthrop's voice calling out some rubbish about light bulbs, and because all these comings and goings were making him nervous he came out on to the landing. Ma Fordyce was going downstairs. As she reached the bottom the front door bell rang. This happened so seldom that it made Mix jump. Of course the light had gone out and tonight it was particularly dark, no moon, not so many lights showing in houses as usual. It was partly the fault of all those tall trees, concealing street lights behind great dark branches. Someone had opened the front door. He heard a man's voice, rich and fruity, and for one moment he thought the impossible: that this was the police. Then Ma Fordyce said, 'Hallo, Tom. It *is* good of you to do this.'

'No problem,' said the fruity voice. 'My pleasure. I brought a bottle of wine. I thought it wouldn't go down badly and when we've wetted our whistles I'll drive Mrs Winthrop home. Can't let her go out alone on a night like this.'

There was silence. They must all have gone into the drawing room. Mix turned round slowly, took a step towards his front door and looking down the left-hand passage, saw the ghost standing at the end in the deep shadows. He clapped his hand over his mouth to stop himself crying out. The ghost stood still and seemed to be staring at him. Then it moved forwards, its hands held out in front of it as if pleading for something, as if begging – or threatening? His front door had been left on the latch; Mix flung it wide open and fell inside the flat, tumbling over the doormat then leaning back, holding the door shut against the ghost. But he could feel no pressure against him and at last, still trembling, he got up and bolted the door top and bottom, something he had never done before.

Tom Akwaa was the first up in the morning. He always was and didn't vary his routine just because he had taken the day off. 'I'll stay till the police come,' he said to Olive when she came down for her tea. 'You want me to remind them you're waiting for them?'

'Would you?'

She couldn't resist starting to clean the kitchen while he was on the phone. Olive belonged to a generation that changed the sheets when the doctor was coming and put on their best underwear before they went on a journey in case they were in an accident and had to go to hospital. Now she tidied and scrubbed the kitchen and wiped all the surfaces in case the policemen went in there for a cup of tea.

It was a relief to Mix to be going away. He might never come back. Not to stay, at any rate. Just to collect his things and get his furniture stored while he found another place. The appearance the previous night of the ghost after a long absence had been the last straw. Compared to that, all these people coming and going didn't amount to much but it was a nuisance, and worrying too. Who had that man been and what was he doing here?

His backache had returned. Not severely, nothing like on that terrible night after his grave-digging, but bad enough. He took two ibuprofen and started to pack. He probably wouldn't stay with Shannon for more than one night. The idea of sharing a room with her two unruly boys, one of them fourteen – she'd had both by the time she was nineteen – didn't appeal. He put in a spare pair of jeans and three shirts. His leather jacket he'd wear. Now to get out of the house before meeting either of those two old witches.

The police needed no reminder once the information given them first by Abbas Reza and then by Olive and Queenie had been compared. A detective sergeant was out in the garden with Tom Akwaa when Olive saw Mix Cellini coming down the stairs. She waited for him in the hallway, though she had no intention of telling him of the policeman's arrival.

'Where are you going?' she said in her best high-handed tone.

He had his backpack over one shoulder. 'No business of yours but since you ask, I'm off to see my sister in Essex.'

'I haven't seen your car about lately.'

'No, you haven't, Nosy Parker, because it hasn't been here. I've sold it.'

He opened the front door and slammed it hard behind him. Olive abandoned her cleaning and began searching through the cluttered drawers in the drawing room furniture to see if Gwendolen had a key to his flat. It took her a long while but by the time Queenie arrived she had found eighteen keys of various shapes and sizes.

'It's not any of those,' Queenie said. 'She told me once, she kept – I mean "keeps" – important keys in the tumble-drier.'

Olive was distracted from her task by this fascinating sidelight on Gwendolen's peculiarities. 'What happened when she used it? The drier, I mean.'

'She never did use it, dear. Not for the purpose it was designed for, anyway.'

They went into the kitchen. The natural place for a tumble-drier would have been the washhouse but Gwendolen had kept hers between the oven and the fridge. From the window they could see the policeman, who had been joined by a second one, poking a long thin stick into a weed-grown mound in what had long ago been a herbaceous border. Queenie opened the porthole on the tumble-drier and brought out a netting bag, which had probably once held onions or potatoes, but which now contained a dozen keys.

'It'll be that one,' Olive said, picking out the newest key, a shiny brass Yale.

The two policemen with Tom Akwaa came in through the washhouse.

'There'll be some chaps coming to dig up the garden,' said the detective sergeant.

'Dig up the garden!'

The detective sergeant looked as if he might explain why and then thought better of it. He and the other man began climbing the stairs, Tom following, and behind him Olive and Queenie taking the flights slowly. At the top Queenie could hardly speak but Olive rallied when one of the policemen started ringing Mix's doorbell.

'He's just gone out.' She decided to lie and hoped Queenie would have the sense not to blurt out a denial. 'Here's his key. He left it with me in case you wanted to look round.'

'Really?' The detective sergeant was only twenty-eight and he hadn't known many murderers but he would hardly have expected a killer to invite the police in to search his premises in his absence. Still, never look a gift horse in the mouth was his philosophy, so he took the key, unlocked Mix's front door and they went in. That is, the police did. Because it had been made plain they wouldn't be wanted, Tom with Olive and Queenie went into the bedroom next door. It was unsufferably stuffy and dusty. Tom, who had an unusually acute nose, sniffed and looked suspicious, sniffed again.

'What's that nasty smell?'

'I can't smell anything, Tom.'

'Nor can I.'

A kindly soul, Tom Akwaa wouldn't have dreamt of telling them that their faculties might have declined with age, so all he said was, 'Well, I can.'

The policemen joined them, the younger one with an armful of books on John Reginald Halliday Christie. Olive, a reader, looked curiously at their spines, several of them adorned with a photograph of Christie's gaunt face.

'Can you smell anything funny in here?' Tom asked.

The bearer of Mix's library, a very tall young man, laid the books on the dressing table and bent almost double so that his nose was nearly touching the floor. 'God, yes,' he said as he straightened up.

When they had all gone but Queenie, who was making coffee in the kitchen, Olive set about taking the sheets and pillowcases off the beds she and Tom had used the night before. She was glad of something to do, for she felt very unsettled and shaky. After all, as people constantly told her, she was not so young as she had once been. The sight of that young man poking a stick into that grave-shaped mound had begun it. Then the smell, though she couldn't smell it. Strangely, those Christie books had been the last straw, the books, that man's face on their covers, and the implication of them. She was afraid of bursting into tears but she had managed to control herself. Her hands, trying to pull the top and bottom sheets off Tom's bed, shook like thin papery leaves in the wind.

Gwendolen was dead, she had no doubt of it now. Although she hadn't much liked the woman she called her friend, she felt the enormity of it, the threatening awfulness of violent death. A tear started in each eye and rolled down her cheeks. She wiped them on one of the sheets and bundled it into a pillowcase to take home and wash.

Outside the door she heard a footstep above her. Had Cellini come back? She set the pillowcase laundry bag down and listened, hoping that her hearing wasn't going the way of her sense of smell. Another footfall. Olive's instinct was to flee, to get down those stairs to Queenie as fast as she could. But she stood her ground. Cellini couldn't have come back, not come into the house and got up the stairs and into his flat without one of them seeing and hearing him. The police had only been gone ten minutes and Tom less than that. Olive set her foot on the bottom step of the tiled flight and began to climb. It was the bravest thing she had ever done.

She would have crawled up the last five stairs if she hadn't been afraid Queenie would come up with the coffee and see her. As it was, she stopped at the top, hung on to the newel post and looked for the source of the sounds. To the right, then to the left. Olive screamed.

'What is it? What's happened?'

She ignored Queenie's voice but she didn't scream again. The sound refused to come. Trembling, she stared at the man with Christie's face. It was quite a lot like the photograph on the spines of those books. He was coming towards her, holding out both hands. She would die, she would have a heart attack and die.

'Please, do not fear.'

He spoke with a strong foreign accent. Not a bit like Christie would have, thought Olive. She closed her eyes, opened them again and said in a whisper, 'Who are you?' She cleared her throat and her voice came out more loudly and clearly. 'Who are you?'

'I am called Omar. Omar Ahmed. I am from Iraq.'

'The war's over,' said Olive. 'Were you in the war?'

He shook his head. She noticed now that his eyes were of a velvety blackness never seen in Anglo-Saxons and his hair black, though peppered with grey. Don't they all have moustaches? she asked herself, and coincidentally he said, 'I shaved my beard so not to look like Middle Eastern man.'

'Are you an asylum seeker?'

He nodded, then shook his head. 'I like to be when I come but I do it wrong, I do no register, so now I am illegal immigrant. I want to go home now, now I can and will be safe, I go back to Basra.'

I don't know about 'safe', she thought. 'Have you been living here?' She didn't wait for an answer but said, 'Come down and have some coffee with my friend and me.'

Queenie was shocked when she was first told, and feared he might be dangerous. But she listened to his story. He had come into England clinging on to one of the carriages of the Eurostar, jumping off it at Folkestone. From the first he was certain that everything he was doing was illegal. That was why he had failed to register as an asylum seeker until the time for so doing was up and it was too late. He hitched a lift to London on a lorry from Prague driven by a Czech. These two were almost unable to communicate, the Czech man having no English and of course no Arabic and Omar having no other languages but his own and a certain amount of English.

In London he slept on the street and begged by day. He watched houses, seeking those which were empty or those with just one solitary owner-occupier, preferably someone old or out a lot. He found St Blaise House and Gwendolen and when the weather grew so cold that he thought he must die if he spent another night on the street, he looked for a way in.

Here Queenie asked why he had come, why he hadn't stayed at home. When he said the name Saddam Hussein and spoke of his wife and children who had disappeared, she nodded, put out her hand to touch his and asked no more.

'I climb across the roofs,' he said. 'It was easy. I get through a window and that too is easy.'

'When was this?'

'Oh, a long time. February, March, maybe. It was cold.'

He had begged by day for money to buy food. Once, in Notting Hill Gate, he saw 'the man who live here' and thought it was all up with him but the man had seemed more frightened than he was. He was always afraid of him on the occasions they inevitably met, Omar didn't know why. He would have told him everything and asked for help, only the man was so frightened of him. The only living creature he had ever had much contact with since coming to London from Folkestone was a cat who lived in the house and who took a fancy to him and slept on his bed, probably because of the fish and meat leftovers he gave it. In the cellar he found an old record player and some records. These he had played softly because without music he felt he couldn't exist.

One night, not long ago, he had heard a bumping

sound and when he came out had seen the man dragging something wrapped in a sheet up the stairs. If it had been in Basra he would have thought it a dead body but not here, not in England.

Queenie gave a little scream but Olive said, 'You must tell the police what you heard and saw. You must tell them when we all go to them and you ask them how you can go home to Iraq.' When Omar looked nervous, she said, 'They'll be glad to get you home. Once it's safe they'll help you to get home. I promise.' I hope you like it when you get there, she said under her breath.

# Chapter 29

The train for Norwich, calling at Witham, Colchester and Ipswich, was scheduled to depart from platform thirteen. For a moment he thought of giving up the whole trip or leaving the station and trying to go by coach instead. No, he'd bought his ticket and a terrible price it was. The last time he had travelled by rail he had sat in first class but things were different now. He had to be careful. It was coming up to lunchtime. He walked down to the buffet car, bought a burger and chips and a can of Coke. Then – thinking, what the hell? – had a miniature of gin to put in his drink.

It was going to be grim at Shannon's. I hate children, he thought, and felt nauseous at the idea of sharing a bedroom with those kids of hers. The younger one, he remembered, had a perpetual cold and was always sniffing. They never washed, either of them, and Shannon was too overworked and too tired to check up on them. Suddenly it came back to him, the day he had tried to kill her. But had he? Had he really? Was that what he really meant, to beat her to death with that bottle? He hadn't actually touched her, Javy had got there first.

When he came to think of it, all his troubles had started with Javy's flogging him for that. Then his hitting his mother so that he had to leave and fend for himself. That was two things. After that, what? Working for Fiterama in Birmingham had been OK but he should never have accepted promotion and moved south. He hadn't much cared about Crippen but still it was a disappointment to find his house gone, though nothing to the shock of Rillington Place. Moving to Notting Hill was a mistake and doing up that flat another. Self-pity washed over him until he felt a stinging behind his eyes.

His whole life had been dogged by ill-luck. He'd gone to Shoshana's Spa and his fate had made him meet Danila and she'd incriminated him by forcing him to kill her. The Indian had told Chawcer about seeing him digging the garden, his back was so injured it would never be the same again and he'd killed a woman who was already dead. Now he was in a train which left from platform thirteen.

He'd been counting as he reflected on his misfortunes. Thirteen. There were thirteen of them. Not meaning to, he let out a low groan and a young woman sitting opposite him stared.

'Are you all right?'

He nodded, tried and failed to force a smile. Thirteen steps down to where he was now, jobless, his money dwindling, haunted probably for the rest of his life, deserted by his friends. Thirteen steps, like the flight down from his flat to her dark domain. And what lay in store? Shivering, he poured the gin into his half-empty can of Coke. The girl who had asked if he was all right was darting anxious looks at him and whispering to the boy with her.

He should have been used to it, but the gin and Coke mixture knocked him out. He felt exhausted. Though the carriage was full of people, mostly very young people and all of them eating and drinking the sort of food he'd had, dropping greasy wrappings and cans on the floor, he dropped off to sleep. He couldn't keep awake.

In the dream he had he was at the top of those stairs, looking down. A voice in his head was telling him not to go down but to step back. Stay where you are, even the first step will be fatal. But something seemed to be pulling him, drawing him forwards and downwards, one, two, three . . . He took a step, then another, and now at the bottom he could see Reggie waiting for him. He woke up with a cry. The girl opposite him wasn't sympathetic any more. She was whispering to her boyfriend and Mix knew she was saying he was drunk.

Perhaps he was. The air of outside would clear his head and maybe it was just as well there would be no drink at Shannon's. A voice over the public address system said, 'The train will shortly be arriving in Colchester. Colchester next stop.'

Mix took his bag down from the rack and moved towards the door. It was already crowded with young people loaded with backpacks and bags and surrounded by more. The train came slowly into the station and the alighting passengers jostled each other out and on to the platform. Mix stepped down but he didn't get very far.

No one put a hand on his shoulder. That was only in the movies. That was for TV. The words the older policeman spoke to him he'd heard a hundred times on TV, he knew them by heart. All of the stuff about saying what you had to say now or you might harm your defence if you wanted to rely on it in court. Well, he'd want to rely on it because it was true.

'The girl was in self-defence,' he said. 'And the old woman was dead before I touched her. I'm not a murderer, I'm not Christie.'

Olive had lost her reading glasses. The only pair she had dated from fifteen years before and they no longer did the job. She was on the point of ringing her optician for a new pair when she remembered she had very likely left them behind in St Blaise House.

For a week it had been forbidden ground, accessible only to the police, to pathologists and forensic experts. They had all gone now, Michael Cellini had been charged with the murder of Gwendolen in the magistrates' court, and things had quietened down. The police were saving up the death and burial of Danila Kovic, Tom said, in case he got off and they'd have another murder to charge him with. Olive let herself into the house, resolving that before she left, glasses or no glasses, she would leave the key behind. Perhaps put it where important keys were kept, in the tumble-drier. Restoring it to this ridiculous place, honouring as it were its former owner's bizarre wishes, seemed to her to be a tiny tribute to Gwendolen.

Olive went into the drawing room, wondering what would happen to this house. Was there anyone to inherit it? Gwendolen had never spoken of relatives except some old cousin of her mother's who had been at her funeral. But Mrs Chawcer's funeral was fifty years ago this year. Gwendolen had been the only child of, as far as Olive knew, only children. Had she even made a will? St Blaise House would be worth millions to a property developer.

She tried to remember where she had been during the hours she had spent here. In the drawing room, of course, in the kitchen – she wouldn't have needed reading glasses there – up in the bedroom she had slept in. She climbed the stairs. Queenie had wept over Gwendolen but she hadn't, she had been angry, but glad too that Cellini hadn't been anywhere near her when the truth came out. I'd have attacked him, she said to the empty house, dragged my nails down his face. Keeping them long and pointed would have been well worth it just for that. She went into the sad, dirty, neglected bedroom. Searching it took about three minutes and then she had to wash her hands.

The glasses came to light in the drawing room. They were under one of the armchairs in a little enclave of dust and fluff and dead flies. She went into the kitchen and was about to wash them under the tap, when the doorbell rang. Some vendor of fish or sharpener of knives, she thought as she went to answer it.

An elderly man and a middle-aged woman stood there. Two of Gwendolen's forgotten relatives?

'My name is Reeves,' the man said, all smiles. 'Dr Stephen Reeves. I happened to be in the neighbourhood and thought of dropping in on Miss Chawcer. This is my wife Diana, by the way. Is Miss Chawcer about?'

'I'm afraid not.' Olive realised she would have to say why not, though in expurgated form. 'Gwendolen has passed away. It was very sudden.'

Dr Reeves shook his head, attempting to look sad. 'Dear, oh dear. Well, she was getting on. It comes to us all. We just thought we'd look in. As a matter of fact –' he allowed his smile to break through '– we're down here on our honeymoon.'

# The Rottweiler

## Ruth Rendell

'In the world of contemporary crime fiction,
Rendell really is top dog'
Donna Leon, *The Sunday Times*

The first girl had a bite mark on her neck but they traced the
DNA to her boyfriend. But the tabloids got hold of the story
and called the killer 'The Rottweiler' and the name stuck.

The latest murder takes place very near Inez Ferry's antique
shop in Marlylebone. Someone saw a shadowy figure running away past the station, but the only other clues are that
the murderer usually strangles his victims and removes something personal – like a cigarette lighter or a necklace . . .

Since her husband died, too soon in their relationship, Inez
has supplemented her income by taking in tenants. The mur-
derous activities of the sinister 'Rottweiler' will exert a profound influence on the lives of this heterogeneous little
community, especially when the suspicion emerges that one
of them may be a homicidal maniac.

'In Rendell's expert hands, you'll want to keep reading
until dawn – with the light on'
*Red*

'Rendell skilfully crafts her characters and they breathe
feverishly through her imagination'
*The Times*

arrow books

# The Babes in the Wood

## Ruth Rendell

### A Chief Inspector Wexford Novel

There hadn't been anything like this kind of rain in living memory. The River Brede had burst its banks, and not a single house in the valley had escaped the flooding. In the midst of all this, two teenagers – Giles and Sophie Dade – and Joanna Troy, the woman who had been looking after them, have vanished. The Subaqua Task Force could find no trace of them, but Mrs Dade was still convinced her children were dead.

The investigation would call into question many of Wexford's assumptions about the way people behaved, including his own family . . .

'A complex saga of family relationships, remorselessly exposing neurotic inner lives'
*Scotland on Sunday*

'Superb plotting and psychological insight make this another Rendell gripper'
*Woman & Home*

'*The Babes in the Wood* extends the conventions of the whodunit, going beyond a cool analysis of how and why a crime was committed, and building into a convincing, often troubling exploration of the way violence infects and damages everyone it touches'
*Sunday Times*

arrow books

# THE POWER OF READING

**Visit the Random House website and get connected with information on all our books and authors**

**EXTRACTS** from our recently published books and selected backlist titles

**COMPETITIONS AND PRIZE DRAWS** Win signed books, audiobooks and more

**AUTHOR EVENTS** Find out which of our authors are on tour and where you can meet them

**LATEST NEWS** on bestsellers, awards and new publications

**MINISITES** with exclusive special features dedicated to our authors and their titles

**READING GROUPS** Reading guides, special features and all the information you need for your reading group

**LISTEN** to extracts from the latest audiobook publications

**WATCH** video clips of interviews and readings with our authors

**RANDOM HOUSE INFORMATION** including advice for writers, job vacancies and all your general queries answered

**Come home to Random House**

# www.rbooks.co.uk